"The doctor said no sex. He didn't say no kissing."

Nash ran a fingertip from her ear to her chin. "You're so beautiful. My breath caught in my chest the first time I saw you."

Kasey's common sense told her to pull away with an excuse, but she was mesmerized by those dark brown lashes lying on his high cheekbones. She didn't even realize that she'd rolled up on her toes and moistened her lips until he drew her close to his chest and his lips closed on hers.

The first kiss was sweet, but then it grew hotter and hotter, turning her knees so weak that she had to lean into him to keep from falling. Her arms slid up around his neck, fingers playing in his thick black hair as he teased her mouth open with his tongue.

Finally, he took half a step back. "Much more of that and I'll tell the doctor to take his orders, pour barbecue sauce on them, and eat them for supper."

High Praise for Carolyn Brown

TOUGHEST COWBOY IN TEXAS

"One of the best feel-good reads I've had the pleasure of reading yet this year! It tugged on your heartstrings and had you cheering for true love." —*Once Upon an Alpha*

"Top Pick! A beautiful second-chance love story that has humor, HOT cowboys and an amazing HEA." —*Harlequin Junkie*

"Terrific...an emotional star-crossed-lovers tale with tangible depths and an attitude that's relatable to real life." —*RT Book Reviews*

"The *Toughest Cowboy in Texas* is a delightful, fast-paced novel full of dynamic and lively characters and, more important, white-hot romance!" —*Romance Reviews Today*

THE LUCKY PENNY RANCH SERIES

"A nice blend of warmth, down-home goodness, humor and romance. Lively, flirty banter and genuine, down-to-earth characters are the highlights of this engaging story...The flirty banter between Deke and Josie is amusing and heartwarming, and the chemistry between them sizzles." —*RT Book Reviews* on *Wicked Cowboy Charm*

Long, Tall
Cowboy Christmas

Also by Carolyn Brown

The Happy, Texas series

Toughest Cowboy in Texas

The Lucky Penny Ranch series

Wild Cowboy Ways
Hot Cowboy Nights
Merry Cowboy Christmas
Wicked Cowboy Charm

Long, Tall Cowboy Christmas

Happy, Texas Book 2

Carolyn Brown

FOREVER

New York Boston

Copyright © 2017 by Carolyn Brown
Excerpt from *The Luckiest Cowboy of All* copyright © 2017 by Carolyn Brown
Cover design by Elizabeth Turner.
Cover copyright © 2017 by Hachette Book Group, Inc.

Forever
Hachette Book Group
1290 Avenue of the Americas, New York, NY 10104
forever-romance.com
twitter.com/foreverromance

First Edition: September 2017

Forever is an imprint of Grand Central Publishing. The Forever name and logo are trademarks of Hachette Book Group, Inc.

The publisher is not responsible for websites (or their content) that are not owned by the publisher.

The Hachette Speakers Bureau provides a wide range of authors for speaking events. To find out more, go to www.hachettespeakersbureau.com or call (866) 376-6591.

ISBNs: 978-1-4555-9747-5 (mass market), 978-1-5387-5989-9 (Walmart exclusive edition), 978-1-4555-9746-8 (ebook)

Printed in the United States of America

OPM

10 9 8 7 6 5 4 3 2 1

*To the men, women, and families
who serve in our military…
thank you for your sacrifices.*

Dear Reader,

Sometimes even for an author, a story comes along that sinks deep into my heart. *Long, Tall Cowboy Christmas* is one of those stories. As Nash and Kasey told me their stories, I realized that this would probably be one of the most emotional books I'd ever write and it really was. I hope that I've done it justice.

As always there are people that I want to mention, those who helped me take the book from a diamond-in-the-rough idea to the book that you hold in your hands today. When I went looking for inspiration for the kids in this book, I didn't have to go far. My great-grandson, Silas, was exactly who I saw when I thought about the little boy in the book with blond curls, and his brother Kyce was exactly the right age for Rustin's new buddy at school. Kyce and Silas have an uncle Zayne just a little older than they are, so he fit right into the story line, too. So thank you to those three little boys who are always at my house on Easter and Thanksgiving, and watching them gave me lots of ideas for this story.

Thank you to Mr. B, my husband of fifty-one years, who is always ready to change his plans to fit with whatever I need to do to go on a research trip or attend a conference. It takes a special person to live with an author, and he fills those cowboy boots amazingly well.

I could never do this job without my team at Grand Central/Forever. My editor, Leah Hultenschmidt, deserves a diamond crown for all her dedication and for helping me to bring out every tear and giggle possible in this story. And Melanie Gold, in managing editorial; Elizabeth Turner in the art department (still squealing over the cover); and Michelle Cashman in publicity—y'all are all fantabulous.

And my agent, Erin Niumata, who's worked with me for almost twenty years...you and Folio Management are appreciated more than mere words can ever begin to tell.

And (I love that word because it means there is more on the way) to my readers. Bless every one of you for reading my books, talking about them, and reviewing them. I have the best fans in the whole universe.

When I finished this book it was with a sigh and the wish that I could give you just one more chapter. I hope you feel the same way when you reach the end. As those commercials say on television—but wait, there's more! *The Luckiest Cowboy of All* will be out in January with Jace and Carlene Varner's story, so keep your boots on and your reading glasses right close.

Until then, happy reading,
Carolyn Brown

Long, Tall
Cowboy Christmas

Chapter One

Nash could taste the sand in his mouth despite the bandana covering his face. Thank God that tomorrow he would be headed back to Texas for a month-long leave. He was looking forward to the green trees, fishing in the Big Cypress Bayou, and his grandmother's cooking. But right now a little boy needed his help. And there was no one to save him but Captain Nash Lamont.

The whirr of helicopter blades above the base meant that it was time to leave. Three of his six-man team would be going home in flag-draped coffins—one of them had been married and had children. He'd been the one who saved Nash's life at the expense of his own, but the captain couldn't think about that now. There was a child in danger out there beyond the base perimeter. He could hear the mother screaming her son's name somewhere in the dust behind him.

Nash rubbed the sand from his eyes and focused on the

child outside the command center. He yelled at the kid, and the kid waved and nodded. He kicked the inflatable ball he'd been playing with all day toward Nash, but wind picked it up and twirled it back at him like a boomerang, floating over his shoulder and landing twenty feet behind him. Nash couldn't take a chance on the boy running through that minefield, so he took off in long strides and threw himself on top of the little boy. Then in a flash, he was on his feet with the boy slung over his shoulder. With a kicking and screaming kid beating at his back, he prayed that he'd make it through the gates without stepping on an IED.

When they were inside the gates, Nash set the boy down and let his breath out in a long whoosh. He'd saved him— this time Nash had saved the kid. The boy might be upset, but at least he was in one piece. Everything was going to be all right. He had failed in his mission and half his team was going home in caskets, but he'd saved the boy.

* * *

Kasey tightly held the red bandana across her face and bent her shoulders against the wind bringing half of the dirt in New Mexico across the border into the Texas panhandle. When the storm hit she'd gone to the back door and yelled at her six-year-old son, Rustin, to get inside the house. When he didn't come running, she'd yelled again and again and finally with worry and fear mixed, she'd started out to find him, stopping every few feet to scream his name.

He'd been kicking a ball around inside the yard fence the last time she checked on him. She searched the barn first, but no one was there. Then she remembered the last time he'd slipped off that she'd found him over at the ranch next door. His dog, Hero, had run away and Rustin had gone looking for him. Hoping that's what had happened this time, she made a beeline down the rutted path leading that way. She'd moved to Happy the spring before to live close to family and to raise her kids in the wide open spaces of a ranch but it was times like this that she missed living in town with a fenced yard and close neighbors.

A quarter of a mile to the barbed-wire fence didn't seem like far unless there was a fierce wind blowing dirt everywhere. When she reached the fence separating Hope Springs from the Texas Star Ranch, she found a piece of Rustin's jacket stuck in the wire and flapping in the wind. She was on the right track. Hopefully, he was holed up in the barn and out of the driving, miserable dirt storm.

She crawled through two strands of wire and then called Hope, her grandmother, to tell her that she'd be back to the ranch house soon with the runaway. Shielding her eyes, she could see the barn through the sand. Who was that in the doorway? He was too tall to be Adam's father, Paul, her children's grandfather who leased the ranch property from Henry's sister. She took another step and rubbed the dirt from her eyes.

Oh, no! Whoever it was had raced out and grabbed her son. He'd thrown himself on top of Rustin, then stood up with the boy thrown over his shoulder like a sack of chicken feed. Rustin was kicking and screaming out for her the whole time. She took a deep breath and started coughing when her nostrils filled with dirt. Feeling as if she was running in boots filled with lead, she could hear Rustin bellowing as she fought against the hard wind trying to knock her backward.

"What the hell!" She gasped for breath when she was finally inside the barn. "What are you doing to my son?

Put him down right now!" She shouted as adrenaline rushed through her body like fiery hot whiskey.

Kicking and screaming, beating the man on the back with his fists, Rustin didn't even see her and turned on her when she grabbed him away from the man. She put her boy behind her and faced the tall, dark cowboy. "Who are you and why were you kidnapping my child?"

Dirt dusted the stranger's dark hair, but his near-black eyes looked blank, as if he was seeing but not seeing, if that made sense.

"I was saving him. You are safe now, Ahmid." The man looked as if he was sleepwalking.

Kasey snapped her fingers in his face, and he quickly grabbed her wrist. She jerked it free and took a step back.

"I'm not Ahmid. I'm Rustin." Rustin wrapped his arms around her waist and peeked around her side.

The cowboy's brow furrowed in a frown. "You aren't Farah. You have red hair."

She jerked off the bandana, letting it hang around her neck, and shook her hair out of the stocking hat. "I'm Kasey McKay and this is my son, Rustin." She took a step back and looked into his dark brown eyes. "What are you doing in this barn?"

He shook his head slowly. "I'm sorry. I fell asleep out here and when I woke up the sand—I thought I was back," he stammered. "That's classified. I am Captain Nash Lamont and I just saved this boy from—oh, no!"

He squared his broad shoulders, standing at attention, but after a few seconds they sagged and he ran a hand over his angular face. So this was Nash. Everyone in Happy had been talking about how he'd taken over Henry's old ranch. He'd moved into the old house last week, but no one had seen him. Not at the café or at church the previous Sunday.

Folks wondered if he might be like his great-uncle—a harmless hermit.

He was well over six feet tall, his black hair brushed the collar of his denim duster that strained at the shoulder seams, and those dark brown eyes darted around the barn as if he wasn't sure where he was. His broad chest narrowed down past a silver belt buckle with the state of Texas engraved on it. Faded jeans, cowboy boots, a felt hat thrown over there on a hay bale said he was proud to be a cowboy. Yet he'd identified himself as Captain Lamont, and that was definitely military.

"You deserve an explanation." His accent was a blend of Texas drawl and something even farther south, maybe Louisiana or Mississippi. "I was in the army and did some work in Afghanistan, Kuwait, and Iraq. There was an incident involving a young boy who had kicked a ball outside the gates in dangerous territory. I tried to save him but didn't get there in time and wound up with a head wound of my own. I came out here to check on the sheep and the sandstorm hit. I thought—" He shrugged.

"You thought you were back over there, right? The sandstorm and the kid out there in it gave you a flashback?" Kasey understood, but she still kept Rustin behind her.

Nash nodded.

Kasey had lost her husband, Adam, when he was on a mission somewhere over there in what the guys called the sandbox. Before that, she'd held him many nights through the nightmares that his job caused, so she understood. But it didn't take away the fear that had tightened her chest so that she couldn't breathe when she thought he was abducting her son.

"Mama, I'm okay," Rustin said in a steady voice. "Cowboys don't hurt little kids."

"I would never harm a child, and I'm very sorry for the misunderstanding, Miz McKay." Nash's deep voice had a dose of deep-seeded southern in it.

"Have we met before?" she asked.

"I heard about you living on the next ranch over." His gaze went over her left shoulder and landed on the barn door.

There was no doubt that he had been a soldier. Shoulders ramrod straight and squared off. Chin tucked back and eyes ahead. Filled with respect. Ready to do battle. No one stood like a military man, especially one who'd been a cowboy before he enlisted.

"Well, then, we'll be going home. Welcome to Happy, Nash." Kasey knew she should invite him to Hope Springs for coffee or supper, but she wasn't feeling too hospitable, not with all those memories of Adam flashing through her mind. Not to mention dealing with a son who was in big trouble for wandering off when he was explicitly told not to leave the yard.

She pulled the bandana up over her nose again and stooped down to zip Rustin's jacket, making sure that the collar protected his nose from the roaring wind and dirt.

"I'll drive you home. My truck is sitting right there." He motioned toward a black Chevy Silverado parked to one side of the barn. "It's still blowing like crazy out there. It's the least I can do for scaring you. And again, I'm very sorry."

"Apology accepted, but—"

"Mama, I don't want to walk home in this stuff," Rustin whispered.

Kasey took one look out the door and realized her son was right. Visibility was practically zero. "Maybe we should just wait it out a little while right here in the barn until it lets up," she said. She cast a glance at Nash as she pulled her phone from her hip pocket and quickly called her grandmother, gave her the news that she'd found Rustin and that the neighbor would bring them home as soon as the wind stopped blowing.

Nash smiled while she talked, but it didn't reach his eyes. He sat down on a hay bale and a big white cat meandered out and hopped up in his lap. He started to rub her long fur and she curled up, as if she belonged there.

"That's the white cat that Aunt Lila talked about. Can I pet her?" Rustin left his mother's side and took a few steps toward Nash.

"Sure. You can even hold her if you want," Nash said. "Sit right here and I'll put her in your lap. She's real tame."

"My sister would love her. She's purrin'," Rustin said when the cat was in his lap.

"So you have other children?" Nash looked up at Kasey.

"Two. Emma is three and Silas is eighteen months." She kept a close watch on her son, sitting so close to a stranger.

"And where do you live?" Nash asked.

"On the ranch right next door," Rustin answered.

"Hope Springs, with my two brothers, Brody and Jace," Kasey said. "Where did you live before now?"

"The last two years out south of Jefferson, Texas, on my grandmother's little spread."

"And before that?"

"Wherever the military sent me."

His dark eyes were boring holes in her. Not like a man who was hitting on her but more like someone trying to place her in his mind. Like he'd met her before and couldn't quite remember her name. But he did because he'd called her Miz McKay a few minutes before. When he did look up, his dark eyes were veiled. It was impossible to see exactly what he was thinking, but there was definitely something haunting Nash Lamont.

A couple of *baa*s caused Rustin to cock his ear toward the stalls on the other side of the barn. "Is that sheeps I hear?"

"Yes, they are. I heard we might have a dust storm so I brought them inside. Want to see them?"

"You bet. I ride the muttons at the rodeo grounds sometimes," Rustin said.

The veil on Nash's dark eyes seemed to lift a little as he watched Rustin run from one stall to the other looking at his small flock. "Look, Mama, this one has babies."

Kasey edged around Nash, careful not to get too close, still not fully trusting him, even if the white cat and her son didn't have a problem with him. "They're cute little things, but you do know this is cattle country, right?" she asked.

He straightened up and towered above her. "Yes, ma'am. But I've always liked sheep, so that's what I'm raising right now." He wandered over to the door and looked outside. "I think the wind is dying down. Please let me drive y'all home."

"Come on, Rustin. We have to get home," Kasey said.

Rustin took time to stick his hand into the stall and pet one more lamb before he ran to the truck. With long strides, Nash hurried ahead of them both and swung open the doors. Rustin climbed up into the backseat without a moment's pause, but before Nash could slam the door, the boy's dog, Hero, jumped right into the truck with him. Kasey hiked a hip on the seat and pulled the seat belt across her chest.

Nash slung open the double barn doors and then hopped into the truck, slammed the door shut, and fastened his seat belt. "Hope Springs? I drive to the end of my lane and turn right? I guess that dog belongs to you?"

Kasey bobbed her head twice.

"His name is Hero and he's got a sister, Princess, and a brother, Doggy. They belong to Emma and Silas, but they ain't as smart as Hero," Rustin said enthusiastically. "I think he likes you."

"He looks like a good dog."

Hero flopped his big black head over the seat and licked Nash's face from chin to ear then lay down with his head in Rustin's lap. If it was true that children and dogs knew who to trust and who to back away from—everything would be just fine.

Nash sat rigidly straight in the truck seat, reminding her again of Adam's posture, even if they didn't look anything alike. Adam had topped out at five feet nine inches, and that was with his cowboy boots on. He'd had clear blue eyes and blond hair. He'd always looked so young that he was carded anytime he ordered a drink, and he had a smile that would light up the whole universe.

The man sitting beside her with a death grip on the steering wheel was a silent, brooding type who had a lot of darkness inside him. He might be late twenties or maybe early thirties, and no one would ever mistake him as being underage.

He drove slowly to the end of the lane, made a right, and then another one a quarter of a mile down the road. The first big raindrops fell, mixing with the dust to create mud that hit the windshield in splats. The wipers couldn't work fast enough to keep the smears from the windows, so Nash backed off the gas and took them the rest of the way at five miles an hour.

"Rustin, you go straight to the bathroom and shuck out of those clothes. And you"—Kasey turned toward Nash—"you do not have to be a gentleman and open doors. Thanks for the ride."

"You're welcome," he said. "And thank you, Kasey, for not shooting me. I apologize once again."

"Didn't have my pistol," she answered as she bailed out of the truck and ran through the nasty rain toward the house. Dripping mud, she stopped inside the front door and kicked off her boots.

Wiping her hands on an apron tied around her waist, her grandmother, Hope, came out of the kitchen with Silas, Kasey's youngest son, and Emma, the middle child, right behind her. Their little eyes widened out like they were looking at a monster.

"Mama, did you and Rustin have a mud fight?" Emma was totally aghast.

"Mommy all yucky." Silas's nose twitched.

Hope giggled. "Got to agree with them, Kasey. You look like you lost a mud-wrestling match. I was about to call to check on you when Rustin came through here like a shot and headed toward the bathroom."

"I told him to go straight to the bathroom and get cleaned up. It's practically raining mud out there with that dust storm." Kasey pulled gobs of wet mud from her naturally curly red hair when she ran her fingers through it.

"Ick," Emma said. She grabbed Silas's hand and dragged him toward the living room. "Let's go build a Lego princess castle."

"Yep." Silas nodded seriously.

"So, you got to see Nash Lamont, huh?" Hope sat down in a ladder-back chair beside the foyer table. "What does he look like?"

"He's every bit as tall as Brody. Dark eyes, dark hair. Military for sure. He doesn't talk a lot, but he seems nice enough." Kasey started on down the hall.

"Did he mention his great-uncle Henry?" Hope fingered

the gold locket around her neck with a wistful look in her eyes.

"No, but he had Rustin slung over his shoulder like a sack of potatoes. Scared the devil out of me."

Hope clucked like an old hen as she stood up and brushed her hair back with her hand. She wasn't much taller than Kasey, had gray hair and bright green eyes, and was still the queen bee of Hope Springs, even if she had turned most of the day-to-day operations over to Kasey's brothers, Brody and Jace, the spring before. Her face and attention to style belied her seventy-two years. "I got to go call Molly and tell her that you almost killed the new man in town."

"Granny!" Kasey's green eyes, so much like her grandmother's, popped wide open. "I didn't even try to kill him. I might have if he'd been kidnapping my son, but he was having a flashback to the war stuff. Adam did that more than once. I felt sorry for him."

Hope headed for the kitchen. "Might be wise to stay away from a man who's got problems like that."

Kasey couldn't agree more, but then there was something in those dark, brooding eyes that made her want to know more about him. She dropped her dirty clothing on the bathroom floor and stepped into the shower. She lathered up her hair three times before the water ran clear. With a towel wrapped around her body, she peeked out the door before she darted down the hall. She almost made it to the wing of the house where she and the kids lived when the front door opened.

"Hey!" Her sister-in-law, Lila, grinned as she removed a mud-splashed yellow slicker and laid it across the chair where Hope had been sitting. Not a single bit of dirt stuck to her jet-black ponytail, and her brown eyes glimmered. "I heard that you had a confrontation with the new neighbor. I also heard that he's quite a hunk."

Kasey wiped a hand across her brow. "Granny didn't waste a bit of time, did she?"

Lila followed her back to the bedroom. "I was out in the barn helping Brody when the storm hit. Thought I'd come get the whole story from you."

Kasey told it again as she got dressed.

"So the part about him being downright sexy is true?" Lila asked.

Kasey shook out her curly red hair and started to brush it. "You ever read *Wuthering Heights*?"

"Of course. I used to be an English teacher, remember?" Lila nodded. "Is Nash a Heathcliff?"

"Oh, yeah, exactly." Kasey nodded.

* * *

Nash parked outside the two-story, white frame house and ran inside with mud slapping against his shoulders and head the whole way. He'd seen massive sandstorms when he'd been on missions and he'd endured tornadoes in east Texas and central Louisiana. He had even lived through hurricanes, but never had he seen it rain mud until that day. Maybe it was an omen that he should have never taken his grandmother's advice and moved to Happy, Texas, to find some peace and quiet on the old family ranch. He left his boots and coat at the back door and padded straight to the bathroom in his socks.

His great-grandmother, Minnie Thomas, had died more than twelve years ago, and even though he'd been a teenager when he attended the funeral, he remembered that every flat surface in the house had been covered with ceramic angels and animals of all descriptions.

That was back when Uncle Henry lived there after his

thirty-year military stint. His dad had gotten sick, so he came home to take care of him, not planning to stay five years, much less almost twenty.

"I guess Great-Granny Minnie needed help runnin' this place, but why did you leave the second time?" Nash muttered. "And if you were going, why did you put away all of Grandma's stuff? Guess if I was meant to know you'd tell me."

It sure looked different now—flat-out stark with only the necessities. No fancy candy dishes or feminine touches anywhere. He dropped his dirty clothing on the floor outside the tiny downstairs bathroom. It had a wall-hung sink, a shower so small that he could barely turn around, and a potty—all crammed together so tight that his jeans and shirt covered the entire floor.

The upstairs bathroom was a lot bigger, with a claw-foot tub and a double sink vanity. It even had room for a ladder-back chair beside the tub to hold a stack of towels. But there was no shower, and Nash relished the spray of scalding hot water.

Sending up a silent prayer that all the mud didn't clog the drains, he looked down at the swirling water around his feet and was reminded of all the blood that day.

No! He wouldn't go there. He made himself think about something else as he kept his eyes away from the shower floor. Forcing himself to go over what all he needed to do the next few days, he finished and then bumped his head on the curtain rod as he stepped out.

"Dammit!" He swore under his breath as he tucked a towel around his waist and tossed his dirty clothing in the washing machine before he went to the master bedroom located right off the foyer.

He glanced around the room and realization hit him.

His uncle Henry, who'd lived here with his ailing parents, had been a career military man. All that clutter that Great-Granny had everywhere must've driven him crazy. That's why the place had changed so much. When Great-Granny died, Uncle Henry had done a job on the place, turning it into what he'd been used to when he was in the army.

"And I'm just like him." Nash groaned as he glanced around his bedroom at the bed made so tightly that a quarter would bounce right off it. Not a wrinkle in sight. Table with only a lamp and the book he was reading beside a recliner. His foot locker at the end of the bed with a go-bag still packed sitting on the top of it. Half a dozen shirts and a few pairs of jeans hung with exactly the same distance between the wire hangers in the closet. If a five-star general did a surprise inspection, Nash would pass with flying colors.

The window shades were pulled up to let in as much light as possible—at least on days when the wind wasn't slinging mud balls against the windows. Sinking down in the recliner, he sighed and pulled the lever to raise the footrest. His grandma had decided that a nice quiet little ranch in the panhandle of Texas would be a good place to get his head on straight. She'd moved away from Happy more than sixty years ago, but she still had fond memories of the Texas Star Ranch, where she and her brother, who was also Nash's great-uncle, Henry had grown up.

He went to the kitchen window and stared out across the flat pasture separating the house from the barn, which was just a blob in the distance. His sheep were probably unhappy in there, but at least they wouldn't have mud balls embedded in their wool.

Two years ago he'd been discharged from the army. Within weeks, his dad and his grandfather had both died and he'd gone to his grandmother's place outside of Jefferson,

Texas, to help her out on the ranch. One of her neighbors had had an orphan lamb, and he wound up taking care of it. Two years later he had ten in his little flock.

He was deep in thought about putting up better fence around the pasture from house to barn when his phone rang and startled him. He managed to work it out of his hip pocket and answer it on the fourth ring.

"Hello, Addy," he said and imagined his grandmother sitting on the sofa in her new place. "How are things in Jefferson?"

"I'm adjusting to town life. It's sure different from living five miles out on a ranch." She laughed.

The sound of her voice put a smile on his face. "It's raining mud here in this part of Texas."

"I saw that a couple of times when I was young. I remember once Mama had white sheets on the line when it hit. Come out of nowhere, but in them days we didn't have all this technology to tell us when the weather was going to be bad. How are you doin' there? Have you called your mama?"

"I met Kasey and her son, Rustin, today," he said bluntly. "I don't remember her from the times when I came here as a kid. And no, I haven't called Mama but I promise I will."

"I wouldn't expect that you ever met her or her brothers. We usually only stayed a couple of days and you trailed around after my dad most of the time. And he never left the ranch unless he had to. You settlin' into the town?"

He managed a chuckle. "It's almost a ghost town. If it wasn't for those grain silos, I imagine the wind would have blown the whole place away years ago. Even after living on the ranch outside of Jefferson the past two years, this is still a cultural shock."

His grandmother's name was Adelaide, and that's what

he heard folks call her when he was a little kid so he'd just shortened it to Addy. Not Granny Addy or even Grandma Addy, but just plain old Addy.

She giggled. "What's the size of the town matter to you? You're practically a hermit so what are you missin'? Town could be as big as Dallas and you'd stay on the ranch just like you did here. But you did promise to stay there a year."

"Addy, there's one café, a school, two churches, grain silos, and lots of ranches. I'm a man of my word, but..."

"I didn't promise easy when I sent you there, but it's a good place to find yourself and figure out if you want to be a soldier or a rancher, grandson. You can't ride two horses with only one ass." She laughed at her own joke.

"Addy!" His deep southern drawl raised an octave.

"That is not a dirty word. Jesus rode one into town, remember, but he wasn't foolish enough to try to ride two."

"Okay, you've made your point. Did you know that Kasey McKay was living right next door?"

"I talked to her grandmother, Hope, a while back, and she mentioned Kasey had come back. We were visitin' about me selling her the Texas Star. Is livin' close to Kasey goin' to be a problem?"

"Probably not, since we won't see each other," he answered.

"You're right about that. Got to go now. Keep in touch. And call your mama."

"Will do. Love you, Addy," he said as he hit the end button.

To keep his word, he hit the numbers to his mother's place in Louisiana. She answered on the third ring. "Hey, son, how's it going? Great minds must think alike because I was just about to call you."

"I'm beginning to settle in. I met Kasey McKay today, Mama."

"You can do this, son. It might not be easy but it'll bring closure," Naomi Lamont said.

"I hope so," Nash said. "I really do hope so."

Half an hour later he ended the call but he still felt a drawing into that dark place where he didn't want to go. One year wouldn't be easy—not with Kasey McKay living next door—but keeping secrets was part of his job description. Had he known that she was anywhere near Happy, Texas, wild horses couldn't have dragged him here.

Chapter Two

The church was packed that Saturday afternoon when Kasey did her slow walk down the aisle toward the front and took her place. Then the traditional wedding music began, and Lila appeared at the back in a long, fitted white dress. A circlet of white roses held a short veil, but she'd opted not to wear it over her face. Her mother, Daisy, walked her down the aisle and put Lila's hand into Brody's.

"I'm not giving my daughter away today, but I'm willing to share her with you. Just know that if you ever hurt her in any way, you have me to answer to. Now be happy," Daisy said.

"Yes, ma'am. You have my word that I will love her with my whole heart forever," Brody said.

"Good," Daisy said and took her place beside her two co-workers, Molly and Georgia, in the front pew.

Kasey was happy for her brother and for his new bride

as they stood at the front of the church that Saturday afternoon and said their vows. But there was a tinge of sadness,
too. In that same church a little more than eight years ago,
Kasey had been the one in a sweeping white satin dress with
her handsome groom beside her in his army uniform. And
then six years after that, she'd worn a simple black sheath
dress and stood before the closed casket bearing her precious Adam's body. She'd been pregnant with their third
child, trying to hold herself together and be strong for little
Rustin and Emma.

Today, Kasey held the bouquet as her brother married the
only woman who'd ever truly held his heart. He and Lila
had taken a long, curvy road back to each other after twelve
years apart, but they were finally together now. And from
the look in her dark brown eyes and his crystal-clear blue
ones, it was one of those matches made far above the white
fluffy clouds in the sky.

Lila had chosen a simple dress that hugged her curves.
With a side slit, it made for easy walking and showed off
a pair of red cowgirl boots. Her dark hair floated in loose
waves halfway down her back. Leave it to Lila to do things
her way and not even give two hoots about what folks in
Happy, Texas, might think about it.

Kasey kept a smile on her face through the ceremony, but
making it reach all the way to the depths of her heart was
impossible. She glanced down at the first pew where her
mother sat with the children. Emma in her cute little ivory
lace, and the boys in their bow ties were behaving, which
was a pure miracle. When the service ended and everyone
had gotten out of the church, Jace waved at her from over
the tops of heads and mouthed her mother had the children
with her.

Kasey made her way through the crowd to her minivan,

where she couldn't hold back the tears any longer. She wept for what had been and what would never be again. She cried for her three precious children—who had amazing uncles in her brothers, Brody and Jace, an awesome aunt now in Lila, and priceless grandparents, but would never have a father. And she sobbed for her own emptiness. A heart needed to be shared, not locked away in solitude.

When she reached Hope Springs, she made a quick run through the bathroom, dried her eyes, reapplied makeup, and headed down the path from house to barn to greet family and friends with a brilliant smile. Fall leaves from the pecan tree in the backyard crunched under her feet. A brisk breeze flipped strands of her hair into her face, and she wished that she'd put it up into a ponytail while she was in the house. She drew the gold-colored wrap that matched her bridesmaid's dress tightly around her shoulders and lengthened her stride.

"Are you okay? You look like you've been crying." Her grandmother met her at the barn door, looped her arm into Kasey's, and led her toward the food tables.

"Allergies," Kasey said.

"Allergic to memories of your own wedding and Adam's funeral right there in the same church? You might be able to fool some folks, but not your granny. I love you, and it hurts me to see you in pain like this. It's time to move on, my child," Hope whispered.

"I've got three kids, and besides, I can't even look at another man without feeling like I'm cheating on Adam." She took a deep breath. "Does Mama still have control of the kids?"

"All but Silas. Gracie's taken charge of him for the rest of the day, and you know how he loves his nana, so don't worry about him."

Adam's mother, the sweet Gracie, was Nana. Kasey's mama, Valerie, was Grandma, and Hope, the kids' great-grandmother, was Granny.

"Thank you." Kasey hugged Hope tightly and then kissed her on the cheek. "I love you, too, Granny."

Hope pulled a tissue from the pocket of her fancy dress and dabbed at her eyes. "Guess I've got allergies, too. Before we destroy each other's makeup, I'm going to go get myself a stiff drink. Want one?"

"You bet." Kasey nodded. She had never lacked for family support, no matter what the situation, and for that she couldn't be more grateful.

* * *

Nash could see the lights and hear music floating across the barbed-wire fence separating the Texas Star from Hope Springs. The Dawsons were having a party of some kind over there for sure, and Rustin's black Lab pup, Hero, evidently didn't care much for it. The critter had been sprawled out on his porch when he went back to the house after checking on his new baby lambs in the corral behind the barn.

Nash pulled his denim jacket tighter and hunched his shoulders against the north wind. The little guy was so excited that he jumped around his legs, whining and wiggling, just begging to be petted. Even though the temperature had dropped drastically in the past hour and it was bitter cold, he sat down on the porch and scratched the dog's ears.

The pup rolled his eyes up at Nash when he stopped and whimpered.

"I'm not feeding you. You belong to that little boy and he'd be heartbroken if you decided you liked it better here."

Hero looked up at him with such begging eyes that Nash had no choice but to either feed him or take him home, so he scooped him up in his arms and headed for his truck.

"I'll take you home, boy, but you need to stop coming over here," he told the dog as he put him into the front seat of his truck and slammed the door.

When Nash got buckled into the seat, Hero had his head down and a paw over his nose. "You need to stay home. Do you hear me?"

He could see a pasture full of cars and trucks when he parked in front of the house at Hope Springs. There were no lights on in the house, so he set the pup inside the rail fence surrounding the yard and drove away. About half-way down the lane he saw a movement in his rearview and hit the brakes. That blasted pup was following him home. If it got out on the main road, it would be killed for sure when all those folks started to leave. He pulled over, and by the time he opened the door, Hero was doing a happy dance around his legs. He picked Hero up and carried him all the way back to the Dawsons' house. Maybe if he sat on the porch with him until the dog went to sleep, he could sneak off.

"Shut your eyes. If these people come home and find me with you, they might shoot first and ask questions later. They'll think I'm tryin' to steal a little boy's dog for sure," he whispered.

"Hello. The reception is down at the barn." A gray-haired lady appeared from around the end of the house. "Don't think I know you. Are you a friend of Lila's?"

Nash quickly put the dog down and jumped to his feet. "Sorry, ma'am. I'm Nash Lamont from the ranch next door. Rustin's puppy showed up at my place and I brought him home, but he got out again and started following my truck, so I thought it safest to stay with him. Poor little fellow seemed lonely."

The lady stuck out a hand. "I'm Hope Dalley, Rustin's great-grandmother. Welcome to Happy."

"Thank you, ma'am," Nash said.

"Well, I was just making a quick stop to change my shoes. My grandson Brody Dawson got married today."

"Congratulations, ma'am."

"You know, why don't you come back with me to the reception? I believe you've already met Brody's sister, Kasey."

"Oh, I wouldn't want to intrude. If you could take this pup inside, I'll be on my way," Nash said.

"Nonsense. There's no better place to meet most of the folks who live in Happy than at this reception." Hope waved that idea away with a flick of her wrist. "I'll put this critter in the utility room." She reached down and picked up the half-grown dog. "You wait right here and I'll be back in a split second."

"But I'm not dressed for a wedding, ma'am." Nash looked down at his faded jeans, work boots, and jean jacket.

"Oh, no one cares about that. We're not all that formal. I won't take no for an answer," she said.

Nash felt as if he should snap to attention and salute, but he only nodded. He'd walk her back to the reception, stick around long enough for her to disappear in the crowd, and then sneak out a back door. With a crowd like that, someone would be willing to drive her back to the house when the party was over.

"I'll be glad to escort you back, ma'am, but then I'd really best get on back to my place," he said when she returned.

"Young man." She pointed her finger at him. "Do not argue with me."

"Yes, ma'am." He came to attention and just barely stopped his hand before he saluted.

She smiled and patted his shoulder. "We're going to get along just fine, like neighbors should."

He held out his arm for her, and she looped hers into it.

"So how are you settling in over on the Texas Star? Rustin tells me you have sheep."

"That's right. Ten and two lambs right now. So you knew my great-grandparents?"

"Yes, I did. They were good neighbors. Adelaide was older than me and Henry by ten years. I was just a little girl when she left town but I remember her singing in church. She had a lovely voice," Hope said.

"Still does," Nash said. "So you and Uncle Henry were about the same age?"

"That's right," Hope said.

They were silent for a few moments and then Hope said, "Have you heard anything from him lately?"

"No, ma'am."

"Did your uncle Henry come to visit y'all very often after he moved away from Happy?" Her voice softened to a whisper.

"Last time I saw Uncle Henry, I must've been about sixteen or so. He just stayed a day and a night if I remember right. That would have been a few months before he left Happy."

Nash stopped at the barn door and held it open for her. "So you've lived on this ranch your whole life?"

"I have. When my folks died, I inherited the place. My husband, Wes, and I ran it together until he passed on and then I managed it with the help of my grandsons until last spring."

Nash didn't want a history lesson. He wanted to ask

when Kasey had moved back, but that would simply cause more conversation, so he kept his mouth shut.

"Now, let's go inside. I'll have to sit at the head table, but you can go on and get some food and find a place to get acquainted with the folks. For the most part we're a likable bunch."

Checking out the whole barn with one glance, he noticed an exit at the back and a doorway leading up to a loft in addition to the wide doorway where he and Hope had entered. Delicious aromas from food tables on the right and an open bar just beyond that called to him. It had been more than a week since he'd had something that didn't come out of a can or go into the microwave. Hope said something and he nodded, hoping that he wasn't agreeing to something he couldn't deliver, because he hadn't understood much over the sound of the band firing up with an old Travis Tritt song.

His stomach growled and the food looked good, so he filled a plate and escaped up to the loft where he could watch the festivities without actually having to talk to anyone. He sat down on the bottom of three risers, and balancing the plate on his knees, he gazed down at the crowd. A tall guy sitting beside the groom stood up, tapped his glass with a spoon, and then picked up a microphone.

"A toast to the couple. I'm Jace Dawson, Brody's brother. All I can say is bless Lila's heart. It'll take a saint to live with Brody, so she's got her work cut out for her."

A round of laughter and applause and then Jace went on. "Here's to Brody and to Lila. Welcome to the family, Lila. We're glad you're one of us."

He'd barely taken his seat when Kasey popped up. "Y'all all know me. I'm the kid sister that no one talks about."

Another round of laughter. "I want to make a toast to the couple but mine is mainly to Lila. I love you, Brody, but you've got to take a backseat for a little while. Lila, I've always wanted a sister just like you. I admired you before you ever moved away and I'm glad that now I can claim you for my own. If Brody isn't nice, I've got two shovels out in the barn. They'll never find his body."

"Hey, now!" Brody said.

"Sisters stick together." Kasey raised her glass. "I love you both and have no doubts that you'll be together for the long haul. Here's to all of us raising another glass when we celebrate your fiftieth anniversary."

Nash had thought Kasey was downright cute with dust all over her, her voice all loud and demanding and in her mama bear mode protecting her son. But with the candlelight reflecting in her gorgeous red hair and a voice that sounded like whiskey laced with a drop or two of honey, the whole scene took his breath away. He leaned forward to get a better look and to hear every word and had to scramble when his plate began to slide right off his lap.

"Whoa, cowboy!" he muttered.

* * *

A prickly feeling on the back of her neck told Kasey that someone was staring right at her. She scanned the room, but she couldn't see a single set of eyes trained her way. Lila and Brody were on the dance floor for their first dance as a married couple. Gracie had rustled up a high chair for Silas, and she kept wiping barbecue sauce from his hands and mouth. The dance ended and the lead singer for the band invited everyone out onto the dance floor. Emma wasted no time dragging her uncle Jace out there so she could stand on his feet for the next country waltz. Rustin and his grandpa, Paul, were in a serious conversation, most likely about dogs or maybe about how he'd been grounded to his room and barely got to come to the wedding.

Kasey couldn't shake that antsy feeling, so she pushed back her chair and stood up. That gave her a new perspective, but she still couldn't meet anyone's gaze. She meandered through the barn toward the buffet table and got a small bowl of blackberry cobbler.

"Ice cream on top?" a server asked.

"Yes, please," she said.

No one seemed to even miss her as she circled around the outside of the barn and tiptoed up to the stairs to the loft for a few moments away from the crowd. Move on, everyone said, but that was a hell of a lot easier said than done, especially when that would mean forgetting, and Adam had been so wonderful as a husband and father. It wasn't like she was going to throw those memories into a big bag to take to the Goodwill store. She treasured each and every one of them entirely too much.

Kasey took off her high heels on the bottom step and padded barefoot up the stairs. Seeing Nash Lamont sitting on the bottom bleacher brought her up short in her tracks. She blinked half a dozen times, but he was still sitting there with an empty plate sitting beside him.

She stared at his scuffed cowboy boots and let her gaze travel upward to the jeans that hugged his thighs, to his silver belt buckle with a longhorn bull engraved on it. From there up to his neck all she could see was a camo flak jacket.

"Why are you hidin' out up here?" she asked.

He looked up slowly, his eyes meeting hers. "I don't belong down there. I wasn't dressed for a fancy party. I brought Hero home, and your grandma insisted that…" He let the sentence hang in the air.

"She gets her way almost every time." Kasey sat down a couple of feet down the wooden bench from him.

"The food was good." He nodded toward the empty plate. "I should be going."

"Why?"

"I'm intruding."

"Nonsense. Stay and talk to me. I'm a third wheel no matter which way I turn."

"Okay," he answered. "It looks like a nice reception."

"It's the way Lila wanted it," she said. "When I married my husband, Adam, we had a reception here, too. It was a lot like this one, just a country wedding."

"And then?"

"Then we moved to Lawton, Oklahoma, where he was stationed in the army. We thought we'd see the world, but he never got orders to go anywhere else, at least not where I could go," Kasey said.

"Oh?" Nash asked.

"Classified missions popped up a few times a year, and he'd be gone a week or two. Once he was deployed for six months. He was killed two years ago while on one of those secret missions." She had no idea why she was telling a complete stranger about her life.

"I was in the army," he said.

"I gathered that you'd been in the service when you introduced yourself as Captain Nash Lamont. How long have you been out?" She dug into the cobbler and was on the third bite before he answered.

"Two years."

"So what took you so long to get to Happy? I'm naturally nosy. You can tell me that you don't want to answer my questions and I won't be offended."

A smile almost turned his mouth upward but it didn't

reach his eyes. "I was in therapy, and my doctor didn't think I should leave the area. But Addy, my grandmother, who was raised up on the Texas Star, thought that..."

"Grandmothers can be pushy like that, but they're usually pretty wise about things. Did you have PTSD?" Kasey asked when he left the sentence hanging.

His head bobbed once, but he kept his eyes on the dance floor rather than looking at her. Was he the one who'd been staring at her earlier?

She laid a hand on his shoulder. "I understand. I was married to an army guy and—well, I know. He couldn't tell me a lot, but a wife knows."

"At the time things happened, it was horrible. But I thought I was strong enough to come home and forget it all, but it didn't happen that way," he said hoarsely.

She removed her hand and held it tightly in her lap. The touch was supposed to bring comfort to him, not create a soft flutter in her heart. "The mind doesn't work like that, though. It remembers the horrors as well as the good times and usually at the craziest times. I can be walkin' across the kitchen floor and a memory pops into my head that makes me want to sit down and cry. Or I can remember something during a prayer at church and almost burst out laughing."

He nodded. "When I'm in the pasture or the barn is about the only time I can find real peace. Taking care of my sheep puts quiet into my soul. I don't usually talk so much. I'm sorry."

"Don't be. I totally understand."

Another nod. "I was in the Future Farmers of America when I was in school and showed both steers and sheep. If I had my way, I'd be an old-time shepherd and live back in the hills with a whole flock."

"I know cows but not sheep. Don't know many folks

around here—other than a few kids in FFA at school who have them—no one raises them for market," Kasey said.

"Your kids goin' to be in FFA?" Nash asked.

"Probably," Kasey said. "Rustin already wants to grow up and be a cowboy just like his uncle Brody. I expect he'll start showing steers in 4-H and then move to FFA when he's old enough, like we all did."

Another nod. Evidently Nash Lamont was a man of few words, but the silence wasn't uncomfortable. Kasey folded her hands in her lap and watched Lila and Brody dancing together again. He gazed down into her eyes and said something that made her roll up on her toes and kiss him.

"Ever been married?" she finally asked.

"No, ma'am."

Kasey leaned up for a better look at the dance floor when Rustin tapped Brody on the arm and asked to cut in for a dance with the bride. Brody stepped back and held out his hand to three-year-old Emma, who reached up to him. He took her up in his arms and moved around the floor to a fast swing dance. Rustin did a good job of holding Lila's hand and dancing with her for the last minute of the song.

"They're cute," Nash said. "You said earlier that you've got three, right?"

She nodded. "Thank you and yes. Rustin, Emma, and Silas."

"Nice family."

"They keep me on my toes."

He stood up. "I really should go now."

"Hey, the party isn't nearly over. Come on downstairs and meet the town folks," Kasey said.

"Thank you but..." He hesitated and his eyes darted around the place, as if trying to avoid even looking down at all the people.

"Don't do crowds too well?" she asked.

A slight shake of the head. "Not so much."

"Well, you could ease into Happy by coming to Sunday dinner over here on Hope Springs after church tomorrow morning," she said.

He reached for the dirty plate. "Thanks, but I've got other plans."

She laid a hand on his. "I'll take it when I go. Go right when you reach the end of the steps and there's a little side door if you want to sneak out. It's right across from the restrooms."

She hadn't felt even a tiny spark in two years, and two in one night shocked her. It had to be the setting. A wedding nearly always made single folks think about white dresses and three-tiered cakes.

He quickly pulled away his hand. "Thank you."

"I'm sorry, Adam," she whispered as she picked up Nash's plate.

That irritating voice in her head immediately started an argument. *Why should you be sorry? Adam told you more than a dozen times if he ever did not return from a mission that you were to move on and not be lonely.*

She set her jaw in a firm line. *It's the wedding that caused me to react to Nash Lamont. That's all. I'll prove it the next time I'm around him. I'll deliberately touch his arm or his hand. It won't happen again.*

Chapter Three

Wearing a plaid pearl snap shirt, creased jeans, and polished cowboy boots, Nash timed it so that services had already started when he pulled into the church parking lot. After all, he'd promised his grandmother that he'd show up, not necessarily that he'd be on time. His plan was to sneak in, sit in the back pew, and get out in a hurry the minute the last amen was said. He shook the legs of his jeans down over his boot tops and made it to the church foyer.

The sweet strands of the congregation singing "It Is No Secret" glued his feet to the floor, and he couldn't force himself to go inside. The lyrics said that God would pardon him and it was no secret what God could do. His grandmother believed that, but Nash had his doubts. God might be able to work miracles and magic, but so far Nash hadn't seen much of either. He turned around and slipped away, closing the door gently behind him, and drove back to the Texas Star.

Guilt followed him into the house because he'd told his grandmother that he would go to church that Sunday, and he was a man of his word. He turned on the television and flipped through the channels to one that played old western movies, then watched a little of a John Wayne that he'd seen a dozen times. After a few minutes, he turned off the television, grabbed a light denim jacket and his cowboy hat, and wandered out to sit on the porch steps. It was a lovely fall day, a nice brisk breeze ruffling what was left of the leaves on the trees surrounding the house. But he drifted back two years to that place where sand and heat surrounded him. The vehicle in front of him was blowing up in slow motion and there wasn't one thing he could do to prevent it. He shook his head so hard that his cowboy hat flew off and landed out in the yard.

"Replace those thoughts with something good." He repeated his therapist's words out loud.

The fall leaves lying on the ground caught his attention. The burgundy ones reminded him of Kasey's red hair. A few were the color of her emerald green eyes and the shimmery gold ones were like that gold satin dress that hugged her curves.

He did not have the right to use Kasey as his go-to bright spot to help him crawl up out of the dark places. He left the porch, picked up his hat, and settled it on his head. Then he started toward the barn, only to find Hero at his heels when he'd gone about halfway.

"I'm not taking you home this time, boy. I'm not feeding you or letting you inside the house. If you want to snoop around, that's fine, but you do not live here," he said.

Hero followed him into the barn and sniffed around while Nash did repairs on the six stalls. Usually, fixing something put his mind at ease, but that morning, it didn't work so well. His thoughts kept going back to Kasey in that gold dress and every single word that had come out of her mouth.

His stomach growled and he checked his phone for the time. Noon. He'd been working on the stalls for two hours and Hero had disappeared. The white cat that he and Rustin had petted together wandered out of nowhere, then went back toward the tack room. He made a mental note to pick up a bag of cat food next time he was in Amarillo. A cat in the barn would help keep the mouse population down.

Shivering against the cold north wind that had kicked up while he'd been busy with a hammer and nails, Nash pulled his collar up and headed toward the house in a slow jog. He hung his jacket on a nail inside the back door and removed his hat. He made a ham sandwich and carried it along with a bag of chips through the door into the other room. He turned on the television and flipped through the channels, but nothing kept his attention for more than a few seconds.

The place felt empty, so he put his jacket back on, set his hat on his head, and took off in long strides toward the corral on the backside of the barn where the sheep were. Propping a foot on the fence and his arms on the top rail, he counted them—one ram, nine ewes, and two lambs. They were at peace but he wasn't, and there was nothing that needed his attention right then. He started walking toward the back corner of the property where his little herd of Angus cattle had been grazing this past week. A small creek ran through the Texas Star—good, clear water that meant he didn't have to sink a well or keep a tank filled for the cattle. It cut through at an angle and then widened out as it bubbled its way over to Hope Springs on just the other side of the barbed-wire fence.

One second he was on his side of the fence, the next he

was following the creek to see where it led. A few minutes later he came to a place that took his breath. Clear, cold water tumbling over rocks, a grassy bank, and a big weeping willow tree, still with a few leaves attached to the drooping limbs, all beckoned to him. He squatted down and stuck his hand in the water but removed it when it got so cold that it ached. Straightening up, he made his way to the willow tree. He sat down with his back against the trunk and began to hum "Amazing Grace." A rare smile appeared when the words played through his mind saying that he once was lost but now was found.

"I'm in church, Addy, but not in a building. I am lost, but if I could have the peace I feel right here, I could possibly find my way home," he mumbled.

* * *

Any day that Kasey had fifteen minutes to herself was a rarity. But that Sunday afternoon after church, she had two whole hours. A luxury in any mother's book, even if she did love her children. Tradition was that they decorated for Christmas the Sunday after Thanksgiving, but since Brody and Lila wouldn't return from their very short honeymoon until Monday, it had been postponed until Tuesday evening. Sunday dinner had been over at her mother's place, the Prairie Rose Ranch.

She was ready to go home when she and her mother found Emma and Silas both asleep on the sofa. Rustin and Jace were watching a football game together, and he'd offered to bring all the kids home after the game and naps were done.

She'd thought about taking a long, warm bath with candles, bubbles, and a good romance book. No kids to knock on the door every five minutes wanting her to settle a fight or to hurry up and get done so she could make them a snack. Then she'd entertained the notion of going to the café and sitting in a back booth all alone with a big chunk of Molly's pecan pie and a cup of coffee, but she'd just had dinner and she wasn't hungry. She drove back to Hope Springs and settled into the recliner with a book but not even the steamy scenes between the cowboy and the sassy lady kept her attention.

Finally, after restlessly pacing around the living room and dining area a few times, she shoved her feet into a pair of worn work boots, her arms into a canvas work coat, and headed out the back door. A long walk would do her more good than a long bath anyway, especially after the huge Thanksgiving dinner, the wedding reception dinner, and then another big meal that day over on Prairie Rose.

With Rustin's half-grown dog chasing along in front of her and his two litter mates coming behind her, she walked over to the fence separating Hope Springs from the Texas Star. With Nash in the house now and his sheep in the corral behind the barn, kids wouldn't go there on Saturday night to play loud music and hang out with their friends. Country kids respected animals, so they wouldn't spook the livestock. Henry had never kept cattle up close to the barn and neither had Paul McKay, Adam's father and also the rancher who'd leased the land after Henry had disappeared.

The old sheet iron building had been the place to go on Saturday nights. At least that's where they'd hung out when she and Adam were teenagers. Drinking a few beers when they were underage, dancing to country music turned up as high as someone's truck radio would go, making out in the loft—that was Saturday night fun.

"Oh, Adam, I miss those weekends we spent there." With

a long sigh she turned around and started walking back toward the house, but when she came to the fork in the path, she took the right one and headed toward Hope Springs. Checking to make sure her phone was turned on so that Jace could call when he got home with the children, she whistled for the dogs. They bounded out of a copse of scrub oak trees and ran out ahead of her again, eager to continue the adventure.

When they reached the springs, all the dogs didn't waste a bit of time getting to the edge of the water for a long, cool drink. Kasey parted the bare branches of the willow tree so she could sit awhile and listen to the peaceful bubbling water. Her eyes widened and her heart kicked in an extra beat when she realized that Nash Lamont was sleeping soundly under her tree.

She eased down, sitting a couple of feet from him and stared her fill of the long, tall cowboy. Heavy black lashes rested on cheekbones so chiseled and perfect that they'd make a sculptor swoon. His big hands were folded in his lap and his legs stretched out so far that the branches touched his boots. Her eyes followed the length of his body from eyelashes to toes and back again. He had to be at least six feet three inches tall because he was taller than Brody. He didn't look so dark and intense in sleep, but reminded her of a little boy like Rustin with his dark hair and eyes.

His eyes fluttered open and his head jerked around so quickly that his hat fell off to one side. He combed his black hair back with his fingertips and cut his dark brown eyes around toward Kasey. "Guess I'm trespassing."

"Neighbors don't trespass. They're welcome." She smiled.

"Thank you. I didn't mean to fall asleep. It's just so peaceful here with the sound of the water and the willow branches." He covered a yawn with his hand. "Excuse me. I haven't slept like that in two years."

"I've always felt like when I get under these drooping branches that none of the world or its problems can reach me," she said. "Believe me, I've taken lots of naps right here and worked through lots of problems. I thought we might see you in church this mornin'."

"I was there but I couldn't make myself go inside," he said, honestly.

She reached across the space separating them and laid her hand on his shoulder. "It's okay. When you feel like it, we'll make you welcome."

There it was again—that little flutter in her gut. So it hadn't just been the balcony in the barn or the aura around the wedding.

A faint smile turned up the corners of his mouth. "I like this church better."

"So do I, but my mama and grandmother would have a fit if I declared that I'd be spending Sunday morning out under a tree appreciating God's handiwork in Mother Nature," she admitted.

He nodded and reached for his hat. "What time is it?"

"Getting close to three," she answered.

"I should be going and let you have your time here," he said. "Have to start feeding the sheep in about an hour."

"Stay awhile," she said. "If you like ranchin' so much, whatever made you go to the army?"

"Felt like my country needed me."

"My husband thought that same thing, but he planned to come back to Texas when he retired and ranch the rest of his life."

Nash nodded but didn't say anything.

Sitting there with him without talking should have been awkward but it wasn't. Her mind wandered to her own thoughts about Adam, but she kept sneaking peeks at Nash.

At one time his brow was furrowed so deep that she feared he'd never get the wrinkles out. At another, a tiny smile tickled the corners of his lips.

Had he had a wife at one time or maybe a girlfriend? Did the memories of times they shared make him happy, or was he thinking of that when he frowned? Nash Lamont was certainly not an open book like Adam had been or her brothers, and he intrigued Kasey. She wanted him to talk to her, to tell her stories, especially those of what kind of life he'd had when he was in the sand pit, as Adam called it.

Maybe karma or fate or God—whatever anyone wanted to call it—had sent him to Happy to talk to her about what life was really like over there. If she knew, then maybe she could move on.

* * *

"So did you and Adam used to come out here?" Nash felt guilty the minute he said the words. He had no right to bring up what had to be a painful subject.

Before Kasey could answer, three half-grown black Labrador dogs flopped down on one side of him. One laid his head in Nash's lap and looked up at him with big round eyes, begging to get his ears rubbed. The other two were so close to him that he could feel their little hearts doing double-time.

"They were gettin' a drink the last time I noticed them. I guess they've been out chasin' squirrels or rabbits," Kasey said. "And to answer your question, Adam and I never came here at all. We swam in the springs on the hottest days of summer when we thought we could stand the cold water, but we never sat under the willow tree," she answered.

He didn't want to interfere with precious memories, but

that she hadn't shared this place with Adam made the black cloud that was ever present rise above his head—only a few inches, not a whole mile, but he couldn't wait to tell the therapist on his next visit.

"Which one is that?" He pointed at the dog wagging her tail.

"That's Princess, Emma's dog. And this one is Doggy." She smiled.

"I'm guessing Silas picked Doggy, huh? And I can understand why your daughter chose Princess, but why Hero?"

"Rustin likes Superman, Batman, and all the superheroes. He couldn't decide which one to name the dog because he didn't want to hurt the others' feelings. He pondered over it for a whole day before he finally decided if he named his dog Hero it would cover the whole lot of them," she explained.

Nash stroked their fur, giving each one equal time. "Labs are good dogs for kids."

"Yep." Kasey nodded. "Doggy lets Silas wallow all over him, and trails along behind him like a babysitter. You got a dog over on your place?"

Nash shook his head. "Not yet. If I stay after this year, I might look for a blue heeler. They're pretty good with cows and sheep both."

"If you stay?"

"I promised my grandmother that I'd stick it out for a year, so I'm committed to that much." He stood up so fast that he was a blur. Talking to her was good—maybe too good—but the flight mode was twisting his heart into a pretzel. It didn't hit often these days, but when it did, he had to be alone. "Have a nice afternoon. I'm sure we'll meet up again."

"Right back atcha," she said, nodding. "I've got to get

back to the house, too, so I'll walk with you to the fork in the pathway."

"What path? I came by way of the creek."

"There's a shorter way for you to get home. I'll show you." She started off in the opposite direction of the way he'd come.

So much for running away. His therapist said that he should face his problems head-on, take them by the horns like they were a bull and spit in their face. Maybe this was one of those times, but Nash just wanted to get back across that barbed-wire fence and crawl back into his own little safe world.

"This way," she said.

Shortening his stride so that she didn't have to do double-time, he stole sidelong glances at her. The afternoon sunlight highlighted the curly red ponytail that whipped from side to side as she walked. Her body was that of a woman, not a young girl—just the right size for a man to hold. Full lips were made for kissing and her bright green eyes for mischief. He wished he'd known her years ago, maybe even before she and Adam had become an item.

No, no, no! That aggravating voice in his head screamed. *Don't even begin to think like that. It's not right. This is not grabbing the bull by the horns at all.*

* * *

"Well, here's where we part ways unless you want to come over for a cup of coffee and some cookies left over from Thanksgiving," Kasey said when they reached the division of the rutted pathway.

"Better not," he answered.

"About a quarter of a mile down that way, you'll come to the fence that separates our two ranches. From there it's just a little ways to your barn," she told him, wishing that he'd have a change of mind.

With a tip of his hat and the slightest nod, he left her there in front of an old oak log and lengthened his stride. She watched his swagger until he was completely out of sight and wondered what he'd been like as a younger man.

"And I bet all the girls went crazy over that southern drawl," she muttered.

In a few minutes she was back at the house. She'd kicked off her boots and was hanging up her coat when the front door opened. Rustin and Emma rushed in, and when Jace put Silas on the floor, his chubby little legs tried to catch up with the other two. Jace helped Kasey remove their coats and hang them on the hall tree before he went right back out the door to do evening chores.

"I wanted to go outside and play with Hero. I bet he missed me today," Rustin said.

Emma folded her arms over her chest and tapped her foot. "And Princess needs me."

Silas headed toward the hall tree for his coat. "Doggy?"

"Your dogs have been out running all afternoon and they're asleep in the barn right now. I took them for a walk and they're very tired, so figure out something to play with. Remember, Rustin, you go back to school tomorrow, and Emma, you're going with me and Granny to the church to help get things decorated for Christmas," she said.

"I thought we were decorating our house tomorrow," Rustin said.

"That's on Tuesday after your Uncle Brody and Aunt Lila get home," she said. "Right now you can each bring a toy or a book from your room and play in the foyer or the living room. But when you get done, you have to take that one back before you bring anything else out."

"That's great mothering." Hope made her way into the kitchen through the back door. "Your mama sent over the leftover roast. I thought maybe we'd pull it apart and make hot beef sandwiches for supper. Maybe some macaroni and cheese and fried apples to go with it. Silas loves those two things." She hung her coat on a hook by the back door and went straight to the pantry. "I'll peel the apples if you'll start the water for macaroni. There ain't nothing crankier in the world than a hungry kid."

Kasey looped an apron over her head. "Or a hungry cowboy. Jace is doing chores by himself since Brody is off on his honeymoon, and they've let all hired help go until spring. So he's going to work up an appetite."

Cooking had always been Kasey's escape, even as a teenager. Give her a kitchen and a mixing bowl or some pots and pans and she could solve any problem.

"So what did you do with your little bit of free time?" Hope asked.

"What did you and Mama do while the kids napped?" Kasey said, avoiding the question.

"We talked about the future. Think a dozen apples will do?"

"Maybe you should add a couple more. Jace really loves them."

Hope eyed her. "And now, what did you do all afternoon?"

"I took a walk to the springs and sat under the willow tree."

"Did that make you feel better?" Hope asked.

She put a pot of water on the stove to boil for macaroni. "Than what? I haven't felt bad or haven't been sick."

"You've acted strange since the wedding reception last night. I'm worried that it stressed you out with memories about Adam."

Kasey nodded. "I did have a few moments, but I wouldn't ever want Brody or Lila to know. It was their day and it should have been perfect, just like mine and Adam's wedding was. I only hope that..."

Hope patted her on the arm. "I know, baby girl. Both of us want their marriage to last until they're old and gray and that neither of them will be jerked away in the prime of their youth. But, Kasey, it's past time for you to move on and get a life outside of ranchin' and your kids. You need to start dating again."

"Have you moved on? Grandpa's been gone twelve years. I don't see you dating."

"I'm past seventy and there's a lot less future than past in my life. Not so with you. I know that it's something that you have to do on your own, but if there's anything I can do to help at any time, I'm here."

"Nash Lamont was at the springs," Kasey blurted out.

"And?"

"He's a man of few words."

Hope chuckled. "Like his uncle Henry. That man couldn't hide a single emotion, but he didn't talk a lot."

"What?" Kasey frowned.

"His expressions were written all over his face. If he'd have been a poker player, he'd have lost Texas Star for sure," Hope answered.

Kasey's head bobbed as she remembered the frown on Nash's face and then that very slight grin. He might not have a lot to say, but his face was a whole storybook of emotions, chapter after chapter. She wondered if she spent more time with him just how it might read.

Emma pulled on her apron tail. "I want to cook with you. Rustin is mean and Silas is a baby."

Kasey pulled a chair up to the counter and gave Emma a handful of elbow macaroni. "You can look at these real careful and make sure there's not a single black mark on any of them. You know how Silas hates it when he sees a dark spot and it will help me so much. Why is Rustin mean?"

"He wants to play cowboys."

"And you want to play dolls, right?" Hope asked.

Emma pushed her little red curls behind her ears and set about the job. "I want to do a puzzle."

Hope finished peeling the apples and tossed them into butter melting in a cast-iron skillet. "I'm glad that you and Adam had more than one child."

"Me, too." Kasey smiled.

Emma eyed every single piece of macaroni before she put it into the bowl.

Silas pushed a big yellow truck into the kitchen, around the table, and out of the kitchen, making engine sounds the whole time.

Rustin argued with imaginary bank robbers in the living room.

Had Adam lived, they'd planned on at least four and maybe six children. He'd been an only child and they both wanted a big family.

Is Nash an only child?

Now, where had that thought come from? She shouldn't be thinking of him and Adam in the same moment. She felt as if someone had suddenly dribbled ice down her back, like Adam used to do to tease her.

Hope poked her on the arm with the handle of a wooden spoon. "Water is boiling, and, honey, you don't hide things so well either."

Chapter Four

Monday started out just fine. Nash put in two new fence posts out near the road and stretched new barbed wire between them. Then he drove into town where he bought enough feed to last a month for his sheep, brought it home, and unloaded it into one of the empty stalls in the barn.

He hummed along with the country music song in his head as he headed toward the house at noon. His stomach let him know that it had been awhile since breakfast and that the bowl of oatmeal he'd had was long since gone.

He was almost to the porch when something orange and moving like lightning brushed past his leg and right behind it a blur of black did the same thing.

"Dammit! Hero!" he yelled. "You aren't supposed to chase the kittens."

The dog plopped down on his butt at the base of the huge oak tree at the edge of the back porch and looked up, daring the poor little orange kitten to come back down.

"Am I going to have to put up 'no trespassing' signs?" he asked the dog as he headed back to the barn for a ladder.

Hero yipped but stayed in his place. The kitten had set up a heart-wrenching wail, so Nash jogged all the way out there and back.

He propped the old wooden ladder on the tree and was on the top rung, reaching out toward the kitten, when it scooted another foot away. He leaned toward it and stretched his long arm out and snatched the furry kitten by the scruff of the neck. It went limp and he held it close to his chest as he started down the ladder, slowly, one rung at a time.

Everything was under control until Hero threw back his big black head and howled. The kitten flipped around, dug its claws into Nash's chest, and wiggled free of his hands. It jumped away from him and hugged the tree like a long-lost brother. When Nash grabbed for it, it scampered down the bark to land on the ground and made a mad dash for the barn, with Hero right behind it. That's when Nash took another step and the rung of the old wooden ladder split. He reached out for anything to break his fall, but all he got was a handful of air. His whole life didn't flash before his eyes in that split second before he hit the ground, but a picture of Kasey did.

Red hair tickled his nose when he awoke.

"Nash, are you alive? Wake up and talk to me." Her voice sounded as if it came from the bottom of his grandmother's old well, but he was imagining things or else Kasey was really bending over him. He slid one eyelid open enough to see the glint of the sun flashing off her gold wedding band. Thank God she was there. She'd know what to do; she always did.

"I'm not dead, darlin'. Don't fuss at Rustin because Hero chased the cat. It wasn't his fault." His eyelids fluttered and he slipped back into the darkness.

The next time he awoke, he was moving but it was okay because Kasey was right there beside him, holding his hand. With his thumb, he checked to be sure her wedding band was still there. He couldn't remember their wedding day but that was okay. The explosion had caused some memory loss, but it would all return as long as Kasey was beside him. His brow furrowed into deep lines as he tried to figure out exactly how she'd gotten there but as long as she was there beside him she'd fix everything.

"Open your eyes, Nash. I'm so sorry about all this. I'm going to have Jace build a dog pen so Hero won't run away anymore," Kasey said.

"I'll build our dog pens. Jace don't have to do that. Just get me stitched up and home and I'll take care of our family," Nash muttered.

A bright white light greeted him a few minutes later when he awoke. He'd died and was on his way into eternity. He couldn't be dead. God would have to send him back to earth. His life was not finished. He had to build dog pens because he'd promised Kasey that he would, and a man was only as good as his word.

"Mr. Lamont, you need to lie still," said a man in white beside him.

Angels didn't look like that. They had red hair and green eyes and sexy bodies. The only difference between them and Kasey was that they had wings and a visible halo. He tried to sit up, but strong hands held him still.

"Kasey!" he yelled so loud that it echoed off the walls.

She leaned over him and he reached up to touch her face. He hadn't died. He was in the base hospital. "Tell me I didn't lose a leg or an arm."

"No bones are broken, and there's no blood," she answered.

"Tell them to turn me loose then. I've got to save the boy and my team and then we're going home to build dog pens."

"It's a concussion," the doctor said. "We'll keep him overnight for observation."

Panic set in. He couldn't stay. If he did Kasey would disappear and he couldn't bear to tell her good-bye, not even for one night. He'd been on this mission so long that sometimes he had trouble remembering her face.

"No, I can't! Send me home. I can't stay here." His heart raced as he brought her hand to his lips to kiss the knuckles. "Take me home, Kasey. I need to be home. We've got to build Hero a dog pen. The kids need me."

"I need to talk to the doctor first to see what we have to do if we take you home." Kasey pulled her hand free. "I'll only be right outside that door."

His eyes followed her finger. "Promise you won't leave without me."

"I promise. If they make you stay here, I will stay with you."

"I want to go home. My sheep and my team need me."

The doctor wasn't much taller than Kasey, had a baby face that guaranteed he'd be carded in any bar in the whole world, and blond hair. He carried a tablet with him and checked all the information before he even spoke.

"I can release him, but only if he has someone with him. PTSD, right? I've treated lots of veterans with these symptoms, especially after a head injury."

Kasey nodded. "I'm his neighbor and I'll be glad to stay with him tonight."

"It could stretch into more than tonight. He'll need someone there until he gets his rightful mind back. Might be in twenty-four hours and it will all come back in a rush. Could be in a few days or even a couple of weeks and return in tiny bits and pieces. Right now he's grabbing at bits and pieces of memories. Some from his past and some that could be totally imaginary. He thinks that you're his wife," the doctor said.

Kasey inhaled deeply and let it out slowly. "How am I going to handle that?"

"How well do you know him?"

"He lives on the ranch next door to mine, but..." She hesitated. "It was my son's dog that caused the accident, and my grandmother was good friends with his great-uncle. But what am I going to do about this wife thing? I don't mind helping him out until he gets his memory back, but..." She threw up her palms.

"Small towns." The doctor chuckled. "He shouldn't climb ladders. And you can tell him that I said no sex until I check him in at least three weeks." He touched the screen on his tablet a few times. "I'll see you on December fifteenth at ten thirty. My clinic is a block down from this hospital. The nurse will give you his paperwork with the appointment card. If you need anything or have any questions, my phone number is on the card. Good luck."

"Thank you." Kasey's phone rang and she quickly answered it.

"How is he?" Hope asked. "Are they going to admit him?"

"They want to keep him, but he's refused. He's definitely disoriented and Granny..." She inhaled so deeply that she shivered. "He thinks I'm his wife. The doctor says that he can leave but only if someone is around to watch over him. If I stay with him tonight, can you and Jace manage the kids until tomorrow morning?"

"I've sent Emma and Silas to your mother's place. She's tickled to get them, and Paul and Gracie are picking Rustin up at school and taking him to their place for tonight and tomorrow. I figured you'd want to stay with Nash in the hospital, since it was Hero that caused the problem. But…" Hope stopped talking.

"But what, Granny?" Kasey asked.

"His wife?" Hope groaned. "How are you going to deal with that?"

"It'll be fine, Granny. I'm sure he'll come back to himself soon." Kasey was glad that her grandmother couldn't see the blush burning her cheeks.

"I'll call Adelaide, his grandmother, for him and tell her what's going on."

"Granny, what am I going to do if it lasts more than a day?" Kasey asked.

"You'll have to stay with him. We'll bring the kids over there after tonight if we need to. Jace and Paul are coming to town for vet supplies, so I sent your van with Jace. He should be there any minute with the keys. He can ride back home with Paul."

"Why couldn't Rustin have wanted a cat or a fish?" She sighed.

Hope chuckled. "All things happen for the best, my child. In ten years you'll look back at this and see the purpose of it in your life."

"I know but…" Kasey sighed. It seemed like every sentence she'd said in the last fifteen minutes had been left hanging.

Just like your life right now, huh? That pesky voice in her head said.

"Exactly," she whispered.

"Are you talking to the doctor?" Hope asked.

"No, myself. Granny, this is going to be such a disruption."

"Sometimes a little disruption in the schedule ain't so bad. If he feels like it tomorrow night, bring him over here to decorate our tree. Maybe that will help jar his memories. Sometimes little things do," Hope said. "Now I have to go call Adelaide."

"Okay," Kasey said. "And thanks, Granny. I see Jace coming down the hallway now."

"Bye," Hope said.

Jace handed off the keys and raised an eyebrow. "So are you spending the night here?" His grin kept growing until he started to laugh out loud as she explained the situation.

She popped her hands on her hips and glared at him. "It's not funny."

"No, it's not—but it is." He wiped his eyes with the back of his hand.

She doubled up her fist and hit him on the shoulder. "Hopefully, he'll be normal and I'll be home by morning."

He blew out a puff of air toward the place she'd smacked him. "Mosquitoes cause more damage than that. You'd best practice your swing for your first fight with your new husband."

"Karma is a bitch, and I will get even," she said.

"Take out your anger on Hero, not me. I'm not even the messenger. I'm just the bringer of the keys so you can start your new life at Texas Star," Jace shot over his shoulder as he headed out of the hospital.

"No! No! No! He can't be dead!" Nash's frantic voice came through the doors leading back into the emergency room.

Kasey rushed into the room and went straight to the bed. "No one died. Hero is back at Hope Springs and the kitten is with its mama." She took his hand in hers and gently rubbed the knuckle with her fingertips.

He gripped it hard. "Okay, I believe you. The boy is alive and my team members getting killed? It was all a nightmare, right?"

"Just calm down and breathe. The doctor says we can go home, but you have to follow his rules."

"He told me." Nash sighed. "We can be good for a little while, right?"

"I believe we can."

"Okay, then, let's go home, darlin'. Where are the kids?"

"They're going to stay with my mom tonight."

"Dammit! A night alone and we can't..." he whispered. "Kasey, I remember going up the tree to get the kitten, but everything else except you and Rustin is a blur. Will you help me?"

"Of course." She managed a smile.

* * *

It was almost supper time when they got back to the ranch that evening. She pulled up in front of the house and Nash got out, cocked his head to one side, and frowned. "Is this where we live? Did you move after I deployed the last time? I don't remember this place."

"It's the Texas Star Ranch here in Happy. Your great-grandmother lived here until about twelve years ago. So did your uncle Henry, but he left after she died. It's been leased out until this last month when you decided to come back here and do some ranchin'."

"Hmmm," he mumbled. "I like ranchin', right?"

"I hope so. You've got sheep in the corral behind the barn. You ready to go inside?"

"We have to build a dog pen and take care of the sheep, right?"

"You have to rest until tomorrow. Doctor's orders. Jace will do the chores tonight and we'll figure it all out a day at a time," she said.

"This place doesn't look familiar at all, Kasey," he said. "Are you sure that we live here?"

"I'm very sure." She hoped that the front door wasn't locked because she didn't have a key. If this was really her house, she'd march right up on the porch. Without a second thought, she'd go inside, shed her coat and boots, and head to the kitchen to make supper.

Like in a play or a movie, I'm a character, she thought. *I'm Kasey Lamont and Nash is my husband. I can do this— maybe I'll even win an Oscar for my performance.*

She got out of the truck and made her way across the lawn with Nash right behind her. Except for that silver dollar-size mark on his forehead that resembled a carpet burn, he looked fine. His coat still had a couple of dry leaves clinging to it, and his T-shirt had a few blood spots where the cat had most likely scratched him, but he hadn't lost a bit of his swagger.

The last time she'd been in the house was when she was fourteen. Minnie Thomas had died, and she had come over with Hope to bring a pot roast. The door opened into a wide foyer with a living room, dining room, and kitchen to the left. On the right there was a master bedroom, bathroom, and a small office. She remembered three bedrooms and a bathroom upstairs.

"Hungry?" she asked as she removed her coat and hung it on the hall tree.

She hardly recognized the place. Minnie had loved knickknacks and they'd been everywhere. Ceramic angels of all kinds and descriptions and animals like bunnies and squirrels with little beady eyes that followed her around the room. Now everything looked practically sterile.

His fingers closed around her arm and he pulled her toward him. "The doctor said no sex," he whispered hoarsely. "He didn't say no kissing."

He ran a fingertip from her ear to her chin. "You're so beautiful. My breath caught in my chest the first time I saw you. I'm the luckiest man in the world that you married me."

Kasey's common sense told her to pull away with an excuse, but she was mesmerized by those dark brown lashes lying on his high cheekbones. She didn't even realize that she'd rolled up on her toes and moistened her lips until he drew her close to his chest and his lips closed on hers.

The first kiss was sweet, but they grew hotter and hotter, turning her knees so weak that she had to lean into him to keep from falling. Her arms slid up around his neck, fingers playing in his thick black hair as he teased her mouth open with his tongue.

Finally, he took half a step back. "Much more of that and I'll tell the doctor to take his orders, pour barbecue sauce on them, and eat them for supper. God, why'd I have to fall off the damn ladder? I want you so bad, Kasey."

"The weeks until your follow-up will go by fast." She turned and walked toward the kitchen, amazed that she didn't fall into a pile of hot hormones right there at the toes of his cowboy boots. "Right now we'd better make some supper. We were in the emergency room all day and I'm starving."

Her voice sounded normal, but her palms were sweaty and her heart fluttered like it had a thousand butterflies inside it. "What sounds good to you? It'll have to be something quick. I hadn't even thought of dinner when I realized you'd fallen." She'd almost said when she sent Emma and

Silas into the house with Hope and went looking for Hero on her own. Not because she wanted to but because Emma was crying about coyotes eating him. Evidently Rustin had told her some tall tale about the coyotes killing baby calves and she figured that if they could bring down an animal that size, poor old Hero didn't have a chance against them. She had no doubt that he'd run off toward the Texas Star again, so Kasey had jogged in that direction and arrived just in time to see Nash tumble off the ladder.

"Breakfast food sounds good to me," he said.

She opened the refrigerator door. "Omelets, bacon, and pancakes?"

"No onions but you know that." He set about making a pot of coffee. "And crispy bacon, but you know that, too."

"Yes, I do. Omelet with cheese and...let me see what's in here. Peppers, tomatoes, mushrooms..." She called out each item and checked his expression with each one. "Tomatoes. No peppers but lots of mushrooms."

"Have I told you today that I love you?" He smiled.

"Probably, but I was so worried about you that I don't remember." She brought out all the ingredients for the omelets and opened a cabinet door, hoping that she was in the right area for pots and pans.

"Not there. Everything else is in the pantry. I'll get the skillet and the potatoes. Let's have hash browns," he said.

"You remembered," she said.

"Crazy, but that's all I remember. That and being in the army. There was a little boy outside the base perimeter and..." His brow furrowed.

"Did you try to save him?"

"I think I did, but it's all a blur."

She patted him on the arm. "It'll all come back. Maybe as soon as tomorrow."

"If I remember, can we go to bed?" He ran a hand down her back and gently squeezed her butt cheek.

"Not until you go back to the doctor." Her voice was barely audible over the whining hormones.

"Well, dammit!" He groaned and opened the door into a huge walk-in pantry.

Yes, sir, Kasey McKay was going to deserve a solid gold Oscar by the time this ordeal was over.

She shut her eyes tightly and sent up a silent prayer, not to Jesus, God, or the angels but to her deceased husband: *Adam, please understand, this is just a role and he's going to be embarrassed about it all when he wakes up in the real world.*

Chapter Five

When Jace knocked on the kitchen door, poked his head inside, and yelled, Kasey wanted to rush into his arms and beg him to take her home. Dinner had been an emotional roller coaster with her guilt about the kissing and Nash flirting across the table all during the meal.

"Anybody home?" Jace's voice floated through across the room. "Hey, I smell bacon. Did you save me some food?"

"Come on in. There's plenty." Kasey jumped up and met him halfway across the room.

He hugged her and whispered, "Are you all right?"

She gave a brief nod. "Look, honey, Jace has come by to see you."

Nash looked up from the table with a blank look on his face.

Her brother towered above her, had dark brown hair and light gray eyes. That he was a Dawson was a surefire thing, but Kasey was a throwback to the Dalley side of the family with her red hair, green eyes, and a faint sprinkling of freckles across her nose.

"Hey, Nash. How are you feelin'?" Jace fell right into the role. "And, Kasey, I can't stay for supper. I was just teasin'. Granny would throw a hissy if I wasn't home for supper tonight. Lila and Brody just came back, and we're all eating together."

"You are..." Nash frowned.

In a few long strides, Jace covered the distance and patted Nash on the shoulder. "Remember, I'm Kasey's brother. Brody is the oldest and then there's me and don't you remember the wedding over the weekend?"

The wrinkles in Nash's brow deepened as he shook hands with Jace. "But Kasey and I've been married for years. We have children. We didn't just get married Saturday night, did we? I'm sorry but I can't remember much right now. The doctor says it will come back, but for right now about all I absolutely know is that I'm married to Kasey and we have a son, Rustin. She tells me that we have a daughter and another son and I'm sure when they come home tomorrow, it'll come back but right now..."

"It was our brother, Brody's wedding," Jace said. "And a concussion works in strange ways. Maybe by this time tomorrow you'll get it all straightened out."

"I hope so," Nash said.

"Chores are done. Sheep have been fed and are all fine. Want me to come back tomorrow morning?"

"Thank you, but Kasey and I'll be able to take care of things by then. This feels so crazy, not knowing my own family," Nash said.

"I can't even imagine." Jace bent down and kissed Kasey on the top of her head. "Call if you need anything. The kids are fine and Lila says she'll drop by in the morning."

"We've got to build a dog pen," Nash blurted out.

"Yes, we do, but not for a few days. Jace is keeping the dogs over on Hope Springs for a little while—just until we get the pen built. Your main job is getting well." She smiled.

"Whatever you say, darlin'."

Jace raised an eyebrow and Kasey shot a dirty look his way, but there was a little spark of heat that flashed through her heart at the sound of his deep southern drawl calling her darlin'.

"See y'all." Jace grabbed a piece of bacon from Kasey's plate and chuckled on his way outside.

Nash yawned. "Supper was great. I'll help with cleanup and then maybe you can tell me about our life together. Maybe it'll set a fire under this memory thing. I'd like to remember your brothers and our children."

Saved by the bell! Kasey thought as her cell phone began to ring. She grabbed it from the countertop behind her and answered Lila's call. "Did you have a happy honeymoon?"

"Short but amazing," Lila said. "We've made an agreement to go back to the resort every year on our anniversary. Now tell me about this situation with Nash. Should I come on over tonight so we can talk it out or wait until morning?"

"Morning is fine or maybe—" She stopped herself before she said that she would be home by then. Nash had started moving dirty plates to the sink, but he could hear every word.

"Maybe you'll be back home?" Lila giggled.

"Hopefully."

"Getting a bit hot in the house, is it? I saw that cowboy from a distance at the wedding. He's really, really sexy. Does he need to lock his bedroom door tonight?" Lila teased.

"You're just home from a honeymoon, so what you have

on your mind is totally different from what's on mine," Kasey said. "I'll see you in the morning."

Nash had stripped out of his plaid flannel shirt and hung it on the back of a chair. Now a white T-shirt hugged rippled muscles that body builders would sell their soul to have. Kasey's hands itched to wrap her arms around him from behind and lay her head against his back, to hear the beating of his heart against her ear.

"He's right there, isn't he?" Lila asked.

"Oh, yes, we've finished supper and Nash is helping with cleanup," Kasey answered in a high-pitched tone.

"Nothing sexier than a man washing dishes," Lila whispered. "I can't wait to hear all about this tomorrow. Lord, girl, you might knock me off the Happy, Texas, bad girl throne. Call me later if you need to talk."

"Brody would shoot me dead if I interrupted your first night home as a married couple. Just because you left that fancy resort with rose petals on the bed and chilled champagne doesn't mean the honeymoon is over. I'll see you in the mornin'. I'll have the coffee ready by ten and you can bring some leftover dessert. Good-bye, Lila."

The phone went dark and Kasey laid it back on the counter. "That was Lila, my brother's new bride. She's coming over tomorrow morning after we get done with chores."

Nash nodded and finished washing the dishes. "All done. I'm going to walk out to the sheep pen."

"It's out behind the barn," she said.

"No, darlin', that's where I'm going to build Rustin's dog pens. The sheep pen is..." He stopped. "Dammit! Do I even have sheep? Jace mentioned them, didn't he? I hate this, Kasey."

She quickly went to hug him. "It's okay. You're going to wake up in the morning and be amazed at how normal everything is. The doctor said you'd probably be fine in twenty-four hours."

"Maybe." He propped his chin on her hair. "You smell wonderful."

She moved back and inhaled deeply. "You really should rest. How about a movie?"

He pulled her back into his embrace. "How about a make-out session?"

"Probably not a good idea," she whispered.

"Okay, then, let's take a walk. I'm feelin' boxed in. Do I get antsy like this often?" he asked.

"Yes, you do. You like to be outside working, not inside the house. Let me get my coat." She took a couple of steps back and hurried off to the hall. She'd keep him out until it was close to bedtime, and then she'd call the kids and tell them good night.

Kids! Holy smokin' hell. What was she going to do if he didn't wake up in the real world tomorrow? She'd have to bring the kids to the house and try to explain things to them. How did she do that to three kids?

She stomped her feet down into boots and shoved her arms into the jacket and suddenly remembered that she had nothing in the house in the way of clothing—nightshirt, toothbrush, or even shampoo.

"Ready?" Nash stuck his head around the kitchen door.

He wore a denim jacket, and the legs of his jeans were tucked down into the tops of well-worn boots. He raked his fingers through his hair and picked up his dark cowboy hat.

"Yep," she said. "Just need to pick up my phone in case Mama or Gracie either one call about the kids."

He held it out to her with a smile. "I figured you'd need it."

She glanced at a calendar hanging above the wall-hung

phone in the utility room and noticed that the next day, Tuesday, Nash had an appointment in Amarillo with a Dr. Paulson. Eleven o'clock in the morning.

"Doctor's appointment." She pointed.

He opened the door for her. "I thought we didn't go back for three weeks."

"This is Dr. Paulson," she said.

"My therapist," he said, and then his eyes widened. "I remembered something. I'll cancel it."

"I'll go with you," she said.

He tucked her small hand into his big one. "What about the kids?"

"We'll pick them up when we get back from Amarillo. You need to keep this appointment, Nash. Dr. Paulson needs to be aware that you have this concussion." With that sudden intake of breath at the feeling his touch created, she was amazed that her voice sounded even seminormal.

"You'll like her, Kasey. I've only been twice, but she's better than the last one."

"And who was the last one?"

"You know. That older man in the other hospital where we went right after I got out of the service," he said.

"What does Dr. Paulson look like? I haven't ever actually met her," Kasey asked.

"You don't have to be jealous of her, darlin'. She's about my grandmother's age." He chuckled and gently squeezed her hand. "You never have to be jealous of anyone. You're the only woman for me."

"So you think I'm jealous?" she asked.

"Oh, honey, I remember that fight we had about me dancing with that girl at the fall party. You always said the makeup sex over that was how we got our third child." His laugh even had a Louisiana twang to it.

A deep, crimson blush flushed Kasey's cheeks. She had made that comment, but it had been after the fight with Adam and as far as she knew, she'd never told anyone about that night. How in the hell did Nash Lamont know about that?

* * *

Nash couldn't remember much, but he did have a feeling that his world had changed. Happiness filled his whole body, though he knew—somewhere in the depths of his soul—that he'd lived in a black hole of sadness not very long ago. But that was yesterday or somewhere in the past. Tonight he had a family and beautiful wife, and life was good.

"Have we always had sheep?" he asked Kasey when they reached the corral behind the barn.

A big white cat slunk along the side of the fence until she reached them and then rubbed around his legs.

"Where're your babies?" he asked.

"Two of them are over at the bunkhouse on Hope Springs. Lila got them last summer and brought them with her when she and Brody got married. One is black and one is white and they're about half grown now," Kasey answered. "But she's got a whole new litter now. It was one of those that Hero chased up the tree. Do you remember climbin' up the ladder to get it?"

He shook his head. "My first memory is your wedding ring flashing in the sunlight. The sheep must know me. They're all coming this way." He reached inside over the fence and petted each of them as they arrived.

"They should. You spend a lot of time with them. You brought them here from over in eastern Texas where your grandmother, Addy, lives, remember?"

"No, but it's okay as long as you're right here with me." He slipped an arm around her shoulders. The sun had set and the evening was quickly going from the twilight stage to full darkness. However, there was enough light left to see Kasey's beautiful profile. Half of her face was in total shadows, but he could make out the sprinkling of freckles across her nose. He longed to plant a kiss on every one of those freckles, little angel kisses as his grandmother used to call them.

Hey, I do remember something, he thought. *Addy said that about freckles and she moved from the little ranch to town. I remember feeling sad that last day on the place because I felt close to Grandpa there.*

He pulled her closer to his side and reached across with his left hand to toy with her wedding band. A frown covered his face when he realized that he wasn't wearing his ring and there wasn't even an indention where it had been.

"When did I stop wearing my ring? It does match yours, right?"

"Must've been when you left on that last mission," she answered. "And yes, it matches mine."

"I've got to find it. I should be wearing it," he said.

"Hey!" Hope yelled as she got out of a truck she'd parked not far away. "I came over to check on y'all. How're things going?"

"My grandmother, Hope," she whispered.

"Fine, except that I can't remember much," Nash answered.

"I brought a dozen cookies and left them on the table. Thought y'all might like a late-night snack." She leaned both elbows on the top rail of the fence and propped her chin in her hands. "Nice lookin' little flock you got. How tame are they?"

"They're like pets," he answered.

"We might call on you to be part of our live nativity scene the night we have the Christmas program at the church. Real sheep would sure be better than wooden cutouts. You wouldn't happen to have a donkey, would you?" Hope asked.

"No, but I'm lookin' for one. They keep the coyotes away from the new baby lambs. Just let me know if you decide you want me to bring sheep to the nativity. You got a nice shed for the play? I'm pretty good with buildin' things."

A vision of Hope on the front porch of a long, sprawling ranch house popped into his head. There was a dog and she insisted that he drive her back to the barn where there was a party going on. It could have been ten years ago or yesterday because he couldn't get a fix on the date, but he did like her. He shut his eyes tightly, trying to expand the whole memory, but it faded.

"That would be great. Our old lean-to has sure seen better days," Hope said. "Kasey, you left a few things over at Hope Springs when you and the kids were staying there. I put them on the landing at the top of the stairs. I remember comin' over here a lot when your uncle Henry lived here. Nothing much has changed."

"Except the house. Evidently Uncle Henry didn't like all that clutter and cleared it out after my Great-Granny passed away. Did you know Addy, my grandmother? She still worries about Uncle Henry—hey, I remembered something." He beamed.

Hope reached around behind Kasey and patted him on the shoulder. "Yes, I knew your grandmother. I called her this morning. Don't worry about the memories. They'll come back."

"I hope so. Kasey needs a whole husband, not one who hardly knows his name."

"Don't rush it. Just rest and let it come naturally," Hope said.

"This is such a peaceful place to wait it out," Nash said.

"Yes, it is. I'll be going now. Lila says to tell you that she'll be by in the morning for a cup of coffee," Hope told Kasey. "Call if you need anything. Neighbors take care of each other in this part of the world."

"And family," Nash told her.

"That, too." Hope nodded as she headed back toward her truck.

"My head is really starting to pound," Nash said. "I reckon maybe we should get back to the house and I'll take one of those pills the doctor gave me for pain. I know it will knock me on my butt, but I don't want to waste a single minute with you."

"I'll be here when you wake up, Nash. I promise," she said.

"Right beside me where I can just roll over and look at your beautiful face?"

"Maybe not that. I'll sleep upstairs tonight, but if you need me all you have to do is call out for me. I've been a light sleeper ever since Rustin was born," she answered.

"Why can't you sleep with me? I don't like it when we're apart."

"No sex, remember?"

"That doesn't mean no sleeping together if all we do is sleep," he said. "But you're probably right. It would be frustrating to have you that close and not be able to make love to you."

"Exactly." She tucked her hand into his and tugged on it. "Time to tell the sheep good night and take your pills."

He touched his forehead. He hadn't known pain like this since that time when he woke up in the hospital in Afghanistan. He'd been blown backward when an IED right outside the base perimeter went off. His head landed on a rock, knocking the sense right out of him. They said it took a week for him to realize where he was, and by then he was already back in the States.

So this isn't my first time for this rodeo, he thought as they headed toward the house. *I'll need to tell Dr. Paulson about this tomorrow when I visit her.*

When they were in the house, Kasey went to the kitchen table, read the instructions on a bottle of pills, and shook two out into her hand. When she handed them to him, he kissed the tips of her fingers. "You're a good nurse. Did you ever want to be one when you were a little girl?"

"Oh, no! I wanted to ride bulls and broncs like my brothers." She laughed. "Did you?"

"One time was all it took for me to realize that wasn't my dream. So I decided I wanted to be a wife and a mother and maybe run a ranch someday."

He swallowed the pills with a sip of cold coffee from the cup she'd left next to the pot. "Glad I could help you fulfill that dream."

"Me, too," she whispered. "Why don't you rest in your recliner while I go upstairs and have a nice long bath? It's been a hectic day for us both."

"Will you wake me when you get done and give me a good night kiss before we turn in for the night?" he asked.

She patted his cheek. "Of course I will."

He eased down into the recliner and threw the lever to bring up the footrest. Closing his eyes, he went to that place where he'd been trained to go to avoid pain. In seconds, he was on the bayou in a pirogue, bringing up the shrimp nets. Tonight they'd have shrimp boil for supper, and tomorrow morning his grandmother would make étouffée from the leftovers.

Did Kasey like the shrimp dish served over rice? He tried to bring up a vision of the two of them out in East Texas on the Louisiana border, but it wouldn't appear. Damn this headache anyway.

The pipes rattled as hot water started through them and the noise sent him back to the sand pit. Six of them went over there and only three came home. Three dead and one injured. The hurt one being him with that damned concussion that erased everything for weeks and forced a medical discharge on him. Christmas carols were playing in the hospital when he awoke, and the tree in the waiting room where his grandmother came to visit every day was decorated in red, white, and blue.

Where were Kasey and the kids? He frowned as a few memories surfaced. They had to have come around, but he couldn't remember anyone besides his grandmother and mother. His grandmother stayed in a nearby hotel for two weeks, but his mother only visited and went home. He understood. His father hadn't been well in those days, and he needed her at home.

That same hopeless, helpless feeling he'd had back then washed over him. What if he never remembered his kids' birthdays? What if he couldn't see the faces of those three friends who'd died that day when their vehicle exploded?

His eyes snapped open. He could imagine Rustin with his dark hair and blue eyes, but Emma was too far away to make out the color of her hair. He was in a barn looking down at her from a loft—must've been the wedding Jace talked about. He could see Rustin, and Emma looked just like her mother. But which one of those little kids was Silas? He couldn't remember him at all. Just that Kasey was pregnant with him when he left for that last mission. Finally the medicine kicked in and he fell asleep, only to dream of Kasey sitting with him under a big weeping willow tree somewhere near a bubbling stream that flowed down over a small rocky dam.

* * *

Kasey called her grandmother while the water ran for her bath. "Granny, tell me what I'm going to do if he's still in this fantasy world tomorrow. I've checked the bedrooms, and we can get away with sayin' that the kids' things were delivered to Hope Springs and…"

"Slow down," Hope said. "Tell me what Nash was talkin' about when he said that the house was different. Minnie loved her knickknacks. Are they all gone?"

"You are trying to take my mind off things, aren't you?"

"There's that, but I'm nosy, too. Tell me about the upstairs bedrooms," Hope said.

"One bedroom has a double bed and the walls are painted yellow, and another room has two twin beds and is wallpapered in pink and blue flowers. The one I'm sleeping in might have been a nursery because it does have a rocking chair, one twin bed, and a crib that looks like it came out of an antique store."

"Okay, you will sleep in the one with a double bed. The boys will go in the nursery room, and Emma gets the floral room if they have to be there for a few days. I will have Jace bring over enough toys and clothing to make it feel like you've been there a couple of weeks."

"How are you going to pull that off?" Kasey asked.

"You can make an excuse that y'all need to go to town and Jace and Brody can bring over whatever you need to make it work while you're gone," she said. "Just make a list and email it to me."

"There will be talk about me living here with him. This could be a nightmare in the making," Kasey moaned.

"Rosalie Varner already called a few minutes ago to see what was going on."

Kasey rolled her eyes.

"She thinks you are doing a fine thing, helping Henry's great-nephew when he doesn't have family in this area. She said that if he had broken his leg or his arm or been paralyzed from that fall, everyone would understand that as a good neighbor, you were stepping up to take care of him. A head injury is no different. Just hang in there, honey. He'll come back to the real world pretty soon. Until then, just let me know what I can do to help," Hope said.

"Well, thank God that the queen of the rumor mill has passed judgment," Kasey smarted off.

"Hey, now!" Hope scolded. "Rosalie was a friend of my mother's, and her opinion carries a lot of weight around here."

"Sorry, Granny. I'm stressed out to the point of breaking right now. And we're going to the therapist tomorrow. Think Jace and Brody could fix things in the bedroom while we're gone?" she asked.

"Definitely. Just leave either the front or back door unlocked. Want us to bring the kids home for you?"

"No, we'll get them on our way back here after his doctor's visit. Maybe it won't even be necessary. When the pain in his head goes away, he could remember everything in a flash," she said. "Tell Lila I'm looking forward to seeing her."

"She and Brody have already gone to the bunkhouse and Jace is the only one here. I'm about to leave, but I'll let him know what we've got to do tomorrow afternoon."

"Thanks, Granny, for everything."

"Family takes care of family," Hope said. "Good night."

"Night," Kasey said.

Time was when Kasey would do anything for a wounded veteran. They'd had fund-raisers, picnics, lawn parties, and all kinds of events for their men when they needed help. She'd spearheaded a committee to raise money for special needs that the VA didn't cover when she and Adam were in Lawton, Oklahoma. And when one of their own came home wounded, they'd gone into double-time to help out however they could.

So what's the big deal here? asked that pesky voice in her head.

"I didn't kiss any of those guys," she blurted out as she dropped her jeans and clothing on the floor.

She had barely sunk down into the tub when the ring tone said that her mother was calling. She answered it with a sigh, "Hello, Mama. Are the kids okay?"

"They're watching one of their little movies. They've had their baths and we've had our reading time. I've got to admit, I'm worried about you being over there like this, Kasey. If you have to stay very long, there will be talk for sure." Valerie's tone left no doubt that she was fretting about the exact same things on Kasey's mind.

"I know, Mama, but then we've weathered talk before, and Granny says that Rosalie Varner thinks this is a noble and good thing," Kasey said.

"Well, once Rosalie sets her mind, no one is going to change it." Valerie's chuckle was brittle. "I guess us Dawsons are no strangers to the rumors. Do what you think is right and we'll wade through the muck, but as soon as you're able to do so, I want you back at Hope Springs."

"Remember that old saying about whoever stirs the shit pile has to lick the spoon." Kasey giggled at her grandmother's old adage.

"There could be a lot of folks walking around Happy with bad breath even if Rosalie has spoken," Valerie said. "Most will understand if you're only there as long as you have to be."

"I'll be in Amarillo tomorrow. I'll buy extra breath mints," Kasey said.

"Love you, baby girl," Valerie said.

"Love you back. Kiss my babies good night for me."

"Will do. Call me tomorrow or sooner if Nash gets his mind back," Valerie said.

The screen went dark, and in seconds the phone rang again.

Rustin's picture popped up and she hurriedly hit the right icon to talk to him. "Hey, son, how'd school go today?"

"It went great. Gramps told me that Nash fell out of a tree and broke his brain and you got to stay with him. I want to come over there, too, Mama. I like him and if his brain is busted and he can't work, I can help him with the chores."

"His brain is just scrambled, kind of like a puzzle. He's got all the pieces, but he has to fit them together. I'll pick you up at school tomorrow and we'll see about stayin' here a couple of nights," she said.

"Okay. I'll pack up my duffle bag," he said seriously.

"Grandma is going to do that for you. You just bring home all your schoolwork and whatever you took to your Nana and Gramps's house. I love you, Rustin."

"Love you, Mama," he said. "Gramps is going to play

checkers with me now so I've got to go, but Nana wants to talk to you."

"Kasey," Gracie said. "I just want you to know that Rustin is fine and welcome to stay as long as he wants."

"Thank you, but I'm planning to pick him up at school tomorrow."

"You're doing a good thing. Adam would be proud of you for helping Nash. I've talked to Valerie, and we both think you should go home soon as possible. Helping is one thing. Staying past that would cause talk."

Kasey's cheeks burned. Adam would not be proud of her for kissing another man, not even in the present circumstances, and he damn sure wouldn't be glad that she'd liked it. And then a bit of anger rose up. She was twenty-six years old, had three kids, and was a war widow. What gave her mother or her former mother-in-law the right to tell her what to do?

"Hopefully, he'll regain his memory before long, but, Gracie, he can't drive until he goes back to the doctor on the fifteenth, so I'm going to help him until then," she said.

"You can drive him wherever he needs to go without living there." Gracie's tone got colder with each sentence.

"And what if he has a seizure. The brochure said that was possible," Kasey asked.

"We'll talk about this when the time comes," Gracie said. "For now, Rustin is fine, and we'll keep him as long as you let us."

"Thanks again." Kasey didn't want to argue with Gracie, but there was no way rumors were going to railroad her into something she didn't want to do. She could actually feel her heels digging in for the first time since Adam died. She'd let her family make the decision for her to come back to Happy when her lease was up on the house in Lawton. And she'd stepped into the role of chief cook and bottle washer as well as bookkeeper for Hope Springs because that's what she was supposed to do. But enough was enough.

She laid the phone on the ladder-back chair beside the old claw-footed tub. The water had gone lukewarm so she crawled out and wrapped a towel around her body. She groaned when she saw her reflection in the mirror. Granny had forgotten to pack her mousse, so her hair was going to look like corkscrews when it dried.

"Oh, well, maybe that's what will bring reality back to Nash." She dried off and dressed in a pair of gray sweat bottoms and a faded T-shirt that was two sizes too big. It might be all right for her to be there, but Hope Dalley was not going to aid and abet in any hanky-panky.

With a nervous giggle, she checked the rest of the bag she'd found at the top of the stairs. Toothbrush and her favorite toothpaste, jeans and a flannel shirt, cotton underpants and a clean white bra. Nothing sexy and no perfume or makeup.

She wrapped a towel around her wet hair and padded down the stairs in her bare feet. Nash looked up from his recliner and smiled, his face far more relaxed now that he'd had some rest.

"What time is it? Did I sleep all night in this chair?" he asked.

She settled into the corner of the sofa and pulled a quilt from the back over her legs. "No, only about an hour. I talked to the kids, and Rustin can't wait to get home tomorrow."

"I'm lookin' forward to them all bein' here," he said. "My mouth is so dry. Probably from the meds. Want a beer?" He popped the footrest down and stood up, only to sit back down in a hurry. "Wow! Talk about a head rush."

"How about a glass of iced tea instead? Might not be a good thing to mix alcohol and your meds," she suggested as she threw off the cover. "I'll make us both one and then maybe we can watch a movie. This is the time of year they play all the old Christmas classics."

"We've got to get our tree put up and maybe put out some decorations. This place doesn't look like kids and a family even live here. Did we just move in or something? The kids will expect a tree. And have we even started shopping?"

"I've got most of the presents bought already. Tomorrow evening we're helping decorate over at Hope Springs, and after that we go to Mama's for desserts and to see her tree and house. Maybe we can put ours up on Wednesday. Do you remember where it is?" she asked.

His eyes twinkled. "You're testing me, aren't you? In the attic. The door up there is at the end of the upstairs hall-way. My grandmother reminded me when she called the last time."

"Yes, I am testing you, and you just got an A." She threw the words over her shoulder on her way to the kitchen.

But I failed my test today. She glanced down at her wedding ring and felt torn between the past and the present.

Chapter Six

Kasey was so happy to see Lila the next morning that she grabbed her sister-in-law in a fierce hug before she could even remove her stocking hat and jacket. "I'm so glad you're here. Coffee is made. Let's go to the kitchen and you can tell me all about the honeymoon."

Lila stepped back and whipped off the hat, shoved it into her coat pocket before she took it off and tossed it on the sofa. "You're so strung out, girl, that your whole body is humming. First of all, give me a quick tour of this house. I love old two-story places and I've never been upstairs. Brody and I kind of broke into the place and watched a movie when we were teenagers, but the living room was the only place I got to see," Lila said.

"And what's this about 'kind of'?" Kasey laughed as she motioned for Lila to follow her.

"This was back when Henry still lived here, but he and his mama had gone to visit his sister. He'd hired Adam's dad to do his chores for him, so we knew how long they were going to be gone." Lila opened the door and dragged in a couple of big suitcases. "I didn't want to bring these in until I was sure that Nash wasn't in the house."

Kasey clapped her hands and squealed. "Thank God!"

"No, just me. God didn't have time to pack for you this mornin'. He was busy with more important things." Lila laughed.

"Then bless your heart, and I mean that in the best way possible," she said as she picked up a bag and carried it to her room. "I have to take Nash to the therapist this morning, and I hated to wear the rattiest clothes that Granny could find in my closet."

"She said something about hanky-panky." Lila grabbed the other suitcase and followed her.

"I knew it!" Kasey said. "I could hear it in my head when I saw what she'd sent." She unzipped the suitcase and brought out two pairs of decent jeans, a couple of shirts, her western belt, dress boots, and a denim jacket, plus her makeup bag, hair straightener, and perfume. "I owe you big-time. While I change, tell me about you and my brother breaking the law by breaking and entering."

Lila sat down on the edge of the bed. "Well, we didn't actually break in because there was a key under the mat and we didn't hurt anything. We just borrowed the television and DVD player to watch a movie and make out on the sofa."

"Mama would have thrown a hissy if she'd known what you and Brody did." Kasey stripped down to her underwear and redressed. "Now I'll show you around, but while we're lookin' tell me about the honeymoon."

"My mother would have put me in a convent if she'd known half the things we did," Lila said. "The honeymoon was wonderful. The little resort was fabulous."

"And?" Kasey slung open the door right across the landing from her room. "This is going to be Emma's room while we are here. Did you ever leave the bedroom or did you rely on room service to keep your energy up and going?"

"What happens on a thirty-six-hour honeymoon stays in the resort. Emma will love this room, but it needs some of her toys and dolls in it," Lila said. "How are you holding up?"

"Not so good," Kasey admitted. "Nash really thinks we're married and..." Her voice trailed off.

"Sex?"

"The doctor helped me out by telling him there would be no sex until we go back for his checkup, so I'm sleeping upstairs until then. But that only goes so far. No sex doesn't mean no cuddling on the sofa or kisses good night. And I feel like I'm cheating on Adam every time." She slung open a door. "I bet the last baby in this crib was Nash's mother and then only when they came to this part of Texas for a visit. His mother would have been a granddaughter to Minnie, who was his great-grandma. Sometimes family trees get confusing."

Lila nodded. "You're changing the subject, but that's okay. I'd be uncomfortable in your shoes, too. And, Kasey, the first time I went out on a date after I moved away from Happy, I felt like I was cheating on Brody. I can't imagine what you're going through. Now, let's take a look around this room. The crib looks sturdy enough to hold Silas."

"It only has to hold up a few weeks. Once Nash can drive and I'm sure his brain is fine, we'll be back home," Kasey said. "Now on to the room where I'm sleeping." She stood back and let her peek into the third bedroom. "You've been in my room and that's about it except for the bathroom. To tell the truth, Lila, I liked his kisses this morning, and when he whispered that he thought I was beautiful in my"—she made air quotes—" 'no hanky-panky' getup—well, I hate to admit it but my hormones screamed like fire sirens."

Lila giggled. "You're young. It's been two years since Adam passed, and it's okay for you to feel something when a sexy man kisses you or touches you."

"Then why do I feel so guilty?"

"It's built into us, but we can fight it," Lila said.

"I'm not sure I want to do battle with the guilt or that I have the energy." Kasey sighed.

"Anything worth having is worth fighting for."

"But Nash is going to wake up one of these days, and he's going to be embarrassed that he even thought we were married, and he'll realize it was just an elusive dream brought on by his head injury."

Lila glanced inside the upstairs bathroom. "Emma is going to love that oversize tub. She'll call it her swimming pool. What you said about elusive dreams reminds me of that old George Jones and Tammy Wynette song."

"Yep." Kasey's head bobbed up and down. "Granny plays that old vinyl pretty often. I bought her the CD for Christmas last year but she likes the vinyl better."

"Must be a memory that Granny is reliving. You ever think that maybe this whole situation has come into your life to help you and her both move on?"

"Honey, I'm home." The squeak of the back door hinges and Nash's voice floated up the stairs.

"Be right down. Lila and I are up here," Kasey said.

He waited at the bottom of the stairs and slung an arm around Kasey when she hit the bottom step.

"Hi, Nash," Lila said as if she'd known him forever.

"Hello. You must be Lila." His brow wrinkled as he obviously tried to remember. "Kasey said you were coming over this mornin'."

"Yes, I am." Lila smiled. "I'm so sorry about the accident, but we're all hoping that everything straightens itself out real soon."

Nash nodded. "Me, too, and I'm so sorry that I can't remember you, but bear with me because I will." His face lit up in a smile as he kissed Kasey on top of the head. "We've got about half an hour before we go to Amarillo to the doctor's appointment and I should clean up a little bit. You going with us, Lila?"

She shook her head. "No, I've got some computer work to do this morning and dinner and supper to get ready for the guys at our ranch. Granny is going to the church to make final plans for the Christmas play. She and Rosalie have been talkin' about it on the phone all mornin'. She's volunteered me and Brody to be part of the live nativity that evening. Would you have ever thought that the wild child of Happy would be playing the mother of Christ?"

"Wild child?" Nash asked.

Kasey stood up. "I'll tell you all about it on the way to the doctor's office. I need to get ready to go. You sure you don't want to go with us, Lila?"

"Better not. Dawsons get cranky when they're hungry, and I'm not sure either of those cowboys can cook, so I'd better go on back and make sure there's food on the table at noon." She turned back to Nash. "It's mighty sweet of you to move from your side of Texas out here to the flat land."

"I'd go anywhere to make Kasey happy, and my grandmother thought it would be good for us to be close to her family," Nash said.

"Kasey does love her folks. See y'all later." Lila waved as she left.

While Nash was in his room getting ready, Kasey raced

back up to the bathroom, applied a little makeup, and flipped her unruly hair into a messy bun, holding it there with a clip and two bobby pins. She sprayed perfume on her wrists and neck and then started back to the foyer.

Nash was leaning against the wall beside the coat tree at the bottom of the stairs. Despite what Lila said, another wave of guilt washed over Kasey when Nash held out a hand. When she tucked hers into it, he pulled both of her hands up around his neck and began to sing an old George Strait two-stepping tune, "Oh, What a Perfect Day."

He was an excellent dancer and she didn't even mind that a couple of notes were flat or that his deep voice was a hell of a lot more southern than George's. For two minutes she left guilt behind and enjoyed the dance. But when he stopped humming, tilted her chin up with his knuckles, and kissed her passionately the moment came to an abrupt halt. She stepped back and just barely caught herself before she went up to kiss him again.

"Something wrong?" Nash asked.

"We're going to be late if we don't get on the road," she told him.

"Dr. Paulson can wait. Kissing you is more important." His brown eyes glittered with happiness as he opened the door for her.

Whistling the whole way to the truck, he kept a hand on her lower back all the way to the passenger's side. She stopped so quickly that he took two steps before he realized that she wasn't beside him.

"What did you forget?" he asked.

"What did *you* forget?" she asked. "You're not supposed to be driving. So we are taking my van, since the car seats are in it and we need to pick up the kids when we get back into town."

"How long until I can get behind the wheel again?" He groaned.

"Until your doctor's visit in the middle of December and only then if you remember everything, have no flashbacks, or pass out under stress. The doctor will evaluate you when you go back and make a decision then about driving."

"Dammit! I hate being so dependent. Besides, how am I supposed to buy your Christmas presents if I can't drive to the stores?" He shoved the truck keys back into his pocket.

She kept walking toward the van with him right behind her. His hand covered hers when she reached for the handle.

"I may not be able to drive, but I can still be a gentleman and open doors for my gorgeous wife." He grinned. "Now about those presents? I can't remember doing any shopping at all."

"The children's stuff is mostly bought and hidden over at Hope Springs. I still have to get Emma's Santa present, but other than that, it's fairly well done. I've got all the family presents already wrapped even."

"You've always been organized. When are we bringing it all to our place?"

"When we get the tree up," she answered after a split second's hesitation. "And as for what we buy each other, let's do something different this year. Why don't we wait until the last minute and then decide whether we want to buy presents or go to that resort that Lila and Brody went to on their honeymoon? Mama would keep the kids for us, and I bet Jace and Brody would do the chores." She hoped Nash would have all his broken brain cells back in their rightful place long before that and they'd both be glad that they didn't have presents under the tree for each other.

"A whole weekend with just the two of us in a resort.

That's the best Christmas ever." He fastened her seat belt and was whistling when he got into the passenger's seat.

He talked about putting up the tree and asked questions about the kids all the way to the veterans' center where the therapist's office was located. Did they like living in the country or did they miss town life? Should he get a Santa suit? When should they invest in cattle so Rustin could groom one for the show pen?

Kasey's poor brain was so tired of figuring out how to answer him that she sank into a chair as soon as they were in the small waiting room. Looking around the tiny room and seeing that it was completely empty made her even happier. Thirty minutes of silence was going to be heavenly. She picked up a magazine, but before she could even open it the receptionist told Nash it was his turn.

He took Kasey's hand in his and pulled her up with him as he stood. "I want you to go in with me today and meet the doctor."

"You sure about this? I don't think I'm supposed to be there. This is between you and the doctor." Kasey held back.

He tugged on her hand. "I want her to meet you."

"Okay, but then I'll probably have to leave," Kasey agreed.

The doctor raised an eyebrow when she looked up from behind her desk. "And who have you brought with you to-day?" she asked.

"My wife, Kasey. I'm sure I've told you all about her," he answered.

"Yes, you have mentioned Kasey several times. I'm glad to meet you and glad that you could join us today. Sit." She motioned toward the two chairs across from her. "And tell me about your week, Nash."

"Nice to meet you as well, but I can wait out there." Kasey turned to go to the waiting room.

"Please stay." Dr. Paulson smiled. "I'd like it very much."

Nash started talking the moment they were both seated. "It's been an amazing week. Other than falling out of a tree and hitting my head, causing my second concussion and a little temporary amnesia, that is. But hey, I've got a wonderful wife and three kids to help me get my memory all back, and when I go back for my checkup the doctor will probably let me start driving again."

Kasey fought the heat rising from her neck to her cheeks. Why would he have mentioned her in his therapy sessions?

"So you're his chauffer for the next few weeks?" Dr. Paulson asked Kasey.

"Yes, she is," Nash answered for her. "Kasey was there just minutes after I hit the ground and she called an ambulance. She rode in it with me and they did every test there was to make sure I didn't have a brain bleed. But I just scrambled my memories," he said. "When we leave here today we're going to pick up the kids, go to Kasey's family ranch across the fence from our place to decorate for Christmas, and then tomorrow night we're doing our own tree and decorations."

"I see, and how do you feel about all this Christmas stuff?" Dr. Paulson asked.

Nash reached across the room and laced Kasey's fingers into his. "Great. Just great. There's nothing in this whole world that I like better than family."

Kasey wiggled in the leather wingback chair and scanned the office. A big desk separated them from the doctor. To her, it seemed more like they were in a bank, asking for a loan or maybe starting a savings account. This was not at all what she pictured for a psychiatrist's office. Bookcases covered the wall behind the desk with volumes and volumes of thick tomes filling the shelves. The aroma of gingerbread coming from a candle on a fancy little stand in the corner filled the whole room.

"And what about you, Kasey? Do you like Christmas?" Dr. Paulson asked.

"Love it, but then I love anytime that family can be together," she said.

"I know we're on the clock, but I've got to take a little break here and visit the men's room. Be back in less than five." He rose up out of the chair and headed out into the waiting room where the restrooms were located.

"Talk fast and tell me what happened," the doctor said. "He's never been this talkative. I usually have to drag every word from him."

"After he woke up from his fall, he thought we were married and that he's father to my three kids. Maybe because I'm the one who first found him. Or maybe because I'm still wearing my wedding band. My husband has been gone for two years now." She went on to tell the story of Nash's accident, making it as short as possible.

"And his doctor encouraged you to let him live in this pretend world?" the therapist asked.

"Yes, ma'am. Do you disagree?"

"Not at all. He's in a fragile state even yet. Without breaking patient/doctor confidentiality, I can say that I've only seen him twice, but I've been in direct contact with his previous therapist. This is amazing, and hopefully when he does recover his memories, he will realize that he can be happy again. So if you don't mind doing this, then, honey, you might be helping him more than words can say," Dr. Paulson said.

"I have a question, though. What if he likes this world so much that he refuses to leave it?" Kasey asked.

"That's not likely, but how you handle the whole thing

could either break or make his future. He's been in a dark place and to see him happy is a miracle."

"Well, it is Christmas and—" She heard him returning and quickly changed the subject. "Nash may be part of the nativity scene at the church on the night we have the Christmas program. We're hoping he can bring a couple of the sheep."

"Oh?" Dr. Paulson said. "Tell me about that, Nash."

He eased down into the chair again. "I'm looking forward to it. Kasey's brother Brody and his new wife, Lila, are going to be Mary and Joseph. It will be fun."

"Sounds like it. Back to the concussion and memory loss. Are you having headaches?" she asked.

"Had a stinger last night, but this morning it's gone."

"You need to keep your doctor's appointments," she told him.

"Kasey will see to it. She's pretty sassy." Nash smiled. "When do I need to come back here?"

"Maybe in two weeks this time. December thirteenth at eleven. Does that work?" she asked.

"Sounds fine to me," Nash said. "We got anything that day, Kasey?"

"Not that I know about. Your appointment with the trauma doctor is a couple of days after that."

"Good, then we'll see you then." Nash stood up and pulled Kasey up by the hand, took the appointment card, and tucked it into his shirt pocket. "Now let's go find a good Mexican place to eat. I'm hungry."

"So you like Mexican food?" Kasey asked as they left the office.

"You know I do. It's my favorite. Hey, I remembered something else. This is a good day, darlin'," he said.

"Yes, it is," she agreed.

* * *

Nash glanced at the menu the waitress put in front of him and then handed it back to her. "I'm having the double order of fajitas. I'd love a beer with it, but I don't guess that's an option, is it, Mrs. Lamont?"

"Not until the doctor says you can have alcohol. I'll have the loaded nachos and sweet tea." The idea of being anything other than Mrs. McKay sounded really strange.

"Make that two sweet teas and some of those chips and salsa," Nash told the waitress.

"And a side order of guacamole," Kasey said as she gave her menu to the waitress.

"I liked Dr. Paulson. So what are we going to do when she dismisses you?"

"Go back into the service is what I'd planned, but I'm not so sure about that, now that we've moved here. It's really not much of a life for you and the kids, and we have the ranch now. You remember Addy, right?" he asked and went on before she could answer. "She called this morning while I was doing chores and she thinks we should settle down and make a living on the Texas Star. She says if we'll do that she'll deed the whole thing over to me. Would that make you happy?"

"Addy said that?" Kasey asked. "Tell me again why you call your grandmother Addy?"

"When I was little, they tried to get me to call her Grand-mère, which is the Cajun word for *grandmother*, but everyone else called her Adelaide and I picked up on that and she became Addy to me. But why are you asking? You know all that, don't you?"

"Of course. I was testing you again to see what you remember," she said quickly.

"Hey, I am remembering lots of things." He chuckled. "Okay, then what do you think about settling here?"

"I like living near my folks, but we should also consider your family in this decision," she said, cautiously.

The waitress brought their drinks and appetizers and set them on the table. "Your dinner will be out in a few minutes. Can I get you anything else?"

"We're good," Kasey said.

"Yes, we are," Nash whispered. "Couldn't be better, but I can't remember a single thing that we've bought for the kids' Christmas. If I don't have it all together by then, will you make a list so I won't be in the dark on that morning?"

"Of course," she said.

That was his Kasey, the woman whose picture he'd carried all over the world, the one who'd birthed three children for him and who loved him even when his mind was gone. He could always depend on her and trust her with his whole heart.

"Have I told you how much I appreciate all you did while we were still in the army? Medals should be given to wives like you," he said.

"I had a lot of support." She smiled. "The other wives were there on base and we took care of each other. Sometimes I miss that."

"So you'd like for us to be back in the military?"

"I'm not so sure." She dipped a chip in the salsa and popped it into her mouth. "A ranch is an excellent place to raise kids, and military life isn't nearly as stable, but we've got a year to make that decision."

"You got recent pictures of the kids? I looked in my wallet and couldn't find any, which is strange, because when we were in Afghanistan I had a whole string of them. The guys used to tease me about flipping them out so often."

Her smile was so sweet when she locked gazes with him.

"Nash, you've probably changed billfolds three times since those days. What do you remember about being over there in the sand pit as you guys called it?"

"Spoken like a true army wife. Anyone who hadn't been close to someone who had to be there wouldn't use that terminology. I remember the sand everywhere. In our socks. In our beds. In our hair and our ears. I couldn't wait to get home to the bayou. Fish don't grow in sand and I love to go fishin'. What I missed most was grass."

She cocked her head to the side, and a strange expression crossed her face. "Grass, huh?"

"Yep. On that last mission we were there only a week, but the one before that when we deployed for six months, you were a genius when you sent that box of dirt from the yard and grass seed," he told her.

"Well, you did say that you missed walking out across the yard in your bare feet." A cold chill ran up her spine, because she'd sent that to Adam when he was deployed right after Emma was born.

"I let all the guys put their feet in the box of grass I cultivated. And I told them I had the smartest wife in the world." He leaned across the table and kissed her on the cheek.

"Who were the guys on your team?" Kasey asked.

Nash wanted to answer, but no names would come to mind. "Nothing!" He touched his forehead. "Not a blessed thing."

"Where was your team stationed?" she asked.

He frowned as he tried to remember and then his face lit up. "I know! We weren't at the same base. When they needed us for a job, they usually flew us to a central location, and we left from there. It was cold the night we boarded the plane for the last mission I was on, so it might've been winter."

A cold band of steel wrapped itself around Kasey's heart. Adam had left on the mission that had gotten him killed in the winter. Could it be possible that Nash had worked with him or known him?

The waitress brought their food. "I'll be back to refill your tea glasses in a few minutes."

"Thank you. This looks and smells wonderful." Kasey shot a long sideways glance at Nash. He couldn't have been in the same unit as Adam. If he had been he would have told her when they had to sit out the dirt storm in the barn, and his name was different enough that if Adam had mentioned him, she would have remembered.

"Yes, it does." Nash checked his watch. "What time do we need to be at the school?"

"Three fifteen, but we can go to Mama's and get Silas and Emma before that. Then we can pick up Rustin and go straight to Hope Springs. They're already dragging down the boxes of decoration, I'm sure. We'll be putting up trees or having some kind of Christmas fun for the next couple of nights. That should put us all in the mood for the holidays," she said.

"And then the church program. It's going to be the best holiday ever," he said.

The only thing that could make it better was if something would throw the switch in his brain and make everything right. Other than that, nothing could possibly go wrong with his world.

* * *

It was one thirty when they reached Prairie Rose, Kasey's mother's ranch. Nash shut his eyes tightly, pinched the bridge of his nose, and then let go and opened them in a flash. But he still didn't recognize the place. He had to have been there dozens upon dozens of times when he and Kasey dated.

He tried to bring back the first time he met her. He had to

have been visiting Uncle Henry and his great-grandmother. That was the only plausible explanation, since he'd lived on the opposite side of the state. But not a single thing came to mind.

He hoped that when they were inside he'd get a vision of something that would set off a jolt of electricity in his mind. Maybe they'd made out on the sofa or cuddled up and watched a movie. Or they must have slept in her bedroom when they came home for visits.

"Mama, Mama!" Emma rushed outside in her bare feet. She was the image of Kasey with curly red hair and gorgeous green eyes. She jumped from the porch into Kasey's arms and immediately started to tattle.

"Silas has been all whiny-hiney and he won't play dolls with me," she said, pouting.

"Well, let's go inside and talk to him about that. We can't have a whiny-hiney boy on the day that we decorate Hope Springs, now can we?"

"Do we gots presents yet?" Emma cocked her head to the side and stared at Nash. "You came to Aunt Lila's weddin'."

"Yes, I did." He flashed on the little redheaded girl dancing on Jace's feet at the wedding. Kasey was sitting beside him in the loft and they were eating barbecue together.

He opened the door for Kasey, and Silas came out of the kitchen, slung himself around his mother's knees, and pointed at Emma.

"Mean sissy," he said.

His blond curls reached the collar of his little red flannel shirt and his crystal clear blue eyes looked right at Nash with no recognition. Cold chills dug deep into Nash's spine. That child was the image of Adam McKay, one of his team members who hadn't come home from that last mission—the very one who'd saved Nash's life.

"Adam McKay," he whispered.

Everything tumbled into place.

Kasey was Adam's wife. He'd been the one with the string of pictures that he showed anyone who'd stand still and look at them. Nash felt his whole world evaporate in that single second.

"I'm so sorry, Kasey," he whispered.

"For what?" She turned toward him.

"All of it." He reached down, took the truck keys from her hand, and walked out. His first thought when he reached the ranch was to curl up on the sofa and sink down into the familiar black hole of depression, letting both the embarrassment of the past two days plus all the old memories of Adam and the team flood over him like icy cold water.

But he couldn't let himself slip back into that mode of living, not when he'd known such happiness the past couple of days. He bypassed the house and went straight to the barn, where he grabbed a set of hay hooks and started restacking the small bales to make room for the tractor. It needed a tune-up before spring, and that would be his next job as soon as he cleaned out a spot for it.

The memories flashed through his mind so fast that he had trouble keeping up, so he didn't even hear the barn door slide open. It wasn't until Kasey was three feet from him and he felt her presence that he whipped around.

There she stood with Silas on one hip, Emma standing on one side, and Rustin on the other. "What do you mean, runnin' away like that? We've got to put up decorations at Hope Springs this evening."

"Good God, Kasey, I thought…I mean." He jerked off his cowboy hat and raked his fingers through his dark hair. "You know what happened. You should be in here yelling at me and throwing a hissy, not fussin' at me for leavin' you."

Emma crossed the distance between them and put her hand in Nash's. "I like tall cowboys. My uncle Brody and my uncle Jace are tall cowboys, and I like them, too."

He stooped down to look at the tiny replica of Kasey. "I'm glad, Miz Emma."

"Good, now let's go put up our Christmas tree," she said.

"She talks so plain," he said.

"Always has. Don't avoid the issue here," Kasey said bluntly.

"And when we get done," Rustin broke in, "Mama says that we get to come over here and stay for three whole weeks, and that we're goin' to help you put up a tree and I can help with chores. I can't wait to work with sheep. I ain't never got to be around them except for mutton ridin' at the bull ridin'. Someday I'm goin' to be a bull rider like my uncle Brody. Did you ever ride bulls, Nash?"

"No, I didn't." He stood up. "Kasey, a word?"

"Whatever you've got to say, just spit it out. I told that doctor I would drive you and stay with you until your next appointment, and a Dawson does not go back on her word. Jace and Brody have brought over some of the kids' things so they'd feel at home. We are going to live in that house until the doctor clears you for everything. So suck it up, cowboy. You're stuck with us. Now put down those hay hooks and get in the van. We've got a Christmas tree to decorate at Hope Springs."

"It's my house and..." He hesitated when Emma squeezed his hand.

"We want to have a 'venture in your house? My mama said we could." She stuck out her lower lip in a pout.

"Yes, you can, sweet baby girl." His stooped back down to her eye level, and his heart melted when her little chin quivered. "If you want to have an adventure, you're welcome to stay at my house."

"Okay, then." She wrapped her arms around his neck. "Grandma said we can stay with you until Christmas. Santa will bring presents to your house. Do you gots a fireplace?"

"Well, then I guess we better not confuse Santa, and since I don't have a fireplace, we'll have to leave the front door open for him." He looked up at Kasey. "No hard feelin's about... well, you know?" He straightened up, hung the hooks on the wall, and removed his work gloves.

"Not a single one."

"Is your brain all fixed now?" Rustin asked.

"It's workin' on it," Nash said.

"Here, you can carry Silas to the van. He's gettin' heavy." Kasey put the child in his arms.

Immediately the little guy laid his head on Nash's shoulder and said, "Mean sissy."

"What did he say?"

"He's tattling on Emma. They've been at cross horns all day, according to Mama."

Silas smelled like a little boy who'd been running and playing all day and it was pure heaven to Nash. "I'm surprised that he came right to me. I usually have to be around kids awhile."

"My three never know a stranger. It scares me sometimes." She started out of the barn toward her van. "I got to admit I was wonderin' how in the devil I was going to explain to you that these three kids didn't know you or call you Daddy, and explain to them why we were moving to Texas Star. I'm real glad that something jerked you back into the real world."

"So what are we now, Kasey?" he asked as he put Silas into the car seat.

"We're neighbors and hopefully friends by Christmas," she said.

Chapter Seven

Wiping her hands on her apron, Hope came out of the kitchen when she heard the children and hugged Nash. "I hear things cleared up in your head. That's a great sign. Welcome to Hope Springs. The guys have gone out to the tack room to get the tree and bring in all the decorations. Make yourself at home. We'll have some soup and sandwiches soon as they all get back, and then we'll put you busy helping."

"Hey, somebody hold the door for us," Jace called out from the back porch.

"I'll do it if you'll point me in the right direction," Nash said.

Rustin grabbed his hand and pulled him toward the kitchen. "I'll show you."

"Your mama is not happy with you. She wanted you to come home as soon as he got his mind right. Says you can drive him but you can't live there," Hope whispered as soon as Nash was out of the area.

"I know, but I gave my word, and he's not supposed to drive or be alone until the doctor checks him just before Christmas. What if he had a seizure or a relapse and couldn't remember how to even dial my phone. You going to gripe at me, too?" Kasey asked.

"Nope," Hope answered. "You're a big girl. I trust you, and besides I've been talking to Nash's grandmother this afternoon. She says this might be the very thing that cures him."

"Of what?" A cold chill ran down Kasey's backbone.

Hope threw up her hands. "Whatever the hell it is that ails him. That PSDD stuff."

"PTSD. Post-traumatic stress disorder. Lots of veterans suffer from it. I don't know that there is a cure," Kasey said.

"Comin' through," Jace yelled.

Emma and Silas squealed and ran ahead of them into the living room.

Hope stepped into the hallway.

Kasey plastered herself to the wall, but Nash's forearm still brushed against her as he helped carry in the long box holding the Christmas tree. The electricity that bounced around the room proved that there was still chemistry between them—even after he'd recovered all his memories.

They set the box on the floor and headed right back out.

"Nash is going with me to help get more stuff. Brody is on his way with a pickup load. I'm thinkin' that we can get it all in one more trip," Jace said as they went right back outside.

Nash waved but he didn't smile. His dark eyes had a long way to go before they got back to that place of happiness and contentment he'd had before reality set in.

Lila pushed her way into the kitchen right after the guys left. Static made her dark hair fly out to the sides when she removed her stocking hat and coat. "I just got off the phone with Valerie. Kasey, you are at the top of Santa's naughty list."

"Yep, but she'll get over it." Kasey hung her jacket up and went to the living room to make sure the kids' coats weren't thrown on the floor. "Nash needs someone to look after him until Christmas."

"I agree with Kasey." Hope headed back toward the kitchen. "You girls can come in here and help me get things on the table. The soup is ready, we just need to get the meat and cheese platter fixed up. I hear tires crunching on the gravel. That's either Brody bringin' in more boxes or Valerie arriving with a head of steam and a bushel of advice."

"Neither your mama nor Brody thinks what you're doing is smart," Lila said.

"Brody?" Kasey frowned.

Hope handed her a platter and pointed toward several packages of cold cuts. "Take this to the table. You've got to remember, you were only fourteen when your dad passed away, Kasey. Brody thought he had to be your father as well as your big brother. Don't matter how old you get, he probably won't ever change, so keep in mind that he's protecting you."

"I'm a big girl. I can take care of myself," Kasey said.

"Evidently not." Valerie caught the sentence as she made her way to the kitchen. "I brought a platter of pimento cheese sandwiches. And I'm going on record as sayin' this is not a good idea now that Nash is okay."

"But it was fine when he thought I was his wife and wanted to kiss me about fifty times a day?" Kasey argued.

Valerie whipped around. Her eyes bugged out like a

cartoon character, and her head tilted off to the right. Kasey hadn't seen that expression in years, not since she was a teenager and came home late for curfew with beer on her breath.

Hope stepped between them with her arms outstretched like a referee in a boxing ring. "We're all going to have to agree to disagree. Cut your daughter some slack, Valerie. She's a responsible adult, and we're all close by if she needs us."

"What did you do when he kissed you?" Valerie asked.

"I kissed him back," Kasey said.

"You don't know that man. He could be…"

Hope held up a hand. "No, he isn't. I've been talkin' to his grandmother and I know a little about Nash and he's not a bad person. Stuff happened to him in the army—things he can't talk about and other things he won't talk about, but he's a good man."

"Just because you were friends with her brother and his mama was your neighbor, don't mean anything. And Adelaide isn't going to say anything bad about him. He's her grandson, for God's sake." Valerie was barely keeping her voice below a bellow.

"Trust me." Hope smiled. "I know that Nash is a good person."

Emma ran into the room with Silas right behind her. "Rustin says I'm too little, but how come he gets to help Mr. Nash?"

Silas pursed his lips together. "Me helps, too."

Emma's hands went to her hips in a stance that looked exactly like her mother. "Mama?"

"Yes, you can both help." Kasey relaxed.

"Cookies?" Silas beamed when he noticed the food table.

"Desserts are at Grandma's house," Kasey told him and

then hugged Valerie. "He's our neighbor and I told the doctor that I'd be there until he can drive. That's the way it is, Mama."

Rustin strutted into the room, full of oldest child authority. "I'm hungry. Where's the cookies that Emma said y'all made?"

"At my house. Work and real food first. Cookies later," Valerie told him.

"Aww, shucks. I wanted one of them cookies with the icin' on it." He kicked at imaginary dirt with his boots. "Nash said he likes cookies, too."

"He's my cowboy. I got him first," Emma argued.

"Mine!" Silas said loudly.

"He can be a friend to you all. Rustin, you take this bowl of chips to the dining room table. Emma, you can carry these napkins, and Silas, you can show Brody where to sit the boxes that he's bringing in the back door in about...right now," Hope said.

Silas marched to the living room, but Brody stopped long enough to frown at Kasey. "I don't like this, Sis."

"Don't even go there," she warned.

"We'll talk later," he whispered.

Jace and Nash pushed through the kitchen, both with boxes piled high on their arms. Jace was singing "White Christmas," and Nash had that deer-in-the-headlights look when he passed through the path the four women made by standing to the side.

"Don't be singing that song to me," Lila said. "I had enough of the white stuff when I lived up north. I'm hoping that it's warm enough we can play a game of football outside on Christmas day."

"Not me," Hope said. "I want enough pretty snow to cover the ground so the kids can build a snowman. I've even got the sticks put up for them to use to make his arms. Found the perfect ones under the pecan tree down at my place this past week."

"Hey, Jace, have y'all got it all in the house?" Valerie called out.

"What comes into the house is here. The rest is outside decorations, and we put them on the porch," Jace yelled back. "Can we eat now?"

"After grace." Hope raised her voice above the din. "Give us five minutes to finish putting things on the table."

When everything was in place, the family gathered around in a circle and Emma put one hand in Hope's and reached for Nash's with the other. He glanced over at Kasey.

"We hold hands around the table. I'll explain later," she said as she slipped her free hand into Nash's and bowed her head.

Lord, don't let my hand go all clammy and sweaty, she prayed silently.

"Brody, you say the blessing," Hope said.

When Brody finished, Nash squeezed her hand gently and let go quickly. "I like that tradition."

"It started when Valerie was a little girl. I caught her putting her hand in a bowl of peaches while Wes said the prayer," Hope explained. "So from then on I held her hand and then when she got married and had kids, she did the same thing. Now come on, Rustin, and I'll help you get your plate. You kids can sit at the kitchen table with Nash and Kasey. The rest of us can find a place in the living room. Soon as the kids are finished, we'll get this show on the road."

Emma tugged on Nash's sleeve. "You can help me."

"Okay, but you'll have to show me how. I've never done this job before," Nash said.

"Well." Emma cut her eyes around to her mother. "I want tater chips and pickles."

"Emma!" Kasey scolded.

"A sandmich and sweet beans then." Emma sighed.

"That's a sandwich and baked beans, right?" Nash whispered.

His warm breath on Kasey's neck created another spark that made her shiver. Maybe her mother was right about her staying over at the Texas Star with him.

"Yes," Jace said. "She gets a few words crossways, but she's talked plain since she started sayin' words. She's always been in competition with Rustin."

"I'm not 'petition with Rustin. He's bossy," Emma declared.

"And you aren't?" Brody asked.

Emma shook her head. "I'm renorin' you, Uncle Brody."

"If you ignore me, baby girl, there won't be a bedtime story tonight," Brody told her.

"Okay." Emma sighed. "I'm not renorin' you."

Nash chuckled. "I always wanted a sister or a brother."

"You can have Silas and Rustin." Emma led the way to the kitchen table and crawled up in a chair.

* * *

"Hey, I'll call you when I need to go somewhere if you want to stay here. The kids don't need their lives uprooted right here at Christmas," Nash told Kasey when they were seated at the table with the children.

"It's an adventure to them," she said. "Did you even read the papers that the doctors gave us when we left the hospital? Things that could happen with a head injury? Like seizures, relapse of memory, disorientation about where you are or where you're going. What if you were going out to the back forty acres and suddenly forgot who you were or what you were doing? You could fall into the creek and freeze to death."

"No!" Emma slapped both hands on her cheeks. "Don't let Mr. Nash get froze to death."

Nash laid a hand on her shoulder. "I didn't read the doctor's orders. But that's all a CYA for the doctors and hospitals. It's not going to happen. I'll be very careful, and please call me Nash instead of Mr. Nash, okay?"

"But you are old and Mama says we got to call old people Mr. or Miz." She went back to eating her sandwich.

"Ouch!" Nash flashed a grin toward Kasey.

"Don't worry. Anything over ten years old is ancient to her." She smiled back at him.

"What's CYA?" Rustin asked.

"It's short for cover your fanny," Kasey explained to her son. Then she turned to Nash. "And we're already moved in until Christmas. Are you going to kick us out?"

He shook his head. "I couldn't, but Kasey, it's not fair...not after..."

"Life's not fair. If it were, neither of us would be where we are today," she said.

"Amen to that," he said, glancing around the big open space that reminded him so much of the one in Louisiana where he'd grown up. The center of the place had probably been the original house and then it got added on to through the years.

He liked the open space between the living room, dining room, and kitchen, but there was something about the individual rooms at the house over on Texas Star that appealed to him even more. Compartmentalize—keep things in the right space with doors and locks to secure them.

Like your life and heart, right? The aggravating voice in his head sounded off loud and clear.

That's the way I've been trained, he argued.

Only by your past profession. Now you're a rancher, not a soldier, and if you ever want to have a family and a life, you have to be a helluva lot more open.

I don't need a therapist in my head. He frowned.

"Who are you arguing with?" Kasey asked.

"That obvious, huh?"

"Let's just say you don't have a very good poker face," she told him. "So who was it?"

"The devil himself," Nash answered. "But I'm winning the battle."

"Where's the devil?" Emma's eyes grew huge. "I'll shoot him."

"I bet you would, *chère*." Nash laughed.

"What's one of them things? Is it like a monkey? Uncle Brody calls us monkeys," she said.

"It means 'sweet girl' in the Cajun language," Nash explained.

Emma tilted her head up and flashed a bright smile across the table toward her brother. "I'm a sweet girl."

"You're just a bratty sister," Rustin said. "I'm done, Mama. May I be excused?"

"Am not!" Emma argued. "You're a bratty brother."

"Am not!" Rustin declared.

"Me not!" Silas chimed in.

Both of the older kids looked his way and said in unison, "You're just a baby."

"Me nots a baby." He puffed out his chest.

"Enough of that. Rustin, if you're finished, go ask Uncle Jace what you need to do to help. Emma and Silas, you two finish your food," Kasey scolded.

"Hurry up, Emma," Rustin said. "We got to get the work done so we can go to Grandma's and have desserts. Do we get to help put up the tree at Nash's house?"

"Of course you can. A cowboy can never have too many ranch hands," Nash said.

"Me, too," Emma piped up.

"Me, too." Silas joined in the conversation.

"Guess we'll have lots of help with the Christmas tree business." It had been five years since he'd been a part of anything to do with decorating. Three of those he'd volunteered for extra duty work to allow other soldiers to be home with their families and children. The last two—well, he had managed to be gone when his grandmother did all the decorating. But now he was looking forward to everything about the holiday.

"Hey, y'all in the kitchen. You ready to get in here and help us out?" Jace asked from the living area.

Nash pushed back his chair. "What can I do?"

"Help Brody put up the tree while I unpack the lights," Jace answered. "No matter how careful we are when we put them away, they always tangle."

Just like life, Nash thought as he opened the long box and started laying out the branches for the tree. Kasey was not five feet away from him, unpacking a box with tinsel written on the side. Nash's chest tightened when she bent over and her jeans stretched across a perfectly rounded butt. Only a few hours ago, that sexy redhead was his wife, and now she was only his caretaker.

Brody held the lights on his forearms and Lila fastened each one to the branches of the huge tree. To keep his eyes off Kasey, he watched the newlyweds and yearned for a relationship like they had. One where every nuance and gaze had a meaning or a memory, where the chemistry between them could be felt in the whole room. He'd had that for a little while, but it had all been fake, and he wanted the real deal.

His eyes shifted over to Kasey, and the world stopped turning for a moment. She was the one he wanted, the one he'd always wanted from the first time he saw those green eyes in the picture with Rustin and Emma. Or maybe it wasn't Kasey at all but that feeling that he got in his heart when Adam had talked about his wife. Surely that was what he craved and not another man's wife.

When Lila and Brody finished, Kasey held up the garland. "We're next. You want to hold or drape?"

"Hold. I'm not sure I'd be good at the draping business," he answered.

"Okay, then come over here and hold out your arms."

He crossed the room and she slid the gold tinsel from the cardboard over onto his outstretched arms. Her feathery touch set his heart to doing double-time. "We do it just like Lila and Brody, right?"

"Don't tell me this is your first time to do this." Kasey laughed.

"I usually got to put on a few of those icicles when I was a kid, but Mama did most of the other work with a lot of help from Addy. She came down to Louisiana every year for Thanksgiving, and it was a family tradition to get the tree up before she went home to Texas," Nash said as he followed her to the tree.

Other than the past couple of days when he really thought he was a married man, he couldn't remember the last time he'd said more than two sentences. And it had been two years since he'd talked to anyone about his family or memories. His grandmother accused him of losing his ability to speak while he was in the hospital those many weeks after he hit his head on that last mission.

"That's my job," Emma said from the corner where she already had a fist full of silver and gold icicles in her hands. "Granny let me do that. But not Silas."

Silas raised his head and glared at his sister. "Cookies!"

* * *

Kasey tried to hurry with the garland, but either Lila or Hope thought one was stretched too tight or else needed to be looped down farther. She caught a whiff of Nash's shaving lotion every time he moved, and every time he uttered a word in that deep Cajun drawl, she wanted throw the garland out in the yard and drag him off to the barn or the willow tree at the springs for a make-out session.

Good lord! Adam would be so disappointed in her lusting after another man. She'd vowed to love him forever, and here she was with three kids, her mother, grandmother, and brothers, as well as her new sister-in-law right there in the room with her while she wished she was tangled up under a quilt having sex with Nash.

Until death parts us, that was the vow, not all the way through eternity, that pesky voice in her head reminded her. *Adam told you more than once that if he didn't come home that you should move on.*

Easier said than done, especially since he was my first and only love, she argued.

"Just a tad bit lower on that one and I believe it's perfect," Hope said. "Then Valerie and I get to hang the ornaments."

"And then it's my turn," Emma said.

"That was fun," Nash said. "I never was over at Texas Star during the holidays. I wonder if the decorations there are a lot like these."

"Minnie liked the big lights and she always hosted a Christmas dinner for her Sunday school class. I remember her tree very well," Hope said. "Your uncle Henry complained about having to put the lights up around the house when he retired from the military and came home, but I think down deep he really liked the holiday."

"Well, I guess Kasey and I'll see what's in the boxes in the attic tomorrow. It should be fun," Nash said.

Rustin puffed out his chest. "Yes, and I'm goin' to help."

"And me, too," Emma said.

"Me, cookies!" Silas tapped his chest.

"That's right." Nash settled into the corner of the sofa and Emma sat down as close as she could get beside him. Silas toddled over and held up his arms. Nash picked him up and set him on his lap.

"See!" Silas pointed toward the tree as Valerie and Hope hung the pretty ornaments.

"Yes, sir, I do see and they are sparkly and shiny." Nash grinned.

They need a father. Move on! Move on! Move on! The words tumbled over each other in Kasey's head.

Maybe they do, she admitted. *But I'm not so sure that I could ever be happy with another husband.*

Chapter Eight

Uncomfortable was an understatement when they arrived at Prairie Rose Ranch for desserts and to see all of Valerie's decorations. Nash carried Silas inside the house, and Adam's mother, Gracie, immediately took him from Nash's arms.

"Hey, Gracie, have you and Paul met Nash?" Kasey asked.

"We have," Gracie said curtly and carried Silas to the kitchen.

Paul stepped out from behind Jace and Brody with a hand outstretched. "Good to see you again, Nash. I hear that something clicked in your head and you're back to normal. That's good. How are things at the Texas Star?"

"Going well. Sheep are content. And I like it here in Happy," Nash answered.

"And we're putting up a Christmas tree over at Nash's to-morrow, Gramps." Rustin stretched up on his tiptoes to hang his coat on the rack inside the front door. "And I get to help. Emma can do icicles, but I get to do more."

Emma tipped up her chin. "My 'cicles will be pretty."

Silas came out of the kitchen as fast as his chubby legs would allow with a sugar cookie in his hand. "Nashie want one?"

"Yes, I would love one." Nash grinned.

Silas took him by the hand and led him to the dining room. Kasey followed right behind them. That Gracie was angry wasn't even a doubt, and if she went off on Nash, it could throw him right back into a world where he thought they were married. She had to protect her own interests as well as Nash's in this battle.

"Mama makes the best sugar cookies in the whole area." Kasey raised her voice so that Valerie and Gracie would both know she and Nash were close by.

"Kasey, would you please come in here and help me carry out a few things?" Valerie called out.

The decision was made in a split second. She could put off listening to Gracie and her mother's opinion by taking Nash with her or she could ask him to watch Silas and go on and take her dose of bitter medicine. She chose the latter.

"Looks like they need my expert advice in the kitchen. Will you watch Silas while I'm in there? He can slip away in the blink of an eye, so keep him close."

"Sure thing." Nash took Silas by the hand and led him back into the living room.

Silas took a bite of his cookie and pointed to Nash, who did the same. Then his finger shot over to the Christmas tree, all lit up and sparkly. Kasey inhaled deeply and let it out, then did it again before she marched into the kitchen, ready for war.

The moment she cleared the doorway, Valerie led with the first round. "Gracie and I've talked about this and we've decided that since Nash has his mind right again that you shouldn't live over there. We'll send Brody or Jace to drive him when he needs to go to town or to the doctor's office."

"It's not right, and besides, that whole family was a little odd. Minnie Thomas, his great-grandma, was the only one who wasn't, well, slightly off. His great-grandfather, Henry's dad, was strange. Didn't leave the ranch very often and never went to church with Minnie and the kids. Everyone will be talkin' about you, and Adam would not be pleased." Gracie fired the second shot.

"Are y'all finished?" Kasey's tone was downright chilly.

"Not by a long shot, but we don't want to ruin the evening," Valerie said.

"We're only lookin' out for your best interests," Gracie chimed in. "Adam might want you to move on, but not with that man. He would not be happy about this."

Kasey folded her arms across her chest. "Mama, if you've got anything else to say, then do it and then I don't want to hear another word from either of you."

"You're making a horrible mistake," Valerie's whisper came out more like a hiss.

"If I am, it's my mistake to make," Kasey said. "I gave that doctor my word that I'd take care of Nash until he could drive again, and you, Mama." She pointed at Valerie. "You told the kids that Santa was bringing their things to the Texas Star for Christmas. Besides, I actually owe it to Adam."

"You do not!" Grace gasped.

"Yes, I do. If he'd lived, and if he'd been in Nash's shoes, wouldn't you want someone to take care of him if he wasn't allowed to drive? Or what about if he slipped back into a make-believe world and thought he was in a third world country on a mission or if he went out to do chores and couldn't even find his way back to the house?" When she finished she turned around and marched out of the kitchen and straight to the living room.

She stopped in the dining room, put both palms on the table filled with desserts, and inhaled half a dozen times. She hadn't been sure about the whole situation either, but she was damn tired of other people, even family with good intentions, telling her what to do.

You better be right about this or your mama will never let you live it down, Princess. Her father's voice in her head was loud and clear.

With the back of her hand she swiped at a tear that inched its way down her cheek. "I know, Daddy, but my heart tells me this is the right thing to do," she whispered as she straightened up and headed on to the living room.

"Hey, Sis." Jace motioned her over to the sofa. "We're tellin' Christmas stories. Remember that year when Mama and Daddy had a few friends over for a big people?" He made air quotes around the last two words. "Me and Brody went out runnin' around. Brody was sixteen and I was fourteen, but I got to go with him. Mainly because Mama wanted him to stay away from Lila and I was supposed to tattle, but there wasn't no way I was tellin' on them because Brody would have made me stay home."

Kasey put her fingers over her lips. "Shhh! I've got three kids who do not need to hear that story, and besides, I had to stay in my room, remember. I was supposed to get to go to Granny Hope's house, but she and Gramps came over here for the party."

"I'll tell it," Brody said. "She was mad because we got to leave in my old truck and she had to stay home."

"She could have stayed with her best friend that night, but she'd gotten into trouble for sassin' Mama," Jace said.

"And." Brody lowered his voice.

"And what?" Nash's eyes lit up.

"She watched Mama pour a little rum into the eggnog and a touch of vodka into the punch," Brody said.

"Just enough to give it a little kick." Hope chuckled.

"Is that all?" Lila asked.

"No, it's not," Hope said. "I was here helping Valerie, and when we weren't lookin', Kasey snuck into the liquor cabinet, and let's just say the eggnog and the punch ended up having a lot of kick. And I had the first and only hangover in my life the next morning."

Nash caught Kasey's gaze across the room. "Did you get in trouble?"

She settled down on the sofa between Hope and Jace. "Trouble doesn't begin to cover it. I got grounded for a month and had to help these two old worthless brothers do chores the whole Christmas vacation and the worst part of the whole thing was…"

"And that wasn't nearly enough punishment. I was so embarrassed," Valerie said as she and Gracie entered the room and sat down in a couple of rocking chairs.

"There's good and bad in everything." Kasey turned her gaze toward her mother. "Sometimes we'd hurry through chores and go over to Henry's old barn in the evening. It was while I was grounded that Adam and I started dating and I got my first kiss."

"Sweet Jesus!" Valerie threw her hand over her eyes. "Just remember you got a little red-haired daughter that already acts just like you, and you will have to pay for your raisin'."

"Lookin' forward to it," Kasey said.

"When she's twelve, I'll help you put locks on the liquor cabinet." Hope smiled.

"Thanks, Granny Hope."

At least part of her family trusted her to make her own

decisions and to support her—Granny Hope, Jace, and Lila. She didn't worry about her grandmother or her brother. They could take the heat, but Kasey hoped that Lila didn't catch a lot of flack from Brody for her choice. She sure didn't want to be the reason they fought so soon after their honeymoon.

"Maybe Emma will have more of her father's stable genes," Gracie said.

Kasey just smiled and nodded. Gracie didn't need to know that it was a pure miracle that she and Adam weren't pregnant long before the wedding day or that he did love a good party. Silas was the proof of that, since she'd gotten pregnant with him after a big fall social at the base when they were both too plastered to remember to use protection.

"I'd tell y'all a story about Brody and Lila, but it's classified." Jace laughed.

That last word caused a veil to fall over Nash's eyes and Kasey felt an immediate need to get him back to his ranch. She faked a yawn and said, "Y'all had better hold the good stories until Christmas day because I sure don't want to miss a thing, since this is my first Christmas back here in Happy. But right now it's time for kids' baths and bedtime stories and it's past time to get the chores done on Texas Star."

Lila popped up off Brody's lap. "I'll help get their coats and hats on."

"Me!" Emma tucked her hand into Lila's. "You gets to help me."

"I can do my own," Rustin declared.

"That leaves me and you, buddy." Nash carried Silas toward the coatrack. "It's been real nice to be a part of everything tonight, folks. Thanks for a great evening."

"Holler if you need any help with anything. We're just across the fence, and you can throw Kasey back over it if she gets too sassy," Jace said.

"Thank you." Nash nodded. "I'll have to be nice to her or I'll be runnin' the cowboy boot express every single time I want to go to town for anything." He held up his foot to show them a rugged cowboy boot. "The doctor says that I can't drive for three weeks."

"I feel for you." Jace shook his head in mock worry. "Livin' with her ain't easy."

"They are not livin' together," Gracie said curtly. "They are simply sharing a house until his doctor visit."

"Until Christmas," Rustin piped up and stared right at Valerie.

"We'll see," Valerie said.

Lila got Emma's coat fastened and whispered in Kasey's ear, "Ignore her. She'll get over herself."

"See y'all later. It's been fun," Kasey called out as she helped Nash get Silas into his coat and stocking hat and escaped out the door with Emma's hand in hers. Rustin ran on ahead to the van, with Hero right behind him. When he opened the door, the dog jumped inside.

"Let the dog go with us," Nash said softly. "He'll be fine at the house. Tomorrow I'll throw together a doghouse for him. Tonight he can sleep on the porch."

Kasey didn't argue. The crazy dog would be running back and forth between ranches anyway if she left him behind. To have a warm doghouse might be the best thing for him. She crawled inside the backseat of the van and was busy strapping Emma into her car seat while Nash worked at getting Silas all settled into his. In that tight space, his arm was against her thigh and turned her into butterfingers and a bundle of tightly wound nerves.

"There we go, Mr. Silas." Nash finally moved back.

"Tank you, Nashie." Silas grinned.

"So I'm his Nashie and Emma's tall cowboy?" Nash said.

"Looks that way."

"You're my buddy that I get to spend Christmas with this year," Rustin said. "Will you come to my school party with Mama?"

"Maybe." Nash glanced over at Kasey. "You think after tonight that they'll even want me to be a shepherd in the church thing?"

"Granny Hope runs that show with an iron fist, and she's already got you on the roster."

"What about your mama and Gracie?"

She fastened her seat belt. "They're in charge of the Santa end of the thing in the reception hall. You probably won't be asked to be Santa, but then you don't look much like one to me."

He pulled his belt across his wide chest and locked it. "So you're saying I'd look better in a burlap getup as a shepherd than in a red suit as Santa?"

"Exactly," she said. "But you can still wear your cowboy boots. It'll probably be cold."

"Kasey, I don't want to cause a problem—" he started.

"If you do, that's their burden, not ours," she answered quickly.

* * *

Nash's bare feet didn't make the same noise that boots would have, but every other step squeaked when he stepped on it that evening on his way up to the second floor. "Do I hear kids up here?" he called out.

Emma squealed. "In Mama's room."

He stopped at the open door and leaned on the frame, not wanting to presume too much and go inside her bedroom without an invitation. The scene in front of him could have easily been one of those Christmas pictures that folks sent out during the holidays. Kasey was sitting cross-legged in the middle of the bed with Silas in her lap and the other two kids snuggled up against either side of her. They had damp hair from their baths and were wearing pajamas, and their little faces were clear of all the chocolate they'd gotten on them at Valerie's house. But it was Kasey who made his whole body ache with desire. Her faded T-shirt that was at least two sizes too big and her red plaid pajama pants were rolled up at the hems. Her red hair hung in ringlets, and the overhead light made every cute little freckle shine.

"Come on in; we're just reading the third bedtime story," Kasey said.

"I want to go to my room now," Emma said. "Nash can read me a story."

"Me, too." Silas crawled off the side of the bed and would have fallen if Nash hadn't gotten to him in time.

"No! He's my cowboy," Emma protested.

"Mine!" Silas yelled.

"Ladies first, boys. That's the cowboy way. I'll read a book to Emma and then come right over to your room and read one to you," Nash said.

"Yay!" Emma bounced off the bed and ran across the hallway to her bedroom. She grabbed a book from the nightstand, crawled up into the middle of her bed, and held it out to Nash. He handed Silas off to Kasey and wasn't even surprised at the flutter in his heart when their hands touched. Just because he had a clear mind didn't change the fact that she was one gorgeous woman or that she appealed to him in every way imaginable.

"Oh, no, young lady, it's well past your bedtime. You get under the covers with your head on the pillow." Kasey used her free arm to drag a wooden rocking chair up beside the bed. "Nash will sit right here, and when he's finished with your book, I will tuck you in and turn out the light."

"Not all of the lights?" Emma asked.

"I'll leave a night-light on in the hallway and your door open just a little."

Emma shimmied under the covers, plopped her head back on the pillow, and nodded toward Nash. "I know if you don't say the words."

"Yes, ma'am," Nash said.

It had been years since he'd read out loud to a child. The last time had been when he was about fourteen and one of the younger Lamont cousins hadn't felt well at a family reunion. He'd been sent to the living room to rest on the sofa and Nash had felt sorry for him.

"Once upon a time," he started the Cinderella story.

"I love this story." Emma sighed.

Kasey turned around at the door. "You know the rules. No talkin' while the story is bein' read."

"Shhh. Don't tell him that," Emma fussed.

"Don't you shush me and rules are rules, young lady."

"Okay, we'll start all over and you shut your eyes and imagine a land far away where princesses and princes lived." Nash began to read to her.

A little quiver in his heart said that Kasey was behind him before he finished the story. The moment that he said "the end," she slipped into the room and tucked the covers up around Emma's little round face.

He wanted so badly to follow her lead and kiss the child on the forehead but figured he'd best not press his luck. Both boys were already under the covers and waiting when he arrived in their bedroom. Rustin handed him a book about a cowboy and a dog named Boomer. It was a cute little story about how Boomer saved the day when the little cowboy fell off the fence and the dog went for help.

"I hope that Hero grows up to be as smart as Boomer," Rustin said when Nash reached the end.

"And I hope you have a good night's sleep in this new place." Kasey crossed the room and tucked both Silas, who was already sleeping in his crib, and Rustin in for the night. "There's a night-light on and I'm right across the hallway if you need me."

"Where are you?" Rustin looked at Nash.

"Downstairs in the bedroom off the foyer," Nash told him. "Doors are locked. Hero has a blanket on the porch, and he's protecting the ranch. But if you get scared, I'm not that far away."

"I'm a big boy. I don't get scared," Rustin said. "But you will leave the door open just a little, right, Mama, because Silas might get afraid if he wakes up."

"Of course I will," Kasey answered. "Good night, son."

"Night, Mama and Nash."

They left the room together and Nash started down the stairs with Kasey right behind him. "I didn't eat much at either place, but I'm hungry now. How about a grilled cheese sandwich and some tomato soup? I make a mean soup right out of the can," she said.

"Sounds great," he said, glad that she hadn't gone right to her room. The evenings were so long in the big old rambling house when he had to spend them alone.

"What's your secret with canned soup?" he asked.

"A dash of Worchestershire sauce, a drop of hot sauce, and a little garlic powder," she answered as she opened the refrigerator and took the cheese out.

He went to the pantry and brought out the bread and a can of soup.

They worked together to get it all ready and then sat down at the table. Maybe it should have been awkward, but it felt pretty good to have someone there with him.

"So tell me about yourself," Kasey said. "Now that your mind is clear."

"What do you want to know?"

"Were you ever married?"

"Almost," he answered. "Damn fine soup. Restaurant quality."

"Thank you. What do you mean almost?"

"I was engaged when I got the first concussion. It was a lot worse than this last one. I was in the army hospital for almost a month and then they discharged me on a medical release. I threw a fit and said I didn't want to leave. The army was my life and I loved serving. They placated me by saying I could come back if I ever got a certified VA doctor to say I was okay. But after two years, I know it's one of those catch-22's."

"And that is?"

"I'm probably never going to be cleared and I'm accepting it a little at a time." He bit into the cheese sandwich. "What's under that wrapped-up plate?"

"Granny tucked a plate of cookies in my tote bag," she answered. "And if they never let you go reenlist, what then?"

"Then I'll learn to be content right here," he answered.

She snapped her fingers in the air. "Just like that?"

"You do what you got to do when you don't have a choice," he said seriously.

"What was she like?" Kasey caught his gaze across the table.

"Who?" The whole world condensed into two people having a late-night supper and he couldn't remember what they'd even been talking about.

"The woman you almost married."

A picture of Scarlett Rose, with her beautiful long blond hair and dark brown eyes, filled his head. She cried when she came to the hospital and he had no idea who she was or why he'd call her Kasey, and she never came back. Her mother visited a week later to return the ring and to tell him that Scarlett Rose had moved from Louisiana to Maine.

"I'm ashamed of you, Nash," his mother had scolded when she walked into his hospital room that day.

"What are you talking about?" he'd asked.

"You've been cheating on her with some woman named Kasey and it has broken Scarlett's heart. She told me she'd broken up with you and she's given me the ring to give back to you."

When he'd gotten well, Nash called Scarlett to explain as much as he could. Kasey was the wife of one of his team members and he felt responsible for the man's death, so evidently he'd been trying to find her and apologize. But Scarlett didn't believe him and said that she didn't want him calling anymore.

"Well?" Kasey asked.

"I'm sorry. I was wool gathering. Her name was Scarlett and we'd dated for a couple of years. I asked her to marry me right before that last mission, and when I didn't come home a whole man, she gave back the ring and moved on. Literally, to Maine. Mama said that she married a guy from up there last Christmas."

"Well, that had to have been painful," Kasey said.

"Not so much as you'd think. I'm not sure I ever loved her like I should. I wanted a family and it was time to settle down and think about one," he said.

Like most soldiers, he'd learned not to take much time when it came to eating. But that evening, he purposely slowed down so that he could talk to her longer. The soup was lukewarm when he ate the last bite and it was still only eight thirty, which meant it was a long time until he could fall asleep.

"How about hot chocolate to go with some of those cookies? We could have it in the living room," he asked.

"I'd love that." Her smile lit up the whole house. Hell, it lit up all of the state, but then it always did.

"I'll make it. You just sit there and look pretty," he said.

"Do you wear contact lenses? If so, you need to have them changed. I'm about as plain jane as they come." Her laughter was like light piercing through the deepest darkness.

"Beauty, beholder, and all that stuff," he said. "My hot chocolate is almost as amazing as your soup. I start with a package of instant, only I use half milk and half whipping cream instead of water. Then I put in just a drop of peppermint and a squirt of whipped cream on the top."

She took the wrappings from the cookies. "Sounds great. Hey, Mama made brown sugar fudge. I love it better than all the other candies put together."

"Addy makes that every year. It's my favorite, too." He finished the chocolate and carried it to the table.

She handed him the platter of candy and cookies and he took a piece of brown fudge and a chocolate chip cookie. Dipping the cookie into the chocolate and then getting it to his mouth before it all fell back into the cup was a trick, but he managed.

She followed his lead. "Best way to eat a cookie. You're right about this hot chocolate. It's the best I've ever had."

"Addy taught me to make it," he said. "Is Christmas your favorite holiday?"

"It used to be, but two years ago—well, you know. That

year was really tough, and so was last year. But I'm doin' better. Got to keep up a good front for the kids."

"Most kids love the magic of Christmas."

Kasey finished her cookie and got another one. "Adam loved all of it. The tree, the decorations, all the parties."

"Most of us military guys do, because it means family. That's what we miss most. Not so much all the lights and parties but being with the folks we love." He wished he could give it all back to her, even if it meant him being dead instead of Adam. If only he hadn't let Adam talk him into riding in the second vehicle that day, his friend and team member would be alive to love Kasey like she deserved and to read bedtime stories to his children.

She nodded seriously. "I think of all those guys who aren't home with friends and family. I guess it takes someone who's been in the military, either as a soldier or as a wife, to understand what all that means."

"Yes, it does."

She pushed back her chair and carried the dirty cups to the dishwasher. He helped her get the kitchen put to rights. He'd pushed people away for so long that he'd forgotten how great it was to have someone around to share in simple things like visiting over hot chocolate and cookies. But then again, this was Kasey, the woman who'd kept him sane through the first time with memory loss.

His first therapist had said that he'd projected his feelings onto the pictures that Adam had shown him. His way of coping with the guilt and the inability to save that little boy was to think about taking care of Kasey and Rustin, so he'd simply made them his family. It didn't seem fair that the roles had been reversed and she was now taking care of him.

Chapter Nine

Wednesday was one of those days at the Texas Star. If it could go wrong, it did. If it couldn't possibly go awry, it did anyway. Rustin whined that he didn't want to go to school because Nash needed him on the ranch. Emma fussed that she was big enough to go to school, so why couldn't she? Silas was in a fine mood until he tried to climb the stairs, got about halfway, and slid back to the bottom, causing a bloody nose.

Kasey finally got the bloody nose taken care of and set Silas and Emma in front of the television to watch an animated movie. Rustin kicked the dirt all the way to the school bus, but he did turn around and wave at her. At least she thought it was at her until she glanced over her shoulder to see Nash carrying lumber from the back of his truck.

He'd shed his jacket and had a stack of boards up on one shoulder. His long-sleeved knit shirt hugged his body like a glove and showed every ripple in his abdomen as well as his biceps. The sun was out, but the warm rays weren't what jacked the temperature up about twenty degrees, making her think she might break out in a sweat any minute.

"Mama, where are you?" Emma singsonged.

"Right here," Kasey called out as she hurried back inside the house. "Is Silas all right?"

"We want to make cookies," Emma said. "To eat while we fix our tree."

"Okay, but is Silas okay?" Kasey hurried across the living room floor to find Silas ignoring the television and stacking blocks. He pushed them all back and stood up. Grabbing her hand, he pulled her toward the kitchen. His grin reminded her so much of Adam that a fresh wave of guilt washed over her. She should be focused on the kids, not on a sexy cowboy who heated up all her hormones.

One who'd—she stopped in her tracks. Nash was not supposed to be driving. Had he driven all the way to Tulia to the lumber yard without telling her?

"Hey, it's not cold out here. Reckon Emma and Silas would want to come outside and help me build a doghouse? They'll just need a light jacket." Nash's deep voice filled the whole room.

Not ten feet from her, he was standing in the kitchen, a tall silhouette blocking all the light. Silas was going that way with arms uplifted. Emma danced around like a ballerina.

"If you've got time"—Nash picked up Silas—"you could come on out and help us, too."

When he turned so that she could see his features, his gaze caught hers and held. She caught a whiff of his shaving lotion, something slightly woodsy and sexy as the devil. Then she marched right into his space and shook her finger at him.

"You're not supposed to be driving!"

"Hey, it was only from the barn to the house, I promise."

"Where did that lumber come from?" she asked.

"It was stacked up behind the barn. I guess Paul was going to use it for fencing, but I figure we need a doghouse worse, with the cold weather coming in. I promise if I need to drive any farther than barn to house, I'll tell you." He crossed his heart and then quickly kissed her on the forehead.

"We were going to make cookies," she said breathlessly. "And I thought you were making a pen, not a doghouse."

"Ranch dogs need to be able to run free."

"And ranch cats?" she asked.

"God gave them the ability to climb trees. I'll make you a deal. Y'all help me with the doghouse this mornin' and I'll help make cookies this afternoon."

"Yes, yes," Emma squealed.

"Rusty?" Silas asked seriously.

"He can help me with the chores after school and then we'll get all the Christmas stuff put up and eat our cookies," Nash said.

Silas pointed to the back door. "Me go out."

"First shoes and a jacket." Nash winked at Kasey. "We won't get many more days like this."

"You got that right. The weatherman says that a cold front is moving into this area tomorrow and that it's only the beginning of a long line of blasts between now and Christmas. The old folks are saying that we'll have a white Christmas again this year. They had a blizzard in this area last year."

"I wouldn't mind that." Nash talked as he put Silas's boots and jacket on him and then turned around and helped Emma get her arms into her little pink hoodie. "We could build a snowman. We seldom get snow in Louisiana."

"So what kind of cookies?" His brown eyes twinkled, like they did when he thought they were married.

"What's your favorite?" she asked.

"All of them." He straightened up to his full height, removed Kasey's hooded sweatshirt from the hall tree, and held it out toward her. "But peanut butter is my favorite and then chocolate chip and then sugar with icing and maybe ginger snaps."

"Then just about all of them?" She slipped her arms into the sleeves.

He pulled it up over her shoulders. "To my way of thinkin', there isn't a bad cookie. I'm a lot like Silas in that regard."

"Thank you," she said as she zipped the hoodie up and hoped that he hadn't noticed her shiver from his fingertips touching her neck.

Emma headed toward the door in a run with Silas right behind her. A happy Hero met them on the back porch and bounded from one kid to the other. Nash whipped his camera from his pocket and took a picture of them, then quickly turned around and snapped one of Kasey.

She threw up both palms. "I look horrible. No makeup and my hair is a fright."

"Beauty is in the eyes of the beholder, and darlin', you're model beautiful."

"You don't have to use flattery to get me to help build a doghouse for Hero."

One side of his mouth twitched. "You have no idea how pretty you are, do you?"

And you don't know that you could have any woman in the state of Texas with your dark eyes and that body, do you? she thought. *Come Sunday and we go to church, I'll take a back pew to all the women who'll catch your eye.*

"We've got a doghouse to build. Where do we start?"

"Changing the subject, are you?" He grinned. "I already put the skids on the floor, so we'll build it up from there."

"Where are you going to put it?"

"Up near the back porch right here on the Texas Star. Where else would I put it?"

"Well, we will be going back to Hope Springs after Christmas," she said.

"We'll move it over there when we need to," he answered. "For now it's going close to the back porch."

She followed him to the pickup. "That close to the house?"

"If it snows, Rustin will appreciate not having to go so far to feed and water his dog. And the house will give it a little protection against the cold wind."

She lifted her end of the doghouse floor and helped him carry it to the place he'd picked out.

"Mama, where's Princess?" Emma yelled across the yard.

"She's just slow movin' this mornin', *chère*," Nash said. "She'll be here before long, but right now you have to take care of Hero for Rustin."

"Can Princess sleep in the doghouse, too?"

Nash and Kasey set the platform on the ground. "Look at this, *chère*," he said to the little girl. "It's going to be big enough for all three dogs. That way they can keep each other warm in the winter."

"Like when they was puppies?" Emma stepped up on the floor and used a stick for a pretend microphone. "I'm Pistols."

"Who?" Nash asked.

"Pistol Annies," Kasey answered.

Emma got the words tumbled as she danced around on

her own personal stage. But every time she got to the part about hell on heels it came out loud and clear. By the time she took a bow and left the stage, Nash was laughing and clapping for her.

"She shouldn't be saying that word," Kasey said.

"But it's so danged cute when she strikes a pose and says it. Don't fuss at her. I haven't laughed that hard in years."

"I want a stage like that for Christmas," Emma said. "And I want it under the tree and a real mike-a-phone and music."

"Remember that, Kasey, in case I have a relapse. She needs a little stage and a kids' karaoke."

Kasey started back to the truck to unload more boards. "And earphones for us, right?"

"No, ma'am. I could sit and watch her all day. I'll paint it pink and make a little backdrop with her name in glitter."

"Nash, I've already bought all her presents except for her Santa gift. We open up family presents on Christmas Eve night and then Santa brings one gift for each child and it's under the tree on Christmas morning," Kasey said.

He stacked four boards in her outstretched arms. "I'll make her a stage in the spring and she can put it under the pecan tree and we'll watch her perform."

Kasey started back toward the porch. "That's a long time from right now."

"Then you'll let me do it?" There was so much excitement in his voice that she couldn't tell him no. But there was little chance they'd be living there for Emma's first concert.

"My dad used to do some woodworking and I'd help him out. I miss that," Nash said wistfully.

"How long has he been gone?"

"He got lung cancer when I was seventeen but he didn't

die until I was discharged. Lost him and grandpa pretty close together. He was proud of me for serving," Nash said.

"And your grandparents?"

"Dad's parents were gone before I was born. My grand-dad on Mama's side died about the time I was discharged. Addy needed help on her ranch, so I stayed with her for almost two years. She and Mama spend a lot of time together these days. Addy sold the ranch a few weeks ago and moved into town. She should have bought something in Louisiana but she'll never leave Jefferson. Grandpa is buried there, and it's where all her friends are located."

"So you don't have much family?" she asked. "Are you close to your mother? You talk more about your grandma, Addy."

"I am closer to Addy than Mama. Don't know why that is, just that it is," he answered.

"Not on Mama's side, but there's lots on the Lamont side. I'm an only child but I've got a whole *beaucoup* of cousins scattered over Louisiana. My dad had four brothers and three sisters and they took that verse in the good book seriously—the one that talks about going forth and multi-plying. Hold this board and I'll mark it. Once it's cut off, we'll set the first corner."

Nash was proving to be a jack-of-all-trades. He knew enough about cattle to be a rancher. He was a sheepherder, and now he was building a fine doghouse. And he whistled Christmas carols the whole time he worked.

At noon, they both stood back with the two kids beside them and eyed the doghouse. It had three rounded holes in the front to give each dog access and even had shingles on the roof.

"Hero. Princess. Doggy." Emma marched down the front

and pointed out a name for each animal. "Red. Pink. Blue." She turned around and looked at Nash.

"Hey, now," Kasey scolded.

"Red for Hero's name. Pink for Princess's. Blue for Doggy. Right?" Nash asked.

Emma nodded.

"How about we do that in the spring? Paint has trouble drying in this weather," he said.

Another nod. "Silas and me is hungry."

"Y'all have done a fine job of playin' with those dogs and keepin' them out of our way all mornin' so I'm not surprised you've worked up an appetite," Kasey said.

"Let's go down to that café on Main Street and get us a hamburger and then we'll come home and make cookies," Nash suggested.

"Yes, yes, yes!" Emma pumped her fist in the air. "And Tater Tots, too."

Again, Kasey couldn't say no, but—and there always seemed to be a *but* where Nash was concerned—folks in town seeing her with Nash would cause even more rumors when they showed up looking like a family.

* * *

Nash carried Silas into the café and opened the door for Kasey and Emma with the other one when they reached the Happy Café. He picked up a high chair with one hand and followed Kasey to a booth toward the back.

She had the cutest little sway to her walk and her jeans stretched over her rounded butt, nipping in at a small waist that belied the fact she'd given birth to three children. He could have carried Silas and the high chair across the Sahara desert just to watch her.

"Hey, girl!" Molly came from the back of the café to give her a hug. "Who's this cowboy you're runnin' with?"

"Molly, meet our neighbor, Nash Lamont," Kasey answered.

Not much taller than Kasey, the woman had gray hair, a round face, clear blue eyes set in a bed of wrinkles, and penciled black eyebrows that made her look either surprised or scared out of her wits. "Well, now, I heard that Henry's great-nephew had come to Happy. I'm right pleased to meet you, Nash Lamont. I've got to get back to the kitchen. We got chicken fried steaks today for the special and they're keepin' me hoppin'. Hey, Daisy, look who's here," she called out to a couple of ladies on the other side of the café.

"Well, Kasey Dawson, you haven't been in to see us in weeks. And you brought a friend. Is this Henry's nephew that we been hearin' about?" Daisy, Lila's mother and the owner of the café, talked the whole way across the floor.

"Yes, it is." Kasey situated Emma into a booster seat and then slid in beside her.

"So, Nash, are you settlin' in pretty good out on the Texas Star?" Daisy asked.

"Yes, ma'am. Likin' it better every day," he answered. "I can't imagine why Uncle Henry ever left."

"Have you heard from Henry in a while?" Daisy asked.

"No, ma'am." Nash got Silas into the high chair and pulled it up to the end of the booth. "Don't suppose any of y'all have heard about him, have you?"

"Not a peep."

"This is Lila's mama. She owns the place, and Molly and Georgia work with her," Kasey explained.

"Lila looks like you." Nash smiled.

"I'll take that as a compliment." A little taller than Lila, she had dark hair with a sprinkling of gray and dark eyes. "Now, what can I get y'all to drink?"

"Coke," Emma said.

"Milk for these two." Kasey shook her head. "I'll have lemonade."

"Sweet tea," Nash said.

"Nice to meet you, Nash. I'll have those drinks in a minute along with the menus."

"So Lila's mama owns this place?"

"Yep. She leased it out to Molly and Georgia for about twelve years and they were talkin' about buyin' it, but she decided to come back to Happy at the last minute. Lila helps out when they need her."

"And she works at the ranch the rest of the time?"

"Oh, yeah. She's really caught on to the job, just like Granny thought she would. She's a schoolteacher, and Mama offered her a job here at the school. Mama's on the school board, but Granny offered her a better job to help Brody and Jace run Hope Springs. She's good with the book work and loves to be outside with Brody. And she's a damn fine cook," Kasey said.

Daisy returned with the iced tea and lemonade and whispered, "White milk or chocolate?"

"They'd probably rather have chocolate," Kasey said.

"Yes, yes, yes," Emma clapped her hands. "And Tater Tots. Meat and cheese and ketchup 'burger, too."

"I like a girl who knows what she wants." Daisy gave Nash and Kasey each a menu. "And what does the cowboy in the high chair want today?"

"French fries and a burger with meat and cheese only," Kasey said. "And I want a burger basket. Mustard and no onions."

"Me, too, only I want mayo and no onions, please." Nash handed the menu back to Daisy.

This was nice. No, it went way beyond that. It was downright amazing even if it was only having burgers in the local café. Families did things like this and Nash loved the feeling.

Daisy wrote it all down and disappeared behind the counter.

Nash glanced at Emma. "It's like she's a teenager and she's not even four yet."

"Been like that since her first word. No one could understand Rustin until he was well past three years old, and Silas only says a few words, but not Emma. She says the words plain, but sometimes they don't quite fit like they should."

"I is havin' a burger," Emma declared.

"Like that?" Nash said.

"Oh, yeah," Kasey answered. "Have you always liked kids?"

"Love 'em. Someday I want a houseful. If I stay in Happy, I'd like to fill every one of those bedrooms up with them," he said.

An instant vision of kids popped into his head. They romped through the house and followed him around the place. He held on to it, cherishing the lightheartedness that it created in his chest.

"And if you don't stay?" Kasey asked.

"Then I'll lug around a whole van full of army brats wherever I go," he answered. "How about you? How many would you like to have?"

"Six," she said quickly.

"Really?" He wasn't sure he'd heard her right.

"I want some more girls. It's not fun growing up with no sisters, is it, Emma?"

Emma's red hair flopped around her face when she shook her head. "I want a sister. I'll tell Santa."

Nash chuckled. "Santa might not be too good at makin' sisters."

Daisy brought their food and raised an eyebrow at Kasey. "Lila says that you're stayin' over at the Texas Star."

"Yep, I sure am. The doctor says this cowboy ain't supposed to drive until after Christmas, so the kids and I moved in to help out. Gives Lila and Brody some time to get adjusted to havin' the ranch to themselves since Jace has been stayin' with Mama a lot. Her foreman has taken the month off to go visit his kids."

"Smart move," Daisy said. "I heard that one of those pups of y'all's caused him to fall."

"No, the dog just chased the cat up the tree. A step on the old ladder gave way with me about the time that the kitten clawed me. I should've been more careful," Nash said.

"A knight in shining armor." Daisy laughed.

Kasey laughed with her. "Or at least a wounded knight in a big black pickup truck."

Nash chuckled. "Aww, shucks. I'm just a shepherd and a cattleman. I'm not a knight and I wouldn't trade my truck for a horse and a lance for nothing."

"What's a lance?" Emma asked.

"It's what knights use."

"Can I see it? Is it in the doghouse?"

Nash shook his head. "No, ma'am."

"I'm not a ma'am. Ma'am's is old people like Granny and Grandma." She blew on a Tater Tot and then popped it into her mouth.

Nash laughed out loud, and it felt wonderful.

* * *

Nash pulled an ancient tree from a box that had more duct tape on it than cardboard. The kids squealed and jumped up and down, declaring it was the prettiest tree they'd ever had.

Even with the color-coded limbs, it took half an hour to get the tree put together, and when they were done, the shortest one in the box was missing. Kasey looked through the box and under the sofa and asked both Rustin and Emma if they'd seen it.

"No, Mama," they answered in unison and shook their heads.

"Me tree." Silas peeked out from behind the recliner and held it up high.

"How did it get back there?" Kasey asked.

"Me do it," he said.

"Well, it's time to give it to me," Kasey said.

"No!" Silas stomped his foot. "Me do it."

"I know you had it but we've got to..."

Nash slung an arm around her shoulders. "I think I know what he's saying."

He scooped Silas up in his arms and set him on his shoulders.

"Me do it!" Silas said as he poked the limb into place. "Me help."

"Yes, you did, buddy." Nash grinned. "And now it's time for us to put on the lights. You kids can start unwrapping the ornaments from that box over there so we can hang them when it's time."

"Oh, no!" Kasey shook her head. "Those things are practically museum quality. What if they break one?"

"It would be an accident," he answered.

"But they're priceless," Kasey whispered. "Maybe we should let them put on icicles like Mama does."

"Things, like life, should be enjoyed, not worried over constantly," Nash said. "Lights, garland, and then ornaments?"

He was right. Life should be enjoyed without the burden of guilt and shame, but how to do that was a lesson she hadn't learned yet.

"Baby Silas can't do the pretties," Emma said, seriously.

"Me help more." He picked a box of icicles.

"That's right." Nash nodded. "You sit right there and hold those. That's an important job. When we get ready you kids can help us hang ornaments and then you get the icicle job to do all by yourselves. But Silas gets to put the star on the tree because our new tradition is that the youngest child in this house does that job," Nash said.

Silas beamed.

Rustin frowned.

Emma popped her hands on her hips. "Just how's he gonna get the star up there?"

"I'm going to hold him up," Nash said.

Silas held up his arms and Nash picked him up. "Not now, buddy, but in a little while."

Emma leaned back to see all the way to Nash's face. "You're so tall. You can make Silas get up there."

"When I grow up, I'm going to be as tall as you and I'm going to be a cowboy," Rustin declared.

Nash laid a hand on his shoulder. "Yes, you are."

"And I'm going to know how to build a doghouse just like the one y'all built today. Will you help me learn that, Nash?"

"I sure will and next spring we'll put names on the house."

"Red, pink, and blue," Emma told him.

"That's right. Now let's get this garland on so you kids

can help with the ornaments and then we get cookies and hot chocolate, right?" Nash looked over at Kasey.

"Of course. The hot chocolate is already in the slow cooker and the cookies are on the table, but we don't want to hurry too much," she answered.

"Not to break the pretties." Emma's curls bounced as her head bobbed up and down.

"Music!" Nash set Silas down on the floor, hit a few buttons on his phone, and set it down on the coffee table. "Santa Looked a Lot Like Daddy" started playing.

Emma danced around the room for a while with Silas right behind her. But Rustin stood still and listened to the words.

"Mama, does Santa really look like Daddy? I thought Santa had a big belly and a white beard. The picture of Daddy in my room don't look like Santa."

"It's just a silly song," Kasey said.

"Okay." Rustin joined in the dance, holding his sister's and brother's hand.

Dammit! Just when I thought I'd taken a step forward, one little song reminds me again of what this night should be instead of what it is.

"Sorry," Nash whispered.

"No problem," she said. "I've always kept a picture of Adam in their bedrooms. I don't want them to ever forget him."

"That's good. Don't ever let them forget that he was a hero and a soldier," Nash said.

"Thank you for that," Kasey said.

Dolly Parton's voice filled the room with "Santa Claus Is Coming to Town."

"Listen to this one, kids. It says that he knows who's been good or bad. And he's bringin' lots of presents," Nash said.

"Three." Rustin held up two fingers and his thumb fingers.

Emma held up three on one hand and one on the other.

Nash wrapped the garland around his arms and raised an eyebrow toward Kasey.

"Why do we have three presents for each person, Rustin?" she asked.

"Because baby Jesus had three presents," he said.

"And why only one finger on the other hand, Emma?" she asked.

"This one is from Santa Claus." She wiggled the finger on her right hand. "Santa is bringin' me a singin' machine and a cowgirl outfit."

"That's two presents. Which one do you want more?" Kasey asked.

"The singin' machine," she answered.

"I like that tradition." Nash followed Kasey around the tree. "But I do have a question. Is that one thing in each present or can it be two or more as long as it's three wrapped gifts per child?"

"That's one thing. Gold, frankincense, and myrrh weren't all put into one box. Each wise man brought a present," she answered.

"Is that from both of us, or can we each give them three?" he asked.

"You can't skirt around this one, Nash Lamont. It's three presents and one from Santa. We'll go to my mama's, the McKays, and Hope Springs on Christmas Eve. Each place they get one thing. That makes a really big Christmas when it's all added up. They get three here and then Santa will leave them a present under the tree."

"When do they open our presents?" he asked.

Nash had said *our presents* as if they were a family, and strangely enough it didn't seem strange. *Our presents*, she thought, *doesn't necessarily mean anything beyond friend-ship.*

"Well?" Nash asked.

"Sorry, I was off in la-la land," she answered. "Christmas morning and then we go to the other places."

"We follow the star to Nana's, Grandma's, and Granny's," Rustin explained.

"Star?" Nash asked.

"Pray for a clear night," Kasey said. "We need a star to follow like the shepherds did on the night when baby Jesus was born."

"Rudolph the Red-Nosed Reindeer," started playing, and Emma took control of the living room floor. She used a box of icicles for a microphone and belted out the song, some-times a couple of words behind the singer but she was so danged adorable.

Nash clapped for her when the song ended, and when the next one began he picked her up and danced around the floor to Scotty McCreery singing, "Jingle Bells."

When that song ended, he set her down and held a hand out to Kasey. "This can be our song."

"Have Yourself a Merry Little Christmas" was playing when she walked into his arms and he did a slow waltz around the living room floor with her.

"Listen to the words," he whispered softly in her ear when the singer talked about them all being together if they could muddle through.

"Ain't it the truth," she said.

Emma tugged on the tail of her flannel shirt. "Mama, the pretties for the tree."

"It says that our troubles will be far away, but I think maybe some of them are right here." Kasey stepped back. "Thank you for the dance."

"Three presents can be your tradition. Mine will be that you and the kids come over every year and help me put up my tree and decorations," he said.

A shiver shot through Kasey's heart. Had he slipped back into the world where they were still married?

"We'll probably always be neighbors," he said quickly. "So you will come over and help me put up my tree, won't you?"

"I thought you were thinkin' of going back in the military," she said.

"That idea is getting dimmer and dimmer. I like the peace here on the ranch, Kasey. I like having you and the kids around. Please say yes," he said.

"Of course," she answered. "But that's a year away. Let's get this tree finished so we can have hot chocolate and cookies and get these kiddos into bed."

"And we'll always have snacks and the night you help me decorate, you and the kids will spend the night so it's not lonely, right?"

"What if—" she started.

He put a finger on her lips. "Times change. Circumstances change. But Christmas should be the same every year. Traditions, you know."

There was no denying there was chemistry on his side as well as on hers because his eyes went all dreamy and soft as he looked into her face.

Emma tugged on her shirt again. "Mama!"

"Okay, *chère*." Nash dropped his hand and picked up the box with lights written on the side. They'd been wrapped with care around a piece of cardboard. He gently slipped them off and onto his arms. "We'd best get busy, Miz Kasey. These little elves can't do their job until we get ours done."

"Me not elves," Silas declared. "Me cowboy."

"Yes, you are." Nash chuckled.

Clipping lights onto the branches might have been an easy job if every time either Nash or Kasey moved, they hadn't brushed against each other. Elbows set off electricity. Bare hands created bright sparks. Warm breath on her neck sent hot little shivers down her spine.

When they finished to the applause of the children, Kasey had mixed emotions. On one hand she wished they had six more strands of lights to do. On the other, she needed to clear her head of all the images that had played through it in the last half hour.

"Now garland, but it won't take as long," Nash told the kids. "I see you've got all the ornaments unwrapped and lined up."

"I fixed them," Emma said.

"Well, look at you, all organized." Nash grinned.

That she'd grouped them by color didn't surprise Kasey. Emma had been doing that for months with blocks, doll clothes, and all her toys.

The garland was burgundy wooden beads made to represent cranberries and only took a few minutes to string around the tree. But even at that, it seemed like with every step, Kasey and Nash managed to brush against each other in some way.

"Yay!" Rustin jumped up from the sofa and clapped his hands. "Now it's our turn!"

Kasey nodded and started toward the recliner, but Nash laid a hand on her shoulder. "This is a joint venture here. First of all, Emma, you can put this pretty red one on the tree. And every year you can put the first one on the tree since you're the oldest girl in the family."

"Rustin, you can hang this green one. You keep your ornaments up higher than Emma's, since you're a taller cowboy," Nash told him. "Kasey, maybe you can put the ornaments up higher than Rustin's, and Silas and I will do the ones up near the top and then he can put the star on for us."

A gorgeous blue ornament shaped like an oversize teardrop reminded Kasey of all the tears she'd cried the past two years. She hung it above the section where Rustin was carefully deciding where to put his additions. Maybe all this was an omen that it was time for the tears to end and for life to go on. Even with the chemistry between them, Nash probably would never be interested in a ready-made family, but everything kept saying that it was time for her to get on with her life.

Lord have mercy! There is a spark but it's not necessarily for Nash personally. It's just hormones that haven't been satisfied in more than two years.

She glanced over at Nash hanging a green ornament.

"This one is the color of your pretty eyes," he said.

The reaction she had to the warmth in his voice and the twinkle in his eyes said that it was so much more than a dose of hormones. But, hey, she had the chicken pox when she was fourteen and she'd gotten over that, so she could damn well get over this, too.

Chapter Ten

"Hey, anybody in the kitchen?" Lila yelled that Saturday morning.

"Not now, but I can be. Come on in. I was wondering if y'all had forsaken me. Haven't seen anyone in a couple of days," Kasey shouted from the living room, where she'd been picking up toys and tidying up things while the kids were outside with Nash and all three dogs. She tossed the last few wooden blocks into a tote before she rushed off to the kitchen.

Lila handed Kasey a cup of coffee. "I poured for both of us. Granny sent brownies—the kind with pecans that you like. But they're only a ploy. What I've really come to do is spy on you, since no one has heard from you either. What's been going on?"

Kasey took the mug from her hand and motioned for her to have a seat at the table. "I'm surprised that they waited this long to send over an undercover agent."

Lila tucked a strand of black hair back up under a pony-tail. "Your mama and Gracie are still pretty angry that you're staying here. Jace and I have helped Brody to see a little bit of light, and he's comin' around. Got to give Granny some credit on that issue. She really fussed at Brody. The townsfolk are split down the middle. Some of them are siding with your mama and thinkin' that you're crazy for shackin' up with a relation of Henry Thomas, since he was a bit of an oddball. The other half are ready to give you a crown for helpin' out a veteran until he can get his head on straight again. It's Happy, Texas, so that's about right for the rumor squad, don't you think?"

"I thought you were here to check up on me, not give me all the gossip." Kasey giggled.

"I'm a double agent." Lila laughed with her. "Now tell me something to take back to them and then tell me the good stuff."

"So you want two different stories?"

"You got it. I'll tell them what they need to hear and keep the classified stuff for myself," Lila answered. "So spill it. What's been going on over here on the Texas Star?"

Kasey tasted a brownie and then sipped her coffee before she spoke. "Basically, we are settling in. Schedule is pretty much the same as when I was over there, except there's no computer work. There's only the sheep, so Nash takes care of that stuff. This is the first day Rustin hasn't had school since we came over here, so he's taggin' around after Nash. All three kids love him. You should've seen him when we were putting up the tree."

"Okay, then, the gossip stuff I tell Hope is that you're still babysittin' Nash until he can drive again because Hero is the underlying cause of the problem and you feel obligated. Nothing much changed there. The kids and dogs like him and you are his friend, nothing more," Lila said.

"Pretty much," Kasey agreed.

Lila finished off one brownie and helped herself to a second. "Now on to the classified stuff. Spill the beans, girlfriend."

For the past week Lila had been her sister-in-law, but for the past six months, she'd been her best friend. Still she didn't know if she could put into words how she felt and describe the turmoil inside her heart—not even to Lila.

Lila lowered her voice. "Has he kissed you again?"

"No." Kasey sighed.

"Do I hear a little disappointment?"

Kasey pushed back her chair and paced around the table. "Hell, I don't know. When we were putting up the tree, we kept touching. It was all so innocent, but it was hotter'n blue blazes and I don't know if it's just me waking up from a two-year sexual sleep or if there's really chemistry between us."

"It's definitely both. There's definitely vibes between y'all, and you have had a long sexual nap, but what I think what you're strugglin' with is the guilt," Lila said. "We've talked about that before but we can hash it out again."

"When you came back to Happy, you struggled with getting back with Brody. How did it feel?"

"It wasn't guilt but more fear. My situation was different from yours. I didn't have anything to feel guilty about. I did have to admit that I wasn't over Brody and open up my heart to the fact that I had to let go of the past before I could go on to the future."

Kasey slumped back down in the chair. "I don't know how to let go of the past. I've got three children, and Adam was my first love. Until what happened with Nash, I'd never even been kissed by another man. It scares the hell out of me, Lila."

"So you're dealing with guilt and fear, both?"

"Pretty much." Kasey nodded.

"Hey, Kasey." Nash poked his head in the back door. "Is it all right with you if I take the kids out to the sheep pen? I thought we'd do the chores a little early this evening and then go up to Amarillo to that Garden of Lights Christmas show."

"How'd you know about that?" Kasey asked.

"Heard an advertisement for it on the truck radio. Okay?"

"Sure," she said. "Keep an eye on Silas. He can escape in the blink of an eye."

"Will do. Be back in an hour."

Lila carried her empty cup to the sink. "Come look at this."

Kasey left the table and joined Lila, who was looking out the window. Emma sat on a sack of feed in a rusty red wagon that might have belonged to Henry when he was a little boy. Rustin was pulling it behind Nash, who had three bags of feed in a wheelbarrow right along with Silas perched up on top. His blond curls bounced with every turn of the wheels and he looked up at Nash like he was a god or at least a superhero.

"Now that's daddy material," Lila said.

"Or maybe good neighbor slash surrogate uncle material." Kasey sighed. "Lila, I've only known him a little over a week. Until he came into the picture, I didn't even dream of kissing another man, much less anything more serious."

"It's Christmas. Miracles have always happened during this time of year," Lila said. "Whoa!"

Kasey jerked her head around to see what Lila was pointing at. Evidently Silas had gotten tired of the ride, so Nash stopped the wheelbarrow and picked him up. Now he had the toddler in one arm and was using the other to hold a heavy bag of feed on his shoulder. The wheelbarrow had been left behind and Emma had gotten out of the wagon. She ran along beside Nash while Rustin made better time with the wagon now that it was lighter.

"He don't seem so much like Heathcliff now, does he?" Lila asked.

"Sometimes he still goes into that dark place and I worry that he's slipping back into that crazy world where he thought we were married. I wonder why he even thought that."

"Maybe he knew a red-haired girl or someone named Kasey in his past and he transferred it all to you, plus you do still wear your wedding ring. And he did see you that day that we had the horrible dust storm, remember? And then when he opened his eyes after the fall, there you were, wearing a wedding ring, so he got everything all jumbled up in his head."

He and the children disappeared behind the barn and Kasey turned around to refill her coffee cup. "I guess you don't have a lot of drama to take back for the rumor mill, do you?"

"Remember I was a high school English teacher. I can take a simple sentence and turn it into a full-length essay." Lila grinned. "I'll sugarcoat everything I can, but this classified material stays between us. And remember, girl, if you need anything or just want to talk, it don't matter how crazy it sounds in your head, just call me. You were there for me when I was going through the tough times and ever since when I've had doubts. I'm here for you now." Lila hugged her. "Now I've got to get back across the fence and finish up a whole stack of entries into the computer while Brody plows up forty acres to put in a winter wheat."

"Thank you," Kasey said.

"For?"

"For taking care of all my jobs while I'm over here. I know you'd rather be outside with Brody rather than sitting in front of a computer. And for being my friend and understanding," Kasey answered.

"That's what family is for and I'm really glad to finally be a Dawson," Lila told her. "See you in church tomorrow, right?"

"Oh, yeah. I expect there'll be talk when Nash goes with us. Where is Sunday dinner?"

"Why not have it right here and invite Gracie and Paul?" Lila grinned.

"Catch more flies with honey than with vinegar? Sounds like a good plan to me," Kasey said.

"Hey, I was being sarcastic, but I can see the benefits. Why don't you go for it?" Lila slipped into her jacket and headed outside.

Kasey followed right behind her. "I'll make some calls to everyone. I can cook a pot roast and everyone can bring a side dish or dessert. You can bring that corn casserole that the kids love. Betcha Gracie won't come."

Lila looked back over her shoulder. "I wouldn't take that bet for anything. I'd lose my money."

Kasey motioned toward the barn out beyond the yard fence. "I'm going out to check on the kids. Want to come along?"

"I'd best get back and do my spy duties or they might throw me off the ranch and I'll have to go back to teachin'. See you tomorrow."

Kasey watched her drive away in the ranch work truck

and then walked on out to the barn. She found Silas wandering around inside the sheep pen with a couple of small lambs. He had an arm around each of their necks and was leading them around in circles, with the mama sheep following behind him.

"He'll be a natural at training show sheep," Nash said.

She was torn between looking at him, leaning against the fence post, looking all sexy, or watching Silas with the lambs. After less than a minute, he won out over the toddler and the sheep.

"He's really does have a way with animals." Nash moved close enough that she caught a whiff of his aftershave. Something woodsy and oh, so sexy.

"Look at how gentle he is with them," he said.

"Where are Emma and Rustin?" she asked.

His neck bent slightly toward the inside of the barn. "They're training dogs. Rustin is teaching Hero to be a cattle dog by making him learn to sit. And Emma is working with Princess. I think the dog might be going on tour with Emma when she gets on the stage to entertain from what I hear. Princess will wear a pink collar and sit on the stage beside her while she sings. Emma gets to wear a tiara and cowboy boots with lots of shiny stuff on them."

"Welcome to my world," she said. "Make yourself right at home and keep a gun handy to protect your sanity."

He laid a hand on her arm and squeezed gently. "Don't think I'll need any protection. I'll dive right into the deep end of the insanity pool if you'll go with me."

* * *

The air was brisk enough that the kids had to keep the hoods up on their coats that night at the light display, but the stars sparkled around a big old round lover's moon. Nash was glad that Kasey knew exactly how to get to the Garden of Lights Christmas show because he sure didn't know his way around Amarillo. Not yet, anyway. By the time he'd lived there a couple of years he'd know every street and alley.

Two years? His grandmother's voice sounded so real in his head that he turned slightly to see if she was standing beside him. *You stayin' two years?*

He tilted his chin up slightly, like he would if he were really arguing with her. *Maybe I will. I've felt more alive this past week than I have since I got shipped home from that last mission.*

"Ahhh, lookit." Emma pointed toward an archway of lights. "It's my castle."

"Hey, there's Kyce. He's my friend. Mama, can I go say hi to him?" Rustin pointed toward a couple of little boys with their parents.

"Rusty!" Kyce yelled across the distance and raced over to his side. "I didn't know you were comin' to this tonight."

"Me neither, but we did. Is that your brother?"

"Yep, he's in the third grade. His name is Zayne. Can you go with us?"

"Not tonight," Kasey answered for him. "He needs to stay with our family."

"Mama, come and see Rustin's mama and daddy," Kyce hollered and motioned to his parents.

"Hi, Kasey. I heard you'd come back to Happy. Don't know if you remember me," Kyce's mother said.

"Of course I do, Mallory. You graduated with Jace, right?" Mallory had a mop of brown hair, green eyes, and if it was true that freckles were the result of angel kisses, then the angels must have loved her a lot. "This is Nash Lamont, our neighbor over on the Texas Star. We're stayin' with him for a while until the doctor says he can drive again."

Mallory nodded. "This is my husband, Brad. We live between Tulia and Happy on a little spread. Kyce and Zayne go to school in Happy."

"Kyce, like *ice* with a *K*," said the little brown-haired boy with a round face and big brown eyes. "And that's spelled K-Y-C-E."

"And I'm Zayne with a *Y*, too," announced the other little boy with a smile that showed two big teeth that his slim face hadn't grown into yet. "Is Rustin with a *Y*?"

"No." Rustin quickly spelled his name. "And this ain't my daddy. He's our cowboy and we live with him."

Mallory blushed and whispered. "It's a good thing that you're doin', Kasey. Adam would be so proud, him bein' a serviceman and all."

"Yes, he would," Brad agreed. "We've got to get these boys home now, Mallory. We got to get the cake made to take to my parents tomorrow down in Tulia."

"Sure thing," Mallory said. "You should let Rustin come play some afternoon."

"Sounds good. Good-bye, Kyce and Zayne, both with a *Y*," Kasey said.

"Pleasure to meet y'all," Nash said.

"Yes, it was." Brad ushered the boys away.

"So where did you get Rustin's name?" Nash asked as they made their way through the light display.

"It was Adam's great-grandfather's name on his mother's side and he always liked it."

"And Emma?"

"From a book that Granny read to me when I was a little girl about a princess. Her name was Emma and she had blond hair. That's about all I remember, but I loved the name. And before you ask, Silas was my great-grandfather's name on the Dawson side of the family."

"Well, I like all their names and they fit their personalities so well. Is Kasey a nickname for Katherine?"

"No, I'm just plain old Kasey with a *K*." Her smile put all those stars up there and the lights on earth to shame. "How about you?"

"Mama says that she got pregnant with me on her honeymoon in Nashville, so she named me Nash." He took her hand in his and squeezed gently.

"Fits you. And would you look at that?" She pointed toward a cutout figure of a cowboy with a guitar in his hands. Sparkling red lights outlined the guitar and the cowboy's hat.

"And why does Nash fit me?" He didn't drop her hand but kept her fingers laced with his.

"Sounds like a cowboy's name," Kasey said.

"And not an army captain's name?"

Kasey smiled up at him. "Captain Nash Lamont does have a ring to it." It was her turn to squeeze his hand.

"Me sheeps." Silas tugged at her leg. "Look, Mama."

A gorgeous nativity scene was to their right, complete with a blinking star up above the manger. Two wooden sheep were huddled up next to a couple of shepherds, and someone had covered them with real wool.

"Look at baby Jesus, Mama. I want a baby sister," Emma declared.

"Jesus is a boy, silly," Rustin told her.

"I know that." She shot a dirty look toward him. "But I got two brothers. I need a sister."

They walked through an arch into a clearing that looked like the setting for a fairy tale with a gold carriage set in the middle.

Emma clapped her hands and said, "Mama, when the prince takes me away, I want it to be right here."

"What?" Kasey asked.

"Like in the storybook," Emma said. "He'll take me away in that wagon right there."

"Honey, that's a long way in the future," Nash said.

"What's future?" Emma ran over to the carriage and crawled inside. She peeked out the door and waved at the family. "I'm a princess."

"Yes, you are, *chère*, and future is when you are thirty," Nash said.

"Or thirty-five," Kasey said right behind him. "And this is the end of the tour. Are y'all ready for ice cream?"

"Is Granny Hope thirty-five?" Rustin eyed the carriage but he didn't get inside it with Emma.

"No, she's five hundred," Emma answered as she got out and joined them.

"You better not tell her that," Kasey said. "Wasn't this fun, kids?"

"Yep," Rustin said. "But I wish they'd have had a bronc or a bull to ride instead of a stupid old carriage out of a fairy tale."

"It's not stupid," Emma protested.

"Did someone say ice cream?" Nash asked.

"Yes!" Emma shouted.

"Little corn has big ears," Kasey said.

"My grandmother says that same thing." He laughed. "We could call it their night snack and they could go right on up to bed when we get home. I understand that we're having Sunday dinner at our house tomorrow, so we might need to get things ready for that."

"I should've asked you before I made those plans, Nash." Kasey frowned.

"It's your house, too, so you don't have to feel that way. It's the least I can do, since you're disrupting your life right here at Christmas. How many are we expecting?"

"Maybe eight or ten in addition to us," she said with half a groan. "And you aren't comfortable around people and Gracie in particular. I'll call it off as soon as we get home."

The idea of that many people around him made Nash start to retreat inside himself again, but he refused to go there. He took two deep breaths and smiled at Kasey. "I'm glad that Addy sent half a freezer of beef with me when I moved over here. Maybe we ought to lay out another roast or two and invite a few more folks. We could do it all up buffet style."

"We've got plenty thawing out, and we'll have to make it a buffet. There's no way fifteen of us can get around a dining room table that seats six."

I will pass this test. I will go to church and survive being among all those people and then having fifteen at my house for Sunday dinner. I'm going to do this for Kasey and the kids.

"What are you thinking about?" Kasey asked as they made their way back to the van.

"My multiple personalities are ganging up on me," he teased.

"If there's fewer than three they don't have a chance."

"Why's that?"

"You could take on three with one hand tied behind your back," she joked. "And which Nash is winning?"

"The one you rescued." He threw an arm around her shoulders. "Have I thanked you for that?"

"I believe you have," she said.

Silas wiggled in the stroller and reached his arms toward Nash. "Hold me."

"Come on, buddy. I bet you're tired of looking at the world at knee level to everyone. I'll carry you the rest of the way." Nash deftly undid the strap.

Silas giggled and pointed at the lights up ahead. "Me king!"

"King of the mountain! We should play that when we get home," Rustin said.

"I'll beat you this time," Emma said.

"Will not!" Rustin argued.

"Me king!" Silas joined in the fuss.

"Emma is mean when she plays," Rustin tattled. "She hits below the knees."

"Am not! Boys are mean," Emma argued.

"Sure you want a house full of kids?" Kasey asked.

Nash opened the van door and settled Silas into his seat. "Yep, I sure am."

Evidently everyone in the whole Texas panhandle went to the ice cream store after they'd been to the light show because the place was packed and folks were lined up all the way out into the parking lot.

"It'll be midnight before we get them home if we wait in line." Kasey groaned.

"Then let's go at this another way. Hey, kids, how about we stop by McDonald's drive-by window and y'all can have a chocolate milk shake."

"You're a genius," Kasey said out of the side of her mouth. "Lids and straws and no mess."

"With a little help, I get something right every once in a while."

Chapter Eleven

Nash had grown up going to a little white church down in Louisiana, and when he spent time in Jefferson, Texas, with his grandmother, she'd never let him miss a single Sunday. When he first joined the army he'd gone to chapel every Sunday, but then missions began to get in the way. The past two years it hadn't been a time issue but a people one.

When he finally got things unscrambled that first time, he blamed God for Adam's and his other other team members' deaths. There were bad, evil people in the world that should have taken their last breath instead of those who were giving their lives in service. He'd lost brothers in combat and kept the faith, but that day the explosion and then the little boy's death turned out to be the straw that busted the old proverbial camel's back.

After many months, he had come to grips with the fact that it wasn't God's fault but his own. A soldier was accountable for his own actions and took responsibility. Nash could well remember the day that he'd been out in the pasture with his sheep and the realization hit him and everything reversed. He'd been shifting blame over to the Almighty when it all belonged to him. That was the day that the black hole doubled in size.

Sitting in a pew with Silas in his lap, Rustin on one side of him and Jace on the other, he didn't feel the anxiety or the downright fear that he thought he might. God wasn't going to send fire and brimstone down and destroy all these good people because he was angry at Nash for not doing his job right.

The congregation sang a hymn together and then the preacher stepped up behind the podium. "God is love and light and there is no darkness in Him," he said in a deep voice.

"The darkness comes when we allow ourselves to doubt God's wisdom. Some folks blame our heavenly Father for everything that happens in this physical world, but we make choices and we create problems and then when things go wrong we have to have someone to blame so we lay it all on God."

Nash locked gazes with Kasey, who was only a couple of feet away, sitting on the other side of Rustin. Her brief nod said that they were thinking the same thing and that Adam McKay was at the very core.

The preacher went on, but Nash tuned him out and thought about Kasey and the three kids surrounding him. Silas on his lap, Rustin beside him, Emma on the other side of Kasey. It wasn't difficult to pretend that they were a family, but all good things came to an end. He'd proven that many times in the past few years. The time slipped away from him as he went deeper inside himself, but he got a hard jerk back into reality when Jace stood up beside him, bowed his head, and started giving the benediction.

The moment he said the final amen, folks were on their feet and headed toward the doors where the preacher waited to greet everyone as they left. Jace clapped a hand on Nash's shoulder. "Want to thank y'all for having dinner at your place today. I love the way that my sister makes a pot roast, and maybe we can take a tour of the Texas Star after we eat."

"Y'all are always welcome at the Star." Nash shifted a sleeping Silas into a more comfortable position on his shoulder. "And I'd love to talk ranchin' with you after we get through with dinner."

"Can I go with y'all?" Rustin asked.

"Of course you can. A cowboy can't ever start learnin' too young," Nash answered.

"Yay!" Rustin pumped his fist in the air. "Uncle Jace, can I ride with you?"

"Sorry, kiddo. I've got a pickup full. Brody, Lila, and Granny all rode with me. But we'll be there right behind y'all. And we're bringing a chocolate cake and brussels sprouts."

"You can have the russell sprouts." Emma shivered right beside her brother. "They are nasty."

"I'll eat your russell sprouts, and you can have my cake," Nash said.

"Be careful. She don't forget anything and she'll hold you to that promise." Jace chuckled.

"I love those little cabbages, and Kasey made a peach cobbler, so I'm saving room for that." Nash smiled.

He didn't need to look around to know that it was Kasey's hand on his arm. The sheer heat through his long-sleeved plaid shirt told him exactly who was touching him.

"Hey, you want me to take Silas off your hands?" she asked.

"No, I've got him. Maybe we can get him into the car seat without waking him and he can get his nap out on the way home." Having Silas in his arms gave him a sense of belonging. He wasn't a stranger in a strange land but he was needed, if for nothing else than to carry a sleeping child out to the van.

"I'm going to talk ranchin' with Uncle Jace and Nash," Rustin said as soon as they were in the vehicle. "It's 'portant and girls can't go."

"I'm 'portant, too. Mama, tell him I can go," Emma whined.

"Sometimes us girls got things that we want to talk about that we don't want the boys to hear. So you want to stay with the girls or go with the guys?" Kasey asked.

Emma stuck her tongue out at Rustin. "See, girls is 'portant. And I'm not tellin' you nothin'."

"Well, I ain't tellin' you about ranchin'."

Emma tilted up her chin. "I already know."

"Enough arguing or you will both spend the whole afternoon in your room with nothing but a coloring book and eight crayons," Kasey scolded.

"You're generous. I only got four crayons," Nash said.

"I didn't even get that. If I was banned to my room all I got was one book and I didn't even get to choose it," Kasey said.

"Did you walk two miles to school in the snow?" Nash teased.

"Uphill both ways," she shot back.

"Me, too." He lowered his voice. "And it doesn't snow in southern Louisiana very often."

"I kept a stash of my favorite books under my bed," she said out of the side of her mouth.

"And I knew how to climb out on the roof and shimmy down a pecan tree to the ground. Then I'd go to the creek and throw rocks in the water until my arm got tired," he admitted.

"Rebels, both of us," she said.

She wore a green sweater that morning that was the same shade as her eyes and a tight-fitting denim skirt that hugged her butt like a glove. The pictures Adam had carried around in his billfold didn't do the real Kasey one bit of justice.

"You're a gorgeous rebel," he said.

* * *

Kasey didn't know if he was flirting or just being nice but it had been a very long time since a man other than her two brothers had paid her a compliment. "Well, thank you, Nash. You look pretty handsome yourself."

"Have Gracie and Paul said they were comin' to Sunday dinner with us?" he asked, changing the subject so quickly that she wondered if she'd embarrassed him.

She made a right-hand turn toward the ranch. "Oh, yes! Gracie and Mama are teamed up tighter than a couple of thieves."

"For or against you stayin' at the Star?"

"Against," she said honestly. "But I'm old enough to make my own decisions."

"Family is way too important for me to be creating problems, Kasey. Please go on back home. I promise I won't drive. I can call every time I need to go somewhere. I'm basically a hermit anyway, so it won't be very often."

She shook her head. "Don't try to kick me out, Nash. The kids are settled in really well and I'm not moving them until after Christmas. Their grandmother told them that Santa was coming to the Texas Star."

"I'd never do that, Kasey, but..."

She held up a hand. "No buts. I'm not backing down from what my heart tells me is the right thing to do."

"Yes, ma'am." He grinned.

She made a left-hand turn and slowed down to get across the cattle guard, then drove on toward the house. Jace's truck was already there, and Hope, Lila, Brody, and Jace each had a covered dish in their hands as they made their way toward the porch. Kasey and Valerie parked their vehicles side by side.

Her mother was at the side of the van before they even got the door opened. She handed Nash a covered pan with a chocolate cake inside it, and unfastened the seat belt holding in Emma in the booster seat.

"Come and see my room, Grandma. It's up some stairs." Emma grabbed her hand. "Nana, you come, too."

Gracie had rounded the backside of the van and taken Silas out of the car seat. He awoke and reached toward Nash with a whimper. Nash took him without hesitation and threw the diaper bag over his shoulder.

"Welcome to Sunday dinner, Gracie and Valerie. We're glad to have y'all here," he said.

"Silas does look just like his daddy in that cute little blue sweater, doesn't he, Kasey?" Gracie said.

"Nana," Emma demanded as she grabbed Gracie's hand. "Come see my room."

"Silas has always been Adam's mini-me. We all know that," Kasey called out as Emma hurried her two grandmothers across the yard.

The little dig did not go unnoticed, but Kasey was determined not to let her mother or Gracie get under her skin that day. With the progress that Nash was making, the doctor would clear him for driving or anything else he wanted to do when they went back for the checkup, and then she was staying until Christmas. After all, Santa was coming to this place.

"Hey, Sis, any of y'all need any help getting the kids or food into the house?" Brody crossed the porch and yard in a few long strides.

"Looks like there's one more casserole in the backseat of Mama's truck," she answered as she shut the van door.

Brody picked it up and carried it inside. "Mama probably forgot this one. She and Granny are already bustlin' around like bees in there. Lila is setting the table and..."

"Hey, Nash." Jace rounded the end of the house and motioned. "They've run me out of the kitchen and told me not to come back for twenty minutes. Want to take a walk with me out to the barn?"

"Sure thing. I've got a ewe about to give birth. We can check on her," Nash said.

"You're desertin' me in my time of need," Kasey whispered to Nash. "Those women are out for war. You saw their faces and heard that little dig from Gracie about Silas."

"You're tough. Come to think of it, maybe you're desertin' me in my time of need." Nash smiled down at her.

She wanted to roll up on her toes and kiss him smack on the lips just to prove to everyone that she could, but she wasn't quite that brave. And besides, it wouldn't be a bit fair to Nash.

"We need to talk." Brody stepped out on the porch before she even made it across the yard. "Walk with me, please."

"I should get inside and help with dinner. It's my responsibility," Kasey said.

"There's plenty of women in there. I only need a few minutes," Brody said.

"Okay, then. Come on around back and you can see the amazing doghouse that Nash built for the pups." She started that way with him right behind her.

"Sis, we need to clear the air. We miss you at Hope Springs. Lila wasn't plannin' on comin' home from the honeymoon and having to take over the whole operation. We need you to come home. I'm not sayin' you can't help Nash out when he needs a driver, but..."

Kasey rolled up on her toes and hugged Brody. "I love you, brother. You've always been there for me and had my best interest at heart even though sometimes I did want to shoot you right between the eyes. But I'm a grown woman. I have three children, and I'm making my own decisions from here on out."

Brody took a step back. "Are you already sleeping with him?"

Kasey's hands knotted into fists. "That doesn't even bear an answer. And besides, if we're going to sling mud, just remember I can throw it as hard as you can."

"God!" He raked a hand through his dark hair. "You've always been a handful."

"Yes, and who did I learn it from?"

"Trouble is that I like Nash. He's a good guy and you're ruining both y'all's reputations."

She backed up against the doghouse and crossed her arms over her chest. "I'm not leaving no matter what you say. You're my brother. Act like one instead of trying to be the father to a rebellious teenager."

"Then don't come whining to me when you hear what folks are saying and when other cowboys come sniffin' around thinkin' that you're an easy lay," he said.

"Believe me, if I do any whinin', you won't hear a single peep of it. Let's go inside now so I can help get the dinner on the table."

"I'm only concerned because I love you."

"I know, Brody." She hugged him again. "If I fall in a mud puddle it's because I tripped, not because you pushed me. Treat me like you did when Adam was alive."

"You had Adam then," Brody argued.

"Who made decisions when he was gone for a week or a month or even when he was deployed for six months that one time? Did you come over to Lawton and make sure that I didn't do something immoral or illegal or something that would start a rumor or even keep one going?"

"Of course not." Brody's answer took a while.

"Then trust me now."

"Trustin' you isn't the issue here, Sis. This is Happy, and between the Dalleys and Dawsons, we've had the biggest ranches in the whole area for—"

"For more years than anyone can remember," Hope finished the sentence as she stepped outside. "I'm buttin' in and I know it, but here's the way it is: Kasey's heart tells her to stay over here and be damned to what people think or say. Brody, your heart told you not to give up on Lila or yourself. Listening to it brought you happiness. If Kasey doesn't pay attention to what her heart is telling her, she'll always have regrets. I'm not sayin' this is a permanent thing, but she's got to do what's right for her, and as her family, we need to support her. Now put aside all this crap and let's go inside." She pointed toward the barn. "I see Jace and Nash, and we've got things all ready for dinner. We pushed the kitchen table into the dining room and there's room for everyone to sit down."

"Granny, you're not seein' the big picture," Brody started.

Hope shook her head. "This argument is over, whether you like it or not. Crazy thing is that I would have expected the opposition to come from Jace, not you."

Brody stepped around his grandmother and went inside. His jaw was set and his blue eyes flashing, but he didn't try another approach.

Hope looped her arm into Kasey's. "He means well, honey. Menfolk think they've got to be all protective of us women. What they don't realize is that we're tougher than they could ever be."

"Amen," Kasey said.

* * *

The last time Hope had been in the Texas Star ranch house was when Henry's mama, Minnie, died more than a dozen years ago. She'd come over with the other folks in her Sunday school class to bring food for the family. He'd been sitting on the front porch when they arrived and she'd longed to go to him, wrap her arms around him, and console him. She'd hung back, letting everyone else go in before her.

"Hope." Henry had nodded.

"I'm so sorry," she'd said.

"For what? My mother's death or your decision all those years ago?"

"That's a hard question," she'd answered. "I'm sorry that you've lost your last parent, Henry, but the other part, I can't say I'm sorry for that. Are you sorry for the decision you made that night?"

"I am not." He'd brushed past her and gone to the barn.

She'd seen him at the funeral with his sister, Adelaide, her daughter and grandson, Nash, who was a teenager and tall for his age even then, but there were no more words between them. Hope rubbed the little locket around her neck with her forefinger and thumb and wondered again if he was even still living, and if so, where he was.

"You okay, Granny?" Kasey asked.

"I'm fine. Just doin' some wool gatherin'. I haven't been in this house in more than twelve years," Hope answered.

"And I bet it hasn't changed a bit." Kasey laughed.

"It sure hasn't." Hope shook her head.

Kasey let go of her arm and went to help Lila fill glasses with ice for the sweet tea, and Hope stood back in the shadows and took a long look at the place. A dozen years hadn't changed much of anything. It all looked exactly the same as it had that day when they'd brought in food for the family, except that Henry wasn't on the porch, and that Hope had her share of regrets that went back more than sixty years.

Jace and Nash brought a gust of cool air in with them when they arrived. Nash's dark eyes immediately scanned the room until he found Kasey and only then did they light up. She looked up and they both smiled at the same time. Hope remembered having that kind of relationship with Henry. They didn't need words—a look or a gentle touch, sometimes a sly wink, and they understood exactly what the other one was thinking.

She'd had a good life with Wes Dalley, but she'd always wondered about that other path—the one she'd have followed if she'd left with Henry Thomas that night when he had begged her to marry him the next day and leave with him. She'd never know what living the life of an army wife would have been like or if she and Henry would have been happy because she'd put family and what other folks thought before happiness.

"Okay, folks." Kasey clapped her hands to get everyone's attention. "Everyone can sit wherever they want, except for Emma, who will be sitting beside me in the booster seat and Silas, who's on the other side in a high chair."

Folks gathered around the tables, leaving the head seat open for Nash. When they were all seated, everyone bowed their heads. When no one said anything, Hope poked Kasey on the arm and she laid a hand on Nash's shoulder.

"It's your house. Call on someone to say grace," she whispered.

"Brody, would you please say the prayer," Nash said.

Hope bit back a smile. Sometimes things worked out just the way they were supposed to. Brody cleared his throat and quickly said two or three sentences and then the noise began as conversations started and bowls and platters were sent around the table.

Reaching up to touch a small gold locket again that she'd worn since she'd found it again six months ago, Hope took a long look at her family. If she hadn't stayed in Happy and married her father's ranch foreman, Wes, she wouldn't have Valerie or these three grandchildren. There would be no Brody or Lila or those beautiful great-grandkids. And Nash would have no one to help him get through whatever terrible thing had left scars on his soul. Yes, everything happened for the best, even if it left behind hearts that would always wonder about that other road.

Where are you, Henry? Did you find a woman to make you happy in your old age after all? What have you been doing the past twelve years? Do you ever think of the day that you gave me this locket or the day that I threw it at you when you put that ultimatum in front of me?

"Granny, are you okay?" Lila nudged her shoulder. "You look like you're a thousand miles away."

"More like a thousand years. Old people sometimes spend time in the past, you know," she answered.

"When was the last time you were over here at this ranch?" Nash asked from the end of the table. Kasey was to his right and Silas was between them in an old wooden high chair with so much white paint on it that every corner was now rounded. Henry had probably sat in it when he was a baby. Suddenly, Hope had the urge to touch it, just to see if she could feel his spirit, and it would tell her that he was alive and well.

"That would have been the day that your great-grand-mother passed away. My church group brought food. It will be thirteen years next spring," Hope said.

"I was here but I don't remember you being here," Nash said.

"You hadn't arrived back at the house yet."

"The funeral was so crowded, I don't remember many of the faces," he said.

"Small towns are like that," Jace said. "I remember Henry but not so much about his mother. What was she like, Granny?"

"Minnie was a quiet woman who never missed church or an opportunity to help out with a dinner for the needy," Hope answered. "This place doesn't look a thing like it did when she was living here. She would have liked that you've put up her tree and used all her things to decorate it. At least that corner is still the same."

"Thank you," Nash said. "But that wasn't all me. Kasey and the kids did most of it."

"Well, it looks real nice," Lila said. "Like something you'd see in an antique store. If you ever want to get rid of any of those ornaments or those big lights, just let me know."

"I'll probably keep them forever." He grinned, but his eyes were on Kasey. "We started a tradition here and they're part of it."

"Oh?" Both of Hope's gray eyebrows shot up.

"Kasey agreed that she and the kids would help me with decorations every year and that they'd stay the night here at the Star," he said.

Gracie rolled her eyes.

Valerie sighed.

Hope tapped her tea glass with a spoon. "A toast—to traditions, old and new. To friendships—old and new. And to a very merry Christmas—to all of us, both young and old."

"Hear, hear!" Paul raised his glass.

"A lovely toast, Granny," Lila whispered. "With a lot of underlying meaning."

Hope touched her glass to Lila's. "You always were a smart one."

* * *

The Christmas tree lights mesmerized Kasey that afternoon as she attempted to take a nap on the sofa. The children were all down for at least an hour, and Nash had gone to his room. A whole hour with nothing to do was a luxury she didn't get often, but her mind wouldn't shut down. She kept replaying every word and nuance at the dinner table. Had Gracie and Valerie been nicer or were they just planning a new attack strategy? Did anyone else notice those long looks that she and Nash exchanged? Was Brody done trying to control her life?

She heard a whimpering noise and sat up. She was halfway up the stairs when she realized it was coming from Nash's room and not from the baby monitor on the end table beside her. She eased back down the steps and pressed her ear against Nash's bedroom door.

"No, no!" he growled. "No, God, please, no!"

"Nash, are you all right?" she asked through the door.

"Please don't let them be dead..." he whimpered.

She eased the door open to find him sitting up in bed, his eyes wide open and his hands held out as if they were wrapped around a steering wheel. Fearing that he'd had a relapse, she sat down on the edge of the bed and touched him on the shoulder.

"Nash, it's just a nightmare. Wake up," she said gently.

He blinked twice and grabbed her in a fierce, tight hug. "Oh, Kasey, they're dead. Three of them are dead and it should have been me, not them. How can I ever tell their families?"

"It's okay." She gently rubbed his back.

"I don't give a damn if it's classified. Their families deserve to know what happened and that they were heroes. They need to know. Oh, Kasey, they're blown up."

"That was a long time ago, Nash. It's over and done with," she said soothingly.

"I hear a chopper. Maybe some of them are alive. I've got to get to them to help, but we've got to get this man to base...oh, God...that's not a rescue chopper, it's one of the enemies firing on us. I have to drive faster."

She wiggled free of his embrace and clapped her hands several times. "Wake up right now, Nash Lamont."

He blinked rapidly, his eyes taking in the room. "Where am I?"

"At the Texas Star in Happy. You were having a nightmare."

"Kasey? What are you doin' here?"

"I'm staying here, remember."

"It was another bad dream. I hadn't had one that vivid in a long time." The words came out in short bursts between deep breaths. "I'm sorry. Did I wake you? What time is it?"

"It's three fifteen, December third. We had Sunday dinner here on the ranch and when everyone went home, we put the kids down for a nap and decided that we'd take one, also—remember?"

He nodded slowly. "Sometimes the past and the present get tangled up together."

"Let's get a glass of sweet tea and talk about it in the living room," she said.

"I'd rather have a beer."

"Does your therapist have you on meds?"

"No, and I'm not takin' pain pills, so a beer won't hurt me, Kasey."

She wasn't a newbie to the nightmares or to the crazy awake-but-still-asleep mode. Adam had been in that position a few times, especially after that six-month deployment. Talking helped him more than anything, even if it meant leaving out classified details.

Nash followed her into the kitchen and took two beers from the refrigerator, handed one to her, and carried the other one to the living room, where he sat down on one end of the sofa. "I'm sorry that I woke you. After that dinner and your talk with Brody, you needed a nap." He held up the beer and looked at it for a long time. "I can't remember if I'm supposed to have alcohol with the medicine."

"No, you aren't. Some caretaker I am. I'll get you a glass of sweet tea." She took his can back to the refrigerator and returned to the living room with it. Easing down on the sofa, she purposely left a couple of feet between them. "Now tell me about the nightmare."

"It's always the same dream and it's exactly what happened. We were over there on a mission—classified so I can't reveal names—to rescue a high-ranking official who'd been kidnapped. They were demanding ransom and the government does not negotiate with terrorists, but they will send in their best team to bring their man home. Everything went as planned."

He paused and took several long gulps of the tea. "There were six of us plus the guy we'd gotten out of the place. There were two vehicles and I should have been driving the lead car, but..." He raked his fingers through his dark hair.

"But you weren't because?" she asked.

"The guy we rescued had been tortured and was weak from no food, so we laid him in the backseat of the second car. One of the team members thought I should stay with him, since I was the captain of the team. The medic sat back there with him and another one of the team was in the passenger's seat in the front with me."

"And?" She pushed him forward when he stopped. "Tell me the details, Nash, so that you won't have this dream again."

"You sound like a therapist." He finished off his tea and crumpled the can in his hands.

"Have you told someone else about this?"

He shook his head. "I couldn't put it into words, not to a stranger."

"I'm your friend. Tell me," she urged.

Dark eyes, veiled with secrets beyond even what she could comprehend, stared at her for what seemed like an eternity. "How can you be my friend? I've done terrible things, Kasey. I don't deserve a friend like you."

"You defended this country to give me the freedoms that I have. I'm proud to be your friend, and don't you ever doubt that," she told him. "Now, I want to know what happened. The man you rescued wasn't in good shape, so he was in the backseat with the medic. You were driving and someone was riding shotgun. Three people were in the lead vehicle, right?"

"Humvees," he said. "We were all so excited to be going home in time for Christmas. We thought the first car hit an IED, but that wasn't what happened. It was a rocket launched from a hill over to our left. It was awful and I started to pull over, but the other two in the team were screaming at me to go on."

"Could you have saved those men?" she asked.

He shook his head. "They were all dead but we don't leave our men behind. And a helicopter appeared over the ridge and started shooting at us. I had to do some fancy driving to get us to safety."

"Were the bodies rescued and brought home?"

He barely nodded. "They sent out a squad and the bodies, what was left of them, were sent home in flag-covered coffins."

"Did you get to go with them? See it through and go to the funerals?"

A slight shake of his head. "While that was going on, we got the rescued guy to the base and they put him on a plane straight to Germany for treatment. We succeeded in saving one man but lost three. It never seemed fair to me."

"Why didn't you accompany those bodies home?" she asked.

"That evening at dusk just as they were bringing them in, there was a little boy." He paused again and looked blankly across the room toward the tree. "His mother was a translator for the base, and he came to work with her every day. He was kicking around a ball and it flew out of the gates into a bad zone. I went after him but didn't make it. He stepped on a bomb and I was thrown backward, hit my head on a rock, and had a major concussion. I went home with the bodies but never knew it. They took me straight to the hospital, and that's where I stayed for weeks."

"Well, no wonder you have nightmares. What happened when you got well?"

"They discharged me and I went home to Addy's. Grandpa had died, and she needed help running their small farm. She's a firm believer that hard work cures anything. Then a month ago she sold the farm, and after we got her moved to town, she decided that I should move to Happy to get my head on straight. Doesn't look like it's working too well, does it?"

"Patience." She glanced up and locked gazes with him for at least the tenth time that day. "Why didn't you buy the farm?"

"She wouldn't let me. Said I'd have to go into debt and that there was a ranch in Happy that I could have without owin' money. She sold it to my cousin Taggart, who's used his rodeo winnin's to buy the place. But I don't want to talk about ranchin' or farmin' right now."

He leaned forward and cupped her face in his hands. She barely had time to moisten her lips when his dark lashes fluttered down to rest on his cheekbones and his mouth covered hers in a scorching hot, passionate kiss. When it ended, he drew her so close to his chest that she could not only hear his heart racing but also feel it through his shirt and hers.

"You're an amazing woman, Kasey. I'm the luckiest man on earth that you're my friend."

Friends did not kiss friends like that. She should be eaten up with guilt again, but she wasn't. She wanted to kiss him again to see if the next one was even hotter.

"Mama, can I have a cookie?" Emma's voice floated down the steps and into the living room.

Kasey quickly stood up, knocking over her beer in the process.

"I'll take care of the mess while you get the princess a cookie." He grinned. "And Kasey..."

"I know." She quickly cut him off. "We'll talk about it later."

He gave her a meaningful look. "Thank you."

Emma was too young to notice the high color in her mama's cheeks, but Kasey could sure enough feel the heat as she sat her daughter up to the table and gave her a cookie and a glass of milk.

Chapter Twelve

Damn!" Kasey swore as she shot a dirty look toward the black wall-hung phone not six inches from her side. It rang a second time and startled her all over again. She'd been in the house a week and wasn't even aware that the thing worked, since it had never rung.

She grabbed the receiver and took a step only to nearly drop it since it was attached to the base and not a cordless. "Hello," she said cautiously.

"Could I speak with Kasey McKay please?" a voice she didn't recognize asked.

"This is Kasey," she said.

"This is Barbara Dillard, the elementary school principal. We've got a problem with Rustin and need you to come to the school. We tried the phone number on his records and it went straight to voice mail, but I knew that you were helping out at the Texas Star."

"Is he all right? Is he hurt?" Kasey's heart flipped up in her throat and her voice went all high and squeaky.

Nash came through the back door with Emma at his side. Silas toddled in from the living room and, as usual, reached up for Nash to hold him. Nash picked up the toddler and laid a hand on Kasey's shoulder.

"Something wrong?"

Kasey held up a finger and listened to Miss Dillard, agreed that she'd be at the school in fifteen minutes, and turned to answer Nash's question. "Rustin has gotten into a fight at school, and I have to go take care of it. My phone must need recharging so they called the landline."

"I'm going with you," Nash said. "We'll put Silas's coat on him and…"

"Hey, anyone at home in this place?" Jace yelled from the front door.

"In the kitchen," Nash hollered.

His footsteps sounded like gun blasts as he made his way across the hardwood floor to the kitchen. He stopped dead in his tracks when he saw Kasey.

"Who died? You're pale as a ghost."

"Rustin has been in a fight at school," she said. "He's never fought with anyone. I can't imagine him…"

"Go on. I'll take care of these two monkeys while you're gone. How about a movie, kids?"

"*Frozen*?" Emma eyed him.

"Whichever one you want. Let's get your jacket off, Emma, and come here to Uncle Jace, Silas. It's almost dinnertime so we'll make peanut butter and jelly sandwiches and have a living room picnic," Jace said. "You better go with her, Nash. She might need someone to referee if she thinks someone has wronged her boy."

With a nod, Nash handed Silas to Jace and headed to the hall tree in the foyer to get Kasey's coat.

Kasey shoved her feet into a pair of work boots and jerked the denim coat from his hands and talked as she hurried outside. "The principal said that the mother of the other child is there, too."

"You look like you could eat metal fence posts and spit out nails," he said.

"Rustin is not a fighter—except with Emma, and then it's sibling arguments, not fistfights," she said.

"Don't jump to conclusions until we see what happened." He opened the door for her. "Could be that someone else is bullying him."

"Then I'll take him out of that place and homeschool him. Lila is a teacher. She'll help me see to it that he's learning what he needs to." Kasey started the engine and was backing up before Nash even got his seat belt fastened.

"Take deep breaths and settle down," Nash said.

She started the car and turned to face him. "Don't tell me what to do. This is my child and no one is going to pick on him."

"Maybe he was doing the pickin'." Nash's southern drawl should have calmed her but it didn't.

"Not Rustin." She could feel steam coming through her ears as gravel hit the yard fence when she stomped the gas pedal. Nash might be right about her settling down, but she so needed something to be angry about that day and this was just the ticket.

It had been three days—three long days since that kiss on Sunday and he had acted like it never happened. She'd said they would talk about it, but the time was never right, and now it was a great big elephant hanging between them, creating a ball of anger in her chest. Everyone said for her to move on, but when she thought she might be ready, nothing more than one kiss happened.

She tapped the brakes at the stop sign, slowed from eighty-five to eighty, and slid around the corner on two wheels.

"Slow down or Rustin isn't going to have a mama to fight for his rights," Nash said.

"Then his two uncles, his aunt, his granny, and his grandma will do it for me," she snapped.

She parked right in front of the school, hopped out of the van with Nash right behind her. Rustin was sitting in the hallway with four other little boys, and every one of them looked like they'd been the only little chicken at a coyote convention. Scratches, black eyes, and Rustin held a tissue up to a bloody nose.

"Hi, Mama. Hi, Nash. I'm in trouble, ain't I?" he said.

"What happened?"

"Mrs. McKay?" The principal motioned her inside the office. "And you are?" She eyed Nash from his boots to the top of his head.

Her expression said that she liked every inch of what she saw, but Kasey didn't have the time to be jealous.

"I'm Kasey McKay. This is Nash Lamont."

"Come into my office. The other boys' mothers are already here."

Kasey and Nash followed her through the doors and into a small office.

"Kasey?" Mallory Smith looked up and smiled.

Jody Lansing came up out of her chair with her hands knotted into fists as she got right in Kasey's face. "Your child attacked mine, and I want him expelled for bein' a bully."

Jody had been in Kasey's class in school. She'd been

a cheerleader and probably would still be one when she was eighty. That was her claim to fame—that and the fact that she'd married the second-string quarterback the summer that she graduated.

"Sit down, Jody, and calm down. I'm not expelling any of these kids until we figure out what happened. I haven't questioned them until y'all got here," the principal said. "But I'm going to bring them in here right now, and I will be the one asking the questions. I want all y'all to be silent until we see what these boys have to say. Can you do that?" She gave all four of them a long look reserved for elementary students who weren't following rules.

"Of course," Mallory said.

Jody jumped up the minute the boys walked through the door. A full head taller than Rustin and Kyce and almost the same height as Zayne, her son broke into tears and ran to wrap his arms around his mother's waist.

"He hit me and then that other boy hit me and then that big boy dragged me..."

The principal held up a hand. "That is enough, Trey. We'll listen to your story in a minute, but first I want to hear what Rustin has to say."

Kasey's first instinct was to go to her son, but Nash slipped an arm around her waist.

"Let him tell it," he whispered.

"I hit him first," Rustin said, seriously. "And I'll do it again if he says that my mama is stupid."

The whole room went silent.

"Did not!" Trey screamed and started bawling again.

"Did, too," Kyce piped up. "I heard him. He said Rustin was stupid like his mama because Rustin wouldn't let him have the swing."

"I was right there, Miss Dillard," Zayne said. "He really

did say that about Rustin's mama, and Rustin got out of the swing and hit him right in the nose. Then he hit Rustin and got him down on the ground and started punchin' him, and Kyce jumped on his back to stop him. That's when I pulled Trey off Rustin and he started hittin' me with a big old stick."

"Did not! He hit me and y'all jumped on me, too. I didn't hit nobody."

"Why did you call his mama stupid?" Miss Dillard asked.

"Because my mama says that she's stupid to live with a man and think he'll marry her. My mama says that nobody will ever want a bitchy old redhead with three kids," Trey said.

"I did not say that." Jody gasped.

"Yes, you did. You told Daddy that last night," Trey argued.

It started as a weak giggle coming out of Kasey but grew into a full-fledged guffaw that echoed down the halls of the elementary school. Soon Mallory was laughing with her and Miss Dillard was having a hard time keeping her composure. When the laughter stopped, Kasey had a wicked case of hiccups.

She glared at Jody. "I suppose now you'll go out and say that I came in here drunk since I can't stop these hiccups."

"Boys, you can go back out into the hall," Miss Dillard said.

As Rustin was leaving, Nash reached out and patted him on the shoulder. "You should always take up for your mother even if it gets you into trouble. And..." His face went darker than Kasey had ever seen it. "For your information, ma'am, there's lots of men who'd feel privileged and honored beyond words to have this bitchy redhead and her three kids in their lives. But what Kasey does or doesn't do to help a neighbor isn't a bit of your business."

Miss Dillard took a moment and then said, "The policy book says that I have to take away all recess and playground privileges for three days. They will sit in the hallway where they are now during that time, which begins right now. I'm giving Trey one extra day for causing the problem, Jody. If you have an issue with that then you can take it up with the school board. Because Rustin threw the first punch and didn't bring the problem to me with it, I'll have a long talk with him about coming to me if there is a next time rather than taking it into his own hands."

"That's not fair," Jody argued. "Did you see my baby? He'll have a black eye, and I bet it's not gone before the Christmas program."

"I suggest that you either teach him not to repeat things he hears at home or else that you don't say things that you don't want repeated. Now I've got another meeting, so if you will all excuse me, I'm going to tell the boys what their punishment is and then go to it. My assistant will watch them through the present recess time and then escort them all back to class."

"What about lunch?" Jody asked. "I always pick Trey up and take him home."

"Bring him a sack lunch and he can eat it in the lunch-room. The other boys eat in the cafeteria, right?" Miss Dillard answered.

Kasey nodded.

"Then my assistant will bring them a tray and they can eat it in the hallway at the desks we'll have set up out there. We can also bring Trey's dinner to him, Jody," she said.

Jody jumped up so quickly that the folding chair fell against the wall with a thud. "Are you crazy? There are germs in that place. He has low immunity and he takes certain vitamins three times a day."

"Then bring them with his lunch, leave it in my office, and my assistant will give it to him, but you cannot stay with him during that time." Miss Dillard left no more room for argument. "Give me a minute to tell the boys before you leave and I'd appreciate it very much if you didn't stop and talk to them on the way out."

"You will not tell me that I can't talk to my son. This will traumatize him for the rest of his life," Jody hissed.

"If you cause another disturbance out there, I'll add a day to his punishment. My students, no matter how young they are, will learn to be accountable for their actions," Miss Dillard said on her way out.

"This is your fault." Jody turned on Kasey as soon as the principal was out of the office. "You should have never come back to Happy."

"Whoa!" Nash said. "You need to settle down, lady."

Kasey stepped forward until she was nose to nose with Jody. Dozens of smartass remarks came to mind as well as the urge to simply deck the woman or maybe to yank all that bleached blond hair from her head. Her fists were knotted and her mouth opened but words didn't come out, just another giggle.

"Did you come home because you've gone insane?" Jody growled.

"Nope." Kasey stepped back. "You have a nice day now, and don't forget to bring dear little Trey's lunch and pills to him. Let's go home, Nash. And Jody, you might watch what you say because my son might be smaller than yours, but he's a scrapper—guess it's because he works on a ranch with all those germs."

Jody flipped her blond hair over her shoulder and

stormed out of the office. She slowed down when she passed her son but didn't say a word. Trey was a different matter. He screamed for his mama not to leave him, threw himself on the floor, and kicked the assistant when she tried to make him get back in his chair and called her a stupid bitch.

"Bet that gets him a couple more days," Nash said as they passed the boys.

Kasey noticed that Nash gave Rustin a sly wink and a quick thumbs-up sign.

* * *

"I'm proud of you," Nash said as he buckled the seat belt.

"For not taking Rustin out of school?" She started the engine and backed out of the parking lot.

"No, I was ready to help Lila homeschool him if you'd decided to do that," he said. "If he was truly bein' bullied and couldn't take up for himself, he wouldn't belong in that place."

"Then why are you proud of me?"

"For not beatin' the snot out of that Jody woman," he said. "Want to stop at the café for a cup of coffee or a lemonade before we go home?"

"No, Jace will need to get back to Hope Springs. And between us, I wanted to knock some sense into that woman, Nash. I really did, but I know her and it wouldn't have done a bit of good. That kid of hers and her big mouth are going to deal her enough misery without me adding to it," Kasey told him.

"Is Rustin in trouble when he gets home?"

"What do you think?" she asked.

Nash thought about it until they turned into the lane toward the ranch house. "I believe he's gettin' his punishment at school. If you pile on more then he'll think he shouldn't take up for you or his sister, that people can call them whatever they want and he has to stand back and take it without retaliating."

"Good point," she said as she parked the van. "But on a different level, we should talk to him about keeping the line of authority. He should have gone to the principal and told her what Trey said."

"I agree with that. Trey was the one doin' the bullying. Today it was the swing. Next week it could be something bigger like Rustin's lunch money. It wouldn't be long until our boy would be withdrawn and wouldn't want to go to school. He was smart to nip it in the bud, but I bet Trey goes on to pick on another smaller kid and I wouldn't be surprised if Rustin plays Kyce's part in the next fight."

Kasey turned in her seat and cocked her head to one side. "How's that?"

"If Trey picks on another kid, Rustin might step in and help that child whip Trey's ass." Nash chuckled. "I would if I was him."

"So do we talk to him about staying out of other people's fights, too?" Kasey asked.

Nash opened the door. "Might be a good idea."

He walked on air all the way into the house. She'd said that *they* would talk to Rustin, not that he should butt out. A week ago he'd only seen pictures of her and met her twice and now he was considered enough of a friend to be included, and yet Nash found himself wanting more than just friendship.

You're aiming for the stars with nothing but a BB gun, that aggravating voice in his head said. *What Jody said about her could be better applied to you. This whole town thinks that Henry was an oddball and everyone knows you have PTSD. She would never want to tie herself down to a relationship with a man like you.*

"Well?" Jace asked when they reached the living room.

"Where are the kids?" Nash asked.

"Shhh..." He pointed toward a pallet on the floor in front of the television. "They had peanut butter sandwiches and milk and went to sleep watchin' that movie. I called Mama and talked her down, so you are welcome."

"For?" Nash asked.

Kasey slumped down on the sofa. "I hadn't even thought of that. Mama is on the school board and she probably wanted to storm up there and use her position to get Rustin out of trouble. She'll be livid when she finds out why he got into the fight."

"Oh, she already knows. Mallory is at the café."

Kasey threw the back of her hand over her forehead and sank down on the end of the sofa. "I feel kind of sorry for Jody."

"Well, Mama don't feel sorry for that hussy, and me and you both know that you don't piss Valerie Dawson off and expect happy days ahead," Jace said.

"Amen," Kasey said.

"I'm not following." Nash headed for the kitchen. "I'm going to make a sandwich. Can I make one for y'all?"

"Already ate with the kids." Jace slipped his coat back on. "I should be goin' now. Tell Rustin that I'm proud of him for takin' up for his mama and for takin' his punishment like a man. I understand that Jody's kid was a pistol."

"Gossip does travel fast." Nash chuckled.

"In Happy, it runs the speed of light some stiff competition." Jace threw the words over his shoulder as he left the house.

"If you're making sandwiches, I'll have ham, cheese,

lettuce, tomatoes, and mayo." Kasey looked through the doorway at Nash, who was getting things out of the refrigerator. "And thank you."

"Barbecue chips?"

"Yes, please, and something to drink."

"Comin' right up. Living room or kitchen?"

"Right here in the living room."

"I was thinkin' that if it had been Emma fightin' that kid, he would be in worse shape than he is." Nash fixed two plates, carried them to the living room, and went back for two glasses of lemonade. "Now explain to me what this thing is with your mama?"

"Mama might not agree with everything I do, but that's between me and her, not the whole county. Simply put, you don't mess with Mama's kids. And what Jody said about me, well, that means she's on the top of Mama's list, and believe me nobody wants to be there." Kasey sat up and tucked her hair back behind her ears.

Nash would give up his dinner if he could start kissing her at that soft spot right below her ear, whisper how beautiful she was, and then work his way around to that full mouth for more than one real kiss. The pressure behind his zipper grew pretty tight so he quickly pulled his flannel shirt out to cover the problem and kept his eyes on the animated movie playing on the television. *Frozen* was what Emma called it and he couldn't help but wish he had something that cold to take his mind off Kasey.

Kasey sighed when the movie ended.

"You like kids' movies?" he asked. "Or does this thing with Rustin still have your nerves knotted up?"

"Basically all I've seen for the past two years have been kids' movies and yes, this thing with Rustin does worry me," Kasey answered.

"Mama, can we go outside?" Emma asked as she popped up from her nap, eyes sparkling and full of renewed energy.

"Me, too." Silas yawned.

Nash picked up the plates and empty glasses. "Sounds like a wonderful idea to me. I'll take care of this and then we'll get coats and hats on the kids."

The two kids didn't mind the chilly breeze or the gray skies. Emma skipped ahead of them and Silas did his best to keep up. Pretending was a game for children, not grown men looking thirty in the face in a couple of years, but Nash did it anyway. From the house to the barn, Emma and Silas were his children and Kasey was his wife—and it felt really good.

The sheep came to the fence the moment they heard voices and Emma called back at Kasey and Nash, "Look, Mama. They know me."

"Me, too," Silas declared.

"You've been awfully quiet. Are you still thinkin' about Rustin?" Kasey asked.

Nash wasn't about to tell her what he'd really been imagining. She'd freak out and run back to Hope Springs without even looking over her shoulder. He looked out over the corral and counted the sheep half a dozen times. "I'm missing one and look over there in the corner. The fence has a hole in it."

"We better get in the truck and see if we can find her," Kasey said.

"I can do it, Kasey. You don't have to go."

"Oh, no! I'm not going anywhere near a phone for a few hours. Jody is liable to call to cuss at me. And drivin' for you will sure beat sittin' in the house and worryin' until Rustin gets home. Well, would you look at that?" Kasey looked up at the gray skies. "Our first snow of the season. It's too warm to stick or amount to much, but it sure is pretty."

"Kind of sets the mood for the season, don't it?" Nash said. "Okay, Miz Princess Emma, hold my hand and we'll see how many snowflakes we can catch on our tongues as we run to the van."

"I can take Silas if you're going to run with Emma—" Kasey started.

"Already got him on this arm. You dash into the house and get the tote bag and we're good to go, but we should take my truck. This rough ground will ruin your van." He tossed the keys to her. "We'll have to transfer Silas's car seat and Emma's booster over to it."

Kasey caught the keys and jogged toward the house. She grabbed up a tote bag with diapers inside and met Nash back at the van. With only a few deft movements she quickly undid the buckles. In no time she had a car seat in one hand and a booster in the other. With the expertise of a longtime mother, she got each one fastened into the backseat of his truck. If he hadn't already thought she was half magic and the other half miracle worker, he did then. It took a genius to work all those straps and buckles. Give him a tractor to tear down and put back together any day over getting car seats into a vehicle.

"How much land makes up the Texas Star?" she asked as she pulled the driver's seat forward and adjusted the rearview mirror.

"It's only a section. Sixty hundred and forty acres. Not a big place, but it made a livin' for my great-grandparents."

"Big enough unless you want to hire a bunch of help." She backed away from the house and started driving slowly along the fence line.

They'd only gone a few hundred yards when he pointed to a ewe and a newborn baby lamb hiding underneath an old scrub oak tree. The mama was licking the baby, but it wasn't moving. Kasey hit the brakes and Nash hopped out before the truck was fully stopped. He jerked off his coat and wrapped the lamb in it, made a motion with his hand, and started jogging across the pasture toward the barn. The ewe baaed at him a couple of times but then she followed him straight toward the barn.

* * *

Kasey turned the truck around and beat Nash to the barn. "You kids are going to have to stay in the truck for just a couple of minutes. Okay, Emma?"

"I will watch Silas," she said, seriously.

"Just for five minutes and then I'll come and get you out of the seats," she said.

"Silas." She shook his finger at him. "You be good."

"Me is good boy," he said stoically.

Kasey bailed out of the driver's seat and ran to open the barn door for Nash, who didn't stop until he had the newborn lamb and its mother inside out of the weather.

"Holy crap, he's not even breathing hard after carrying that lamb all that way," she whispered as she got the kids out of their seats and ushered them inside the barn and back to the stall where Nash was working with the new lamb.

The ewe followed them inside and went right into the stall with Nash. Using his coat to wipe the ice crystals from the lamb, he crooned to it like it was a human baby, begging it to live. Kasey wouldn't have been a bit surprised if he didn't start mouth-to-mouth on the animal. But finally he pumped his fist in the air, jumped up, and grabbed Kasey around the waist and spun her around in circles.

"It's alive. Look, Kasey, we saved it and the mama can take care of him now. He's a fine boy lamb. As big as he is, I'm shocked that the mama could deliver him. This is her first baby."

Kasey was dizzy when he put her down and her coat was smeared with lamb slobbers and a touch of blood, but she didn't care. They'd saved the baby, and with any luck it could even be a breeder. Every rancher or sheep herder knew that was a big thing. "*You* saved him. All I did was open a barn door."

Silas pointed at the calf that was now on its feet and was having his first meal. "Me baby."

"Yes, you're the baby," Nash agreed.

"No."

"You mean that's your baby?" Nash asked.

Silas grinned and nodded. "Me baby."

"No!" Emma stomped her foot. "Them sheeps outside love him. That's my baby."

"You can both share and love him," Nash said.

"Tay!" Silas grabbed Emma's hand. "Me share."

"All right." Emma sighed.

"Guess we'd better go fix a fence," Kasey said. "So back in the truck, kids."

"You any good at stretchin' fence? We need to mend the corral before any more get out?" Nash asked.

"Are you kiddin'? I had to do everything on the ranch to show my brothers I was as good as they were." She started toward the front of the barn.

"No! Me baby." Silas slipped under the bottom rung of the stall and wrapped both arms around the lamb. The ewe's tongue slurped across his face and he giggled.

A shiver of disgust shot down Kasey's spine. Nash chuckled, opened the gate, and picked up Silas. "We need to go fix a fence so that no more babies will get out. Rustin will be home soon. You can bring him out here to see the new member of the flock."

"Rusty see me baby." Silas wiped at the slobbers on his face.

"You really are good with kids," Kasey said on the way back to the truck.

"Got lots and lots of little cousins."

"It shows," Kasey said.

He'd make a fine father—no, that wasn't right. He would make an amazing daddy. There wasn't anything wrong with a father, but a daddy was so much more.

Chapter Thirteen

Rustin didn't run from the bus to the house that afternoon like he normally did. He dropped down on his knees to pet all three dogs and then kicked a few rocks on the way to the porch. Kasey watched from the living room window as he finally squared his shoulders and marched toward the house, determination written in his expression.

"Me, baby sheeps." Silas met him inside the foyer and grabbed his hand, pulling him toward the kitchen.

"No, you're a little boy," Rustin told him. "Talk big like Emma."

Silas dropped his hand and glared at him. "Baby sheeps!"

"There's a new baby lamb in the barn. We found it and then we fixed the fence," Emma translated.

"No fair. I had to go to school." Rustin pouted. "Mama, why didn't y'all save that job until Saturday when I got home?"

Kasey crooked her finger at him. "I think we need to talk, don't you? And it's not about fairness."

He shut his eyes and inhaled all the way to his boots. "Can I take my coat off first?"

"Might be a good idea," Kasey told him.

She and Nash were sitting on either end of the sofa a few minutes later when he came into the room and stood in front of them. She waited a full minute before she finally asked if he had anything he'd like to say.

"I'm not sorry that I hit Trey. I am sorry that Kyce and Zayne got in trouble. I didn't need them to help me, Mama. I coulda whooped him all by myself."

"Anything else?"

"I'll take my punishin' for what I did, but I ain't goin' to say sorry to Trey, not even if I have to stay in my room for a hundred years."

"Are you going to remember that there is a chain of authority and go to your teacher or Miss Dillard the next time Trey is mean to you?" Nash asked.

Rustin took another deep breath and shook his head. "I ain't a tattletale. And Trey won't be mean to me no more."

"How do you know that?"

"His mama brought him a nasty sandwich that didn't even have meat in it. Miss Dillard brought us a tray from the cafeteria. We had chicken nuggets and French fries and chocolate cake. We threw his dinner in the trash and us other boys shared with him. And did you know she makes him eat pills even when he's not sick. We threw them away, too."

Nash chuckled and Kasey poked him in the ribs. "So y'all are going to be friends with him, then?"

"We got to or that boy is goin' to starve. I bet Hero wouldn't even eat that sandwich with all that green stuff in it," Rustin answered.

"What about that fit he threw when we were leavin'?"

"Well." Rustin sighed. "We had us a talk with him and he won't act like that no more."

"Oh?" Kasey bit back a smile.

"Yep, Zayne told him that if he acted like that, all the boys in the school would call him a big sissy, so he shut up. And I told him he wasn't goin' to talk about my mama like that or he'd take a whoopin' every day."

Nash patted the sofa between him and Kasey. "Come on over here and sit down. Did Trey get mad when you told him that?"

Rustin shrugged. "Nope, he said sorry."

Kasey slipped her arm around Rustin and hugged him. "Well, it looks to me like you boys took care of things like grown-up men, but tattletale or not, you have to let Miss Dillard know if there's another problem so that other kids won't get bullied."

"Does that mean I can't 'fend myself?" Rustin asked.

"It means that you should never start a fight but that you never run from one," Nash said.

"Mama?" Rustin looked up at her.

"That's right. If you start one, you're the bully. If you run from one, then the bullies will never leave you alone. But it's best to go tell Miss Dillard when someone is mean to you," she answered.

"I'll try." Rustin sighed again. "Can we go see the new baby sheep, now?" Rustin asked.

"Yes, but Silas says it's his lamb, so don't argue with him," Kasey said.

"How come he gets…" Rustin stopped midsentence. "Yes, ma'am."

Kasey gave him another quick hug. Growing up wasn't a bit easier than moving forward. Both of them had lessons to learn and there was no guarantee that they'd be easy.

Chapter Fourteen

Nash arose early on Thursday morning. It had been one of those restless nights when he dreamed of Kasey and Rustin. They were in trouble and he tried to run toward them, but in the dream he couldn't move fast. He finally gave up trying to go back to sleep at four thirty since he'd already proven that the dream would start again from the beginning and he'd awake in a cold sweat with fear making his heart thump.

He was sitting at the kitchen table with a cup of coffee in his hands, waiting for daylight so he could go do chores and check on the new lamb in the barn, when Kasey arrived. One look at her blitzed eyes, and he knew that she wasn't well.

"Headache. Really bad one. Call Lila for me," she said.

"Why?"

"She needs to come get the kids." Kasey made her way

to the cabinet and downed a couple of pills with a glass of water.

"I can take care of the children and get Rustin on the school bus. Go back to bed and call me if I can do anything to help," he said.

"Thank you," she mumbled.

"Go rest in my bed. You might fall going back up the stairs," he said.

"Okay." She put a hand over her eyes.

He quickly got up and threw an arm around her shoulders. "Lights hurt, don't they? I'll get you into bed and you can use my extra pillow to put over your eyes."

"Thanks again," she mumbled.

He picked her up and carried her to his bed, laid her down gently, and pulled the covers up over her. She grabbed the extra pillow and covered her eyes as he pulled the window blinds shut. "Don't worry about a thing. Sleep it off."

"All I can do," she whispered.

He'd just sat down at the table when his phone pinged and a quick check let him know it was his grandmother—*you up yet?*

Instead of sending a text back, he called her back.

"Good mornin'," she said cheerfully. "I couldn't sleep last night so I'm on my second cup of hot chocolate, and I've finished off a plate of beignets. What are you doin' up so early?"

"Nightmares, but I'm glad I'm up because Kasey has a migraine and I need to help with the kids."

"Poor *chère*. I had those things when I was younger and they are horrible. You take good care of her."

"I will. Everything going okay with you?"

"You know, it's the strangest thing, but Uncle Henry

called me right out of the blue. Don't hear from him for twelve years and then he calls. Crazy, ain't it? I told him that you were on the ranch in Happy and he said that he liked that idea."

"Wow, that is crazy. Where is he? What's he doing?"

"He's off somewhere down in Florida and he owns an ice cream truck. Ain't that a hoot?"

"Did he say why he left?" Nash asked.

"Just said that he couldn't stand to live there no longer and there wasn't a reason to make him stay after our parents were both gone."

"Guess if he's happy that's all that matters," Nash said.

"He asked all about the Dawsons and the Dalleys and I told him what I knew about the folks in Happy. Asked him when he was comin' for a visit and he said he might surprise us someday. I'll believe it when I see it." Adelaide laughed. "Did you know that he and Hope had a bit of a thing back in the day?"

"For real? Kasey never mentioned it."

"Maybe she didn't know. It was a long time ago. He asked her to marry him and go with him when he went into the military, but she wouldn't leave that ranch of hers. I doubt Hope has talked about it very much to her Valerie. Now tell me about Kasey. Do you like her?"

"I like her entirely too much. You're the only one who knows the whole story. Please give me some advice." He fidgeted with the mug of coffee, turning it around on the table several times.

"Follow your heart. That's the best advice I can give anyone."

"I'd like to do that, but..." He hesitated.

"But you're afraid when you tell her about Adam that she'll break your heart, right?"

"Something like that. I can't live with myself if I don't tell her and yet, I know it's going to change things."

He could shut his eyes and see his grandmother sitting in her favorite rocking chair. The house would smell like chocolate and beignets. Suddenly, he craved a plate of those little sweet Cajun doughnuts.

"Life is one big change after another, but I'm glad you moved to Happy. There's a difference in you."

He checked the time—still a while before he should wake Rustin. "And that is?

"You're comin' out of that dark cave you've lived in for two years. I can hear it in your voice. The ranch and Kasey are both good for you."

"I feel so guilty, Addy. When Adam talked about his family, I wanted what he had."

"Don't punish yourself. You've been ready to settle down and have a family for a long time. It wasn't his family you wanted but your own. Fate has brought you two together so y'all can help each other to move on. Maybe with each other, maybe with someone else, but Adam needs to be put to rest and only you two can do that," she said. "Now tell me about Rustin's fight at school."

"Gossip travels faster than sound." He chuckled.

"Oh, yes, it does, and I want to hear the whole story."

He should have felt better when he hung up after laughing with his grandmother over Rustin's incident, but the weight on Nash's heart was heavier than ever.

* * *

Kasey awoke at noon to the sound of kids' giggles and Nash's deep voice telling them to keep it down a little, that their mama wasn't feeling too good. She eased one eye open to find that the headache was functional. That meant there was still pain, but her vision wasn't blurred and she could bear the light. She rolled over and got a whiff of the remnants of Nash's shaving lotion on his pillow. She pulled it to her body and hugged it tightly.

"God, I miss sleeping with a man and wakin' up to his scent on the pillows," she mumbled.

Things got quiet out there beyond the dark bedroom, and she slung her legs over the side of the bed. Padding out of the room in her flannel pajama pants and an oversize faded shirt, she found Nash washing dishes and no kids in sight.

"Shhh..." He put a finger over his lips. "They just now dropped off for naps. If they hear your voice, they'll wake up."

She frowned and pointed toward the dining room. "What is that?"

"Camping out," he explained.

A white sheet had been draped over the dining room table, creating a tent. Underneath were pillows, books, and two sleeping children.

"They are camping and I'm watching out for bears and skunks," he explained. "Hungry?"

"Starving. I'm always nauseated at the onset of one of the headaches and afterward so hungry I could eat one of those bears if you catch it." She caught a whiff of Italian food. "You cooked?"

"Of course," he said. "Sit down right here and let me work on your neck. Lots of headaches are stress related and come out of the neck."

She eased down into a chair and Nash went to work on her temples first, placing his hands on her cheeks so that his thumbs worked on the spots between her eyebrows and hairline. Making lazy circles and increasing the pressure every few seconds, he kept up the massage for a good five minutes before moving around to the back of the chair. He took her neck in his hands, heating her hormones to the boiling point. Rolling it around in his hands, she could feel the tension leaving her body by degrees. Then he began to massage her shoulders, digging his fingers into the knots and dissolving them. The pain in her head dissolved to half strength and her stomach grumbled.

"Now for food. Spaghetti, garlic bread, and salad. Tea or beer?"

"Tea, please," she said.

"Sit right there and I will bring it to the table."

The last time a man had waited on her was on her honeymoon when Adam brought in the tray from room service. At the time, she'd thought it was the most romantic thing ever.

It wasn't right to compare two very different men, especially when one of them was dead, but when she took a bite of Nash's spaghetti, she decided that a massage and his food were better than the room service on her honeymoon.

"God, this is amazing. Did you make the sauce from scratch?"

He nodded. "Just like my cousin Amanda taught me. She married an Italian, and she's an amazing cook. After eating her marinara, that stuff you buy in a jar at the grocery store is pretty bland."

"What else can you cook?"

"I do a mean shrimp boil and make a gourmet bologna sandwich. That's the extent of my cooking, though," he said.

"You cook and watch kids, run a ranch—what can you not do?" Kasey asked.

"I'm not real good at talkin' to most people. I keep things inside and I don't share things," he said.

"That's not what I see." She almost groaned when she bit into a slab of garlic bread.

"Oh yeah? And what do you see?"

"I see a man who's got some demons, but he's very able to communicate," she told him between bites.

And I see a cowboy who is sexy, charming, and kind, she thought. *One who makes me feel like a queen every time he looks at me.*

He sat down at the table with her. "I didn't used to be this way, Kasey. In the military I was a go-getter, made rank so fast it amazed my superiors. Then everything happened and it fell apart. I didn't want to be around people and I'm still not completely over it. I'm comfortable with you, but with others I answer questions and nod and smile. Your brother Jace wanted to talk last Sunday, but I clammed up, and I really have problems around Adam's parents."

"Why with me?"

He shrugged. "It's complicated. Someday I'll try to put it into words, but right now you need to eat and get rid of that headache. If you're okay, I'm going to the barn. Rustin will be home pretty soon."

"I'm much better now. Thank you so much for today."

He grabbed a coat and disappeared out the back door.

So someday he would tell her why she didn't make him uncomfortable. What would the story be when it became uncomplicated?

* * *

On Friday Kasey awoke with a clear head and had breakfast ready when Nash and Rustin arrived in the kitchen at the same time, both rubbing their eyes, and with that dark hair, even looking a little alike.

"I don't want to go to school today," Rustin said. "I need to stay home and help Nash take care of this place. It's goin' to really snow."

"Tomorrow you can stay home, I promise," Kasey said.

"For real?" Rustin's blue eyes sparkled.

Kasey made a sign over her chest. "Cross my heart."

Nash shot a sly wink her way. Tomorrow was Saturday and there would be no school.

"Okay, then, I need a stack of pancakes and some bacon, *chère*," Rustin said. "And maybe a tall glass of milk to get me through the day."

Nash chuckled and she narrowed her eyes at him.

He threw up his hands dramatically. "What'd I do?"

"He's startin' to sound like you with that southern accent." She pulled down a bowl to stir up some pancakes. "Blueberry, chocolate chip, or plain?"

"Blueberry," Rustin answered.

"Sounds right fine to me, *chère*," Nash teased.

Kasey hoped Nash would hang around and talk when Rustin left to get on the school bus, but he said he had to go take care of something he was doing out in the barn.

"See you at noon then," she said.

She'd learned a long time ago from Adam that a man had to choose his time to talk. Forcing the issue only caused them to clam up even more. She stood in the kitchen window and watched Nash all the way to the barn. She could barely see him through the big open doors but she could tell that he'd hoisted up a bag of feed on each shoulder.

"Like feather pillows," she said. "Nash Lamont is a heavy-duty machine on the outside, but on the inside he's got a big heart and a bigger bag of secrets that he really needs to unload."

"What's a heavy 'chine?" Emma rubbed the sleep from her eyes.

"Me want pandycakes," Silas said right behind her.

"Chocolate chip, blueberry, or plain?" She turned around.

"Chockit chip," Silas said.

"Me, too." Emma nodded.

Kasey thought about Nash the whole time she stirred chocolate chips into the batter. His hands had been magic on her neck and shoulders the day before. He was a hard worker and really good with kids, but the thing that she thought about most was the chemistry between them when he kissed her. She wanted more, but these past days, he seemed preoccupied and ready to get out of the house every time they were alone.

"Maybe he's realizing that he wants a family of his own someday and not a ready-made one," she whispered as she poured batter onto the grill. "Maybe I'm in the same boat with him. I'm ready to move on and he's here so it stands to reason that I'd...oh, stop it!"

"I didn't do nothin'," Emma said loudly. "Silas is a good boy, too."

"Me good boy," he said with a nod.

"You're both being very good." Kasey flipped half a dozen small pancakes on a platter. "Pandy cakes for two hungry little monkeys."

"Not a monkey." Silas frowned.

"Monkeys like chocolate." Emma grinned.

Silas tapped his chest. "Me monkey."

Kasey laughed and poured warm syrup on the pancakes. Her monkeys were growing up so fast that it was frightening. Nash was excellent with them, but when it came down to the wire, he probably wouldn't want a ready-made family. Maybe that's what he was talking about when he said things were complicated.

"Lord, why am I thinking of him in that way? I'm just his friend and we've only shared a few kisses. What's the matter with me?" she muttered under her breath.

"You kissed a monkey?" Emma frowned.

"Of course I did." Kasey bent to kiss Emma on the forehead. "I kiss three of them every day and love all of them."

"Who loves who?" Jace asked as he pushed through the back door.

"Mama loves me," Emma declared.

"You have breakfast? I've got more pancake batter," Kasey asked.

"Already ate. Just came by to see if Rustin is doin' okay?"

"Oh, yeah." She told him about how now Trey was one of the boys' new friends and they were teaching him not to be a sissy.

Jace poured himself a cup of coffee and leaned against the cabinet. "That sounds more like Brody than me or you. And how's things goin' over here?"

"As in?"

He wiggled his eyebrows.

"Come on, Jace. I'm only here to help, not fall in love."

"Me monkey," Silas said.

Jace ruffled Silas's hair. "Yes, you are."

"We were talking about me loving my three little monkeys," Kasey explained.

"I'm so jealous of you that I could just spit," Jace said seriously. "I wish I'd gotten married when I was twenty like Adam did."

Kasey pulled a package of hamburger from the freezer and laid it on the cabinet to thaw. It was a good day for a pot of beef and vegetable soup. She'd make enough to have leftovers for supper, since Rustin loved it so much. "You weren't in love at twenty."

"I was in love with Carlene or thought I was." He sighed.

"Carlene Varner?" Kasey asked. "The girl you took to the prom your senior year. She was really cute, but I didn't think y'all were serious."

He nodded. "We weren't. Not really but it might have gotten serious if I hadn't gone to college and her dad hadn't gotten transferred. Crazy thing is that sometimes a woman with long blond hair will catch my eye and I still think about her."

Kasey cleaned both kids' hands and faces and set them on the floor. "We'll get you dressed in a few minutes and maybe go out to the barn to see the sheep. Isn't she kin to Rosalie Varner? You ever ask her about Carlene?"

"Once, but she said that sometimes it's too late to do what you should have been doin' all along. Whatever that means is beyond me. Don't matter anyway. It's just seeing you happy makes me wish maybe things might have worked out with her so I'd have kids by now." Jace finished his coffee. "I'll help with that and go with you. And I don't mean to pry, Sis. I just like seeing you happy again. Before you came over here you did what you were supposed to do but now...well, I think you're finally moving on."

"I am and Nash is helping me, but that doesn't mean..."

He held up a hand. "I just don't want to see you slide backward after Christmas. I'd rather see you live here forever and be his roommate as that."

"Was it that bad?" she asked.

Jace threw an arm around her shoulders. "To see our sister lose her sass? Yes, it was."

"Thanks for caring. Now let's get the kids bundled up and take them outside for a little while. Did you hear that we're in for a big snowstorm this next week?"

"I did." He grinned. "We sure might have to have the live nativity scene inside the church again this year. And, Kasey, I meant what I said. I'm in your corner anytime you need me."

She hip bumped him. "Love you, brother. Maybe it's time that we both move on."

Chapter Fifteen

Valerie brushed a light dusting of snow from her shoulders when she came into the kitchen through the back door that Saturday morning. Emma was a blur as she ran across the floor to wrap her arms around her grandmother's legs. She wore mismatched socks and a bright red sweat suit with a pink and green tutu over the top.

"She dressed herself this morning," Kasey said.

Valerie stooped to hug her. "And a fine festive job she did of it. Where are your boots, baby girl?"

She ran off toward the living room and came back wearing cowboy boots that had once belonged to Rustin. "I'm ready."

"Rustin!" Valerie called out as she straightened up. "Where are Nash and Silas?"

"Me go, too?" Silas carried his coat into the kitchen and handed it to Valerie.

"You aren't in the program this year," Valerie told him.

He puckered up and his fists went to his eyes. "Peese," he begged.

Valerie picked him up and held him close. "You can go to the church with us and help me in the kitchen while Rustin and Emma practice. Okay?"

"Tay." He sniffled. "Nashie?"

"No, honey, Nash has to stay here. Why is it that the one name he says plainly is Nash?" Valerie muttered.

"Bowdy and Ace?" Silas grinned.

"Brody, Jace, and Nash have to stay home and work," Kasey said. "*N*'s are easier than blended letters and *J*'s, evidently."

Rustin breezed into the room, fully dressed, hair combed, boots on the right feet and his coat on. It might have been buttoned crooked but hey, he'd gotten the rest of it right so that was no big thing.

"Jace says that he sees a difference in you since you came over here. I don't," Valerie said.

"Guess it's all in the eyes of the beholder, kind of like beauty."

"And the beastie," Emma said. "I like that movie."

Valerie set Silas on the floor and buttoned up his jacket. "Everyone ready? It's cold out there. We might have a white Christmas again this year."

"Snowman!" Emma jumped up and down.

"Sandy Claws," Silas said seriously.

"I wish I'd never told them that Santa was coming here. If I hadn't, you wouldn't have an excuse," Valerie said.

"I don't need an excuse or even a reason. I gave my word that we'd celebrate Christmas here and I'm keeping it." Kasey kissed each child on the forehead.

"Maybe I do see a difference, and it's not for the better," Valerie fussed.

"Mama, do you remember how much you hated Lila?"

"This is different." Valerie glared at her.

"I'm not going to marry Nash, but we're helping each other get past some tough times. I miss talkin' to you. Let's agree to disagree. It's Christmas, for Jesus's sake."

"Amen!" Silas bowed his head.

Valerie giggled. "Out of the mouths of babes. Okay, I miss you, too. But I'll be glad when you're back at Hope Springs where you belong."

"It's only a few more weeks." Kasey draped an arm around her mother's shoulders and hugged her. "A wise woman told me two years ago after a very painful funeral that everything happens for a reason."

"That woman should have kept her mouth shut. I need the van keys so I don't have to move car seats."

Kasey moved away from her and pointed toward a nail beside the back door. "The ones with the horseshoe charm. See you at noon, right?"

"No, we're havin' hot dogs at the church for the kids after practice and then I thought I'd take them home with me for the afternoon. I'll have them back by bedtime. We're goin' to make more cookies for the ranch Christmas party. Chocolate chip and peanut butter freeze well."

"Have fun," Kasey said.

"What are you going to do today?" Valerie asked.

"Wrap presents and maybe go to town for groceries," she answered.

"If you get done, I can always use a few loaves of your famous banana bread for the ranch party. Folks love it with that cream cheese stuff you put in the middle of two slices."

Through the kitchen window, Kasey caught sight of Nash coming toward the house from the barn. His strides were long and his wide shoulders were hunched against the cold.

"Will do, Mama," she said absentmindedly.

* * *

"Now's my chance," Nash said to himself as he waved at the kids. "Valerie is even takin' Silas, which means this is the perfect time."

His hands had gone clammy inside the leather work gloves, and although there was nothing on his shoulders, the imaginary weight was far heavier than two bags of feed or even a newborn calf. There was no doubt in his mind that he'd seen the last of the kids and that Kasey would be packed up and gone by noon. He glanced at the doghouse, where three black pups were curled up inside, out of the blowing snow. Later he'd take it over to Hope Springs, maybe under the cover of night so that Kasey or the kids wouldn't have to look at him.

He hung his coat on a nail inside the back door, removed his cowboy hat, and laid it on the cabinet, then peeled off his gloves and put them inside the hat. He poured a cup of steaming hot coffee and carried it to the living room.

"How's the new lamb. Still in the barn?" Kasey removed a cake from the oven and set it on the cabinet to cool.

"Doin' fine. I'll turn him and his mama out into the corral with the rest of the flock as soon as this weather breaks. Kasey, we need to talk," he said bluntly and headed into the living room.

She followed him into the living room. "Yes, we do."

He sat down in the rocking chair and tried to calm the tightness in his chest "It's about this thing between us."

She hiked a hip on the arm of the sofa. "Okay."

"I need to tell you a story that's classified. I swore an oath not to..."

She slid over onto the end of the sofa and propped her feet on the coffee table. "Then don't."

"It's about Adam," he said.

She put her feet on the floor and leaned forward. "Go on."

"This is all in confidence. Please promise me that what is said in this room right now stays in this room."

"You knew Adam?" she said without a second's pause.

"There were six of us that formed a bond in basic training. We went on to different bases, but our superiors had seen how well we worked together as a team and sent us for more extensive training. We weren't the Rangers, but we were a little elite group that they sent in for black ops. Do you know what that is?"

"It was when Adam came in, grabbed his go-bag, and said that he'd see me when he got back. I knew better than to ask questions. Why didn't you tell me that you knew him?" Her voice caught and cracked.

"I knew him before y'all were married. He was part of the team that I've mentioned." Nash wanted to get it all out and over with, but he had to go slow so that she wouldn't be blasted with too much information at one time.

Tears welled up in her eyes. "Why didn't you tell me before now? Were you with him when he died?"

He wanted to rush to her side, hold her, and wipe away the pain, but he sat still. When he was finished, it would be easier for her and him both if she wasn't in his arms.

"I was with him a few minutes before, but I didn't see him go."

"Did he..." Tears streamed down her face.

He shook his head. "He did not suffer, Kasey. He never saw it coming. None of us did."

Kasey wiped the back of her hand across her wet cheeks.

"All he talked about from the day I met him was you, Kasey," Nash said, his throat getting choked up. "And then the kids when they came along. He was the only family man among us, and listening to him gave us hope that someday we would find what he had with you." Nash fought the desire to go to her, but he knew if he did he'd never be able to go on with the rest of the story.

"A high-ranking official in the government had been kidnapped somewhere in France," he continued. "We didn't know the particulars—just that he was being held in Afghanistan and if we didn't pay a big ransom they would kill him."

"The US doesn't negotiate with terrorists," she whispered.

"That's right. They send in a team to rescue the person. We'd done it dozens of times. Adam was a genius who always came up with a simple plan and it always worked."

She held her hands so tightly in her lap that her knuckles were white. "Except that time."

"No, it worked that time, too. I told you part of this before when I had that nightmare," he said and paused a few seconds before he went on. "We got the guy out of the place, but he needed medical help. Our doc got into the backseat of the vehicle with him to keep him alive. Adam volunteered to drive the lead vehicle so I could stay back and better protect the man we'd rescued. We could see a sandstorm comin' on the horizon and knew there was a chance we'd be separated."

"He was like that, always ready to help." She wiped her cheeks but the tears kept coming.

"I truly don't think he ever saw or heard that rocket. It came out of nowhere. I knew there was no way they were alive, Kasey, but it still killed me not to be able to stop and check. My duty was to get our man to safety. And he needed a hospital. It should have been me in that vehicle, not Adam. He had a family and he died because of me."

He couldn't look at her face but he could feel her staring at him. He wanted to meet her eyes, to tell her a thousand times that he was sorry and to hold her while she processed all of what he'd just said.

* * *

She stood up and he did the same. It all made sense now about why he thought she was his wife. He'd seen pictures of her and of Rustin. Adam carried a whole string of them.

"You son of a bitch. How could you not tell me?" She took two steps and beat at his chest with her fists.

He stood there, arms to his side, sadness filling his face and tears in his eyes. "I'm so sorry, Kasey. He was part of my team, but…"

"There's no excuse. Right now I don't even want to look at you or talk to you." She spun around and ran up the stairs, sobbing the whole way.

She threw herself on the bed and wept into her pillow. "Complicated, my ass!" She beat on it like she had on Nash's broad chest as her heart shattered all over again for the loss of her precious husband. Just a mere minute difference in timing and Adam would have been alive today and the rocket would have exploded the second vehicle. Just another hundred yards or maybe even less and he would have been in the delivery room with her when Silas was born.

It wasn't meant to be that way. The voice in her head was Adam's without a doubt. *And it's time for you to let me go, Kasey. My soul can't be at rest if you don't.*

"I can't. You were the love of my life. If it hadn't been for our children I would have died that day they told me you were comin' home in a casket," she whispered.

Nash is a good man.

"But he should be dead and you should be alive." Her hands clenched into fists and she drew back to hit the headboard but thought better of it and beat on the pillow some more. The few times that she'd heard Adam's voice before he'd agreed with her decisions, but today his tone had the same edge that he'd had when they argued.

You need someone in your life to make you happy again. I'll never be far away because we have three beautiful children that will always help keep me in your memory, but it's time for you to live in the present, think about the future and not the past. Give him a chance. I trust him and I forgive him. I made that decision. He didn't.

"Don't go," she groaned. "Please, Adam, don't."

She sat up and reached for something that wasn't there. She would never hear his voice again. When Adam said something, it was so final that it could be written in stone, and he'd gone for good this time.

"I can't let you go, Adam," she whispered.

A gentle knock on her door made her want to crawl out the window, shimmy down to the ground, and run so far away that she didn't have to think about what she'd heard.

"Kasey? Are you all right?" Nash's voice broke.

She crossed the room and slung open the door. "No, I'm not all right. Everything is wrong and I'm confused. Why would God do this? Why didn't you tell me? I'm so mad at you that I'm seeing red spots."

"You've got a right to be angry with me, but don't blame God. He didn't take Adam. Those terrorists did. I've wished a thousand times a day that the explosion would have taken me and left him with you. Can I come in?" His eyes were as swollen as hers.

"No. Go away. I don't want to look at you—not yet." She turned her back to him and drew the curtains back to stare out at the ugly gray sky spitting snowflakes.

His voice was soft and each word came filled with pain. "I will, but you need to hear the rest of the story. When I got that first concussion, I thought I was married to you that time, too. The psychiatrist said that it was transference issues. In my mind, I'd killed Adam and thought that I had to take care of you to atone for it. I kept begging for the doctors to go get you to come to the hospital. That's what broke me and my fiancée up."

She stared out the window, refusing to look at him. "Why did you move to Happy? You had to have known this was where Adam was from."

"We used to tease him. Living in Happy. Being so happy with you. It was like a fairy tale. I had no idea that you'd moved back here or that you'd live on the ranch next door. Addy talked about Hope Dalley, and I didn't even know that was your grandmother. I told her about Adam, but I always called him Happy, not Adam. I had no idea what your maiden name was, Kasey. I only knew you as the gorgeous redhead in the pictures that Adam showed anyone," he said. "And somewhere in the back of my mind during two different times, you belonged to me."

The snow came down harder and had begun to stick on the bare tree limbs. "And when your mind is clear?"

"The first time, I felt guilty for even thinkin' such things. Now that you're more than a pretty face in a wallet-size picture, I like you, Kasey. I like everything about you—you're a fine mother, a wonderful person, and I like your sass and determination. I'm sorry that I didn't tell you all this earlier, but I didn't want to burst this bubble we've been living in. I know you'll probably want to leave now, and I damn sure can't blame you. But I want you to know that this has been the best two weeks of my entire life. So thank you for giving me the best Christmas present I could ever get."

Adam's words as he walked out the door to go on that last mission echoed in her mind. *Don't worry, darlin'. I've got the best team in the whole world. I trust them with my life.*

Guilt, grief, shock, and every other emotion rolled up into one tight ball and lay in her heart like a stone. She shut her eyes. "I just needed some time to process this whole thing."

"I'll be in my room. It will hurt me too much to see you leave and I don't know that I'll ever get over the guilt of all this," he said.

She heard his door shut on the first floor. When she opened her eyes all she could see was big, beautiful snowflakes falling silently and the silhouette of the barn out there in the distance.

Suddenly the walls felt as if they were closing in around her, stealing all the oxygen out of the air and creating a vacuum where she couldn't breathe. With a soul so overwhelmed with emotions, she hurried down the steps, grabbed her coat, and slammed the kitchen door behind her. She was on her way to her van when she realized that her mother had taken the van. She didn't have a vehicle so she ducked her head and followed the path to the barn.

"Why didn't he tell me? Why did Adam have to die? Why do I have to be in love again?" She demanded over and over again even after she'd slipped inside and could hear the new little lamb in one of the stalls.

Inside the barn was just as frigid, but at least she was out of the driving wind and stinging snow. She remembered that the tack room had a small space heater to keep the pipes from freezing, so she went in there and plopped down on the futon. But it still didn't do much to warm her cold insides.

Her phone pinged in her hip pocket, but she didn't want to talk to anyone. Then again, what if one of her kids had fallen and broken an arm or needed stitches?

She checked the text message to find that it was from Lila:

We need to talk.

Oh, no! What if Granny had a heart attack?

She quickly hit the number and Lila picked up on the first ring. "Did you hear that Rosalie Varner died?" Lila said without even saying hello. "And she left instructions that there's to be no funeral or memorial or anything else. She's given her body to science. Granny is angry as hell because she says that…"

Death. Those men coming to her door. Driving for hours and hours in cold weather and crying the whole way from Lawton, Oklahoma, to Happy with two little kids in the backseat.

Funeral. Sitting there in front of a closed casket knowing that the baby she was carrying would never know Adam.

Burial. Watching them lower the casket into the ground, taking her heart with it.

Kasey sobbed.

"Oh my. I didn't know you were close to Rosalie. I'm so sorry I just blurted it out," Lila said.

"It's not Rosalie." Kasey blurted out the whole story of what had happened between sobs.

"Oh, Kasey, I'll be right over."

"No, you stay with Granny. I've got to get through this on my own, but thanks for listening. And don't tell anyone, please. I need some space and you know my brothers. They'll be ready to rush over here on their white horses to rescue me," Kasey said.

"You got it. Call me later?" Lila said.

"I promise," Kasey said in a hauntingly calm voice. There were no more tears and only a big empty hole where her heart had been. She tossed the phone on an end table and curled up in a ball on the futon.

* * *

Nash paced the floor in his bedroom until he heard the door slam and then he went upstairs, backed up to the wall outside her empty bedroom, and slid down to the floor. He caught a faint whiff of her perfume, probably left behind when she ran out of the house. One of Silas's stuffed animals was lying on the floor not three feet from him. He picked up the little brown horse and hugged it to his body. Emma's door was open and he could see her dolls all lined up across her bed. Lord, he was going to miss the kids, but nothing could compare to the big empty space that Kasey had left behind.

He'd expected her to be angry, and she had every right to be. But he never thought that the guilt and retelling of what had happened would rip his heart out of his chest again and leave nothing but a shell behind. To see that disappointment in her eyes killed him.

Standing up, he made his way to the foyer and shoved

his heavy arms into a jacket. He didn't know where he was going but Kasey damn sure didn't need to ever look at his face again. He'd drive until he was too tired to go another mile and then he'd stop and—he stared out the kitchen window without seeing anything. Her van was gone and even though her mother's truck was there, he hadn't seen Valerie hand over the keys to it. That meant she was out there walking somewhere with the north wind whistling through the trees and something akin to a blizzard right in the middle of it. He ran out the back door and yelled her name, but like a boomerang the fierce wind brought it back to his ears.

He hunched his shoulders against the snow, which stung his face, and started toward the springs. She said that she went there to think, but then he noticed that the barn doors were closed even though he'd left them ajar earlier that day. So he jogged back that way.

Easing open the door of the tack room, he saw her on the futon, curled up and staring straight ahead without focusing on anything. She was safe and she'd made it plain how she felt. He'd just leave now and stay in a hotel in Tulia until she got her things out of the house. That would make it easier for her.

"Nash," she whispered.

"I'm leaving. You..."

"Please come here."

Even if she shot him through the heart with a bullet, he couldn't refuse her. He walked over to the futon and she tilted her head up to look into his eyes.

"Closure hurts like hell. Help me heal," she said.

He held out a hand, and she put hers into it. It was the biggest blessing that God had ever granted to him. "Only if you'll help me do the same."

She nodded and he pulled her up. Her eyes never left his

and instead of pulling her hand free, she tucked her other one into his, also. "I'm sorry."

"You have nothing to apologize for, darlin'. I'm the one who does. I should have told you earlier, but I was so happy. I finally felt like I'd found myself again." He pulled a hand away and traced the tearstains on her cheeks. "I will never break your heart again, I promise."

* * *

Kasey rolled up on her toes and moistened her lips just in time for his to meet hers in a kiss so full of hunger and passion that it was like balm for the ache in her heart.

Keeping his lips on hers, he gently removed her coat, tossed it toward the work bench, and then in one swift motion, she was in his arms and they were on the futon in each other's arms. With fingers tangled in his thick dark hair, she snuggled in even closer to his chest and hoped that the kisses never ended.

His hands found their way under her sweatshirt and massaged her back from the neck to the waistband of her jeans. There was no way she could say a word—to tell him to stop or to take off the damned shirt—not without breaking up his delicious kiss.

"I want you," she said simply.

"Kasey, we don't have to..." he started.

"Yes, we do, Nash. Oh, yes we definitely do." She tugged at his hand when she stood up.

He followed her lead and in one swift movement the futon became a bed. Her hands went to his shirt, where she slowly undid each button, taking her time to run her fingers through that soft dark hair on his chest. They had all day and she was going to savor every single moment. While she pulled the shirt free, he eased hers up over her head and carefully unfastened her bra.

Slipping the straps down, his eyes never left hers. She undid his belt buckle and he unfastened the top of her jeans. "Nash, I think you should know it's been more than two years, and I was never with anyone but Adam."

"You deserve so much. Let me take care of you. " He gently laid her on the futon, finished stripping out of his clothes, and then carefully removed what was left of hers. Then he stretched out beside her and pulled a throw from the back to cover them.

"Our own cocoon," she whispered.

He mumbled something that she couldn't understand. Suddenly he was turned around in the bed and working his way from the arches of her feet all the way up her thigh with strings of kisses. When he reached her lips and gently bit the bottom one, she rolled him over and stretched out on top of him.

"You're so special, Kasey." He pushed her hair back with his hands and cupped her cheeks, staring into her eyes with such unbridled passion that it took her breath away. "I've waited my whole life for this moment, to meet my soul mate."

"You are definitely a romantic," she said.

"Never have been before, but..." He brought her face to his and covered it with kisses. "But, Kasey, I'm speechless at this moment. Let's just lie here like this all day."

"I've got something else in mind." She smiled and reached between their bodies to circle his erection with her hand. "Oh, my!"

"If you want this to last longer than a millisecond, you might want to..." he started.

With one deft movement she guided him into her and sat

up, bracing her hands on his chest and began a slow rhythm. "First time might be a sprint. Second can be a marathon."

"And the third?" He rolled her over and they rocked together.

"The third, darlin'," she panted, "is going to last…oh, my god…until…sweet Jesus, Nash…"

"Until?"

"All day long," she squealed.

He brought her to the edge of the climax and then slowed down the rhythm. She felt like she'd been dancing a fast swing dance that left her breathless and then the music changed to a slow country waltz. If this was what happened after a two-year gap, then sweet lord, the next round wouldn't be over until midnight.

"Like that?" His warm breath caressed her ear as he put everything into second gear. "Or this better?" He slowed down again.

"All of it," she answered.

"This." He gently traced her jawline with his forefinger, sending her hormones into a frenzy. "Or this?" His lips latched onto the part of her neck right under her ear.

"Both," she panted.

"Protection?" He groaned.

"I'm on the pill," she told him.

"Thank god." Suddenly he kicked it into fifth gear and she wrapped her legs around his body and hung on for a ride that took her to heights that she'd never climbed before. She left the world behind and took a swan dive from the top of the highest climax she'd ever experienced.

"That…"—she gasped—"was…"

"Intense." He rolled to the side and cradled her in his arms.

"I can't breathe."

"Are we alive?" he managed between dragging air into his lungs.

She propped up on an elbow and brushed a strand of his dark hair away from his eyes. "Nash, tell me this isn't wrong. That it's okay to heal, that we aren't..."

He wrapped both arms around her and quieted her with a sweet kiss. "I don't know, Kasey. All I know is that it feels damn right."

Chapter Sixteen

Kasey was in church, for God's sake. She should be paying attention to the sermon, not replaying every single scene of the day before in her mind. She looked down at the place where her wedding ring had been that morning. There was still an indention and probably would be for a long time, but she felt no guilt about removing it. The time had come, and although she would always love Adam, her heart wasn't closed off to another relationship.

It might not be with Nash, but she'd always be grateful to him for telling her the truth about Adam and for helping her to face the future. She glanced across the top of Rustin's head and caught Nash's gaze. For a long time they both talked without words, remembering the day before.

They'd spent the whole day in his bedroom. It should have been downright weird and awkward talking about Adam while they were both tangled up in a chenille bedspread after that first bout of sex, but it wasn't. When the conversation had gone to other things, like ranchin' and goals and dreams, she opened up to him more than she had to anyone in her whole life.

Her thoughts in church were interrupted when Rustin tapped her on the leg and whispered, "Can I go to the bathroom?"

"Go that way." She pointed toward the end of the pew toward the wall and not the center aisle. "And come back the same way."

Nash drew his legs to the side to let him pass and his knees brushed against Kasey's. Even though the denim of his jeans and her blue-and-green plaid skirt, the heat shot through her veins like she was hooked up to an IV of pure old Kentucky bourbon. He quickly moved his knees away, but it took a long time for her body to cool down.

Rustin returned with wet spots on the butt of his jeans where he'd dried his hands on them, and after what seemed like hours and hours, the thirty-minute sermon ended.

"Before Paul McKay gives the benediction, I'd like to remind everyone that the school Christmas program is tomorrow night at six thirty. It's going to be cold, but these kids all need our support, so bundle up and go to the auditorium for a couple of hours of entertainment. I understand there will be refreshments in the cafeteria following the program. And now Paul will pray for us."

The moment after the final amen, Rustin hopped up and eased past Kasey to get to the center aisle with his grandfather. Even seeing her son with Adam's parents didn't send Kasey on a guilt trip like she thought it might have. Nash closed the space where Rustin had been sitting and crooked his little finger around hers.

"Let's go to the café for lunch today," he suggested.

"Can't." She shook her head. "Mama told me right before services began that we are all going to Gracie and Paul's place today."

Nash dropped her finger and shook his head. "Not me."

"You need to talk to them, Nash. You don't have to tell any of the classified stuff, but it will help them to know how their son died and that you were there with him," she said. "Just that much, nothing about that first concussion or the little boy getting killed. But talk to them about Adam. Tell them his nickname. By the way, what did the team call you?"

"Bayou," he answered. "I don't know if I can do this, Kasey."

"It would sure bring peace to your heart and closure to theirs," she said.

"You sound like my therapist," he said.

"Smart woman, ain't she?" Kasey grinned up at him.

"I'll go, but if they start pullin' out pistols, I'm gettin' the hell out of Dodge."

She looped her arm into his. "And I'll be right ahead of you, so don't run over me."

* * *

The tension in the McKay house was so thick that a wild, longhorn bull couldn't have penetrated it when Kasey and Nash came inside behind the three kids. Gracie shot a look toward Valerie, and Nash wouldn't have been surprised to see her reach in a cabinet drawer and pull out a sawed-off shotgun.

"Mr. and Mrs. McKay, could I please have a little visit with you privately, and then I'll leave. It's plain you don't want me here, and I sure don't want to spoil your time with your grandkids and friends," Nash said.

He'd called his mother, Naomi, that morning and she'd agreed with Kasey. He had to be up-front and honest, as far as possible, with the McKays. Telling them would help bring closure to them but it would also help him.

"Grandkids and family," Gracie sniffed.

"Whatever you've got to say, I expect you can say it in front of these good folks, so pull up a chair and start talkin'," Paul said.

"It's a little personal, so I'd rather tell my story just to y'all," Nash said.

"We've shared pretty much everything since our son married into the Dawson family. So speak or just go on home, like you said you would," Gracie said coldly.

"Okay, then." Nash squared his shoulders, came to attention with his hands behind his back, and sucked air into his lungs. "I was Captain Nash Lamont in the United States Army. Your son and I were on a six-man team together that I commanded. Most of our missions were classified, so I can't talk about them. But what I did want to tell you is that we called your son Happy, since he came from this town and since we never knew him on a day when he wasn't happy. He inspired the whole team, and I was privileged to serve with him. I was there when he died and I wanted to tell you a little about it." The words came out in one big rush, like Nash was afraid if he didn't get it all out then he never would.

Gracie sat down in a wooden rocking chair with a thud. "Go on."

"He was instrumental in saving more than a dozen lives. On the day he was killed we had just completed a mission. A rocket was launched from a hill and it hit his vehicle.

Thanks to him, the hostage we rescued is alive and well today. But Happy paid with his life, along with two other soldiers in that vehicle with him. I'm very sorry and I feel guilty that he died when it should have been me in that lead vehicle." He stopped to catch a breath and then turned around and looked from Gracie to Paul and back again. They exchanged a long look and then Paul went to her and wrapped his arms around her, letting her weep on his shoulder.

"Stay. Don't go, Nash. Why didn't you tell us this before?"

"Classified," he whispered.

Gracie pushed back and dried her tears on a tea towel that she'd been holding. "Please stay. Tell us the stories that you can tell."

"Are you sure?" Nash asked.

"Very." Gracie's voice broke.

"Take off your coat. We're about ready to sit down to dinner," Paul said. "But until then, you can join me and these other two guys in the living room."

"No stories until I'm in the room. I want to hear everything that you can tell me about my son." Gracie managed a smile.

"See, I told you," Kasey whispered.

"And what would they think if they knew about yesterday?" he asked.

"That's classified, too." She winked at him as she turned to the kitchen to help put the dinner on the table.

Nash didn't need a degree in psychology to know what the McKays would think if they knew how many times he'd coveted what Adam had in his life, how many times Nash wished that he had a beautiful wife, two kids, and another on the way. He would become David from the Bible in their eyes. He saw what another man had, yearned for it, and caused a man to die so he could have the prize.

So don't tell them that part, the aggravating voice in his head said loudly. *This is all fate. You had no idea that you'd ever even be in a position to meet Kasey in person, so that burden is not yours to bear.*

"Well, now that was a crazy twist of things," Jace said. "Why didn't you tell us you knew Adam when we first got to know you? Had that fall knocked those memories from your head?"

If falling off a ladder would permanently erase that from my mind I would have taken a dive from one a long time ago, he thought.

"I didn't even meet you guys until after the ladder incident. Happy talked about his family and Kasey a lot, but I had to wait for the right time. I needed to come clean with Kasey first and I did that yesterday," he explained.

"How'd that work out for you?" Brody asked.

"Not so well at first. I figured she was going back across the fence to your place, Brody. I never expected her to stay after... well, you can imagine," Nash answered.

"That's Kasey," Brody said. "She'll take a bullet rather than go back on her word. She said she would stay and wild horses couldn't carry her off."

"She says it's a Dawson thing," Nash said.

"Mostly." Jace chuckled and looked at Brody. "But I remember once when you didn't keep your word and it came back to bite you square on the ass."

"Right back at you," Brody growled.

"No teeth marks on my butt." Jace grinned.

"Details?" Nash settled into a wooden rocking chair.

"He asked Lila to go on a real date with him. Dinner, movies, and the whole shebang on the night before she and her mother left Happy. It was a couple of days after their high school graduation. And he stood her up," Jace tattled.

"You mean, Lila and her mama moved away from here?" Nash asked.

"Yes, they did. They left Happy and we didn't hear from her again until last summer. That means Brother Brody here almost lost the love of his life. He had to do some fast scrambling to get her to marry him." Jace laughed at the dirty looks Brody shot toward him.

"Your day is comin', so don't gloat too loudly," Brody told him. "And I'm going to tell you *I told you so* a million times."

Gracie stepped to the door and motioned to Paul. "Dinner is about ready. You cowboys get washed up."

* * *

Hope sat across the table from Kasey and Nash with Emma between them and Silas in his high chair on the other side of Kasey. Hope thought they looked like any normal family, the way that Nash helped with Emma. He had always been good with the kids from day one, but there was a different, more familiar air, between him and Kasey.

Oh. My. Goodness. They've been to bed and I don't mean to nap. She covered her mouth so the words didn't sneak out for everyone to hear.

She could always tell when a relationship went from friendship to lovers. There was a difference in the way two people talked to each other and there was always, always the way they looked at each other, exchanging words with nothing more than a glance.

She touched the gold locket around her neck and

wondered if her mother had known when she and Henry had lost their virginity that night in the hayloft, the night he'd given her the necklace for her sixteenth birthday. She could see a lot of Henry in Nash. The dark hair and eyes and more than anything, that serious nature.

"Tell us when you first met Adam," Gracie said as soon as Paul finished saying the blessing for the food.

He took a long gulp of sweet tea and looked over at Kasey. Hope didn't know the silent words they exchanged, but she well remembered talking to Henry with her eyes. Kasey nodded slightly, evidently giving him courage, and Nash set the tea glass down.

"They lined us up when we first got to the base and the drill sergeant started his spiel. I was right beside Happy—sorry, I mean Adam—and from that day on we were lined up alphabetically. Lamont, McKay, Nelson, and so on. Those six weeks we had to learn to work as a team or we'd have never made it. Happy and I helped Nelson get through a tough night when his girlfriend broke up with him. In the end there were seven of us who made up a pretty good team and they sent us on for some special training along with our career field. One guy washed out when he broke his leg and got a discharge, leaving six."

Henry had been a man of few words except with Hope. Then he could talk for hours about everything, how much he didn't like ranching, how he wanted to get away from the panhandle of Texas to see the world beyond, and always how much he loved her. Hope wondered if Nash had gotten his wandering soul from his great-uncle or if he'd settle down on the Texas Star. If her past had taught her anything at all, it was that she would never interfere with Kasey's decisions if she and Nash did get into a permanent relationship.

"That was Adam, always ready to help someone," Hope said.

"Happy was the glue that held us all together. He kept things positive. That cowboy could make us laugh even in the worst situations. One time we were goin' into a bombed-out building, up a narrow flight of stairs, and he told me to go in sideways so I didn't get stuck."

No one laughed or even grinned.

"You'd have had to be there," Nash said. "They called me Bayou because of my accent, but my other nickname was Shrek. I've always been a giant. Happy could go into places that I couldn't ever wedge my big body into."

Still no smiles or laughter.

Hope had seen the animated cartoon about the ogre Shrek many times with the great-grandchildren. Nash didn't look a thing like that big old green hunk, but with his size, she could see why the soldiers would have tagged him with that name.

"Oh, come on." Hope giggled. "That is funny."

Valerie managed a smile. "I was trying to imagine Nash with those silly ears."

"Or green?" Gracie said.

Emma's chin pointed toward the ceiling and she cocked her head to one side. "Not Shrek. Not green."

"Right." Nash patted her on the shoulder.

"I think Nash is more like John Wayne," Rustin said.

"*The Cowboys* is one of his favorite movies," Kasey said.

"Mine, too," Brody and Nash said in unison with Jace coming in only a second behind them.

"Well, thank you." Nash smiled across the table at Rustin.

The smile sure enough reminded Hope of Henry Thomas's, especially back when he'd caught sight of her sitting under the willow tree at Hope Springs. That and his daddy's barn had been their two meeting places. His folks wouldn't have minded them dating right out in public, but her father wouldn't have it. No, sir. Henry Thomas was on the strange side and he wouldn't have his only daughter mixed up with that boy.

"So what happened when you got to the top of the stairs?" Paul asked.

"We got to the top room where the terrorists were holding the hostage, rescued him, and I carried him down the stairs, thrown over my shoulder like a sack of feed because we didn't want to take time to untie him. We made it back to the helicopter and were on the way before Happy told him that he had to buy us all a round of drinks as soon as we were back in the States," Nash glanced at Kasey. He hadn't told her all of the story before but she didn't look like she was angry and for that, he was grateful.

Hope would bet dollars to cow patties that Nash hadn't talked that much since he'd gotten out of the service.

"My son did not drink," Gracie declared.

"Oh, yes he did, but I could put him under the table," Kasey said.

"Kasey!" Valerie gasped.

"It's the truth, and I can outdrink both my brothers, too. Ask them."

Brody nodded.

Jace shrugged. "Can't deny it or she'll give you a demonstration."

Just like me. A smile tickled the corners of Hope's mouth. *The first time Henry and I sneaked some of his daddy's peach moonshine out to the barn, he was woozy after two drinks, but not me. I wonder if the liquor store sells that these days. I'd sure like another triple shot of it.*

"Mama, what are you thinkin' about?" Valerie asked. "You look like the cat that just ate the canary."

"I did, feathers and all, and it tasted pretty fine," she said.

"Did the man buy y'all a drink?" Paul asked.

"No, they swept him into the hospital for tests and debriefing, but he sent the team a bottle of Pappy Van Winkle the next day."

"That's a pretty good thank you," Brody said.

"It was mighty fine and Happy said, and I repeat word for word, 'My wife would damn sure like this stuff.' Then Hap—I mean Adam—went on to tell us about sharing his first beer with her out in Henry's barn long before they were even old enough to drive."

Jace held up a hand. "I was there."

"Jace Dawson!" Valerie fussed.

"Mama, there wasn't much to do but go to Henry's old barn and hang out with our friends, drink some beer, and kiss on our girlfriends," Jace said.

"I'm not so sure I want to hear any more." Gracie sighed. "You sure ain't like your Uncle Henry. He was a quiet man who hardly ever said a word to anyone."

Oh, Gracie, you just didn't know him like I did. Hope sent the platter of hot rolls around the table again.

* * *

Hearing stories about Adam sent Kasey into a spiral of confusing emotions. After the funeral everyone had walked on eggshells around her, as if they were afraid to even say his name. Today opened a floodgate of memories, and knowing how he'd died, hearing his voice telling her a final good-bye the day before—those things had brought closure.

She'd expected Rustin to ask for more stories about his daddy when they went back to the Texas Star that afternoon, but all he wanted to know was when he could have his first beer.

"When you're twenty-one and not a day before," Kasey told him.

"But you—"

"Doesn't mean you get to and if I catch you drinkin' before that, you don't even want to know what will happen," Kasey said.

Rustin shivered. "I have to stay in the yard for a week, right?"

"Nope, until your twenty-first birthday."

Rustin slapped his hands on his cheeks. "Noooo!"

Emma was yawning and Silas was fighting sleep when they reached the house.

"Nap time," Nash said.

"Not me. I'm too big for naps. I go to school." Rustin yawned.

"Me, too," Emma said.

"Do not! You ain't old enough for school," Rustin said.

"No arguments," Kasey said sternly. "Rustin, you may read a book on your bed while Emma and Silas take a rest. No one has to sleep, but you have to lie still and let your bodies get recharged for an hour."

"Kind of like our games when you plug 'em in?" Rustin asked.

"Exactly," Kasey told him.

"Well done. Bet they're all snoring in less than five minutes," Nash said out of the corner of his mouth.

"From your mouth to the sandman's ears," Kasey said.

The kids were all asleep when Kasey went back downstairs, where two cans of beer were waiting on the end table.

Nash patted the sofa beside him. "It might not be the prettiest sofa in the world, but it sure is comfortable. Join me." He motioned toward the mugs. "Thought you might like a cold drink. I know I do. My mouth is dry. I haven't talked that much in my life, not even to the therapist."

She reached for the same can at the same time he did, and they both jerked their hands back. He waited until she had one in her hands before he reached for the one that was left.

He popped the top and took a long gulp. "How did all that affect you, Kasey? What does it do to us?"

"Adam is always going to be a part of our past and our future, since he is my children's father, but..." She pulled the tab on her beer and downed a fourth of it. "I loved him, Nash, but, and this is going to sound just plumb crazy, but sometimes I could hear his voice in my head. Yesterday he told me to let him go and move on and that he wasn't going to talk to me anymore."

"Doesn't sound crazy to me," he said. "I've had mental conversations with him, too. And he basically told me to wake up and face reality and to get on with my life and stop wallowing around in a pity pool."

She nodded and they finished their beers in silence.

"Is all this talking going to make it weird between us?" he finally asked.

"What is 'us'? Friends? Friends with benefits?"

"I don't know, but I don't want to mess up whatever it is. My heart was shattered and you've helped me put it back together by being there for me."

"Me, neither. I guess we'll have to wait and see what happens. If someone would have told me where I'd be staying over the Christmas holiday this year, I would have figured they'd been hittin' the moonshine bottle too much."

"Ain't it the truth?" He took her hand in his and leaned his head back on the sofa. In only a few seconds, his breathing slowed and he was sound asleep.

She laid her head on the wide sofa arm and shut her eyes. Though it had to be the ugliest sofa left on the face of the earth, the thing sure was comfortable, but the house needed some feminine touches to make it a home.

It's his house and you won't be here in two years. This time it was Brody's voice in her head, but what was the use in arguing when he was right.

* * *

She awoke with a start, not knowing if it was morning, afternoon, or night. Whimpers said that one of the kids was awake, so she knuckled her eyes, worked the kinks from her neck, and stood up. Then she realized for the second time that the noise wasn't coming from upstairs but was right beside her.

"Dammit! I can't go on and leave them," he said hoarsely.

She eased back down beside him and shook his shoulder. "Wake up, Nash. It's another dream."

No doubt it had been brought on by all the talk that day. He pushed her hand away and opened his eyes wide, but there was no evidence that he was awake. "We can't leave them." He looked through her and then at her and wrinkled his brow. "How did you get here?"

"We're in Texas." She snapped her fingers.

He went from past to present in the blink of an eye. "I'm sorry."

"Don't be. You can't control the nightmares, but hopefully someday they'll be gone for good."

He slipped his arms around her and drew her close. "It's better if you're here when I wake up, Kasey."

She kissed him on the cheek and started to say something, but he put a finger over her lips. "Don't say anything. Just let me hold you."

She snuggled down into his embrace until they heard Rustin and Emma arguing as they hurried down the stairs. Even then she only moved a little bit and didn't shy away from his hand in hers.

Chapter Seventeen

Kasey fidgeted with her hands and wiggled in her seat. The auditorium was packed and the whole family was there. Rustin had two lines and would be singing three songs with his class. He wasn't a bit nervous when she'd left him backstage in the care of his teacher, but she had more butterflies flitting in her stomach than she'd had on her wedding day.

Valerie touched her on the arm. "Be still. It's just a school play, and everyone will think he's adorable no matter what happens."

"How did you ever live through three of us? Ballgames, rodeos, fairs, and school events?" Kasey asked.

"With lots of pride and many prayers. Once a mother, always a mother. It's even more binding than marriage."

"I believe it," Kasey said as the lights in the auditorium dimmed.

Nash tucked her hand into his when the curtains opened. At his touch, all the jitters left her body and she immediately settled back in her seat to watch the prekindergarten and the kindergarten classes take the stage for the first scene in the program. Wearing cute little red stocking hats, all the kids were gathered around the teacher who was sitting in an oversize rocking chair with a huge book in her hands.

"'Twas the Night Before Christmas," she said.

Evidently the children had been told to speak up because Rustin held the mic close to his mouth and his voice echoed off the walls when he said the next two lines of the poem. He waved at his family when he handed off the mic to the little girl sitting next to him.

"Rustin yelled!" Emma said loudly on the other side of Valerie.

"He was just speakin' up so we could hear him," Valerie said.

"We can relax now," Nash whispered into Kasey's ear.

"You were nervous?" Kasey asked.

"Oh, yeah, I was. He'd be so disappointed if he didn't do his part well."

Each child said a line or two and then the whole group stood up and got into a line. According to Rustin they were to stand up straight and tall, but several kids got so involved in "Jingle Bells" that they danced around the stage. Then when they went into "Frosty the Snowman," Rustin had stood still as long as he could and he began to sway to the music. By the time they started "Rudolph the Red-Nosed Reindeer" Rustin and the whole class had lined up and were doing a simple line dance.

"He didn't tell me about that," Nash said.

Kasey shook her head slowly. "Me, either."

Emma clapped her hands and sang right along with the group. Silas, who was sitting on Brody's lap that night, got about every fifth word but he was singing just as loudly as his sister.

The timing was horrible, with some kids singing a line behind and others half a line ahead, but they were so cute that the whole crowd gave them a standing ovation when they held hands and bowed at the end.

When the program ended and all the kids were turned loose, Rustin made a beeline for Nash. "Did you hear me? I said my part real loud."

Nash laid a hand on Rustin's shoulder. "You made us all very proud the way you spoke right up and the way you sang your songs."

"Mama, did you hear me? How'd you like our dancin'?" Rustin asked.

Kasey hugged him. "Oh, yes, loud and clear. You didn't tell us about the dance."

"Me and the kids been practicin' at recess. We didn't tell nobody, not even the teacher." He grinned.

"Well, I bet she was surprised." Nash chuckled.

A little jealous sting pierced her heart because he'd gone to Nash first. Kasey tried to shake it off, but it didn't work. Rustin was her son, and granted he and Nash had gone over those two lines a hundred times, but she'd practiced all his songs with him.

Emma tapped him on the shoulder. "You yelled. Where's the cookies?"

Silas ran over to his brother and gave him a bear hug. "Cookies?"

Rustin puffed out his chest. "In my room. I will take you. I know the way."

"Hey, Rustin." Brody scooped up Silas. "Where'd you learn those dance moves?"

"Uncle Jace," Rustin answered with a nonchalant shrug.

Kasey cut her eyes over toward her brother and was met with a big grin. "You're welcome. He wanted to surprise everyone, so he and I worked up a little line dance."

"Well, next time you come to me, son," Brody said. "I'm a better dancer than Uncle Jace."

"Will you take me to the cowboy bar to learn?" Rustin asked.

"He will not!" Lila put a ton of emphasis on the last word.

"The boss has spoken." Brody chuckled.

"Aunt Lila is boss?" Emma slipped her hand into Lila's.

"Sometimes." Lila smiled. "And sometimes Uncle Brody is boss."

"But most of the time, Granny Hope is the boss," Jace said.

"Too many bosses. Mama can be my boss." Emma skipped along beside Lila.

Kasey patted her on the shoulder. "Thank you, baby girl."

Family, it's what it's all about. Kasey forgot about the pang of jealousy and mentally hugged every one of the folks individually. She saved Nash until last in the scenario, and warmth filled her cheeks with a gentle blush. For the first time she had included him in the family and it didn't feel a bit weird.

A Christmas tree was in one corner of Rustin's school room. Decorated totally in paper ornaments and a big loopy chain from strips of red and green construction paper, it had a big glittery star on the top. Santa faces that had been colored by the students lined up, one after the other, on the wall around the tree. A long table had been set up in another corner with trays of cookies and a big bowl of punch.

"Looks and smells just like a school," Nash said.

"Yep." Lila nodded. "Doesn't matter if it's a big one like I taught in over in Tennessee or a little one like this, they all have the same feel."

Jace slipped up behind Kasey and rested his chin on her head. "I'm so jealous of you that I could just spit. I want a kid who dances on the stage and who is so proud of his classroom that the buttons on his shirt are about to bust plumb off. I want a daughter like Emma and a baby like Silas and maybe three or four more past that."

"Well, you're going to have to get serious about things then. Date women who will make a good wife and mama," she said.

"We miss the kids over on Hope Springs, Sis," Brody said. "It's kind of lonely."

"Hey, you can have one, two, or all three anytime things get too quiet. Or"—she slid him a sly look—"you and Lila could get busy and have one of your own. This time next year you could be totin' around a new little Dawson."

Silas pointed at the cookie table. "Me needs!"

"Me, too." Jace took him from Brody and headed over to the refreshments.

"Not yet," Rustin said. "You got to see my desk before you get cookies. That's the rule. And then I get to take my stuff off the tree and put it in the bag to take home." He tugged at Kasey's hand. "Come and see. I cleaned it all up. Right here."

There on the top of his desk was a color sheet with holly around the edges and Santa in his sleigh across the top. Inside on wide lines he'd written his Christmas list in his own tight little handwriting. The first of the three items on the list brought tears to Kasey's eyes. She swallowed hard more than twice as she looked at those two simple words— *a daddy.*

"Oh!" Lila gasped as she looked over her shoulder.

"Guess you've got your work cut out for you if you're goin' to get that done by Christmas," Jace teased.

"How do you get it under the tree?" Hope asked.

"Stop it," Kasey whispered.

"Hey, Rustin, how about you show me which ornaments we need to take off the tree," Nash said. "Maybe if we're real careful we can put them on our tree when we get home. Silas and Emma are getting real hungry for some of those cookies and tell the truth, those chocolate chip ones that your granny brought sure look good to me."

Kasey could have kissed him right there in front of the other parents, her family, and even God for doing that so that she could catch her breath and figure out how to even talk to her son about his list.

"Not long ago Rustin would have been holding my hand, not his," Brody said.

"And he will be again right after Christmas," Valerie said, seriously. "But that's not sayin' that I wouldn't love to have a new baby in the Dawson family." She winked at Lila.

Silas reached his chubby little arms out toward Kasey. She took him from Jace and carried him across the room so he could pick out a cookie. When she had him settled in a chair around a little table, Emma and Lila joined them.

Emma held up her cookie. "Look, Mama, I got one like Santa."

"Me gots Frosty." Silas held up a snowman-shaped sugar cookie.

"Confession time," Lila said as she got Emma pulled up to the table. "I miss school. Not enough to give up the ranchin' and go back to it, but I do."

Kasey stepped back into the corner. "Change scares the devil out of me."

Lila followed her. "You're preachin' to the choir. It took every ounce of trust in my own judgment to make the decision to help Brody on the ranch instead of teach this year."

"Regrets?"

"Not really, just a longing for the old familiar routine. Ranchin' is so different from a structured schedule," Lila answered. "Now tell me about what's going on over on Texas Star. We haven't talked in days."

"Make some time to come by tomorrow or the next day and we'll have a visit." Kasey nodded at Hope and Valerie coming their way with cookies and punch in hands.

"We got extra so y'all don't have to get in line." Hope passed off a plastic cup with a small paper plate on the top. "The iced sugar cookies are all gone."

"I'd rather have this one anyway. Thanks, Granny," Kasey said.

Hope's gray hair had been styled that morning at the local beauty shop and her nails were freshly done. She wore creased jeans and a pair of her fancy cowboy boots. Her ugly Christmas sweater was bright red with a fuzzy snowman on the front. A ranch wife, according to her, had to keep up appearances. Valerie believed in the same thing and that night she was all decked out in a bright green sweater with Rudolph on the front, jeans, and boots.

Kasey's nails were chipped and her red hair was pulled up in a ponytail but several curls had escaped and were tickling her face. She hadn't had time to put on a smidgen of makeup, and her jeans came right out of the dryer. Her sweatshirt had a Christmas tree on it, but several of the sequins were hanging by a thread. Keeping up appearances was tougher when the ranching woman had three kids to get ready every time she walked out the door.

Nash stepped out of a crowd of people with Jace, Brody,

and Rustin. He came right to her side and flashed his brightest smile. "All these people are beginning to box me in," he whispered. "The only way I can manage is to keep my eyes on you. You look like an angel tonight."

"I look like shit," she muttered.

"Honey, you outshine every other woman in this room. We've got Rustin's stuff all in his envelope. He did a good job coloring and cutting his ornaments. We're putting them on the tree when we get home."

"That'll make him feel like a king," she said.

"He makes me feel like one for sure."

Valerie pushed her way between them. "You mind if I take Emma home with me for the night? Rustin's had so much attention, it will be good for her to get to help me tomorrow. We're goin' to make fudge for the ranch party. She's got pajamas and a toothbrush at my house."

"Me, too, Nanma?" Silas asked.

"How about you go home with me?" Gracie quickly left the group of women she'd been talking to and quickly came over to them. "We're goin' to Amarillo tomorrow for a load of feed, so it might be the middle of the afternoon when we get him to your ranch."

Those two words—your ranch—twirled through Kasey's mind in dizzying circles. "Sounds fine to me. He hates it when he's all alone in the day, so that'll work fine."

"Oh, honey, me and his poppa will keep him entertained real good. We've got a litter of kittens in the barn that's just about ready to wean, so he and Paul will have a good time with them. Did you ever notice how good he is with animals?" Gracie asked.

"Yes," Nash answered quickly. "It's like he's got this sixth sense that draws them to him. You should see the sheep with him. They treat him like he's a new baby lamb."

"He's a special baby." Paul joined the group. "Hey, buddy, you want to go home with me and Nana?"

Silas crawled out of the chair and held his arms up to Nash. "Me Nashie come, too?"

"No, baby boy." Nash took him into his arms. "This old cowboy has to stay home and feed the sheep."

"Tay." He nodded and reached out toward Paul. "Kitties?"

Nash shifted him over toward his grandfather.

Paul hugged him closely. "Yes, there are kitties in your Poppa's barn and we'll go see them in the morning."

"Sheeps?" Silas's big blue eyes were serious.

"No, but they'll be waiting when you get home," Nash answered.

"Tay." He sighed. "Kiss Mommy."

Paul held him over toward Kasey and Silas gave her a peck on the cheek. "Nite, nite, Mommy."

"Nite, baby. I'll see you tomorrow."

Silas nodded. "Kiss Nashie."

Paul shifted his position to hold the baby out toward Nash. He kissed Nash on the cheek and said, "Nite, nite, Nashie."

"Good night, cowboy," Nash said, hoarsely.

"Need anything?" Kasey asked Gracie.

"No, darlin'. We keep diapers and pajamas for all of the kids just in case you ever need us." Gracie smiled.

Kasey knew that, but she always asked anyway. She didn't know if the grandparents had seen Rustin's list or not, but she appreciated them that night more than ever before. It would give her an opportunity to talk to Rustin about that number one thing on his Santa list.

"Mama." Rustin tugged on her hand. "How come Emma and Silas get to do a sleepover and not me?"

"It's a school night. They didn't get to be in a play."

"Well, rats!" he pouted. "School is tough on a cowboy, ain't it, Nash?"

"Sometimes," Nash agreed. "Are you ready to go home and put your ornaments on our tree?"

"Yep, I am," Rustin said. "Will you read to me tonight?"

"I reckon I could do that," Nash said.

"Miss that, too," Brody said.

"Love you, brother," Kasey said.

"Right back atcha." He smiled.

* * *

Nash propped his back against the old four-poster headboard in Rustin's temporary room. He was so tall that his feet almost touched the footboard. Kasey leaned against the doorjamb and listened to him read a Christmas book to Rustin that evening. When he read the final page of the story, Rustin was yawning and rubbing his eyes.

"The end." Nash closed the book.

Rustin wrapped both his arms round Nash and hugged him tightly. "G'night, Nash."

"Nite, buddy."

"I like bein' your buddy," Rustin said. "I liked seein' you at my play."

"I liked bein' there." Nash slung his legs over the side of the bed and picked up his boots. "See you at breakfast."

He brushed against Kasey's shoulder as he started out of the room. "Want me to stay for this?"

She shook her head. "I think I'd best tackle it alone, but thanks."

Rustin covered a big yawn with his hand. "Mama, I like bein' on the stage."

"I can tell." She sat down on the edge of his bed. "I want

to talk to you about what you put on your Santa list. Did you mean that you wanted your daddy to come back? That can't happen, son. He's been gone two years and he's in heaven with my daddy and my grandpa."

"No, Mama." Rustin shook his head. "I 'member him a little bit, but not much. I want a daddy of my own like the other kids have. Some of them even have two daddies."

"You mean like a real daddy and a stepdaddy?"

Rustin nodded. "It ain't fair that they get two and I ain't got none."

"You've got Uncle Brody and Uncle Jace and your grandpa."

"They ain't a daddy. If Santa can fly in the sky all over the world, then he can find me a daddy. I want one just like Nash," Rustin said seriously. "I like it here and so does Hero. He told me that he don't want to go back to Uncle Brody's and Granny's ranch."

"I see," Kasey said. "Well, what if Santa can't find you a daddy?"

"Ahhh, Mama." His grin reminded her of Brody. "Santa is magic and he always brings what I ask for. Just wait and see."

Kasey's heart felt like someone had just filled the inside with stones. "Okay, but that's a pretty big order."

"Nite, Mama. I love you." Rustin gave her a hug and then he slipped beneath the covers. "Tuck me in."

She slid off the bed and pulled the covers up to his chin. "I love you, too, son."

"I know it." He laughed. "Mamas love their cowboys and I'm a cowboy."

"You got it." Kasey giggled. "Now go to sleep. You'll be too tired to eat pancakes for breakfast if you don't shut those eyes."

Kasey turned out the light and left the door open a crack, but she'd only gone two steps when she heard him talking. She stopped and took a step back toward the door.

"Okay, God, we need to talk," he said. "I told Santa that I want a daddy for Christmas. One like Nash. But Granny Hope says that you're bigger than Santa, so you need to tell him that's what I want. In Jesus's name, cause that's what cowboys like Nash and Uncle Brody and Uncle Jace say at the end of their prayin' and I'm practicin'. Good night, God."

She made it to the top of the stairs before she sat down and put her head in her hands. In seconds Nash was right beside her, his arm around her shoulders.

"Are you okay?"

"No. He's goin' to be disappointed, Nash, and it's not fair."

"Life is not fair. I saw his list and it breaks my heart for him. Let's go have a cup of hot chocolate and sit on the sofa. We don't even have to talk, Kasey."

Just like Nash. That's what Rustin said more than once. As she put her hand into Nash's she could understand what Rustin saw in him. Nash Lamont was a good man who understood the yearning in a little boy's heart, just like he understood the pain in a woman's.

He led her to the sofa and drew her close to his chest. "I couldn't have gotten through the evening without you."

"I feel the same way. I thought my heart would stop when those curtains opened. He's a natural though. Told me that he likes bein' on the stage."

"Just like Adam. That guy could deliver an inspirational speech that would fire up the whole team. I want him to know his father, so I'm going to make him a picture album with pictures that I have of the team. It'll be something he can go back to when he's feelin' like all the other kids have more than he does. He'll have a real hero for a daddy."

Kasey tiptoed and cupped his face in her hands. "You're the sweetest man in the whole world, Nash Lamont. Thank you."

"You're very welcome. Now, we've had enough emotion tonight. You sit right there and I'll make a couple of cups of chocolate. Want to watch a movie before we turn in?"

"Something funny," she said.

"I've got just the ticket." He grinned. "The second *Home Alone*. That kid reminds me of Rustin, not in looks but in smarts."

"Saw the first one a long time ago, but not the second one so I'm in." She plopped down on the sofa. "Hot chocolate and a movie. Sounds like a date."

"It can be if I can have a good night kiss when I walk you to your door." He threw the words over his shoulder on his way to the kitchen.

"I don't usually give out kisses on the first date."

"Not even if I'm irresistible?"

"We'll see," she said.

She glanced around the room and for the first time considered what she'd do different if she did stay there indefinitely. She would get rid of the sofa, not only because it was ugly but also the springs had broken down, and when she sat down it felt as if she was falling to the floor. Poor old Nash, as big a man as he was, probably felt like he was sinking into quicksand.

Her phone rang and she quickly pulled it from her hip pocket. "What's up, Jace? Is Emma homesick?"

"No, and it was nice to have a chance to read her a bedtime story again. Didn't realize how much I'd missed it. I wanted to know what you told Rustin about that list. You know you can't just marry the first man who comes along so the kids will have a father, don't you?"

"Come on, brother, give me a little bit of credit," she said.

"Just sayin', that's all," Jace replied. "And that reminds me, are you bringing Nash to Granny's big Christmas shindig this weekend?"

"I imagine I will. Any reason why I shouldn't? Has Brody said something?"

"He's comin' around. Give him some more time," Jace answered. "Got to go. The princess needs a glass of water."

"You're spoiling her."

Jace chuckled. "Yep, and enjoyin' every minute. I'm goin' to get me one of those daughter things someday."

"I'll believe it when I see it." Kasey giggled.

Her phone went dark and she laid it on the end table. She glanced around the room. No family pictures or personal touches anywhere. A sofa, end tables with lamps, coffee table, a rocking chair, and a recliner. Kasey had never been a hoarder but a few little changes in the house could sure add some warmth and coziness to it. Even a picture of the kids here and there would make it into a home rather than a house.

Nash put a steaming mug of chocolate in her hands. "What are you thinkin' about? Your brow was all wrinkled up."

"That this place has a lot of potential. The house is old but the foundation seems solid and there's lots of good in it," she answered truthfully.

"But?"

"It needs some pictures or bright colored throw pillows or maybe some family pictures set around here and there," she said.

"When I was in the attic getting the Christmas stuff I

found boxes and boxes of stuff that Uncle Henry must've packed up. They're all labeled. I saw dozens with that word—knickknacks—written on the outside and one evidently has pink lace curtains in it. Made me think of Emma."

"She'd probably love them."

"If you want to put them in Emma's room, I'll bring them down tomorrow. And now, I'm going to put a movie in the player because we need something to laugh about."

The antics of a small boy alone in a big city with a couple of two-bit robbers made Kasey laugh so hard that she figured if the animals and the angels could really see, they'd be giggling, too. When the movie came to an end and the little guy was taking a small ceramic bird to a homeless woman, Kasey got a fresh belief in Christmas miracles.

"I believe," she said simply.

Nash stood up and took her hand in his. "So do I after these past days. Now darlin', it's past midnight. Time for me to be a gentleman and walk you to the door."

When they were in front of her door, he put a hand on either side of her, palms flat against the wall, creating a cage. "Just five more minutes before you go inside your room. I want you to hear something." He pulled out his phone and flipped through a few icons before he pressed a button. Then he laid the phone on a ladder-back chair sitting between the two bedroom doors and held out his hand. "May I have this dance, please?"

She put her hand in his as Tracy Byrd began to sing "The Keeper of the Stars." The lyrics said that it wasn't an accident that he'd found her, that someone had had a hand in it long before they ever knew. Nash was smooth on his feet. His heart did double-time and he sang along when Tracy sang about soft moonlight on her face and how that it took his breath away just to look into her eyes.

She was in a beautiful bubble for five whole minutes and when the song ended, he brushed a soft kiss across her lips. "I believe every word of that song. Good night, Kasey." He picked up his phone.

"Right now, so do I," she whispered.

She watched him disappear into the shadows down the steps. Then she went into her room and fell backward onto the bed. Her phone pinged and she checked it, thinking that it might be her mother or Gracie.

It was a text from Nash with a link but no words. When she clicked on it, "One More Day" by Diamond Rio started to play. She listened to it, watching the lyrics roll up the whole while. She played it again as she got dressed for bed and freed her hair from the ponytail. Then she hit it again and laid it on the pillow beside her head.

"You, Nash Lamont, might be an introvert, but darlin', you're a hopeless romantic and I love that about you," she said as she shut her eyes and hummed the melody from the song.

Chapter Eighteen

It had been a strange week on Texas Star, mundanely routine since the school program but with an underlying tension that Kasey couldn't wrap her mind around. Just when she thought Nash might be coming out of his shell, he did a 180-degree turn. No sweet songs on the phone. No little moments that made her heart flutter. And he stayed out of the house so much that she only saw him at meals and a couple of hours in the evening—but then he was involved with the children.

She'd been raised on a ranch, so she knew that was the way things were most of the time. Her dad hadn't spent much time inside, and when he did, he was usually in his little office taking care of ranch business.

On Wednesday Lila offered to keep the two young kids while Kasey drove Nash to his therapist appointment. Kasey could have written all the words that Nash said on the way to the doctor's office on a postage stamp. He put on a Blake

Shelton CD, leaned the seat back, and shut his eyes. She might have thought he was asleep, but he kept time to the music with his thumb on his thigh.

When they arrived, he didn't ask her to go in with him so she sat in the waiting room for half an hour and leafed through year-old magazines. She'd just finished with one when Dr. Paulson and Nash came out of the office. Nash sat down and the lady motioned for her to come inside.

"I wanted just a moment with you," she said. "He's making such good progress and you deserve most of the credit."

"Today I feel like he's taken six steps backward instead of one tiny baby step forward," Kasey said.

"Oh, no, honey, he's dealing with things and talking non-stop to me. That's amazing. I want to see him in one month, but if you need me sooner, just call and I'll make time for him," she said.

"What'd she want with you?" Nash asked when they were on their way out of the building.

"To tell me that you're doing very well. You might get that clearance if you ever want to go back into the service," she answered.

"She said that?" he asked.

"No, but it seems like things are movin' that way," Kasey said.

The only difference in the drive home was that he listened to an Alan Jackson CD. He didn't even go through the house but made an excuse that he needed to check on the sheep and went out there.

To top off the crazy week, Emma and Silas were total brats on Friday when Kasey was trying to get them ready to go with her and Nash to his doctor's appointment. Any other time, he'd have helped her with the kids. But that day he'd been in his bedroom for the last hour. How long did it take a man to get ready, for God's sake? He'd taken a shower and shaved before he disappeared behind the closed door. All he had to do was put on clean clothes and boots.

Emma crossed her arms over her chest and shook her head so hard that her braids slapped her in the face. "No shots!"

"I told you, Nash is going to see the doctor, not you." Kasey jerked a sweater down over her head.

Emma uncrossed her arms but stomped her foot. "I want to stay with Grandma."

"Your grandmother has to be at the church to help with the program stuff today and you can't go with her."

"Then Nana's?" Emma glared at Kasey.

"Nanma, yes!" Silas yelled and danced around in his pajamas.

"Nana is at the church, too."

Silas stopped and fell down on the floor. "No!"

Emma dropped to her knees beside him.

Kasey backed up and sat down on a ladder-back chair beside the hall tree. "We are leaving in ten minutes and if you're not ready then you won't go to any grandma's house for two whole weeks. It's your decision."

"Lila's?" Emma's tone had softened.

"Not Lila's either, and there might not be ice cream for two whole weeks. And there's a possibility that you won't get to play with your dogs or to make a snowman later on. The weatherman says we're going to have a nice white Christmas so I guess Rustin and Nash will make the snowman and you'll have to watch from the window."

Emma sighed.

Silas got up off the floor, tugging at his pajama top. "Me's ready."

"Emma?"

"Can I wear my pink tutu?"

"Too cold," Kasey said as she removed Silas's pajamas, changed his diaper, and redressed him. "Besides, it wouldn't match your sweater."

She growled.

"One more of those noises and we won't be stopping at the café for burgers after the doctor's appointment."

"Sorry, Mama." Her chin dropped to her chest. "I'll be good. Can we have ice cream at the café?"

"We'll have to see about that."

Finally, Silas was dressed except for his coat and hat, but Emma was only wearing panties and a sweater. Kasey held out a pair of bright green leggings and Emma shook her head.

"We are not negotiating, young lady. Five more minutes until we have to walk out the door."

With a long dramatic sigh, Emma stuck out a foot. "Boots?"

"That's fine," Kasey growled.

"Mommy howlded." Silas giggled.

"I did not," Kasey protested as she pulled Emma's hair up into a ponytail.

Emma wiggled. "Ouch! Grandma don't pull."

"Grandma deals with angels. I work with little demons," Kasey said.

"Who's an angel?" Nash asked as he came out into the foyer.

"Me!" Emma's sent her most innocent smile his way.

"Me is angel!" Silas ran to him, arms raised, as usual.

"Are we all ready to go?" Nash asked as he picked Silas

up. "Looks like you need a coat, buddy, and Emma, don't you look pretty today."

"It comes at a great price," Kasey said.

"Your sanity?"

She quickly finished Emma's hair. "Is gone for the next two years."

Nash tugged Silas's hat down over his thick blond curls and then put his coat on him. "Well, you look beautiful as usual, Miz Kasey."

"Flattery won't get you anywhere after the morning I've had," she said.

He handed Emma's coat to her. "Just statin' facts, ma'am."

Together they got the kids into the van, strapped into car and booster seats. Without a word between them, she slid behind the wheel and he buckled himself into the passenger's seat. It wasn't really raining, but a thin mist fell and froze the minute it hit the windshield. She hit the warmer for both the front and back windows and turned on the wipers, which did little but make a mess until the glass heated up.

"Mama, Silas touched me," Emma whined.

"Me not," Silas declared.

"Burgers at the café or home for a peanut butter sandwich and a nap and no books tonight?" Kasey noticed Nash staring at her. "Don't you say a word."

"Bad mornin'?"

"You have no idea."

* * *

Nash had been on top of the world at the end of Monday night when he kissed Kasey at her bedroom door, but on Tuesday he awoke with a rock as big as a third world country in his chest. He called his mother and she reminded him that hard work usually brought him out of the dark places.

He'd gone to the barn, restacked all the hay bales and cleaned all the stalls, and put down fresh hay to get them ready for any new calves or lambs. It didn't help so he called his grandmother that afternoon and talking to her didn't lift his spirits either.

Wednesday wasn't a bit better after the therapist's visit, so he went back to the barn after chores were done and made a lean-to for the church live nativity program. Hope had said that they usually set it up under the big pecan tree in the churchyard, so he'd made a wooden star to hang above it. He painted it with some gold paint he'd found in the tack room and even found a little vial of glitter in a drawer and applied it.

On Thursday, he'd gotten up feeling worse than ever, so he'd decided to make a manger for the doll that would be used to play baby Jesus. He argued with the voices in his head as he worked that morning.

He'd shared downright hot kisses with Kasey. He'd had amazing sex with her. She'd brought him out of his shell more than anyone, including doctors and therapists. He owed it to Adam to do what he could to take care of his family, but that didn't include kisses or sex, and the guilt had been eating on him all week.

That afternoon he was still wallowing in the heavy thoughts on the way to the doctor's office. Kasey was driving five miles below the speed limit but then the roads were slick. Then suddenly the whole van whipped around and they were headed right back up the highway toward Happy. He grabbed the dash with both hands and looked over his shoulder to see if the kids were okay.

Kasey tapped the brakes two or three times and finally

slowed enough to park on the side of the road. She had a death grip on the steering wheel and her whole body was stiff as a board when she got the van under control.

"Are they all right?" Her chin quivered and her eyes were fixed straight ahead.

"Do it a din, Mommy," Silas said, cheerfully.

"That was fun," Emma chimed in.

"I'd say they're fine. Hit a slick spot, did you? Want me to take over?"

"No, not until the doctor..." Her hand went to his arm. "Did you bump your head on anything? The window, the seat belt thing up there?"

"I'm fine, Kasey. Nothing got broken or even bruised."

He shook his head in disbelief. No flashback to the way he'd driven, fishtailing back and forth through the sand with no defined roads on the day that Adam was killed. With all the adrenaline rushing through him in the terror that one of the kids might be hurt, he was surprised that he hadn't thought of that horrible day.

"Are you sure? Unfasten your seat belt and look at them for me. I'm terrified, Nash," she said.

He did what she asked and found two kids with big grins who looked like they'd been on an amusement park ride. "No trauma. No blood," he reported. "But I think you should let me drive the rest of the way. You are shaking like a leaf in a whirlwind."

"Can't," she whispered. "Doc hasn't released you, and I have to get right back on the horse." She stiffened her upper lip to keep from crying and made a U-turn in the middle of the road. "I can't let you drive or I'll dread getting behind the wheel with the kids in the backseat even worse next time."

"You can go faster than thirty miles an hour," he said.

"No, I can't. We won't be late. Don't worry," she said.

It was exactly ten thirty when Nash went up to the desk and checked in for his appointment. He didn't even have time to sit down in the waiting room before they called him back to an examination room, where he sat for fifteen minutes before the doctor rushed inside.

"So how have you been feeling?" he asked as he sat down on one of the little round roll-about stools. "Got your memory back?"

"Feelin' fine and my brain is functioning at full capacity, sir," Nash answered.

"No nausea, recurring problems like vision loss or seizures?" He pecked away on a tablet without looking at Nash.

"Nothing but wishing I could drive. That's been a pain in the butt," Nash answered.

"Okay, let's look at your blood pressure and check your lungs. Standard stuff, and then I'll sign off for you to drive. You're being honest with me, right? I could do another scan to be sure, but I hate to do them unless it's necessary." He snapped a cuff around Nash's upper arm and pumped it up.

"Well, that looks good." He made a few more taps on the tablet. "Depression, suicidal thoughts, or nightmares?"

"I'm seeing a therapist for PTSD."

"Okay. Which doctor?"

Nash rattled off her name and address. "It's a preexisting condition I brought home from the last mission I was on and has nothing to do with this accident."

"If you have any of the symptoms on the papers I sent home with you, call me immediately. I'll clear you today to drive and go back to whatever lifestyle you had before, but I do advise that you continue to keep your appointments with the therapist."

"Yes, sir." Nash almost saluted the doctor.

"No more falling off ladders," the doctor said with a smile. "And thank you for your service, son."

Nash smiled and shook the doctor's hand, then headed back toward the lobby, where he found Emma and Silas entranced in a cartoon on the television while Kasey flipped through a magazine. He'd admit it—he'd had feelings for her when she was nothing but a picture of another man's wife, but that had been nothing compared to what he felt now when he held her in his arms. Living with her had been a breath of fresh air shot into a dark cell. But in all honesty, he knew he wasn't right for Kasey. The army had already taken one husband from her, and for her to lose two would be cruel beyond what the heart could stand.

So you're going back as soon as you can? asked the voice inside his head as he stared his fill of the woman of his dreams from across the room.

No, I'm not, he answered quickly. But if something happened to me, she'd still be losing two husbands.

Thinking of leaving her put a lump in his throat and another one of those heavy rocks in his chest, but he had to think about her, not himself. She was an amazing woman and mother and she meant too much to him to see her hurt.

"Nashie!" Silas squealed and ran toward him, his chubby little legs a blur.

Emma was right behind him, twirling and dancing like a mixture of a ballerina and a swing dancer. "Watch me dance, Nash!"

Nash stooped low enough that he could gather both of them up in his arms. "Were you good? Do we get to go to the café for burgers and ice cream on the way home?"

"We's good," Silas said.

"That's great," he said, but his eyes were on Kasey, who'd laid down the magazine and was coming their way, laden with a tote bag and three coats. "Let's set you down and get you bundled up so we can get on the road."

The sun had peeked out from behind the dark clouds that had been spitting freezing rain thirty minutes before. Nash helped Kasey get the kids situated in the backseat of the van and then held out his hand.

"Doc says I'm cleared for anything I want to do, including driving," he said.

She shook her head. "I'll take us home."

"But I can drive now, Kasey."

"So can I, and it's my van."

"What's the matter with you?" he asked. "You haven't been yourself all morning and it's more than that little slip on the ice back there. What did I do wrong?"

She got into the driver's seat and snapped the seat belt with a dramatic flourish. "If you don't know, then I'm damn sure not tellin' you."

"Bad, bad." Silas shook his finger at her.

"I'm tellin' Granny Hope," Emma declared.

"Peanut butter or burgers?" Kasey snapped.

"Don't take your pissy mood out on the kids," Nash said.

"They're my kids. Just because they think you walk on water doesn't make them yours," she shot back.

* * *

Lord have mercy! What in the hell was wrong with her? Granted, Nash had been standoffish for a week, but that didn't give her the right to act like a shrew, and damn it, she was so angry at him.

He wouldn't understand if she tried to put it into words.

She felt used and discarded. Kiss her, have sex with her, dance with her, and then hardly even speak to her for five whole days.

"I'm sorry," she said but there was ice in her voice.

"No, you aren't. Just take me home and then you can get on back to your life. I can drive myself now, so you don't have to feel obligated to stay on my ranch," he said.

"No! Café," Emma said.

"Take me to the ranch and then you can bring the kids back to the café. You don't want to be with me anyway. Thanks for all you've done, but I'm a grown man who can take care of himself."

He folded his arms over his chest and stared straight ahead out the window. His teeth were clamped tightly and his full mouth nothing but a thin line. Anger radiated out of him like heat waves on the highway in July.

"If that's what you want, then fine," she said.

What is this fight all about? It was definitely Lila's voice in her head. *It's not about who is driving. That's just the excuse.*

Kasey flipped her hair back over her shoulder. Without a word, not even to correct Emma when she tried to boss Silas, she drove straight to the Texas Star and parked in front of the house.

"Is this the way it's goin' to be, *chère*?" he drawled out the endearment like it was a dirty word.

"Don't call me that when we are fightin' and yes, this is the way it's goin' to be, Captain Lamont," she said.

"So be it." He got out of the van and stomped into the house.

"Hungry to death, Mama." Emma sighed dramatically.

"Nashie?" Silas asked.

"He's goin' to eat peanut butter."

"Nashie bad?" Silas's eyes widened.

"No, he just has to check on the sheep, but we'll go to the café and have burgers." Kasey fought to keep her voice even and held back the tears as she turned the van around. "How about we eat and then go spend the rest of the day with Lila and Uncle Brody?"

"Yep!" Silas yelled.

Paul and his old running buddy, Fred, were in the café with a big basket of french fries between them. Silas ran right to his grandfather and Paul slid out of the booth and pulled up a high chair to the end.

"Let me take care of this one. You and Emma grab that last booth and have a girls' lunch," Paul said.

"Thank you," Kasey said.

"You okay?" Paul asked.

"Fine. Just a stressful day."

"Where's Nash?" Fred asked.

"We just got back from the doctor, and he's been released to drive. He needed to get back to the ranch and I'd promised the kids that we'd eat at the café if they were good," Kasey said past the lump in her throat.

"Well, that's good news." Fred nodded.

Daisy waved from behind the counter. "Be with y'all in a minute. Well, look at who's comin' in the door."

"Lila!" Emma let go of Kasey's hand and ran across the floor. "Eat with me?"

"Sure thing, princess," Lila said. "I was runnin' ranch errands and saw your van, Kasey. Thought I'd stop and have a burger. Where's Nash?"

"Come sit with us." Kasey nodded toward the booth in the back corner.

"Your usual?" Daisy raised her voice above the noise of more than a dozen conversations.

Lila and Kasey both nodded at the same time.

"I'll get our drinks, Mama," Lila said. "Looks like y'all are busy."

"Thanks, kiddo," Daisy said.

Lila brought two tall glasses of sweet tea and a small one with a lid on it filled with milk to the booth. "Okay, talk, sister. You look like you're about to cry. Sadness or anger?"

"A little of both."

"What was the fight about?" Lila asked.

Kasey sipped the tea. "Lettin' him drive home from the doctor's office."

"Who won?" Lila asked.

She stared out the spotlessly clean window at the parking lot filled with trucks and cars. "He didn't drive, but I didn't win."

"Okay, then what's the fight really about?" Lila asked.

Daisy brought three red plastic baskets filled with burgers and fries to the table. "Good to see you, Kasey. You ain't been out much but then you've had your hands full with all this holiday stuff and with Nash, right?"

"You got it." Kasey forced a smile.

Daisy made the telephone sign with her thumb and pinky finger. "Holler at me later, Lila."

Lila removed the paper from her burger and bit into it. "Nothing like a good old greasy burger."

"Yep." Emma took a bite of hers.

"Real argument?" Lila asked between bites.

Kasey's appetite faded after the first bite. "Build up and then let down. Little corn has big ears."

"Later?" Lila asked.

"We're comin' to see you today," Emma said.

"That's great." Lila raised a dark brow toward Kasey.

Kasey shrugged. "Thought we might spend the night and

maybe even the weekend. Help get the ranch Christmas party in gear."

"We can use all the help we can get," Lila said. "And we'll talk later over a bottle of wine."

Kasey pushed back her basket. "Wine sounds wonderful, but there's not much to tell."

"Oh, honey, I've done already walked the road you're on, and I think there's lots to talk about. Especially if it's taken your appetite. *S-E-X*, yet?"

Kasey blushed.

"Yep, we need to talk."

* * *

Christmas truly had to be a time of miracles and magic.

Kasey spent the whole afternoon in the kitchen with Hope, Valerie, and Lila, and no one questioned why she was back at Hope Springs. She had told them that Nash could drive, so she and the kids were going to spend a couple of days away from Texas Star. Of course, Valerie was probably thinking that Kasey was coming home for good, and she might be right. And Hope needed the help for the ranch Christmas party on Saturday night, so she was too busy to question anything.

It was close to midnight when Valerie and Jace went home to Prairie Rose and when Hope said good night to everyone and went to her little house located at the back of the ranch. She'd moved into it when she turned the ranch over to Brody, Nash, and Kasey the spring before.

Brody said he had about an hour of phone calls to make and disappeared into the office.

Lila waited until she and Kasey were alone before she brought out a bottle of blackberry wine. She didn't bother with fancy flutes but poured it into a couple of recycled jelly glasses and motioned for Kasey to follow her into the living room. She handed Kasey one and then touched it with hers.

"To a long talk about why you're really here. So talk, little sister," Lila said.

"He was so sweet after the fight when he told me about knowing Adam and then so, so romantic on Monday night." Kasey went on to tell Lila the details of what had happened after the school program. Then she stopped and drew her feet up on the sofa and sat cross-legged.

"And the next morning?" Lila pushed for more.

"He was coldly indifferent, like nothing had happened between us. Every day has been the same. He stays in the barn or out on the ranch, only coming in for meals."

"Evenings?" Lila asked.

"He watches television or helps with the kids until they go to bed and then he disappears into his room until breakfast," Kasey answered.

"And you let him? What in the hell is the matter with you, Kasey? This isn't the red-haired spitfire that I know," Lila said.

"If he doesn't want to spend time with me..." Kasey defended herself.

Lila didn't let her finish the sentence. "Talk to him and figure out what he's thinkin'. Make him use words, and even if you think you can read him, don't let him get away with that. Brody tried it with me a few times. I asked him if he thought I was a damn mind reader."

"I don't have that right," Kasey said.

"Bullshit!" Lila fussed. "You've been over there takin' care of him and his house and helping on the ranch, so you have every right. Plus you slept with him. If he was just playin' you for a night of sex, then make him say it outright and then slap the crap out of him for it. If he really cares for you, then make him say it. You should go home after the party tomorrow night and walk in there like you own that ranch and you're royally pissed."

"But—" Kasey started.

"Would you have let Adam get away with that?"

"Hell, no!"

"There's the attitude I know. Get your stompin' boots on right after tomorrow's party. We need you until then and he needs to think about things but then you're going to march in there and shoot the elephant that's in the room with y'all."

Her glass made a clunking sound when she touched it to Kasey's again and they both downed the rest of the wine.

"Now." Lila's dark eyes twinkled. "Tell me about the sex. Any good?"

Crimson filled Kasey's entire face.

"That good? Wow! And you're lettin' that get away because you're afraid to stand up for yourself?"

Kasey divided the rest of the wine between them, almost filling the two glasses. "I guess anything worth having is worth fighting for."

"You're preachin' to the choir for sure, darlin'." Lila laughed. "Your whole family, except Jace and you, hated me and thought I was going to be the complete ruination of your brother."

"Yep." Kasey raised her glass. "And they love you now, but Mama is so against me even being over there with Nash because Henry was kind of strange."

"She'll come around." Lila winked. "And now I'm going to bed with that sexy cowboy I married. Keep me posted?"

"Sure thing." Kasey nodded.

She tipped up the glass and finished off what was left. She wanted another glass—hell, maybe another bottle—but she didn't need a headache the next morning. "Adam, you could help me out here," she whispered as she checked on the kids and made her way to the bedroom. She sat down on the edge of the bed and pushed a button to turn on the radio on the nightstand.

Tears started to flow as soon as she heard the first piano notes of "Go Rest High on That Mountain." Vince's sweet voice left no doubt that the message was from Adam. Like the lyrics said, Adam's life had been trouble and that he wasn't afraid to face the devil. Adam had faced more demons that he could ever talk about, but the words said that his work on earth was done.

"Okay, I get it. I should move on." She wiped her cheeks with the back of her hand.

Her phone pinged and she checked the message. It was from Nash, and once again it was only a link to a song. She hit it and Blake Shelton's voice filled the room with "God Gave Me You."

She sent a text: *We'll talk tomorrow after the party.*

She got one back immediately: *Fair enough.*

Chapter Nineteen

Kasey was making the rounds among the newest guests at the ranch Christmas social when Emma tugged on her skirt tail. "Mama, where's Nash? I miss him."

"We're going home tonight, and you can see him before you go to sleep. Where's Silas?" Kasey blinked half a dozen times but it didn't change the fact that she'd called the Texas Star home.

Emma shrugged.

"Where's Rustin?" Kasey asked.

Emma pointed toward the Christmas tree where Rustin and his friend Kyce were huddled around a tablet playing a game. "Boys!" She sighed.

"Is Silas with Uncle Brody?" Kasey scanned the room and located Brody and Lila talking to Gracie and Paul. And there was Jace sweet-talking a pretty blonde in a cute little blue velvet dress. Hope was with Fred and his wife, and Valerie was discussing something with the caterers.

"Silas is gone to get Nash," Emma answered.

"How? What? Are you sure, Emma?" A double dose of adrenaline hit Kasey, making her heart sound like a rock band's drums.

"Yep, that way." Emma's finger shot up toward the kitchen door.

She crossed the room in a hurry and grabbed Jace by the arm. "You've got to come help me. Silas has run away. Emma says he went to get Nash."

Lila laid a hand on her shoulder. "What's goin' on? You look like you're about to faint."

"Will you watch Emma and Rustin for me?" She went on to tell her that she and Jace were going to search for Silas.

"We can have everyone in this place combing the ranch for him in five minutes," Lila said.

Jace shook his head. "Let's not ruin the party. We'll probably find him in twenty minutes or less."

Kasey slung a coat over her little black dress, changed her high heels for a pair of Lila's cowboy boots sitting by the back door. She was already going out of the yard gate when Jace caught up to her.

"Call Nash," he yelled. "Tell him to start toward us."

"My phone is at the house in my purse," she said.

Jace tossed his toward her. "Use mine."

Nash had programmed his number into her phone and she didn't know it from memory. She stopped in her tracks and shut her eyes tightly, trying to remember the house phone number for Texas Star, but nothing came to mind.

"I've got to go get my phone," she said.

"I'll run back and grab it. You keep walkin' and I'll catch up to you." Jace disappeared into the darkness.

"Silas!" she screamed and counted off five steps and

yelled again. It seemed like she'd walked a hundred miles before she heard the crunch of dead leaves as Jace jogged back toward her.

"Had to hunt down your purse," he said. "You take the fork toward Texas Star and I'll go to the barn."

Hero bounded from the path leading to the springs and yipped at Kasey, then whipped around and returned back the same way. She called Nash on the run and he picked up on the first ring.

"Hello, Kasey," he said.

"Where are you?" she asked, breathlessly.

"On Hope Springs property. My sheep found a way out of the corral and I'm tracking them. It looks like they're headed toward the springs. What's wrong?"

"Silas is missing. Jace is going toward Texas Star looking for him. Silas told Emma he was going to get you," Kasey said.

"Oh, my God. Forget the sheep. Where do you want me?"

"Oh, no!" She stopped in her tracks. The Rudolph antlers that Silas had worn all evening were hanging on a tumbleweed. "He's gone toward the springs."

"I'm within a hundred yards of there and I'm runnin'. He wouldn't get into the water, would he?"

"I don't know. He's fearless!" She clutched the phone to her chest as she ran even faster.

Kasey could hear the water rushing over the rocks when the phone rang again. She didn't even check to see who was calling but hit the right icon. "Tell me you found him, Nash."

"It's Jace. I'm at the Texas Star. Looked through the house and even in the doghouse. On my way to the barn right now. No sign of him. How about you?"

"Nash and I are on our way to the springs. I found his

Rudolph antlers and he's headed that way. I think that's what Hero was trying to tell me."

"Let me check the barn and I'll be there soon as I can." Jace's tone had almost as much fear in it as Kasey's heart did.

She wouldn't have known Hero was speeding toward her if she hadn't heard him panting. The black dog hardly even stopped before he reared up on his hind legs and put his paws on her thighs.

"Have you found him?" Kasey asked.

Hero barked once and then was gone down the path again, straight toward the springs. She wanted to call out to Silas, but she was afraid that if her boy was close to the water it might spook him and he'd fall in. So she kept silent and kept running.

"Silas!" Nash hollered not far from her.

"Silas!" She yelled right behind him.

Which way should she go? Nash had stepped out of the darkness and wrapped her in his arms.

"We'll find him, *chère*. I promise." He laced his fingers in hers and together they covered the next thirty yards to the springs.

"He's not here." Ice ran through her veins. Her baby was in that cold water.

She and Nash removed their coats and fell back on the ground to take off their boots. Then Hero growled right behind them. They turned and heard giggles from under the willow tree. Hero wagged his tail and yipped. Kasey took off in a dead run with Hero behind her, pushing the sheep out of the way.

She grabbed Silas up and hugged him tightly. "Why did you run away? That was a bad, bad thing to do," she said as she kissed him so many times that he squirmed.

"See Nashie. Sheeps." He pointed at Nash and then the sheep.

Without letting go of him, she pulled out her phone and called Jace first. "We've got him. You can go back to the party."

"I'm at the fork in the road. Is he okay? Did he get into the water?"

"No, Nash's sheep and Hero were protecting him. It's crazy but the sheep made a circle around him and Hero came back to the ranch to get me," she said. "I'm going to Texas Star, Jace. Can you bring the kids over after a while?"

"Sure thing, Sis. You want me to come help you get him and the sheep back home?"

"No, just tell Lila and Brody that we're fine and make an excuse for me."

"You got it," Jace said. "See you in an hour or so and give that kid a hug for me. I don't know when I've ever been so scared."

"Me, either." Kasey sighed.

She wasn't even aware that Nash had stepped away until he draped her coat over her shoulders.

"Thank you," she muttered.

He took Silas from her so she could put the coat on. "You have goose bumps the size of mountains on your arms."

She shoved her arms into the sleeves and slipped the phone into her pocket.

Nash wrapped Silas in his coat. "How'd you get here, buddy?"

"Nashie!" Silas put his little hands on Nash's cheeks and kissed him on the chin. "Go to party?"

"No, little man. I think it's time for us to go home," Nash answered.

"Sheeps, too?"

"They'll follow us. Why did you run away like that?"

"Me get Nashie. Got cookies." He smiled up at him.

"So Nash needed to eat cookies with you?" Kasey asked.

He nodded seriously. "Go home now, Mommy?"

"Yes, baby, we're goin' home now," she said.

"I'll carry him. He's too heavy for you to tote across rough ground for half a mile," Nash said.

"Can I help with the sheep?"

"Walk right here beside me. The sheep will follow. I'm the one who needs help, not the animals," he said seriously. "But the important thing right now is to get everyone home and warm. We can talk later."

Home.

He was taking them all home. And that's exactly where Kasey knew that she belonged.

* * *

Before they reached the fence, Silas had gone limp and was sleeping soundly. Kasey was silent, probably still in semishock and feeling the effects of the adrenaline rush subsiding. With one foot on the bottom line of barbed wire and holding the top one up with his hand, Nash watched her slip through and then handed Silas over the fence to her.

He palmed a wooden post and hopped over it and took the sleeping child from her. "The sheep will slip through. They'll leave some bits of wool but they'll be fine." He answered the questions written on her face.

With a few bleats they were all on the Texas Star side of the fence in only a few minutes and following him toward the barn. When they reached the yard fence, he handed Silas off to her.

"I'll get them secured in the barn until morning and be right in. There's a pot of soup on the stove if you're hungry," he said.

Are you stupid? Talking about food? The pesky voice in his head yelled at him. *You should be tellin' her that you're sorry for being such a dumbass, making a big deal out of driving and for not going to the café with her and the kids.*

"I couldn't eat a single bite. I can barely even breathe yet," she said as she headed toward the house.

He nodded and led the sheep on out toward the barn. He checked the corral and found the rest of the flock bedded down for the night. There was a small place at the corner where the fence had separated from the post, but he couldn't figure out just how six full-grown sheep had gotten through there, or why the rest hadn't followed them.

Magic. It's the Christmas season. They were needed to protect the child. The voice sounded a lot like his mother and he suddenly missed her. He made a mental note to call her later that week. *A true Cajun wouldn't even question that.*

When he'd finished securing the fence, he brought the ones that he'd penned up inside the barn out to the corral. Maybe his mother was right—they'd escaped to take care of a little boy. It was the season, and all those years ago shepherds followed a star to find the baby. Maybe Silas's little voice had floated across the fields and the sheep heard him.

There had been a nice moon and twinkling stars in the sky when they were walking across the field but now it was all gray. The first sleet pellets hit him in the face as he jumped the rail fence around the yard and made his way toward the back porch. He stopped when Hero barked at him from inside the doghouse, then he bent down and rubbed the dog's ears.

"You done good tonight, boy."

His tail thumped against the walls of the doghouse, as if he understood.

Nash scratched each dog's head one more time before he rushed inside the house. "You guys curl up tight. It's goin' to be a cold one."

Warmth stung his face when he was in the kitchen. Coming in from the cold like that without even a hat, it was no wonder his face was prickly. But the flush that came next had nothing to do with the weather and everything to do with the beautiful woman right there in front of the stove.

"We need to talk," she said.

"Mama, mama! Did Silas find Nash?" Emma tore into the kitchen from the foyer without even stopping to take off her coat. "Yep, he did!" She grinned up at Nash.

"Hey." Jace leaned on the doorjamb. "Kyce and Zayne went home and Rustin was bored so I brought them on home. It's way past their normal bedtime anyway."

* * *

There was that word—*home*—again. Every sign in the whole universe kept pointing right at the Texas Star, not unlike that famous star in the sky that guided the wise men and shepherds to Jesus all those years ago.

"Okay, kids, you had baths before the party, so up to bed with you. I'll give you five minutes and then come tuck you in," Kasey said.

"Can I do that tonight?" Jace asked. "I kinda missed it when you left."

"Hey, Nash. Did you get lonesome without us?" Rustin asked.

Nash laid a hand on the boy's shoulder. "Yes, I did, and I'm sure glad you're home."

"Me, too?" Emma cross the room and wrapped her arms around his knees.

"You, too, princess."

"Okay, Uncle Jace." Emma left Nash and tugged on his hand. "You can read to me tonight."

"No books this time. It's very late and we've got church tomorrow morning, so it's straight up to brush your teeth, get into your pajamas, and go to sleep," Kasey said.

"Next time?" Emma cocked her head to one side.

"Next time." Jace slung her over his shoulder like a sack of potatoes. "Race you up the stairs, Rustin."

Giggles blended with boots stomping on hardwood steps.

"Hey, y'all keep it down. Silas is asleep," Kasey yelled.

"That was a long walk for the little guy. Wild horses running right through the house probably wouldn't wake him," Nash said. "We were going to talk?"

"In a little while, when Jace leaves and when the kids are asleep." Anything they started right then would lose momentum as soon as Jace returned because he'd think that he had to step in and play the role of big brother.

The next ten minutes were the longest of her life. Nash went to the living room and sat down in the recliner. He toyed with the remote but didn't turn on the television. She tidied up an already spotless kitchen, wiping down counters that were shiny clean and rearranging the cans of food in the cabinet.

Jace finally appeared in the kitchen and talked as he put on his coat. "I'm going back to the party. Emma yawned once and went right to sleep. Rustin had his knuckles in his eyes and tried to talk me into reading just one little bitty book to him. And Silas is sleeping sound. See y'all in church tomorrow?"

Kasey nodded and said, "Thanks for bringing them home and for tucking them in tonight. My hands are still shakin' and my heart is just now settling down. When I think of..."

Jace drew his sister to his chest and hugged her tightly. "Don't go there. We'll just have to be sure to watch that critter closer from now on. Up until I was thirteen I was terrified of the dark, but nothing frightens our Silas. He must've gotten that from you. I can't remember you being afraid of anything."

Until now, she thought. *My own feelings scare the hell out of me.*

"Goodnight, Sis." Jace planted a kiss on the top of her head. "You'll be over the jitters by church time tomorrow mornin', and dinner is at Hope Springs. Leftovers from the party, I'm sure, but I'm not complainin'. I love good barbecue." He waved through the door into the living room. "Bye, Nash. See you tomorrow."

"Thanks for everything, Jace," Nash said.

Kasey waited until she heard the engine of the truck start up and then until she couldn't hear it anymore before she took a deep breath and marched barefoot into the living room. She popped her hands on her hips and inhaled deeply.

"You were a jackass, Nash Lamont. You had no reason to treat me like you did," she said.

He sat up straight in the chair, which put them on almost the same eye level. "You had no reason not to let me drive. You know how I've hated bein' dependent on you like I was a little schoolboy."

You're supposed to apologize and kiss me, she thought.

You don't need or even want a wimpy cowboy in your life. That was Lila's voice for sure.

"What's the real issue here? This is too damn big for it to be nothing more than driving home," she countered.

"What do you think it is?" he fired back.

She sat down on the sofa and leaned her head back. When she pinched the bridge of her nose, he immediately left the chair and took a seat next to her. He turned her around to face him and massaged her temples.

"Is it a migraine?" he asked.

"Just a hellacious headache," she answered. "And I'm mad at you."

"I'm mad at you." His fingertips were pure magic.

"What're we goin' to do about it?" she asked.

"Talk about what's really goin' on in our heads. I'll go first," he said. "These past weeks have been the happiest of my whole life. I had always wanted to go back to the service, but now I've changed my mind. I was miserable all day without you here. I was right back in the black hole with no bottom."

"I could never stand in the way of your dreams, Nash," she said softly.

He put a palm on the top of her head and one on the back of her neck and rotated her neck in several circles, then reversed the process, loosening all the tense muscles. "I'm not so sure that's my dream anymore, but if I was to have the opportunity to reenlist—well, you've lost one husband to the war. That's enough for any woman to endure."

She moved his hands and leaned forward until her nose was practically touching his. "And I don't have any say in the matter?"

Holy crap! He'd said husband. He was thinking permanent relationship? That was almost as scary as losing Silas.

"Kasey, let me explain. You're everything that Adam said you were, everything that all of us other members of the team wanted. I know how he felt and how much losing him must have affected you. I can't cause someone to hurt like that twice in a lifetime."

"Again." She said through clenched teeth. "What about how *I* feel? For the first time in two years I'm moving on and it's because of you."

"How do you feel?" He kept his eyes downcast.

She slipped her knuckles under his chin and raised his head so that she could crawl right into his eyes to his soul. "I like you, Nash Lamont. I may even be falling in love with you. You're a good, kind man, and I'm not going anywhere until after Christmas. You can't run me off again. We are going to talk about our feelings, not shove them under a haystack and fight around them. We might find that we don't even like each other, but by damn, it won't be because we were too uptight to express our feelings."

The veil over his dark brown eyes lifted. "You always speak your mind like this?"

"No, sometimes I cuss a little more and yell a lot more," she said. "Why'd you join the service anyway?"

"Did you ever hear that song about where corn don't grow?"

"Travis Tritt." She nodded.

"I wasn't college material. Made good grades but didn't like school. I can't remember when I didn't want to be a soldier and see places where corn didn't grow, or peppers or sweet potatoes or purple hull peas. So I joined the army and loved every bit of it until... well, you know. And I liked the hard work on Addy's ranch, but all I could think about was getting my life and mind together so I could go back into the service where I belonged."

"And now?"

"I'm finding that I've got this chance at happiness and I don't want to let it slip through my fingers. And *chère*, I think I'm fallin' in love with you, too." Without taking his eyes from hers, he picked her up and carried her to his bedroom.

"Are we about to have makeup sex?" she asked.

He hit a button on a stereo and Travis Tritt started singing "Can I Trust You with My Heart?"

"It can be anything you want it to be. Just tell me that I can," he said as he peeled the form-fitting dress up over her head.

"Can what?"

"Trust you with my heart," he said. "I'm not too good with words but country songs are..."

"Yes." With one tug all the snaps on his shirt popped open. "And I love country music."

His smile was all the foreplay she needed. She hurriedly undressed him and pushed him backward on the bed. When she started to throw a leg over his body, he flipped her over and in seconds they were keeping time to the music playing in the background.

Nash pushed her hair away from her eyes and locked gazes with her. Every single song that played on the mixed CD was a message to her from him, and good lord, but it was romantic as all get-out. The sex was like dancing in an old country bar with a live band. His hands were like tender feathers on her neck and ribs one minute and the next they were under her butt, demanding that she meet him thrust for thrust.

She dug her nails into his back and latched onto his neck with her lips, her tongue feeling his racing pulse.

They reached the climax at the same time and she thought her lungs would explode. Did she say his name there at the end or had she told him that she loved him? She'd couldn't remember anything but knowing complete and ultimate satisfaction in the blur surrounding that moment.

"God Almighty!" She finally got out two words.

He cradled her in his arms and kissed her on the forehead. "Intense."

"Wild."

"Yes." She ran her hands over his chest.

"His thumb made lazy circles from her neck, down the valley between her breasts, and around the white stretch marks on her belly. "Every single inch of your body is amazing."

"Who told you that you weren't good with words?"

"I get tongue-tied around you, Kasey. There's got to be a better way to tell you that you're stunning and that you look like a movie star, but my mind gets all tangled up and all I can say is that you're beautiful."

His hands roamed over her body and set a brand-new fire inside her. When he bent and made love to her lips and mouth with his tongue, she thought she would climb the walls. "I need..." she started.

"So do I, but let's slow it down and play a little while," he said. "There's a lot of night left, darlin'."

* * *

Kasey awoke to the aroma of coffee and bacon. She slung her legs over the side of the bed and looked around. She'd gone to sleep in Nash's arms in his bed and now she was in her own room and Silas was standing in the door. Had she dreamed that amazing night of sex?

"Me hungry," he said.

"Me, too. Let's go get breakfast." She started to whip off the covers and then realized she was naked. "Why don't you wait for me on the top step? I'll be there in just a minute."

"Six thirty!" She moaned when she glanced at the clock on the bedside table. It had been after three when he'd rolled her up in the bedspread with him and they'd fallen into a deep sleep together. She didn't have a single recollection of going from his room to hers.

Kasey hurried to the door and shut it. She would have liked to slide down the backside and think about the night before, but it was morning and that meant she was a mother now. She pulled on underpants, a bra, and an oatmeal-colored thermal shirt with a red-and-green plaid overshirt and socks before she jerked on a pair of jeans. Rustin was slow moving in the morning, so she'd have to keep at him... and then she remembered that it was Sunday, not a school day.

"Me hungry!" Silas frowned up at her when she opened the door.

"Relax, little man, I'm here." She gathered him up and carried him across the hallway to change his diaper before they went down to the kitchen. Rustin's bed was empty and Emma's giggles drifted up the stairs along with the delicious aroma of bacon.

"Rusty?" Silas looked over at the empty bed beside his crib.

"I hope he's in the kitchen." She gathered him up in her arms and left the bedroom the two boys shared.

"Nashie?" Silas asked.

"I hope he's in the kitchen, too." She bit back a groan.

If that was Granny Hope or Lila making breakfast, they'd take one look at her and know exactly what she'd done all night. She checked her reflection in the mirror out in the hallway. Yep, there was a hickey the size of a silver dollar shining on the side of her neck. She quickly popped up the collar of her shirt, but it wouldn't stay put so she flipped her red hair over her shoulder to cover it.

Nash must've heard them coming because he met them halfway across the kitchen. "Good mornin'," he said but his dark eyes said much more when he locked gazes with her. They said that he wanted to draw her into his arms and maybe even take her back to the big king-size bed in his room to welcome the new day in a much more personal way.

"Good mornin'," she said without blinking.

Silas reached out his hands toward Nash. "Hun-gee!"

"Well, big guy." Nash took him from Kasey and put him into his high chair. "We've got bacon and eggs and waffles. What looks good?"

Silas waved his chubby little hand to include all of it.

"That's a cowboy after my heart." Nash chuckled.

Kasey set about making a plate for Silas.

"We waked up and Nash was cookin' and we let you sleep," Emma said. "I want to wear my red dress to church."

Rustin hardly let her finish her sentence before he said, "I get to help feed this mornin'. Nash is goin' to let me."

"How?" Kasey whispered to Nash.

"I carried you up a couple of hours ago. Rustin is old enough..."

"Yes, I am," Rustin said. "I gots to learn if I'm goin' to be a cowboy rancher."

"And that's why?" Nash grinned.

"Thank you," she mouthed and then added, "for letting me sleep and making breakfast."

"Thank you," he whispered.

"What did Mama do?" Emma asked.

Nash smiled at her. "Your mama worked very hard at the party yesterday and then had to get out in the cold and walk a long way to find Silas when he ran away. She was very tired, so we let her sleep a few extra minutes this mornin'."

Man, he was quick on his feet. The only answer Kasey could come up with was the truth—that she'd spent the whole night having amazing sex and didn't even wake up when he carried her upstairs to her own bed. And you damn sure didn't tell a three-year-old that.

Chapter Twenty

Hope could see and feel the difference in Kasey and Nash that morning. They sat with Jace, Brody, and Lila in the pew right in front of her and Valerie, Gracie, and Paul. It was nothing that she could put her finger on, but his dark eyes were full of life instead of pain, and Kasey—well, she looked alive instead of just living. That little sliver of a hickey that she almost hid with her turtleneck sweater said that they'd come to an understanding and at least part of it had been in bed or maybe a hayloft.

Hope's thoughts went back to the days when she and Henry had argued and then made up. She even had a few close calls when it came to covering marks on her neck. Her mother would have died a lot earlier than she did if she'd ever seen a sucker bite on her daughter's neck.

And here I sit in church of all places wanting to applaud them both, Hope thought as she opened her hymnal to the congregational song that morning. She sang along with everyone else and tried to pay attention to the preacher, but memories of Henry flooded her mind. Nash reminded her so much of his great-uncle. He was taller, but those dark eyes and that head of black hair were the same, plus he had that same swagger and quiet way about him. Kids had always flocked to Henry after church, even when the adults kept their distance because they mistook his introverted personality for strangeness. Nash had that about him—Kasey's kids loved him and he appeared to really care about them.

As the preacher cleared his throat and everyone began to get ready to leave, Hope left the past behind and came back to the present. But it was a good thing that getting through the pearly gates of heaven didn't depend on the scores she'd make on a test on the sermon that morning. If it had been, she'd have been looking forward to an up-close-and-personal visit with Lucifer, himself.

"Just a reminder that we will have our church Christmas program on Wednesday night. Right now the weatherman is sayin' we'll have a clear night, even though it will be cold. So the stars should be shining bright to bring our shepherds and wise men to the live nativity scene and the folks out to the special night we have planned. The nativity will be up from five to seven, and then the inside program will be presented. Afterward there will be refreshments in the fellowship hall. And now, Brody, will you please give the benediction."

With Silas still in his arms, Brody stood up and bowed his head. "Thank you for our blessings, even those that we thought were obstacles…"

Hope smiled and nodded. Brody was accepting the situation with his sister, and that was good. Lila could take part of the credit for that, since she'd stood her ground on the issue from the beginning. Hope wrapped her arms around her body and hugged herself. Who would have ever thought that Henry's nephew would come to Happy and that he and Kasey would have a chance at happiness?

Maybe that's what God or fate or karma, whatever a person calls it, had in store all along. Hearing Henry's voice in her head made her eyes pop wide open. It was so clear and definite that she glanced over her shoulder to be sure he wasn't on the pew behind her. She reached up to touch her little gold necklace.

There probably still would have been a Nash even if I'd gone with you and left Hope Springs behind, but there wouldn't be a Kasey. So you're right, Henry. It was a plan far above what we had any control over, wasn't it? Someone with far better future sight than we had or will ever have knew that Kasey would be the only one who could give Nash life again, and that he was the only one who'd understand her. Hope swiped a lonely tear from her cheek.

"You all right, Granny?" Kasey asked as they all made their way to the center aisle. "Are you cryin'?"

"I'm fine, honey. Never better. There was something in my eye. Let's go home and have some dinner," Hope said.

"We're going to take the kids to the Amarillo mall for pictures with Santa this afternoon. Want to go with us?"

Rustin jumped up and down half a dozen times. "Why didn't you tell me? Did you know, Nash? Emma, we get to see Santa today and whisper in his ear."

Emma hugged Rustin in a tight squeeze. "And sit on his lap?"

"No, thanks." Hope grinned. "I'm going to take a long nap. After yesterday, I've had enough excitement for a few days. I have to save my strength for getting things all ready for the church program on Wednesday, but you might pick up a couple of gifts for me while you're at the mall."

Kasey fell in behind Hope. "Just make a list."

That Nash kept his hand on her shoulder or that her granddaughter's green eyes had more sparkle in them than she'd seen in two years did not escape Hope. *Yes, Henry.* She touched the gold locket around her neck again. *Someone does see the future much better than we do.*

She and Valerie got to the ranch before anyone else and went straight to the kitchen to pull the barbecue from the warm oven. Valerie had been talking nonstop about the upcoming church program and how much they still needed to do when Hope butted in.

"I've got something to say before all the kids and Gracie and Paul get here. You're going to crawl down from the soapbox that you've been on about Nash and Kasey," Hope demanded.

Valerie opened the refrigerator door. "Now, Mama, don't start on me."

Hope slammed the door shut. "They've been to bed."

"No!" Valerie squealed. "Did she tell you that?"

"Look at her when she gets here. She's smiling and it reaches her eyes for the first time since Adam died. So step back and let her alone. She's a grown woman."

"But what if—"

"She's a big girl. She can make her own decisions and accept the consequences for whatever they are. We're family and we need to support her, not fight her when it's evidently bringing her happiness," Hope said.

"Who are we supporting?" Brody came into the kitchen through the back door.

"Your sister," Valerie said bluntly.

"It's not easy, but Lila has made me see the light, Mama. Kasey will always be my little sister and your baby girl. She's happy. I can see that Nash is good for her.

Nothing might come of it, but that's for her to decide,"
Brody said.

"And you all know Kasey," Hope said. "If we fight her,
she'll set her heels and then it'll be our fault if she makes a
wrong choice."

"Amen to that," Valerie said. "I hear little feet runnin' on
the porch, so here they come."

"Brody? You goin' to make things right with her?" Hope
whispered.

"Yes, Granny. I'll find a minute to talk to her today."

"Good. A house divided cannot stand." Hope patted him
on the arm and opened the refrigerator door for Valerie.
"Now you can get the cold stuff out."

* * *

Dinner was over. Dishes were done and Kasey was herding
the kids into the foyer when Brody appeared out of the west
wing of the house and cornered her. "Can I have just a
minute?"

Lila stepped out of the bathroom. "I'll gladly get them
ready to go see Santa. Mind if me and Brody follow y'all in
Amarillo? I've got some last-minute shopping to do and I'd
love to snap a picture for my first Christmas album of all the
kids."

"I'd love that. Granny gave me a list of things to pick up.
It would be great to have help with that or with the kids."
Kasey turned to Brody. "What's up?"

"Are we okay?" he asked.

"You tell me."

"I'm sorry that I've been a jackass."

"Apology accepted. Which of these kids do you want for
the afternoon?"

"Rustin. I think Silas belongs to Nash." Brody smiled. "And FYI, I don't like sharing you."

"And FYI, you aren't. I will always be your little sister no matter what other title I get bestowed with, Brody Dawson." She tiptoed and threw her arms around him. "And I'll always need a big brother in my life."

"Just not an overbearing father figure, huh?"

"Something like that. And while we're on the subject, is Mama sick?"

He removed her jacket from the coatrack and held it out for her. "Not that I know of but"—he lowered his voice—"Granny took away her soapbox this morning."

"Well, bully for Granny." Kasey slipped into the coat he was holding and turned to Nash. "You'd better hurry and get your denim jacket on because Silas will want you to carry him to the van."

"Who's driving?" Nash asked.

"You are." She grinned. "It'll be nice to look at all the holiday decorations on the way up there without having to worry about running off the road."

"Hey, Rustin, you want to ride with me and Lila?" Brody asked.

"Naw, I think I'll just go with Nash," Rustin answered.

"And there you have it." Brody sighed.

"Same thing applies that I just told you. He'll always need you and Jace to fill the spots for the greatest uncles in the whole world, just like I need two wonderful brothers," Kasey said softly.

"You really are happy, aren't you?" he asked.

"Yes, darlin' brother, I am." She slipped out the door behind two kids.

Nash was right behind her with Silas in his arms. They got everyone buckled into the backseat and were ten miles up the road when a car whipped around a semi in a no-passing zone. Kasey squealed and grabbed the dash for support and saw a small portion of her life flash before her before Nash jerked the wheel to the right and braked hard, coming to an abrupt stop just as the car and the semi sped past.

"Is everyone all right?" he asked, hoarsely.

"What happened?" Rustin asked.

"Thank God for seat belts." Kasey could barely force words from her mouth.

"Or they'd have been thrown around like marbles in a tin can. Are you okay, Kasey? No bumps or blood?" All the color had left his face and his eyes were as big as saucers.

"I'm fine. You?" she asked.

"Will be when my heart slows down. What in the hell was that driver thinkin'? I'd like to get my hands around his rotten throat about right now." Nash doubled up his fist and shook it at the windshield.

She covered his right hand with her left one and brought it down. "Let's just sit here a couple of minutes and get our bearings."

"I don't want a bear from Santa," Emma declared loudly. "I want a singin' machine."

"Me wants sheeps and cookies!" Silas then said.

Rustin puffed out his chest. "Mama said bearings, whatever that is."

"*Bearings* means until we feel better about going on. That kind of shook me and your mother up," Nash explained.

"Otay." Silas nodded seriously.

If Nash said it then it should be written in stone. Kasey was suddenly green with jealousy. She'd had Silas all to herself since the day he was born. Sharing him with Brody and

Jace had been one thing, but the relationship he had with Nash went far deeper.

And it happened so quick, she thought.

"All goes to show that we better take advantage of opportunities while they are in front of us," Nash said.

"Life can do a one-eighty in nothing flat, can't it?" Kasey could finally feel her nerves unwinding.

"Lesson learned." Nash brought her hand to his lips and kissed her knuckles. "On to enjoy Santa Claus and maybe even buy some presents."

"Yay!" all three kids yelled from the backseat.

* * *

Kasey's hands were still shaking when they reached the mall, but when Nash laced her fingers in his on the way from the parking lot until they were inside, all the jitters settled right down. The first persons she saw when they were inside the doors were Brody and Lila. He waved and motioned her over.

"We were about to send out the military to find y'all," he said.

"We had to get bears," Emma said.

Lila frowned. "Bears?"

"Bearings. We had a narrow escape with a car passing a truck and Nash had to brake hard and pull over or we'd have had a crash," Kasey explained.

"And then bears before we could see Santa," Emma declared in her most authoritative tone.

"I see. Well, I'm glad no one was hurt," Lila said.

"You okay, Kasey?" Brody asked.

"Fine now. Shook up for a minute."

"Scared the hell out of me," Nash admitted.

Brody clamped a hand on his shoulder. "Would've me, too, especially with kids in the car."

"Sandy Claws!" Silas pointed.

"Let's get in line," Kasey said.

When it was his turn to sit in Santa's lap, Silas had a change of heart and the only way they could get a picture of him was if Nash held his hand. When Santa asked him what he wanted for Christmas he took a deep breath and said loud enough that the whole place could hear. "Nashie. Me wants Nashie."

"Is that a puppy dog?" Santa asked.

Silas shot a go-to-hell look at him. "No!"

"I betcha we can find a Nashie at the North Pole and I will do my best to bring him to you for Christmas," Santa said and they moved on to the next child.

"Well, that was an experience." Nash grinned when he joined Kasey and the rest of the family.

Brody chuckled. "I want to see Santa shove you down into his bag of toys."

"I'll do my best not to break anything," Nash said. "How about we take these kids to the play area and let the ladies do some shopping? I bet they'd all love that."

"Please, Mama! Please. I hate to go in the stores!" Rustin said.

"I want to shop." Emma pouted.

"Then it's boys to the jungle gym with us guys and girls to the stores?" Nash looked over the kids' heads at Kasey.

"Sounds like a good plan. Let's get goin', Lila, before they change their minds."

Lila rolled up on her toes and kissed Brody. "See you in an hour."

"Or two." He laughed.

"Take your time." Nash didn't kiss Kasey, but the slow,

sexy wink he sent her way brought up scenes from the songs from the night before and put a nice blush on her face.

"What's that all about?" Lila asked when they went into the nearest western wear store to fill Hope's list first.

"What?" Kasey tried to act innocent.

"Spill it, sister. You had makeup sex, didn't you?"

Kasey nodded. "You ever had music sex?"

"What's that?" Lila laid two leather billfolds on the cashier's counter while Kasey gathered half a dozen pairs of wool socks.

"Country music mixed CD and the…well, if it's a fast song…and if it's a slow one…it's a horizontal dance that keeps up with the beat with…" Kasey blushed all over again.

"I get it and no, but it damn sure sounds like fun. How long does the CD last?"

"The one he'd made lasted an hour and it ended on 'God Blessed Texas.'" She giggled.

"Oh, I've got to give this a try for sure. A whole hour? Did you replay it or did you fall asleep?" Lila asked.

"We didn't replay it, but we didn't fall asleep the next two times and when I woke up he'd carried me upstairs and put me to bed so that the kids…and now I feel like my face is on fire."

"Wow! That's pretty damned impressive." Lila paid the bill and shoved the receipt into the bag with the items. "So is this going to get serious?"

"He's not avoiding me this mornin', so maybe."

They started out of the store when Kasey remembered that she didn't have a thing under the tree for Nash. He should have three presents like everyone else, and then a Santa present. But what on earth did she buy for him, especially when Lila was with her? Socks were warm but so impersonal. A billfold was the same, and besides that's what grandmothers gave to her grandsons—definitely not what she should give Nash—especially after last night.

"Can you believe it's only a week and a couple of days until Christmas?" Lila asked.

"What have you bought for Brody?"

"Nothing yet, but you can bet your fanny that he's getting a mixed CD for one of his presents. Let's go into that store right there. I really like that plaid shirt in the window." Lila pointed. "Don't worry, I'll let Brody think the music sex was all my idea."

"Thank you!" All the air left Kasey's lungs in a loud whoosh. "I probably shouldn't have told you that, but it's been a long time since I had a friend I could talk to about anything. In the army, the wives had to be close as sisters and we...well..." she stammered.

Lila draped an arm around her shoulders. "I never had a girlfriend that I could be this open with and it's pretty awesome."

"Yep, it is," Kasey agreed.

Chapter Twenty-one

A stiff breeze rattled the limbs of the old scrub oak tree, but the stars were bright in the dark sky that evening. Nash couldn't see any sign of a moon, but one star did look brighter than the others. If modern-day shepherds were on their way to see the new baby, he doubted that it was shiny enough to lead the way.

If someone had told him six weeks ago that he'd be sitting in front of a manger that held one of Emma's baby dolls all wrapped in swaddling clothing with Kasey McKay next to him, he would have told them they were insane.

"I keep expecting a lightning bolt to flash through the sky and zap me, pretending to be someone as holy as Joseph," he said out of the corner of his mouth.

"It'll get me first," Kasey answered.

"Y'all are supposed to be quiet," whispered Jace, dressed as a shepherd.

"I'm glad I don't have to do this every day," Rustin said.

Paul chuckled. "I don't think I could be a wise man for more than an hour a year."

"Shhh..." A second wise man, Fred, shushed them. "If we talk, then everyone who walks by will want to visit with us."

Nash drew Kasey close to his side when she shivered. She wore jeans and a turtleneck sweater under the robes, but it was getting colder by the minute. Lila and Brody had been supposed to play the parts of Mary and Joseph in the live nativity, and he'd been slated to be a shepherd so he could take control of two sheep. But the couple who were helping with the inside program got sick at the last minute and Hope made changes. Nash didn't think that she'd checked with God about putting him and Kasey in the roles of Mary and Joseph or how the whole town of Happy would feel about it, but there they were, kneeling beside a box made with old weathered barn wood filled with hay and a doll baby with blond hair. The crazy thing was that he couldn't think of a place he'd rather be unless it was sleeping with Kasey beside him.

There had been no nightmares the past three nights, no cold sweats or waking up with a head full of miserable memories. With Kasey in his arms, he'd slept like the proverbial baby. They had learned to set an alarm, and she was either in her room or the kitchen by the time the kids were awake.

"Mama, I got to go to the bathroom," Rustin whispered.

"You know where it is," Kasey told him as she reached under her robe and fished her phone out from her pocket to check the time. "And it's only ten minutes until we finish here, so you don't have to come back. Find Nana and stay with her."

"This wise man's knees are about to fold, so I'm going

inside, too," Paul said. "Gracie is watching Silas and Emma, so we'll add Rustin to the mix."

"What about the sheep when we get done here?" Fred asked.

"They're tied so they should be fine until we go home," Nash answered.

Home.

He'd used the term before.

Going home to Louisiana for leave from the military. Going home to his grandmother's farm from the feed store or the grocery store. Going home to the base from a mission. But never had the word sunk into his heart and soul like it did that night. For the first time in years, he really felt like he had a place to settle down and grow old.

But Kasey damn sure deserves more than a little spread with a little flock of sheep, he argued to himself when he thought of her never leaving the Texas Star.

"Time!" Kasey finally said. "And Paul's knees don't have a thing on mine right now. Who would have thought dirt could feel like concrete?"

Nash stood up and extended a hand to help her. The now familiar jolt that rushed through him even at the touch of her palm didn't surprise him, but he did wonder if it would be like that when they were two old people sitting on the porch in rocking chairs.

He shook the negative voice from his head as the whole group from the nativity hurried inside the fellowship hall out of the cold.

"Is it okay if we take all this garb off now, *chère*?"

"I'm shuckin' out of mine," she said as she unwound the long scarf that covered her hair and shook it loose. "I would not have made a good woman in that age."

He wiggled his dark eyebrows. "Why?"

"You know better than anyone else. In those times they would have already taken me out in the street and thrown rocks at me."

"I would have protected you." He slipped the long robe over his head and folded it neatly. "What do I do with this?"

"Just lay it on the table over there. Gracie and Granny know where to store all the costumes." She nodded toward the place where the little drummer boy's outfit and one of the wise men's were lying.

"Here, I'll take it." Fred held out a hand. "Y'all done good and the real live sheep did a better job than those painted wooden ones we've had for years. And that star was a nice touch. Next year, do you reckon you could get a donkey and get it trained?"

"It's an idea. That painted one looks kind of flat," Nash answered.

Fred slapped his leg and laughed loudly. "It is kind of skinny, ain't it?"

"Y'all need to feed it better. I'm surprised that it's not dead." Nash kept up the joke.

"Amen to that. Kasey, you tell Hope Dalley that next year she's going to have to find a younger wise man. My old bones don't take to the chill anymore," Fred said.

Kasey nodded toward the refreshment tables. "You tell her. She's right over there."

"Time to go find a seat now?" Nash asked.

"We need to get Silas. Emma and Rustin have a little part in the program," she said.

We.

Like home, that was another short word with so much meaning. Maybe it took the *we* to make a home, because a house was only an empty shell without someone to share it with.

"Wait right here. I'll get him, and, honey, I can see part of that hickey on your neck," Nash whispered.

* * *

Kasey turned around and deftly adjusted her sweater so that the mark was covered and then flipped her hair over it to be doubly sure. She'd been considering getting one of those cute little chin-length bobs, but this definitely was not the time to make that change.

The church was packed when they got inside the sanctuary. They'd have been standing or sitting in folding chairs that had been set up in the narrow side aisles if Jace hadn't saved them part of a pew. The space was tiny enough that Kasey was pressed so tight against Nash that light couldn't get between them, and Silas had to sit on Nash's lap.

"Full house," Jace whispered.

"Never seen it like this before," she said.

"Me, either. Did you hear that Mrs. Anderson, the fifth-grade teacher and little kids' Sunday school teacher, has been diagnosed with early Alzheimer's? She decided to retire effective immediately. Mama and the rest of the school board have a week to get someone hired and to find someone to teach her class here at the church."

"Don't look at me," she said. "You can volunteer."

"Not me," he declared.

"Maybe they'll hire a teacher who will lead you to the altar and you can start havin' all those kids you've been talkin' about. Now that would sure enough cause another packed church. The great Jace Dawson finally roped and tied." She giggled.

"Not damn likely," he muttered.

Nash leaned forward and said, "Never say never."

Before Jace could say anything else a dozen little children marched out from the choir loft. Led by the preacher like little puppy dogs, they each stopped on a piece of tape stuck to the floor. The preacher went on to stand behind the pulpit.

"Welcome, everyone, to 'Jesus Is the Reason,' the title for this year's program. In this part of the world we tend to think that when we gather for weddings, funerals, programs, or even after church on Sunday, that there should be food involved. But then Jesus fed the multitudes and even fried fish for his disciples so maybe it's just following his example when I tell you that immediately following the program, the ladies have set up refreshments in the fellowship hall. Now I'll turn this over to Mrs. Anderson, who tells me this is her last time to chair this program."

Everyone applauded when a gray-haired lady took the podium. The pianist hit a few chords and then the children all sang "Joy to the World." After that they said their memorized verse, each one telling a little about the birth of Jesus. Rustin was the last one to deliver his line, and he spoke right up just like he'd done at school.

Then Emma's little group took the stage, each carrying an ornament, and as Mrs. Anderson read a sweet little story about how a star got to sit on top of the tree, each child hung his or her ornament on the tree. Then they sang "Hush! There's a Baby," and Emma's voice drowned out everyone else's, even Mrs. Anderson's.

The rest of the program lasted about an hour, but Kasey had trouble keeping her mind still. There wasn't room to wiggle, but she did cross and uncross her legs so many times that Jace finally frowned at her.

"We need to get those lace curtains out of the attic for Emma?" Nash whispered softly in her right ear.

Now what in the devil brought that on? she wondered. They were listening to kids read passages from the Bible and talk about Jesus being the whole reason for the season and Nash was thinking about pink curtains?

She nodded.

"What made you..."

"Emma looks like an angel and my mind circled around to those things," he explained. "One of the boxes has ceramic angels written on the side? Maybe we'll put some of those in her room."

Another nod. "She'd probably like that. Got any sheep for Silas and Rustin's room?"

A smile spread across his face. "Probably. Do they like bunnies? I saw one box of those."

The responsibility behind what he'd just said was pretty damned weighty. They were about to make decisions that would involve both of them. She brushed that away and mentally began to redecorate the living room. That ugly brown braided throw rug in front of the coffee table was going to be the first thing replaced. It would make a really nice dog bed inside that new house Nash had built for Hero, Princess, and Doggy.

"I forgot to buy the dogs a present," she whispered.

"Unforgivable!" Jace chuckled. "Whatever made you think of that?"

"Long story, but the kids will throw a fit if the dogs don't have a present on Christmas," she said.

"I'll take care of it. How about new food dishes and a rawhide bone for each of them?"

"Great!"

Hope tapped them both on the shoulder from the pew behind. "Shhh...no talkin' in church."

Jace nudged her and winked. They didn't need words.

The queen bee of the program had spoken and they'd better listen. No one crossed Hope Dalley, least of all one of her own grandchildren.

Silas had fallen asleep by the time the program ended, and he awoke in a sour mood. But he turned the frown into a bright smile when Nash told him that there were cookies and candy waiting just for him. Nash had a way with kids and should have a dozen of his own.

Rustin and Emma ran across the room, holding hands and both talking at the same time. Silas wiggled until Nash set him on the floor, and the three of them took off over toward the Christmas tree where brown paper sacks were lined up on the floor. Each would contain an apple, an orange, candy bars, and cookies so that the kids would have something to take home that evening. Hope Springs had brought them for the past fifty years, but not many people knew where they came from.

Valerie hugged Kasey from behind. "The kids did really good. Emma's going to be a natural. We might see her in Nashville before too many years."

"Don't say that. She's growing up too fast as it is."

"Darlin' daughter." Valerie chuckled. "It was just yesterday that you were just her age, so don't blink."

"I told her that I'd build her a stage," Nash said. "When spring gets here, we should have a concert with her as the main attraction."

"That would be fun and, Nash, that lean-to you built for the nativity scene was really nice," Valerie said as she moved on over to help the ladies with the food tables.

Spring.

Concert on the Texas Star.

Everyone was on board with this whole thing with Nash and suddenly, out of the dark night, Kasey wasn't so sure about any of it. It was moving too fast, and she felt pressure behind her eyes.

Reverse psychology.

That's what it was. Lord only knew, she'd used it enough on the kids to recognize it. Valerie had thrown a good old-fashioned southern hissy fit when Kasey moved over to the Texas Star. That didn't work, so now Valerie had done a one-eighty. It was so that Kasey would feel exactly like she did right then, that she'd question her own feelings and would move back to Hope Springs.

"Well, it won't work," she muttered.

"What?" Nash asked.

"Nothing." She smiled. "Let's have a snack and then take our sheep and kids home."

Warmth filled her heart when she realized she'd said *our* sheep and kids, and there wasn't a bit of guilt mixed in with it.

"I'm sure ready for that." Nash nodded. "I get a little antsy in big crowds. I'm lots more comfortable on the ranch with you and the kids."

"Me, too," she said and meant it.

Chapter Twenty-two

Nash had set the box with the pink lace curtains to the side and was on the fifth one marked knickknacks. He'd chosen three ceramic angels for Emma's room, all with touches of pink to match her curtains. Now he was looking for something that might look nice in the boys' room. Finally, he found one with cute little lambs for Silas.

"Yes!" He pumped his fist in the air like one of the children.

"Jackpot!" he yelled when he discovered a collection of cowboy boots in the last one.

He was putting three into the box with the curtains and lambs when something rattled inside the largest one. He turned it upside down and a small black velvet box fell out at his feet. The corners were worn and a few places on the box were completely bare. He flipped it open to find a set of wedding rings inside.

Touching the center diamond, he thought about how the engagement ring would look on Kasey's finger. Without thinking he stood up so he could get his phone from his hip pocket and bumped his head on a rafter.

"Ouch!" he yelled.

"You okay up there?" Kasey yelled from the bottom of the narrow staircase.

"I'm fine. I found the curtains and some other things for you to look at."

"I'm putting the soup on the table in five minutes," she said. "Maybe this afternoon we can hang the curtains?"

"No problem," Nash said as he hit the right icon to call his mother.

"Hello, Nash. What's goin' on?" she answered.

"Mornin', Mama." He lowered his voice. "I'm in the attic going through boxes and I found a set of wedding rings in a velvet box. They were tucked down in an old ceramic boot. Were they Granny Minnie's?"

"In a black velvet box that's old as dirt?" she asked.

"That's right."

"I can't believe you found them. Yes, those were Granny Minnie's rings. She had to take them off when she got sick because her fingers swelled. You say they were in a boot?" Adelaide asked. "Look on the bottom. Does it have *MT* scratched into the heel?"

He turned it over. "Yes, it does."

"I remember when she and Hope's mama and Rosalie Varner took a ceramic class years and years ago. Granny Minnie made that boot for grandpa's birthday and he kept it on his desk with pencils in it."

"Do you want me to send the rings and the boot to you or to Addy?" Nash asked.

"Lord, no! You keep the rings and the boot. Maybe you'll need those rings someday," she said.

He could picture her smiling and crossing her fingers.

"Nash." Emma's voice floated up from the bottom of the stairs. "Mama says soup is on the table."

"I heard that," Naomi said. "If your grandmother and I didn't have this cruise planned over Christmas I would come to Happy and meet the kids and Kasey."

"Door is open anytime you want to come," Nash said.

"I appreciate that. Bye now," Adelaide said. "And I'm glad you found those rings. I've often wondered what happened to them."

* * *

Kasey hummed a Christmas carol that morning as she pulled a pan of cinnamon rolls from the refrigerator and slipped them into the oven for a special breakfast. Not only was it Christmas morning but it was her last committed day on the ranch. Unless Nash asked her to stay longer, she would be going back to Hope Springs the next day. "Until after Christmas," she muttered as she put on a pot of coffee and got out juice and milk for the kids.

Would she stay longer if he did mention it?

On the one side, the folks in Happy hadn't taken her out and stoned her for living with an unmarried man for the past month. Times had changed, and living with a guy wasn't nearly as big a deal as it had been twenty-five or even ten years ago. But they could always change their minds and gather up the rocks or a length of rope if she continued to stay there, now that he no longer needed her help. But then did she really care what anyone thought?

She set the table with the pretty Christmas dishes from the top cabinet shelf. It would be one thing to date Nash, quite another to live with him in a town the size of Happy. Plus, she had Hope Springs to think about, as well as Prairie

Rose. She couldn't throw away good names and reputations on a whim.

But is it a whim or is there something besides great sex here? she asked herself.

It took only a split second to decide that it was more than sleeping with Nash—a lot more. It was all the kindness and sweetness in that man's heart. Not all guys would have built a huge doghouse for animals that would only be there three weeks, or a nativity set, or let three kids trail after him any-time they wanted to go with him to the barn. Or help her find closure for Adam. No, whatever it was that she had built with Nash this past month had already grown roots much deeper than the naked eye could see.

She glanced at the tree with the presents under it and the Santa presents displayed out in front. Nash had put together the bicycle for Rustin along with a set of steer horns at-tached to the front that he'd found in a specialty store, the little red wagon with a bag of cookies that he'd remembered were Silas's favorites, and had bought a couple of back-ground tapes to lay on the top of Emma's singing machine. He'd abided by her rule of only having three presents each for the kids and wanted no recognition for the little things he'd done for the Santa presents.

That was father material for sure.

"Merry Christmas." His arms went around her waist and he buried his face in her hair. "Something smells amazing. The way it's snowing out there, the kids just might get to build a snowman this afternoon."

She turned around and slipped her arms around his neck. "Merry Christmas to you. I thought you were still sleeping."

"I couldn't sleep after you left our bed, so I got up and did all the morning feeding chores. Now we can enjoy

Christmas with the kids without leaving the house." He brushed a kiss across her lips.

"Mama," Emma called from the top of the stairs. "Did Santa come? Is it mornin'?"

"Sandy?" Silas yelled.

"Excitement is about to begin." Nash held her hand, and the two of them went to the bottom of the steps.

"It's mornin'. Go wake up Rustin and Emma, and Silas, you stay right there until I can change your diaper."

"I'll peek and see if Santa has come." Nash's tone was even more excited than the kids were.

"You could change the diaper and let me check for Santa," Kasey teased.

"No problem. I got lots of nieces and nephews, so it wouldn't be my first turn around a squirmin' child." He started up the stairs.

She grabbed him by the belt loop. "I was teasing. I'll take care of that if you'll get things all situated to film them with your phone as they go into the living room."

He stopped on the second step and turned. "Deal, but I do have a really good camera that'll make a better video."

She nodded and took the steps two at a time, very aware that he was watching her backside as she did. Rustin and Emma waited on the landing until she got Silas changed and ready, but they were fairly well humming with excitement.

"Did he come, Mama? Did you look and see if he brought us a present?" Rustin asked.

"He did. I know it." Emma wiggled like she was dancing.

"Sandy come, Mommy?" Silas yawned.

"Don't know yet, but let's go see." When they reached the bottom, she set Silas on the floor. "Emma, honey, you hold Silas's hand. Nash is taking pictures of y'all so we can show Granny and your uncles, since they aren't here this morning, okay?"

"Tay." Silas's blond curls bounced as he nodded vigorously.

Rustin sniffed the air. "It smells just like Christmas."

"Cinnamon rolls!" Kasey gasped. "Wait right here until I get them out of the oven."

They were perfectly browned and slid out of the pan beautifully. She quickly spread a coating of butter cream frosting on the top, left the bowl and spatula on the cabinet, and rushed back to the children. Kasey stopped in the doorway when she realized that Nash was stooped down in the foyer already doing a video.

"Emma, what do you love about Christmas most?" he asked.

"Presents," she said.

"What about you, Rustin?" he asked.

"This year Mama isn't cryin'," Rustin said. "Hi, Mama. I see you back there behind Nash. Can we go see our presents now?"

Kasey swallowed hard three times and nodded. No way could she say a single word after that comment.

"Just one more, please, guys. Silas, what do you like about Christmas?" Nash asked.

"Nashie." Silas rubbed his eyes with his fists.

The lump in Kasey's throat doubled in size.

"Okay, Rustin, count to twenty and then y'all can come and look under the tree." Nash rose up and hurried into the living room, where he switched on the lights and took a knee in the corner to film the kids when they came through the door.

"One, two, three, four," Rustin counted slowly.

"Ten, eleventeen," Emma said.

"Twelve, thirteen." Rustin laughed.

"Tenty!" Silas yelled.

They stopped at the doorway and all three of them clamped their hands over their mouths. Their eyes widened and for a long moment, the whole room was as silent as a tomb. Then Emma's squeals bounced off the walls, followed by Silas's and then Rustin's as they raced across the room to their Santa presents.

"Lookit, Mama, it's got horns. It's the best bike in the whole world and I bet I can ride it without the little wheels real soon," Rustin said.

"I'm a star!" Emma picked up the microphone and hugged it to her chest.

Silas crawled into the wagon and turned to look right at the camera. "Nashie, pull Silas, tay?"

"In just a minute, buddy. But you've still got presents to open," Nash said.

"Do you want to sit down and open your other presents now or have breakfast first?" Kasey asked.

"Can I eat my breakfast on my wild bull bike?" Rustin asked.

"No, you can't." Kasey shook her head. "Bulls don't come to my table."

"Presents!" Emma said without letting go of the microphone.

The children sat down in a circle and she passed out their three gifts. But when she finished there were six more presents under the tree. Three that she'd slipped in there last night for Nash and three pretty red ones with green bows, all professionally wrapped and shoved toward the back.

"And three for Nash," she said.

He turned the camera off and joined the kids on the floor. "I've had the best Christmas ever just having you and the kids here. I didn't need presents, too."

"Can we go now, Mama? Please!"

"Just five seconds." Nash kissed Kasey on the neck when he reached around behind her to get his camera.

Paper flew everywhere as the children made short order of their presents. Toys were what they always got for Christmas and their birthdays. According to Adam, since they limited the number of gifts, then each one should be something they really wanted and would last, because they did not get toys every time they went to the store. Ice cream was a treat for being good when they had to go shopping with their parents, not toys.

Silas carried each thing to his new wagon as he opened them and set it down gently beside his cookies. When he finished he pulled the wagon over to Nash and crawled into it with his gifts.

"Can you sit right there until Nash opens his presents?" Kasey asked.

"And until Mama opens hers?" Nash said.

"Yep." Silas's head bobbed up and down.

"You go first." Nash scooted over a couple of feet and handed Kasey three gifts.

She found a little gold locket in the first one.

"I saw you admiring the one that your grandmother wears all the time," he said. "Open it."

Inside she found a tiny little picture of her three kids with a herd of sheep in the background. "Oh, Nash, it's beautiful. Put it on me."

His big hands trembled as he fastened the delicate gold chain around her neck. "You really like it?"

"I love it. Are you aware that the one she wears was given to her for her sixteenth birthday by your uncle Henry?"

"No," he said.

Kasey fingered the heart-shaped locket that dropped to exactly the right place. "It's beautiful."

"Not as much as you are," he whispered.

Her second present was a lovely wooden picture frame with FAMILY IS THE GREATEST GIFT painted in bright yellow letters. And the third, a blinged-out alarm clock with a crown at the very top of the minute hand.

"For the queen of the Texas Star," he said.

And he didn't think he was romantic enough?

"Thank you so much, Nash. You've put a lot of thought into these, but when did you..."

"A little online shopping bought some of it and the necklace was when you and Lila were shopping and we watched the kids. Brody and I traded turns with the kids and did some buying of our own." He grinned. "So you really like them? It was so hard to keep it down to three. You deserve so much more."

"Mama." Emma waded through the paper and bows and threw her arms around Kasey's neck. "My new baby and me is hungry. Can we eat?"

"Nash needs to open his presents first, and I bet that the cinnamon rolls are cooled down by then."

"No eat. Pay." Silas had opened up a big blue bucket of blocks and was busy stacking them.

"I'll try to hurry, princess," Nash told Emma.

He opened the first one so carefully that the paper didn't even have a tear in it. "Oh, Kasey, this is so nice. It looks just like the ranch brand." He held up the bolo tie with a gold star slide. "I know just the special occasion that I'll wear it first."

A vision of him wearing nothing but that flashed through her mind and put a scarlet blush on her face.

He was a little less patient with the second one, a fluffy oversize throw the same color as his dark brown eyes. A wicked smile turned up the corners of his mouth. "And I've got a picture in my mind for this."

So did she.

It didn't involve watching movies with the kids in the room. But rather wrapping up in it after a bout of really hot sex and falling asleep together.

Tucked inside a little tin box with a Christmas tree on the front, the third present was a gift card to a steak house in Amarillo. "Why, Kasey, are you asking me for a date?" He raised his voice over blocks falling, Emma talking baby talk to her new doll, and Rustin making engine noises as he floated his remote-control helicopter over the Christmas tree.

"If I was, what would the answer be?"

"Name the day and we'll use this card." He grinned.

Silas left his blocks and crawled into Nash's lap. "Hungee?"

"Yes, I am buddy, and those cinnamon rolls are just like an extra present," Nash answered. "Ask Mama if we can have breakfast now?" He slipped her hand in his and squeezed gently. "Thank you. I wasn't expecting presents, but they are all perfect. I can't tell you..."

She leaned over and kissed him on the cheek. "Neither can I. Let's have breakfast. We're supposed to be at my mama's for brunch at nine, then at Gracie and Paul's for coffee and cookies at ten thirty."

"And Granny's?" Emma followed Kasey's lead and kissed Nash on the other cheek.

"Back to Granny's at eleven thirty for presents and to help get the family Christmas dinner on the table at two o'clock," she answered.

"Then home so I can ride my bike?" Rustin asked.

"It's snowing, buddy," Nash said. "But we can take it out to the barn and you can ride it up and down the aisles and I bet we can set up a couple of hay bales so you can fight them with the horns."

"Me, wagon?" Silas asked.

"And I'll pull you all over the barn." Before he could say anything else, his phone rang and he mouthed "Uncle Henry" as he answered it.

"Okay, then. We'll leave the back door unlocked. We'll be at Hope Springs for Christmas dinner at two o'clock."

"And you are invited," Kasey yelled.

"Yes, it's fine," Nash said. "We understand, but we hope you change your mind." He put the phone back in his pocket and shook his head. "He says not to expect him but that he'll see us this evening. His flight is going to be late, and then there's the bad weather from Amarillo to here."

"I'm ready to eat." Emma smiled.

"Looks like we've got a full day." Nash helped Kasey to her feet.

And then all of this comes to a screeching halt, she thought with a sigh.

* * *

The morning after Christmas, Nash and Kasey took the wagon and the new bike out to the barn to let the kids play with them. Emma, of course, had to take her karaoke machine and sing to the sheep. Then they went back to the house where Kasey made a pot of coffee for her and Nash while the kids played with their other toys.

It was past time for Nash to ask Kasey to stay, way past time to admit to her that he'd flat-out fallen in love with her, but as he sat there across the table from the most beautiful woman in the world, the one who'd stolen his heart, he was tongue-tied that morning.

"Hey, Nash." Jace burst through the front door. "That ram of yours is out on the road. I was on my way back to my place with a load of feed. Tried to get a lasso on him, but he's a wily old boy. Maybe you'll have better luck."

"You got time to watch the kids, Jace? I'll go with him and help. The sheep know me pretty good, so maybe I can sweet-talk him a little," Kasey asked.

"Sure thing, Sis. But remember, we're supposed to be at Granny's for leftover dinner, so hurry up," Jace answered.

Kasey tossed Nash's coat across the room. "That's an hour from now. Shouldn't be a problem."

Nash threw on his coat and followed Kasey outside into the blowing snow. "They were all in the barn half an hour ago. I can't imagine how he got out."

Kasey was already in the driver's seat of the van. "Maybe he jumped out of the stall and..."

"Dammit!" Nash slapped his thigh as he buckled up. "I bet I didn't close the barn door all the way. I was in such a hurry to get the kids back to the house that I might have left it open a little bit."

"Let's just hope that none of the others got out."

"I'm so sorry," Nash said.

"No problem."

The north wind whipped the snow across the road in waves and the windshield wipers couldn't keep up even on the highest speed.

"I don't want you to leave Texas Star," he blurted out.

"I don't want to go, either, but...hey, there he is." She pointed to the ram, who must've gotten turned around. With his head down, he was in the middle of the road coming right toward them. She stomped the brakes and the van fishtailed all over the place before it came to a stop not ten feet in front of the critter.

Nash bailed out of the van and grabbed the animal by the horns. He pulled him off the road and yelled. Kasey rolled down the window. "Did you say something? I can't hear you above this wind."

Nash motioned with his hands for her to go back to the ranch. "We can't put this smelly old sheep in your vehicle."

She shook her head. In seconds she was beside him, snow collecting on her stocking hat and shoulders. "I'm not leaving you out here in this mess. I'll toss the kids' car seats into the back and we'll put him in the van. It's not that far from here to the barn."

Nash pulled on his horns but the crazy thing wouldn't budge. "What if he..."

"We'll clean it up." She threw the words over her shoulder as she hurried back to the vehicle.

He threw the two-hundred-pound ram over his shoulders and carried it to the van. Kasey had already gotten things ready but the animal came alive when he put him inside the warm vehicle. Kasey put her hand on his head and quickly slammed the door shut.

"Quick thinkin'." Nash panted. "I hope he doesn't kick out any windows on the way to the barn."

"If he does, we'll be eating mutton until spring. Get inside fast so he doesn't jump over the seats and try to get out one of the front doors."

Nash wanted to continue the conversation about her not leaving, but the crazy sheep put up a noise all the way to the Texas Star. He was still rolling his eyes and bawling when Nash hopped out and opened the barn door wide enough to let Kasey drive inside and then closed it tightly.

They'd come a long way from the day he'd met her during a dirt storm a month ago. If it wasn't the stupidest idea in the universe, he would propose to her today. He loved her and didn't want to spend one day of the rest of his life without her. He reached into his coat pocket to finger the velvet box he'd tucked there…but there was no little box. His chest tightened and his heart fell to the barn floor.

She crawled out of the van. "What's wrong? Are you all right? Flashbacks?"

"You know, I haven't had any nightmares since you've been sleeping with me," he answered honestly, but his mind was on that spot where he picked up the ram and evidently lost the velvet box. It would be completely covered in snow by the time he got back there, but he had to go find it. How was he going to explain why he couldn't go to Hope Springs with her?

"Okay, then let's put this boy back in his stall. I bet he'll be happy to stay put after that little escape into the real world." Kasey laughed.

Nash picked a halter off a nail on the wall and slung open the van door. The ram stepped out like he owned the world and marched right back to his stall without so much as a single bleat.

"You might be right." Nash sighed.

"What's the matter with you?" Kasey opened the gate and the ram wasted no time going to his feed bucket.

"He's learned his lesson."

"Not him." Kasey shut and locked the gate. "You're acting strange."

Nash shrugged and shoved both hands into his coat pockets. And there the box was in his left pocket. He remembered putting it there earlier than morning in case he needed to tuck Silas's sippy cup in the right one.

"We started a conversation, but…" He let the sentence drop.

She crossed the distance separating them and wrapped her arms around his neck. "Nash, I don't want to leave Texas Star either. When I came back here to live at Hope Springs, it was like I went backward eight years. I was just

Brody and Jace's kid sister again. But since I've been on your ranch, I'm a grown woman who's capable of making decisions and living a real life and..." She paused.

"And what?" He tipped up her chin and stared deeply into her beautiful green eyes.

"And it's not just because I'm a whole person again and have you to thank for that as well, or that the kids love it here. It's because I've fallen in love with you, Nash," she said.

He moved back a few steps.

She stammered, "You don't have to say it right now. It's insane for me to say it, since we've only known each other a month but it's the truth..."

"Honest? Are you in love with me?" His heart was beating so fast that he thought it might leave his body and thump around on the floor at his feet.

"Yes," she whispered.

He pulled the box from his pocket and dropped down on one knee. "You have given me back my will to live, Kasey. When we come to the end of our lives, I hope that we make the jump into eternity together. I love you more than living one more day without you, and I'm in love with you, too. Kasey, will you marry me?"

He popped the lid open to reveal the rings. All shiny now from a secret trip to the jewelry store, they sparkled even in the dim barn.

"Yes," she said without a moment's hesitation. "But only if we can live together until spring."

"Anything you want, *chère*," he said as he slipped the engagement ring on her finger and then put the box with the wedding band back into his pocket.

"It's beautiful and it fits perfectly," she whispered and then her lips were on his in a kiss so passionate that it warmed the whole barn.

"It was my great-grandmother's. I'm so glad you like it. And on a little side note, can I tell Rustin that Santa brought him a daddy for Christmas?"

"As soon as we get back to the house, but only if I never have to take this ring off. And since the whole family will be at Granny's for leftovers, we can tell everyone at once."

He drew her into his arms and then his lips found hers and all was right with his world. "I do love you," he breathed into her hair when the kiss ended.

"And we're going to have a beautiful life together," she whispered.

* * *

Jace was so eager to get to his place, unload the feed, and not be late to Hope Springs by noon that he didn't even notice the ring or the grins on both Nash's and Kasey's faces. He blew his sister a kiss and disappeared within two minutes of the time they walked through the back door.

"Hey, Rustin," Nash called from the bottom of the stairs. "Y'all kids want to come down here. We got something we want to tell you."

In a matter of seconds Rustin and Silas appeared at the top of the steps with Emma right behind them. Rustin tucked Silas's hand into his to help him, and Emma held on to the rail.

"Easy now, brother. Your legs ain't as long as mine so we'll go slow," Rustin said.

"Mine is long as yours," Emma said.

"Are not!" Rustin argued.

They were halfway down when Silas let go of Rustin's hand and yelled, "Here me comes, Nashie." And he flew through the air, arms out and a smile on his face, right into Nash's arms.

"Silas McKay!" Kasey squealed.

"Nashie gots me." He grinned.

Nash flashed a brilliant smile at Kasey. "Yes, I do, forever, amen."

"Don't you ever do that unless Nash is right there, promise," Kasey fussed.

"Yes, ma'am," Silas said.

"Well, he got that down plain enough," Nash said.

"First thing a little cowboy had better learn to say to his mama when she's either mad or scared out of her wits." Kasey held up the ring to catch the light coming through the window. "It's so beautiful, Nash."

"What's beautiful?" Emma asked as she slipped her hand into Nash's free one.

"My new ring that Nash gave me," Kasey answered. "Come on in the living room and we'll tell you all about it."

Nash sat down on the sofa and Silas scrambled off his lap to the floor to stand with the other kids. Kasey snuggled up close to Nash's side, and he tucked her hand into his.

"What was on your list for Christmas that you didn't get, Rustin?" Nash asked.

Rustin dropped his chin to his chest with a sigh. "A daddy. I really wanted a daddy."

"Well, I asked your mama to marry me, and she said yes. So if it's all right with you kids, I'll be your new daddy."

"Really?" The hope in Rustin's face was almost heartbreaking.

"You'll still have your daddy in heaven, of course, but I'll be your daddy here on earth," Nash explained.

"A daddy, for real?" Emma squealed.

"Yes, a daddy for real," Kasey said, tears shimmering in her eyes.

"We don't have to move?" Rustin asked.

"Nashie, daddy?" Silas frowned.

"Yes!" Emma threw herself into Nash's arms. "Nash is going to be our daddy. Do we get to call him daddy?"

"Only if you want to," Nash said.

Rustin slung an arm around Nash's shoulders. "I just can't believe it. I asked God every night for you to be my daddy."

Silas crawled up into Nash's lap with Emma. "Yes. Nashie is daddy."

"Guess that settles it then. How about a March wedding?"

"Anytime you want, *chère*. Tomorrow, next year, March or June. Just don't ever leave me." Nash leaned around the kids to kiss her.

"It's real." Emma sighed. "He kissed her just like in the Cinderella movie."

* * *

"Where are those kids? Dinner is almost ready." Hope took a big crock bowl from the cabinet. Like always, her gray hair was styled perfectly, makeup done impeccably, and her cute little holiday bibbed apron covered a pair of black dress slacks and a pretty bright blue sweater.

"They're probably having trouble getting that sheep back to the ranch. An old ram can be cantankerous," Gracie answered.

"Do y'all think she'll move back home tomorrow?" Valerie pulled a pan of hot rolls from the oven.

Lila started filling glasses with ice and sweet tea. "Home? I believe that Texas Star is her home now and that if she does come back here, she won't stay more than a few days."

"Well, we all wanted her to be happy, didn't we?" Hope said.

"That's a really pretty bowl, Hope," Lila commented.

"I love this bowl. My mama always put the mashed potatoes in it for Christmas dinner and it reminds me of her."

"I always wondered why it didn't match your other Christmas china and crystal," Valerie said.

"A reminder that the odd lookin' in our lives might hold the best things." Hope smiled.

"I do love your mashed potatoes." Valerie hugged her mother. "I'm going to call Kasey and see what's keeping them."

Hope nodded toward the kitchen window. "I see them driving up now. They'll be coming through the door any minute."

"You're just in time," she announced as Kasey and her family piled in the back door. "We're ready to start putting everything on the table."

"Guess what, Granny!" Rustin yelled the minute they were in the kitchen.

"We got a daddy!" Emma squealed. "We got him for Christmas even if it was yesterday."

"Nashie, daddy!" Silas joined in the excitement.

Kasey held up her ring. "We're engaged."

"Congratulations!" Hope set the bowl down and hugged them both at once. "Jace, Lila, and Brody. Come on in here. Kasey and Nash have some exciting news," Hope yelled and then motioned for Valerie to join them in a group hug.

"Welcome to the family, Nash," Valerie said.

Hope took a step back, tears in her eyes as she took in everyone together, everyone so happy. Family, indeed, was the greatest Christmas gift of all.

When Jace Dawson hears Carlene Varner is back in town, he'd like to pick up where they left off on graduation night years ago. But Carlene's got secrets—including the identity of her daughter's father—and the truth might tear them apart…

A preview of
The Luckiest Cowboy of All
follows.

Chapter One

Sometimes it's too late to do what you should've done years ago. Aunt Rosalie had said that so many times that it should have been in a book of famous quotes.

"I get the message loud and clear," Carlene whispered around a lump the size of an orange in her throat.

"You okay, Mama?" Her daughter, Tilly, ran from the porch out to the minivan. "Here, let me take that box. It says stuffed toys, so I can carry it inside."

Carlene shifted the box into Tilly's hands and picked up a heavier one to carry inside the little two-bedroom frame house. With its peeling paint and hanging rain gutters, it looked like the last wilted rose of summer right now, but come spring she'd put a coat of fresh white paint on it, maybe plant some bright colored flowers around the porch, and it would look better then.

A bitter cold north wind whipped her long blond hair around into her face, reminding her spring was a long way off as she headed from her bright red minivan to the porch. Tilly opened the door for her and then closed it behind her.

"I made you a cup of tea."

"Thanks, baby girl." Carlene smiled. "Did you make one for you?"

"I made me some hot chocolate," Tilly said. "I liked our house in Florida better than this one."

"Why?" Carlene pulled a wooden rocking chair up closer to the coffee table and picked up the mug of steaming-hot chamomile tea. Too hot to drink, it warmed her hands. Tomorrow, when she and Tilly made a grocery store run to Amarillo, she'd have to remember to buy gloves for both of them.

"This place smells funny," Tilly said.

"We'll burn candles this afternoon and air it out on the first day with some nice weather. When we get settled, we'll start giving it a face-lift. You'll be surprised what new paint and a little fixin' up will do."

"And we'll get rid of the dead Christmas tree." Tilly glanced at the brown pine tree in the corner.

"Of course," Carlene said. "If you want, you could start to unpack what's in your room and I'll get those last three boxes while my tea cools."

"Okay. I'll have to take all that stuff off the shelves. I'll put my animals on the bed and then use the boxes to put Aunt Rosie's things in." Tilly carried her cup of hot chocolate to the bedroom.

With five moves in her eight years, Tilly was a pro at the moving business. Now her daughter was in the third grade, and it was time for them both to put down roots. So when the job offer came from Happy right after Aunt Rosalie died and left the place to her, Carlene did what she should've done years ago. She came back to the town that she should've never left.

Carlene nodded and leaned her head back on the rocking chair. It had been ten years since she'd been in the house. In those days Aunt Rosalie bragged that she'd never met a speck of dust she couldn't conquer. Looking around, evidently when her aunt died, all the dust she'd fought with over the years had reappeared and brought more with it. It would take days, possibly weeks, to get the house whipped into shape.

"That's tomorrow's work. Today's is getting Aunt Rosalie's things sorted through to make room for ours. Happy New Year's to us." She raised her cup of tea and then set it on the table.

Carlene drew her jacket closer around her chest and headed back out for the rest of the boxes. "Thank you, Aunt Rosalie, for leaving me everything in your will. At least I own the house, have a place to live, and don't have to pay rent."

She stepped off the porch when she heard tires on the gravel road. With the house the only one on a short dead-end road, she was pretty sure the visitor would be pulling into her driveway any second. She tucked her hair behind her ears and shivered.

Shading her eyes against the bright winter sun, she watched a big black crew-cab truck came to a stop right beside her minivan. Cowboy boots were the first thing that appeared when the door opened and then a very familiar figure followed. Jace Dawson tipped back his hat and waved. In a few long strides he was close enough for her to catch a whiff of Stetson aftershave—a scent that still created a stir in her hormones every time she smelled it.

Happy, Texas, had a population of fewer than seven

hundred, so it was a given that she'd run into Jace someday, probably sooner rather than later, but the first day she was there, before she could even get unpacked, meant that the gossip vines had not died in ten years.

"Carlene, I heard you were coming back to town. Here, let me help you get those into the house." He picked up all three of the remaining boxes and headed off toward the porch. "So you're going to be the new fifth-grade teacher, Mama tells me."

"That's right."

He filled out those Wranglers even better than he had in high school and had maybe even grown another inch or two.

"Been a long time," he said. "Where you been all these years?"

She opened the door for him and he set the boxes in the middle of the living room floor. "Here and there. Moved around a lot. California, then Georgia and Oklahoma, back to Florida and then here."

"You plannin' on livin' here? Mind if I sit down?"

"When did we get to be so formal? Of course you can sit." She kicked off her shoes and padded barefoot across the cold hardwood floor.

He avoided the rocker and sat on the sofa. "Look, I don't know how to tell you this..." He hung his head and looked into his hands, taking a deep breath. "I'm real sorry to have to say it, but I bought this place from Rosalie last year. She was planning to check herself into a nursing home and said she needed the money." He removed his hat and laid it on the coffee table.

"No!" Carlene sank down into the other end of the sofa and felt the color drain from her face. "She didn't...she wouldn't...she said..."

"I can bring the deed to show you. You goin' to be all right? I'm so sorry about this misunderstanding." Jace raked his fingers through his dark hair and his gray eyes were filled with true remorse. "And I'm real sorry for your loss. I know that you spent a lot of time with her when you lived here."

"Sell it back to me." Carlene met his eyes across the short distance separating them. "That shouldn't be too difficult. I have enough savings for a down payment, and we can get a loan at the bank for the rest."

Jace inhaled deeply and let it out very slowly. "Even though it's not fit for you to live in, I would sell it to you if I could and I'd even be willin' to help remodel it, but I can't. It's all been deeded over to the rodeo association. I bought it for that reason. We're going to expand the grounds next door and build a new concession stand and bathrooms right here on this property." Another deep breath. "Demolition is scheduled for February fifteenth. The contractors are starting the new buildings right after that."

"Dammit!" Carlene swore.

Jace had always had one of those faces that couldn't hide what he was thinking, and it was plain that he was not lying to her. Still, surely to God if Aunt Rosalie had sold the property she would have told Carlene. They talked every single Sunday evening from eight to eight thirty, and she always said that her greatest wish was to die in the same house where she'd been born. That her roots were in the place and it would make her life come full circle.

"The papers and the letter the lawyer sent are in that box. I'm going to dig them out right now. She must've gotten senile at ninety-five because she would've told me." Carlene left the sofa and ripped the tape from the top of the box marked IMPORTANT PAPERS.

"I have the deed, the papers that the rodeo folks signed, and everything in a folder at home. I'll be glad to bring them over to you," Jace said.

She pulled a big brown accordion file from the box and flipped through the tabs until she found the one she wanted. Removing a manila envelope from it, she shook out the letter from the lawyer saying that she'd inherited Rosalie's personal belongings and had even sent a key to the house so she could "get what she wanted out of it."

"See, here's her handwritten will, dated two years ago giving me everything that she owns." Carlene held it up.

"I bought the place a year ago," Jace said. "And I turned it over to the rodeo the next day with the understanding that we couldn't start to build until Rosalie had passed or she went to a nursing home."

She turned up the envelope and shook it, but nothing else fell out. She opened it wide and for the first time saw another little folded piece of paper at the bottom. Another fierce shake didn't bring it out, so she ripped the side away and carefully removed the letter. With dread in her heart she read it out loud:

My dear Carlene,

The lawyer says I don't need to redo my will. It does leave all my possessions to you, but I should tell you that I've sold the house to Jace Dawson or maybe it's to Prairie Rose Ranch. I don't know what bank account the payment came from. The money is in the Happy bank and if you'll remember you've been a joint member on that account for a couple of years. Do with it what you want. I just didn't want you to be burdened with selling this place. It needs lots of work and should be torn down, but I was born here and it's my wish to die here. My memories are all tied up in this place. Jace donated the land to the Rodeo Association. That's a good thing and it makes me happy.

Love, Aunt Rosalie

"Well, now what?" She laid aside the letter and threw up her hands in defeat.

"Now, you can live here until the wreckers come if you want. There's not much rental property in town that's fit for you to live in, but there are a couple of places for sale if you're plannin' to stay."

"I'd thought this would be my last move," she said. "I'm ready to put down roots, and I always liked this small town."

"We'll find you a place, I promise." He reached out, as if to touch her, but dropped his hand in his lap. "You've got my word on it. I should be going unless you've got more boxes to carry in."

"I thought you were going to college and . . ." She wanted to cry, not talk about the past.

"Went to college, figured out my heart was in Happy, not off somewhere in a big city with a desk job." He smiled.

Anger boiled up from her toes. "Dammit, Jace."

"What?"

"Nothing."

"Hey, I remember that look in those pretty brown eyes and you're mad as a wet hen after a wild Texas tornado," he said. "Spit it out."

"I'm mad about this house," she said through clenched teeth. It wasn't a lie. She was furious that she couldn't even buy it back from Jace. Understanding the whys and wherefores didn't make it a bit easier to accept, but what she was most mad about was the decision she'd made to leave. It had been based on his dream. "I thought the place was mine. I was already figuring out ways to remodel it."

"Honey, it'd take more than paint and curtains to make this place livable. The plumbing and wiring all would have to be replaced, and the worst thing is that the foundation is termite infested and barely hanging on by a thread. If it don't fall down around your ears in six weeks, you'll be lucky."

She got up and stomped around the boxes, out into the kitchen and back to the living room to the window where she stared out at the two vehicles sitting side by side. "There's no way you can ask the rodeo people to sell it back to me?"

"Sorry." He shook his head as he stood up. "I should be going now, Carlene. But like I said, it's no problem for you to stay here until the day before the wreckin' crew arrives. And if I can help you move or help find a place or anything, call me."

"Thank you," she said.

His heart was still as big and kind as it had been in high school. He'd been witty and charming, an amazing boyfriend and sexy as hell, but it had been that sweetness about his heart that had drawn her to him from the beginning.

She turned around and padded barefoot across cold hardwood floors, stepped on a few bits of dead needles from the dried-up Christmas tree in the corner. "Ouch! Why did she always have to have a live tree?"

"Let me help you." He knelt beside her and gently removed the dried debris from between her toes.

His touch sent delicious shivers all the way to her scalp, just like it had when they were dating in high school. His forefinger tracing her jawline in those days would have her ready to drag him off to the hayloft in Henry's old barn.

"There now." He rose to his feet. "Want me to help you get rid of this thing? I can haul it out of here as it stands."

"Thanks but no thanks. There's several ornaments on there that I'll want to keep, so I'll take care of it later."

He headed for the door and stopped in the middle of the floor. "Mama says you still go by Varner. You ever get married?"

She shook her head. "You?"

"I'm still holding on to the most eligible bachelor in the panhandle." He grinned.

"With that much power, surely you could sweet-talk the rodeo folks into selling me this house," she said.

"Can't do it, Carlene," he said.

"Hey, look what I found." Tilly burst into the living room, but stopped short at the sight of Jace. "Who are you?"

Her hair was all tucked up under a stocking cap with the Florida Gators logo on the front, and big green sunglasses covered half her face.

"I'm Jace Dawson. And you are?" He stuck out his hand.

She shook his hand. "I'm Tilly Rose Varner. Look what else I found." She brought out an official stuffed alligator from the Florida football team. "I haven't seen him in a whole year. I guess Aunt Bee packed him for me."

"She probably found him under your bed," Carlene said. "Surely you aren't finished unpacking all those boxes."

"Nope, but I'm hungry. I'm going to make a peanut butter and jelly sandwich. You want one?" She laid the stuffed animal on the sofa and started toward the kitchen.

"Your little sister or niece?" Jace asked.

"No, I'm her daughter." Tilly giggled as she whipped off

the stocking hat and a cascade of curly red hair fell to her shoulders.

An icy chill chased up Jace's backbone. "How old are you, Tilly Rose Varner?"

"I'll be nine on February ninth." She removed the oversized sunglasses and looked up at him with gray eyes sprinkled with gold flecks. Eyes that were exactly like his.

Suddenly, there was not a single doubt in his mind that Jace Dawson was staring at his daughter.

About the Author

Carolyn Brown is a *New York Times*, *USA Today,* and *Wall Street Journal* bestselling romance author and RITA® Finalist who has sold more than 3 million books. She presently writes both women's fiction and cowboy romance. She has also written historical single title, historical series, contemporary single title, and contemporary series. She lives in southern Oklahoma with her husband, a former English teacher, who is not allowed to read her books until they are published. They have three children and enough grandchildren to keep them young. For a complete listing of her books (series in order), check out her website at www.carolynbrownbooks.com

Fall in Love with Forever Romance

NEW YORK TIMES BESTSELLING AUTHOR
CAROLYN BROWN
LONG, TALL COWBOY CHRISTMAS
A HAPPY, TEXAS NOVEL

LONG, TALL COWBOY CHRISTMAS
By Carolyn Brown

A heartwarming holiday read from *USA Today* bestselling author Carolyn Brown. Nash Lamont is a man about as solitary as they come. So what the heck is he doing letting a beautiful widow and her three rambunctious children temporarily move in at Christmas?

Kasey Dawson thought she'd never get over the death of her husband. But her kids have a plan of their own: Nothing will keep them from having a real family again—even if it takes a little help from Santa himself.

Fall in Love with Forever Romance

THE TROUBLE WITH CHRISTMAS
By Debbie Mason

The Trouble with Christmas is the first book in the *USA Today* bestselling Christmas, Colorado series by Debbie Mason. This special reissue edition will feature bonus content never before in print! Resort developer Madison Lane is trying to turn Christmas, Colorado, into a tourist's winter wonderland. But Sheriff Gage McBride is tasked with stopping her from destroying his town. After meeting Madison, he can't decide if she's naughty or nice, but one thing is for certain—Christmas will never be the same again.

Fall in Love with Forever Romance

MAYBE THIS CHRISTMAS
By Jennifer Snow

One more game is all that stands between hockey star Asher Westmore and a major career milestone. But when an injury sidelines him for months, the only bright spot is his best friend and physical therapist, Emma Callaway, whose workouts improve his body *and* his spirit… Fans of Lori Wilde will love the latest from Jennifer Snow!